Em... F...

M... ...ance for Mills & Boon. S... ...en
over twenty-five books and has twice been a finalist
in the Australian Romantic Book of the Year Award,
which she won in 2013 for her novel *Sydney Harbour
Hospital: Bella's Wishlist*. You...
Emily at emilyforbes@intern...
website at emily-forbesauthor...

Sue MacKay lives with her h...
beautiful Marlborough Sounds, with the...
doorstep and the birds and the trees at her back door.
It is the perfect setting to indulge her passions of
entertaining friends by cooking them sumptuous meals,
drinking fabulous wine, going for hill walks or kayaking
around the bay—and, of course, writing stories.

London Hospital Midwives collection

Cinderella and the Surgeon by Scarlet Wilson
Miracle Baby for the Midwife by Tina Beckett
Reunited by Their Secret Daughter by Emily Forbes
A Fling to Steal Her Heart by Sue MacKay

Available now

Also by Emily Forbes

Reunited with Her Brooding Surgeon
Rescued by the Single Dad
Taming Her Hollywood Playboy

Also by Sue MacKay

Redeeming Her Brooding Surgeon
Taking a Chance on the Single Dad
The Nurse's Twin Surprise

Discover more at millsandboon.co.uk.

REUNITED BY THEIR SECRET DAUGHTER

EMILY FORBES

A FLING TO STEAL HER HEART

SUE MacKAY

MILLS & BOON

First Published in Great Britain 2020
by Mills & Boon, an imprint of HarperCollins*Publishers*
1 London Bridge Street, London, SE1 9GF

Reunited by Their Secret Daughter © 2020 by Emily Forbes

A Fling to Steal Her Heart © 2020 by Sue MacKay

ISBN: 978-0-263-27962-7

MIX
Paper from
responsible sources
FSC® C007454

This book is produced from independently certified FSC™ paper
to ensure responsible forest management.
For more information visit www.harpercollins.co.uk/green.

Printed and bound in Spain
by CPI, Barcelona

REUNITED BY THEIR SECRET DAUGHTER

EMILY FORBES

MILLS & BOON

For Scarlet, Tina and Sue,
my fellow *London Hospital Midwives* authors.
What a team. We did it!
Love
Emily

CHAPTER ONE

'HAPPY BIRTHDAY, DEAR LILY! Happy Birthday to you!'

Chloe Larson blinked back tears as Lily blew out the candles on her birthday cake. She couldn't believe she had a three-year-old daughter.

She pulled the candles from the cake and picked up the knife. 'Shall I help you cut it up?' she asked.

'I want Granny to help me,' Lily said.

Chloe tried not to be hurt. Ever since Chloe had found out she was pregnant at the age of twenty-four and had chosen to be a single mother, her own mother had been supportive. Chloe knew she couldn't have raised Lily without her help, and she tried not to mind when Lily turned to Susan as easily as she turned to Chloe, but sometimes she wished that life had been different.

She held back a sigh as she passed the knife to her mum. There was no point in wishing for something that wasn't to be.

'Make a wish, Lily,' Susan said as she guided her granddaughter's hand to slice through the rainbow cake.

'Don't touch the bottom, Lil,' Chloe's brother Tom prompted.

Lily carefully lifted pieces of cake onto pink paper

plates. 'Uncle Tom gets one first,' she said as she handed cake to her guests. 'When will Uncle Guy get here?'

'You saw him this morning, Lil. He's working tonight. We'll have to save him a piece.'

'Can you take me for another ride now, Uncle Tom?' Lily asked as she put a final piece of cake aside for Guy.

Chloe's brothers had given Lily a pink bike, with streamers dangling from the handles and a set of stabilisers on the back, for her birthday and Lily had spent most of the day riding up and down the driveway with Tom close behind.

'Sure.'

At twenty-one, Tom had plenty of energy, despite his job as a paramedic, and he doted on Lily as all Chloe's family did. Chloe knew how lucky she was. People said it took a village to raise a child, and Chloe was grateful to her mother and brothers for their support. And to her girlfriends. She had a lot to be thankful for.

'Come and watch me, Granny.'

Lily skipped outside followed by Tom and Susan, leaving Chloe inside with two of her best friends.

'Okay, who will join me in a glass of wine or a G&T? Esther?'

'Wine, please,' Esther replied as Carly, who was in the early stages of pregnancy, said, 'No wine for me, but I wouldn't say no to another piece of cake.'

'What would you wish for, Chloe, if it was your birthday?' Esther asked her when she returned with the wine and Carly cut more cake. 'How about your own happily ever after?'

Chloe looked sideways at Esther. The three women had been friends since they'd undertaken their midwifery training at the Queen Victoria together, and along with Isabella, who was currently overseas, the four of them had formed a tight-knit unit and sometimes Chloe was sure they could read each other's minds. But surely Esther wouldn't have guessed that Chloe was wishing for a different life?

'I'm already happy,' Chloe replied. She always insisted that she was happy with her life. She'd made a choice and she didn't regret it, even if it hadn't always been easy.

'How about satisfied, then? Couldn't you do with a white knight to come riding into your world?'

That was the trouble now that Carly and Esther had each found their perfect match and were deeply in love—they were both soon to be married and wanted everyone else to have their own happily ever after. But serious relationships were not for her; in her experience they only led to heartache. She'd be happy for Esther and Carly—she *was* happy for them—and she'd be a supportive friend, but she wouldn't make the mistake of believing she could have her own happily ever after again. She'd been in love once before and it hadn't ended the way she'd hoped.

'I'm fine,' she insisted.

Her life was busy and she was rarely alone even if she was sometimes lonely. Her days were spent either at work in Accident and Emergency at the Queen Victoria Hospital where she was surrounded by patients and colleagues or at home with her daughter. Home was her childhood house where Chloe's youngest brother, Tom, and her mother also lived. Chloe had never moved out, although that had been her intention. She'd finished school and stayed home while she completed her nursing and then midwifery training but her unexpected pregnancy had derailed her plans and here she was, three years later, still living in her mother's house.

It sounded depressing, it sounded as if she hadn't achieved a great deal, but she paid rent and her share of the bills. She was a flatmate in a sense, not a free boarder. Plus she had a good relationship with her mother and Lily benefited from having family around—she loved her granny and her uncles. The arrangement suited everyone and Chloe was happy enough. She couldn't deny that sometimes she wished for companionship, and yes, sometimes she wished for more sex too, but she didn't believe in one-night stands and she didn't believe in people's ability to maintain long-term monogamous relationships so she was caught between a rock and a hard place. It would take someone pretty special to make her believe in happily ever after again. She thought she might have missed her chance at finding her 'one.'

'How long since you've been on a date?' Esther asked.

'It's been a while,' she admitted.

'Can you be more specific?' Carly asked with a smile.

'November.'

'*November!* It's already March!'

'I know. But everyone is busy over Christmas and then, in the middle of winter, I can't be bothered going out.'

'Maybe you should try online dating,' Carly suggested. 'At least that way you can start the process from home. You can peruse the menu in your pyjamas, so to speak.'

But Chloe had heard too many bad stories about

online dating. She wanted to feel that spark of attraction from seeing someone in the flesh. She knew that existed. It had happened to her before. She didn't want to flick through online sites judging people on their photoshopped looks or their fabricated profiles and she certainly didn't want people judging *her* anonymously. She shook her head.

'You should think about it, Chlo,' Esther said. 'I'd love you to bring a date to my wedding.'

Esther had told her on numerous occasions she was welcome to bring a guest but Chloe couldn't imagine where she'd find someone she wanted to be her 'plus one.'

'I could ask Harry if he knows anyone or maybe you'll meet someone at the wedding,' Esther said before turning to Carly. 'Or maybe Adem has some nice single friends?'

Chloe's blood ran cold at the idea of being paraded around to all the single men. 'I know you mean well, but I'm okay on my own. Really.'

Esther and Carly both looked a little sheepish. 'Sorry. You know we love you and we just want you to be happy.'

'I am,' she insisted again. 'Don't say anything to Harry or Adem on my behalf but I'll let you know if I change my mind about a date. Okay?'

Maybe she should take a date with her, even if it was just someone to provide a shield, some protection, if necessary. But she had no idea where she would find such a person.

Chloe put Lily's favourite bedtime story book down and wriggled carefully out of her daughter's bed, trying not to disturb her. She pulled the covers up and took a moment to watch her sleeping.

Lily was the spitting image of her at the same age. Her riot of strawberry blond curls fanned across the pillow framing her round face. A scattering of freckles ran over her nose, little dark spots on her pale skin. She had one arm thrown up beside her head and Chloe knew there was a graze on her bony elbow and another one on her knee. She reached out and touched one of Lily's curls. Chloe had always hated her own hair, especially as a teenager, and the minute she could afford to she had bought a straightening iron and had dyed her hair blond, but now she loved her daughter's strawberry curls. Chloe still dyed her hair, although she had given up straightening it except on occasion. Straightening her hair took time and that was a luxury she didn't have much of any more.

The only differing feature between her and her daughter at the age of three was the colour of their eyes. Chloe's were dark brown, Lily's were grey, and in Chloe's opinion Lily's were far more striking especially in contrast to her pale auburn curls.

She searched her daughter's face looking for any resemblance to the man who had fathered her. She liked to think there was something of him in Lily but as more time passed it was becoming harder to remember all the little details. Lily definitely had her father's grey eyes but she couldn't see those while Lily slept. She wondered if Lily ever wished that her father was around. Was something missing in her life? She seemed happy enough and she had good male role models but was that the same thing?

Chloe knew it wasn't. Chloe and her younger brothers had been raised by their mother after their father had died when Chloe was seven. Chloe loved her mum and she knew she'd done a brilliant job raising three kids on her own but that had never stopped Chloe from missing her father. Lily had never met her father; maybe that would be enough to stem those feelings of loss, but Chloe doubted it. It might not matter to Lily now but what about when she got older?

She wondered for the thousandth time what had happened to Lily's father. To Xander.

To the man who had captured her heart in the Australian outback four years ago.

He had looked like a blond Nordic god and she'd known from the moment she'd met him that he was damaged, wounded, but he was gorgeous, irresistible, and she'd been certain she could handle him. She'd been on a study exchange with the Australian flying doctor service and hadn't been looking for anything more than a holiday romance.

Initially everything had been fine. Manageable. On paper, their affair looked perfect. She was young and footloose and Xander had just been through an acrimonious divorce. Neither of them had been looking for anything serious and they'd both been happy to have a light-hearted liaison, something to satisfy their mutual physical attraction and desires. Their time together had lasted less than four weeks. That was all the time she had left in Australia. It was enough time to have some fun but not long enough for heartache.

At the end of the month she hadn't been ready to leave but she figured she'd forget about him in time. A holiday romance wasn't meant to be for ever. She missed him but she figured she'd get over it.

She would focus on her career, on getting a contract with the Air Ambulance Service, and Xander Jameson would become part of her past. A memory to take out and relive from time to time.

But she hadn't expected the emptiness that gnawed away at her. The ache that felt like a lump of lead in her chest. She'd never fully given her heart to anyone—in her experience men had a wandering eye and had trouble staying faithful, and she protected her heart zealously, careful not to give it away—but Xander had caught her by surprise.

She certainly hadn't planned to fall in love. In her experience love didn't last. Her parents' marriage had crumbled under the weight of her father's infidelity and Chloe's one semi-serious relationship at the age of twenty-one had suffered the same fate. In her experience falling in love only led to heartache. But that didn't stop it from happening to her.

She hadn't counted on meeting Xander.

And she hadn't counted on falling pregnant.

She had been back in London for a month before she realised. At least that situation explained her unexpected feelings. She wasn't in love, she told herself, just overwhelmed by a flood of hormones.

She tried to contact Xander—she knew it was the right thing to do—but he'd disappeared.

She'd wanted to find him; despite her strong views on serious relationships and their longevity she let herself get carried away with a fantasy, creating all sorts of happily ever afters in her mind, and part of her hoped for a miraculous happy ending even though she knew there were no such guarantees.

She only realised when she was trying unsuccessfully to find him how little she really knew about him. They hadn't spent much time talking about anything important. She knew he'd grown up in Adelaide in South Australia but he had no social media identity and his work colleagues had either been unable or unwilling to give her any useful information. Her letters had been returned to sender, unopened. He seemed to have disappeared off the face of the earth.

But she had never stopped wondering if her life would have been different if she'd found him.

Would he have wanted to make them a family?

He had told her his marriage had ended because his wife had wanted children and, although he'd never voiced the words, Chloe took that to mean that he didn't.

She'd been relieved in a way not to find him. What would he think of Lily? She was glad she hadn't had to find out. The decisions about her pregnancy were hers alone to make and her dreams of a happily ever after remained just dreams.

Once Lily was born she'd had no time to continue her search and she'd doused the flames of her dreams and focused on the job of raising her daughter. But she'd never forgotten him.

She sighed.

How could she forget him when she was reminded of him every day? Every time she looked into her daughter's eyes.

She'd tried to forget and she'd tried to convince herself she hadn't been in love with him. If anything, her experience with Xander was just more proof that everlasting love was not meant for her.

She had her daughter, her miracle, her precious Lily. That would have to be enough.

She left Lily's night light on and the door ajar as she slipped out of the room while her mind continued to wander. If she'd realised the consequences of their affair would she have been more cautious?

She loved her daughter and she had absolutely no regrets about having her. She was always going to keep the baby—her mum had raised three kids with minimal help and Chloe knew she could raise one. She had never considered giving Lily up. She had no regrets about the choices she had made but she did sometimes wonder about a different future.

Maybe the fact that Esther and Carly were both about to settle down and join the ranks of the happily married was making her reassess her own life. Maybe she did need to get out on the dating scene. Maybe she would like some company. Now that Lily was three maybe Chloe's life would calm down, perhaps she would get some time to herself, a day that wasn't all consumed by motherhood and her career. Perhaps there would be some time for her to have a social life beyond an occasional drink or dinner with Carly and Esther. Nothing serious—casual dating would be fine. She wasn't going to dream of anything more than that. She and Lily were fine on their own and she wasn't prepared to settle for anyone ordinary. It was better to be single than to be with someone who wasn't perfect for her. And for Lily.

Still she wondered if Xander could have been that person.

She had been on a few dates since Lily had been born but no one had lived up to her memory of Xander. She was sensible enough to realise that her memory may have altered over the years. She was remembering all the good things, looking at him through rose-tinted glasses, but he couldn't be perfect. Four weeks just hadn't been long enough for her to get annoyed by his flaws.

But what if she had found him?

Where would they be now?

She shook her head. She couldn't survive on 'what ifs.' Even if she'd found him, he might not have been the person she wanted him to be. They'd had amazing chemistry but who knew if that would have been enough to sustain a happy, long-term relationship. She was certainly none the wiser.

She was sure there was a simple explanation to Xander's apparent disappearance but, whatever it was, she'd never been able to find him and now, here she was, almost four years later, still single, and Lily was still without a father.

Should she let her girlfriends set her up? Chloe wondered as she hurried through A&E to fetch another bag of saline. Was that the answer?

The idea of going on a date wasn't completely unappealing but the logistics of it wasn't as simple. Most days after a long shift at work and then coming home to a toddler, she barely had the energy for housework. She couldn't imagine having the energy to get ready and dressed up for a date.

She returned to the treatment cubicle and her patient, pushing all thoughts of dating aside.

'All right, Penny, this should help you feel better,' she said as she connected the bag of saline to the drip.

'Can you tell me again what the doctor said is wrong with me?' Penny asked.

'You have a condition called hyperemesis gravidarium,' Chloe told her as she updated Penny's chart. 'It's a medical term for severe morning sickness that unfortunately doesn't just hit you in the morning. I know you feel awful and while it can be serious it's not life-threatening and it will pass.'

'When?'

'It's usually much better by about halfway through your pregnancy.'

'That's another three months away,' Penny groaned, and reached for the bowl and proceeded to vomit again. She'd presented to A&E in the late afternoon, badly dehydrated, having vomited all day.

Chloe held Penny's hair back from her face and took the bowl from her when she finished, swapping it with a cool, damp flannel.

'Is there anything I can do to make it stop?' Penny asked.

'Some expectant mums find that drinking your food instead of eating it can help,' said Chloe. 'Making shakes and smoothies for example and a diet high in protein and carbohydrates is better than a fatty diet. Ginger and vitamin B6 can also help.'

Scans had shown that Penny was pregnant with only one baby and blood tests hadn't detected a virus or anything else untoward. She had low blood pressure and a rapid pulse but the nausea and dehydration were the main concern.

'Does the vomiting harm the baby?'

'Vomiting itself isn't harmful but it is important not to ignore the symptoms. If you're unable to keep food down, then you're not getting the nutrition you need and neither is the baby and sometimes this can cause a low birthweight. You do need to take care of yourself.'

Chloe didn't want to frighten Penny unnecessarily but it was important to stress that she needed to monitor her condition. 'A lot of pregnant women with this condition find they need regular fluid top-ups to combat the dehydration. Anti-nausea medication as well and, very occasionally, hospital admission. I'm going to give you the details for the Early Pregnancy Unit here at the hospital. It's open every day during office hours. That's the place to go if you're feeling unwell. You'll get seen faster than here in A&E and you're less likely to pick up any bugs. I think you should pop in there for a check-up in the next day or two as they will be able to suggest some strategies to help you through this.'

Chloe pulled a notebook from the pocket of her scrubs and wrote down the phone number and details for the EPU as well as the scientific term for Penny's diagnosis. As she tucked it into Penny's bag the A&E manager stuck her head into the cubicle.

'Chloe? The air ambulance has called for a midwife. Can you go with them?' Shirley asked. 'I'll reassign your patient.'

Chloe nodded. 'Penny's notes are up to date. She's all set for the moment.'

Chloe was one of three midwives who worked with the Air Ambulance Service on an as-needed basis. The service had their base on the top floor of the Queen Victoria Hospital with a rooftop helipad, and Chloe had applied for a position at the hospital specifically to work with the service. She loved the work and wished she could do it full time but that would mean doing general nursing and not midwifery. She didn't want to give that up so this was the compromise; she felt it gave her the best of both worlds.

She threw her gloves into the bin and hurried to the lift, not wanting to waste time. Protocol dictated that the crew would aim to take off within four minutes of receiving a call.

She got out one flight before the roof and stepped into the pair of orange overalls that were handed to her. She zipped them up over her scrubs and ran up the stairs and out onto the roof. She jogged across to where the helicopter sat on the helipad, its rotors turning. She ducked her head instinctively even though she wasn't tall enough for the blades to hit her and climbed into the chopper and took her seat. Neil, one of the two fire officers on deck, slid the door closed behind her.

She reached up and unhooked a helmet that was hanging above her head. She tugged the elastic band that tied her unruly curls into a ponytail lower down on her neck so she could pull the helmet on. Sitting opposite her was Rick, one of the service's paramedics.

She hadn't been called for a job in over a month and she felt the familiar thrill of nervousness and anticipation as she fastened her helmet strap and reached for her harness. She worked quickly, not taking the time to glance at the other seat where one of the doctors would be sitting, as she knew the pilot was waiting to lift off.

'Chloe, this is Dr Alexander Jameson.' She slid one arm into her harness as she heard Rick introduce her to a new doctor. 'He's covering for Eloise while she's off after her knee surgery.'

Chloe felt a shiver down her spine and her heart rate increased even as she told herself she'd misheard. She *must* have misheard. She'd been thinking about Xander and must have imagined Rick had said his name because why would he be *here*? She kept her head down, taking longer than usual to click her harness together.

'He's just come down from Wales.'

Chloe breathed out. He was Welsh. Not Australian. It wasn't him.

But when she lifted her head she was looking directly into a pair of familiar grey eyes.

It *was* him.

Xander.

Her vision blurred as everything around her shifted. She squeezed her eyes shut, trying to clear her vision, but when she opened them she found Xander still looking straight back at her.

His eyes ensnared hers and held her motionless and she felt the air rush from her lungs as if she'd been punched in the stomach.

She stared at him. At the helmet that covered his head but not his perfect oval face with its angular, high cheekbones. At his full lips that were outlined by designer stubble and at his forehead that was slightly creased. She remembered that expression; so often serious, he usually looked either like he carried the weight of the world on his shoulders or was deep in thought.

She wanted to reach over and smooth the crease from his brow.

His grey eyes, which still held a trace of sadness, were wide, framed by thick, dark blond lashes, and they stared straight into her soul.

How could she have forgotten how gorgeous he was?

She was immediately transported back to a hot Australian day, to the first time she saw him. He had the same effect on her today as he'd had then. She couldn't breathe. She couldn't think. She couldn't stop staring at him. From the moment she'd first laid eyes on him almost four years ago she'd fallen hard and she could feel herself tumbling again.

How could she have forgotten the intensity of her feelings?

She felt light-headed, dizzy, and was grateful that she was already sitting down.

She had spent months trying to find him. Months thinking of all the terrible things that could have happened to him and here he was, apparently fit and well, sitting in her chopper.

CHAPTER TWO

'XANDER, CHLOE IS one of our on-call midwives.' Rick was still introducing them as if they didn't already know each other. As if Chloe's world hadn't just tipped on its axis.

Her heart was racing and her hands were shaking. She tucked them into her lap, hoping Rick and Xander didn't notice her reaction.

'Chloe.' He nodded. Once. Briefly.

He didn't deny that he knew her and he didn't pretend that he was meeting her for the first time but he certainly didn't appear too thrilled. He gave her nothing. She consoled herself with the fact that it wasn't the time or place for a personal conversation.

Would he be expecting one?

He probably hadn't thought about her once in four years. He would have no idea that she thought of him daily. He would have no idea of the impact he had made on her life.

She studied him fleetingly, trying not to stare again. The orange jumpsuit that was the uniform for air ambulance medical staff was not the most flattering shade but Xander wore it well. His face was slightly tanned, making her wonder where else he'd been. Surely he hadn't got a tan in Wales? His shoulders were still broad, his legs long and lean. He looked thinner than she recalled and she wondered if his hair, beneath the helmet, was as thick and blond as she remembered. Four years ago he had worn it swept to one side, always looking as if he'd just finished running his fingers through it.

When she had left him behind, they'd had no plans for anything to go beyond a brief holiday fling. He had no idea that she'd spent months trying to find him.

She pushed the memories of their time together aside, before they could come flooding back. She couldn't afford to be swamped by the past. She had a job to do.

She could be professional. She *was* professional.

She'd waited years to speak to Xander. She'd given up on ever finding him. She could wait a few more hours to catch up.

She turned to Rick, hoping he was the one with all the information about the job and focused on the task at hand.

'Where are we headed?' she asked.

'Stabbing. Domestic dispute. Thirty-year-old woman, fourth pregnancy, thirty-eight weeks. Paramedics are on site. The woman and her partner are both being treated for injuries. The woman is in labour.'

Chloe digested the scant information. Details about the job were relayed to them by the co-pilot, Jeff, and were usually minimal. She knew the job was likely to be complicated but that was normally the case. The air ambulance wasn't called for simple incidents. But they wouldn't be the first pre-hospital team at the scene and she knew more information would be forthcoming once they arrived. The team had plenty of emergency medicine experience between them and were used to gathering information as they went.

Out of habit she checked the supplies stashed in the seat pockets beside her while her mind wandered.

She could feel Xander's eyes on her but she didn't dare meet his gaze. She needed to collect her thoughts before she connected with him and checking the supplies gave her something to occupy her throughout the short flight.

She needed to control her nerves. She concentrated on counting supplies, willing her hands to stop shaking. She was equal parts excited, nervous and worried.

She needed to focus but she was dying to know what he was thinking. What had he been doing? How was he? Did he ever think of her? And what did his arrival mean for her? For them? For Lily?

It was only a few minutes before she felt the helicopter begin the left-hand bank turn and knew they had reached their destination. The pilot, Simon, would be giving Jeff a chance to identify a safe landing site.

The house was easy to find; from her seat Chloe could see an ambulance, a police car and a police van parked out the front.

The chopper landed on a vacant block that looked as if it may have once been a tennis court. A few kids scattered to the footpath as it descended but then hung around, mouths open and eyes wide, to watch the scene unfold.

Rick slid the door open as the chopper touched down. Chloe reached for one of the kit bags only to find Xander had reached for the same one. Their hands touched and as Xander's came to rest on top of hers she jerked hers away as if she'd been scalded. Her skin was on fire, her breathing rapid. She kept her gaze averted and picked up a second bag as she tried to get her nerves under control.

She strode off, carrying the bag, quickly putting some distance between them. She needed to keep him out of her line of sight while she pulled herself together.

Two policemen emerged as they approached the house and between them Chloe could see a man in handcuffs. The husband? The police officers pushed on his head, forcing him into the back of their van before slamming the door. She gave him a cursory glance as she walked past before following Rick into the property.

The house was identical in appearance to several others in the street. A small front garden in need of some attention separated the house from the street. A short flight of steps led to the front door set in a narrow two-storey building. Chloe knew the floor plan—she'd been to many houses just like this one—and there was nothing to indicate from the outside what went on behind closed doors. Houses where domestic violence occurred could look like any other from the outside.

The front door opened into a tight hallway. There was a staircase on their right, an empty lounge on the left. Looking past Rick's shoulder Chloe could see a kitchen at the end of the hall. The air ambulance crew crowded into the small room.

A woman lay on the floor. Her shirt was ripped and bloodied and blood pooled on the linoleum. Her skin was pale and her breathing laboured. Two paramedics knelt on either side of her and one looked up as the team entered the room.

'This is Shania. Stab wound to the right chest.'

The paramedics had cut through the woman's top and the one who spoke was just finishing applying a dressing to the lateral side of the woman's chest.

'We've only just been able to get to her,' the paramedic continued. 'We had to wait for the police to subdue her partner.'

'She is complaining of difficulty breathing. She's hypoxic, absent air sounds,' the other paramedic said as he lifted the stethoscope that he'd been holding against the woman's chest. 'Rapid heart rate and sharp stabbing chest pain. I think she may have a tension pneumothorax.'

The air ambulance team all had their job roles emblazoned on the front left of their overalls. The paramedic holding the dressing reached into the kit that was beside her with her free hand and passed gloves to everyone before handing a stethoscope to Xander.

'She's thirty-eight weeks pregnant. Fourth pregnancy.' The paramedic repeated the information that the air ambulance team had already been given. 'She's in labour but we haven't had time to assess that.'

Xander knelt beside the woman. He placed the stethoscope against her chest and listened. Chloe was happy to defer to him. She knew there was no point asking the woman any questions about her labour until her chest pain was sorted. If she was having trouble breathing, she wouldn't want to talk. The woman's labour wasn't the priority. A tension pneumothorax was life-threatening.

Xander lifted his head. 'I need a large-bore needle, fourteen-gauge,' he said.

The paramedic handed him an angiocath along with an alcohol wipe. Xander swept the wipe across the woman's ribs and Chloe watched as he palpated for the intercostal space in the mid-clavicular line with slender fingers. His blond head was bent over the woman, the smooth skin on the back of his neck exposed as he leant over his patient.

He was talking to the woman, explaining what he was about to do.

He was calm and methodical. He worked quickly but smoothly. There was no panic, no hurried movements, nothing to alarm or frighten the woman, who was already on edge.

Chloe watched his profile as he worked, noting the angle of his jaw, the blond stubble that covered it, the sharpness of his cheekbones, his flat, shell-shaped ears. She remembered how much she'd learnt from him when they'd worked together in Australia. His calmness, experience, patience and bedside manner were some of the many things that she'd found attractive but they hadn't been the first things she'd noticed about him. She hadn't even known he was a doctor, let alone that she'd be working with him, when she'd first seen him. It had been one of those moments you read about: their eyes had met across a room and she was done for. She'd fallen hard and fast.

She blinked and cleared her mind as she took a deep breath and told herself to focus. There were more important things to think about than what had happened between her and Xander. Those days were long gone. She was a different person now, no longer carefree, no longer independent. She had a job to do and other things to consider. She needed to get herself under control. She couldn't let her hormones unsettle her. She needed to take stock of the situation—even if she couldn't make sense of it yet.

She had to try to ignore the fact that Xander was kneeling just inches away from her. She had to resist the temptation to reach out and place her hand on the back of his neck. To feel the warmth of his skin under her fingers. She had to pretend he was just another colleague, not the man who she'd once thought could be the love of her life.

She forced her attention back to the tableau in front of her, concentrating on the woman's chest instead of on Xander.

He'd found the space he wanted and she watched as he inserted the needle between the woman's ribs. They all heard the air as it flowed out of the chest cavity. He removed the needle after a few seconds, leaving the plastic tube in situ, and reviewed the woman's observations. Her oxygen sats improved as her chest re-inflated. Xander listened for breath sounds before taking a chest seal from Rick and applying it.

Rick and Xander worked smoothly together, inserting a drip, administering pain relief and hooking an oxygen mask over Shania's nose and mouth while Xander kept up his explanations.

They didn't need Chloe's help but she kept herself busy, finding the things she might need for a delivery and making sure they were close to hand. Focusing on anything but Xander.

'How are you feeling now, Shania?' Xander asked. 'Do you have any pain? Can you tell me where it is?'

'Ow!' Shania clutched at her stomach and Chloe could see the tell-tale ripple of a contraction pass across Shania's abdomen. Treating a tension pneumothorax always gave immediate relief and Xander had relieved Shania's chest pain so successfully that she was now complaining about her labour pains.

Xander caught Chloe's eye and gave her a quick smile, uniting them in their treatment of their patient. But his smile did more than that. Chloe thought he was handsome when he wore his usual brooding expression but when he smiled he was something else altogether. No longer wounded, or sad, the shadows in his eyes disappeared and it was like watching the sun come out after a long winter. His smile instantly transformed his face and made Chloe's world tilt. It had been almost four years since she'd seen his smile and it knocked the wind out of her all over again.

'Looks like it's your turn,' he said as he stood preparing to swap places with Chloe. Space was at a premium and Chloe was very aware of how close to her Xander was standing. How she had to brush past him in order to reach their patient.

She took a deep breath and mentally shook her head as she knelt on the floor.

'Shania, I'm Chloe. I'm a midwife. Let's see what's going on with this baby of yours, shall we?' She strapped a foetal heart rate monitor around Shania's belly and waited anxiously for the reading, hoping it would fall between one hundred and ten and one hundred and sixty beats per minute.

One hundred and two...

'We need to get her to hospital,' Chloe said. The baby appeared to be in distress and Chloe was concerned about oxygen deprivation given Shania's injuries.

'I'm not going to the hospital,' Shania protested.

'We need to transfer you,' Chloe insisted. 'You have

a chest wound and you're having a baby. This is for your safety. And your baby's safety.'

'Who will look after my kids?' Shania asked as another contraction gripped her.

'Where are they?' Xander asked.

'With one of the neighbours.' A policewoman stood in the corner of the kitchen. Chloe had barely been aware of her until she replied to Xander's question.

Xander looked over to her. 'Can you see if the neighbour is happy to keep them for a while?'

The policewoman nodded and left the room and Chloe indicated to Rick to follow her. She needed him to fetch the stretcher.

She bent her head and resumed her examination. 'Let me have a quick look to see how far along your labour is.' The contractions were less than a minute apart and Chloe was worried. She looked up at Xander. 'I don't think we're going anywhere right now. She's fully dilated.'

The baby's head was crowning. There was nothing Chloe could do now to slow down Shania's labour. This baby was coming whether they were ready or not.

'I want to push!' Shania cried out.

'Okay, Shania, ready when you are.' The pain relief Xander administered was enough to lightly sedate Shania, enough to calm her down but not enough to make her unable to push.

Shania bore down and Chloe eased the baby's head out. 'Well done, Shania. Take a breath now,' she said as she felt for the cord. Everything seemed clear. 'Wait for the next contraction and I'll get you to push again.'

The baby came out in a slippery rush. A girl. She didn't appear to be injured but everything was silent. No crying and Chloe didn't think she was even breathing. She quickly wrapped her in a soft cloth and rubbed her vigorously and was rewarded with a muted cry.

'Congratulations, Shania. You have a daughter.'

Chloe clamped and cut the cord and did a quick Apgar assessment. The baby's hands and feet were blue, her respiration slow, but she scored an eight out of ten, which was great, all things considered.

Chloe wrapped her against the cold and slid a cap onto her head to retain warmth. 'Do you have a name for her?' she asked as she handed her to Shania.

'Tonya.' Shania was gazing at her daughter, all pain forgotten.

Shania was oblivious to her surroundings now as Chloe delivered the placenta and put it into a bag. Shania still needed to go to hospital and Chloe needed to take the placenta with them.

Rick returned with the stretcher followed by the policewoman. Chloe could see the surprised look on her face. The baby had arrived faster than anyone anticipated. The policewoman spoke to Shania. 'Shania, your neighbour will mind the children while you go to hospital.'

Shania was too tired to argue as Chloe took the baby and Rick and Xander transferred her to the stretcher.

Chloe did another quick check of the baby and increased her Apgar score by one. Despite the dramatic circumstances surrounding her birth she was doing remarkably well. Chloe carried Tonya out to the chopper and held her as Shania's stretcher was loaded on board and Rick connected Shania to the monitors. Simon lifted the chopper into the air as soon as Rick gave the all clear.

'The police asked me to let you know you'll need to make a report,' Xander said to Shania. 'They want to know if you want to press charges.'

Shania shook her head. 'I'm not going to press charges.'

Xander looked incredulous. 'What? Why not?'

'If I'm in hospital I need Greg at home to look after the other kids. I can't have him locked up overnight. They'll keep him until he sobers up and then they'll let him go. I just hope he goes home and not back to the pub.'

'The police have arrested Greg. I don't think they're going to be too quick to let him go.' Xander was speaking slowly, as if he was worried that Shania wasn't understanding the situation. 'Has he been physically violent towards you before?'

'I started it,' Shania replied, and Chloe noticed she avoided answering Xander's question.

'How do you figure that?'

'I was going to the next-door neighbour's. I was going to ask her to drive me to hospital because Greg had been drinking, but Greg got angry. He didn't want the neighbours to know he was in no state to drive and he insisted he was okay to take me. I knew he wasn't and when I tried to get past him he blocked my way. I grabbed a kitchen knife and threatened him but he took it off me and, when I tried to push past him, the knife stabbed into me. I shouldn't have taken the knife in the first place and then none of this would have happened.'

Chloe could see by Xander's expression that he wasn't pleased with Shania's answer. She also knew he wouldn't be pleased that there was nothing he could do about the situation. She knew he was driven by the same overwhelming desire to help people, to fight for the underdog, to improve people's lives, as she was. 'Shania, the knife didn't stab you, your husband did. That is *not* okay.'

'Do you have kids?' Shania asked.

Chloe should have anticipated the question. It was one she got asked by almost every labouring mother when they were looking for some common ground or reassurance that Chloe knew what they were going through, but she hadn't been prepared to have to answer that question in front of Xander. Her heart rate spiked but thank God she didn't have to answer as fortunately Shania was addressing Xander and not her.

Xander shook his head. 'No, I don't.' He kept his head turned away and Chloe wasn't able to see his expression. When she'd last seen him four years ago he hadn't wanted kids. Had anything changed? Would he want Lily?

'I have three kids,' Shania continued. 'Four now. I don't work. Where would I go?'

Xander looked up and Chloe took over from him. She knew he'd be wanting to offer advice but she guessed he wasn't sure how the system worked in the UK.

'There are options,' Chloe said. 'I can organise for a social worker to come and see you and we can see what measures we can put in place.' It was often a difficult process. Resources were scant and Chloe knew that a lot of mums preferred not to uproot their children. It was a catch-22. She'd start with getting the social worker visit while Shania was in hospital but she knew from experience that there was little they could do if Shania wasn't on board with the idea. She was sure Shania had heard it all before but she was pleased to see her give a very slight nod of agreement just as the large red *H* of the hospital helipad came into view beneath them.

The hospital roof became a hive of activity as the helicopter door slid open. Surgical and neonatal teams were on hand to meet them and transfer the patients and Chloe lost sight of Xander as she went with baby Tonya to the neonatal unit.

Her hands shook as she transferred Tonya to the neonatal stretcher. Her heart rate was still elevated and she knew some of it was due to adrenalin from the job but the rest was wholly and solely because of Xander.

She remained on tenterhooks for the rest of her shift waiting to see if Xander would appear in A&E even though she knew his shift must have finished well before hers. The air ambulance helicopter only operated during daylight hours and it was long since dark. Once the helicopter was out of action, road crews took over and Xander would have gone home. The only reason he would have to come to A&E would be to see her.

She was partly relieved and partly disappointed when her shift ended with Xander nowhere in sight.

Xander sat at the bar and nursed his drink as he mulled over the day's turn of events.

He wasn't thinking about work or Shania. He was thinking about Chloe. Seeing her had completely blindsided him and had brought back memories he'd thought long buried.

He hadn't let himself consider the possibility of seeing her again even though he was in London. But was it really such a surprise?

They'd met when she was on a study exchange, working with the flying doctor, and he knew that the London air ambulance was the UK equivalent but he'd had no idea she was working with them. He hadn't let himself hope that he'd see her again.

But here she was.

It had been almost four years but she'd barely changed. Maybe she wasn't quite as thin but, if anything, the few extra pounds suited her. She still looked young—she was seven years younger than him so she must only be about twenty-seven—but there was a maturity about her now. In both looks and manner. He saw it in her eyes and he'd seen it in her work today. She'd been confident, assured and capable.

He closed his eyes as he pictured her.

Her thick blond curls had been pulled back into a ponytail today, but he could remember how it had felt to slide his fingers into her tresses, how her hair had felt splayed across his bare chest. How she'd felt lying nestled into his side, how he had felt when she'd taken him in her arms. The cool, silkiness of her skin, the softness of her lips and the smell of shampoo and sun in her hair. He recalled it all.

It had been almost four years but he remembered her as if it was yesterday.

She had been a good distraction, an *excellent* distraction, at a time of his life when he'd needed distracting.

He'd had a tumultuous two years and he had still been trying to process what had happened when she walked into his life. He'd encountered two of life's major stresses simultaneously. A serious health scare and a marriage breakdown. His cancer diagnosis had been a shock, his wife's infidelity equally so. Going through chemotherapy had been confronting and exhausting without the additional stress of a divorce. A divorce that he hadn't seen coming. Those past two years had left him shattered and numb and he had been struggling to find his new identity in a future that didn't hold marriage or fatherhood. His dreams had been crushed, leaving him with nothing except his career.

He had been physically and emotionally exhausted when he'd met Chloe. He'd been through the wringer and, although he knew a stranger would look at him and suspect nothing, he felt a shadow of his former self.

She'd made him feel better but she hadn't been able to mend him.

Chloe had given him a chance to forget about the previous two years. Some respite. She'd allowed him a chance to ignore what had happened but, he could admit this now, that hadn't helped him to deal with it. Denial and acceptance were two completely different things.

But he did know that the last time he'd been truly happy had been when he'd been with Chloe. She had calmed his soul and brought peace and happiness to his life at a time when he'd desperately needed it. And then taken it all away with her again when she'd left.

He hadn't anticipated that her departure would leave such a big hole in his life—after all, they'd only known each other for four weeks—but the loneliness he felt had surprised him and it was only after she'd gone that he wondered if he should have confided in her. Could they have had something more if he hadn't been so emotionally wounded? So damaged.

He would never know.

Confiding in her would have meant talking about what had happened, talking about his feelings, and he wasn't ready to do that. He was happier in denial. They'd shared a bed but not their minds. His wife, ex-wife, whom he'd known for ten years, had betrayed his trust and he hadn't been in a position where he could bring himself to trust anyone else with his story. Not even a virtual stranger.

He'd needed time.

And time was something they didn't have then.

He may have denied them the opportunity of getting to know each other better but he consoled himself with the knowledge that Chloe was only ever in Australia temporarily. He told himself that nothing he could have said or done would have changed that but it didn't stop him from sometimes wishing that things had turned out differently.

They'd had no plans for a future together, although he had found himself imagining one, but he knew he wasn't in a position to offer her anything permanent. The future. Permanency. They were words that he'd been afraid to consider. His fate was still uncertain. He'd enjoyed Chloe's company but he'd known, in his soul, that he wasn't what she needed even while he thought she might be exactly what he desired.

But he had to sort himself out first. He had to find some level of acceptance for what had happened to him. To his life. He couldn't move forward until he'd done that.

He didn't know what his future was going to be, so instead of searching for her he'd gone searching the world, looking for a substitute. Looking for something to fill the space she'd left behind.

He'd thought he would find something to fill that void but today, seeing her again, he wondered whether his search had been in vain. Could anything fill that void or could it only be filled by someone?

She'd been the perfect tonic for him at one of the lowest points of his life but what about now?

Was he in a better place?

Four years on and he'd thought he was better but his feelings today took him by surprise. He'd felt an extraordinary sense of calm when he'd seen her today. As if, for the first time in years, he could breathe deeply and fully.

He'd considered asking her out for a coffee or a drink but had hesitated at the last minute. He needed some time to understand what this chance meeting could mean. Was it just that? A chance. It didn't need to mean anything. He didn't need to act on it. He needed time to digest this situation. To figure it out.

Being in the same place again was just a coincidence and he didn't believe in coincidences.

But he couldn't deny that it had been good to see her again.

He swallowed a mouthful of beer as he recalled the first time he'd laid eyes on her.

He'd been sitting by himself at the bar in the Palace Hotel in Broken Hill—some things never changed, he thought wryly, although he had been waiting for a colleague. He'd been drinking too much, blocking out the previous two years. He'd already had one beer and was on to his second when she walked in.

The late-afternoon sun had silhouetted her in the doorway of the hotel and her golden curls had shone like a halo around her head. She was slim and elegant with a dancer's posture and a graceful walk.

He'd sat, mesmerised, as she'd walked towards him. He hadn't stopped to wonder why she was heading his way; at the time it had made perfect sense, as if his mind was willing her to come to him, as if she could read his thoughts. It was only when she joined him at the bar that he noticed that Jane, a Royal Flying Doctor flight nurse and one of his colleagues, was with her.

Jane introduced them and the news that this vision, Chloe, was going to be working with him for the next month was the best thing he'd heard in a long, long time. From that moment on he was scarcely aware of other colleagues and patrons coming and going around them. He was struck, not only by Chloe's natural beauty but by the joy that seemed to radiate from her. He'd been enthralled by her smile, her lips, the light in her brown eyes and her exuberance.

He had no idea of how long they'd stayed in the bar. All he knew was that he wasn't leaving until she did and eventually it was just the two of them, alone. One by one the others had left but Chloe had stayed on and, therefore, so had he.

She didn't have anywhere she had to be.

She'd flirted with him. Touched him on the arm. The thigh. Playing with her glorious hair. He thought he was too old for her, he was about to turn thirty but he'd felt ten years more than that; he *was* old but not so old that he didn't recognise the signs of mutual attraction.

He'd wondered, briefly, if it was a bad idea to let her know he was interested too but he hadn't wanted to resist. Hadn't been able to. Chloe had been very convincing and he hadn't fought against her for too long. He had behaved for one night but they both knew what was going to happen.

He remembered the anticipation.

Being with Chloe was the first thing he'd looked forward to for months.

He had been working with the Royal Flying Doctor Service for six months. It had long been a dream of his that had been squashed by his ex-wife, but when he'd finally made it to the service he'd felt a sense of relief that he was starting to put the past behind him rather than the sense of excitement he'd always hoped for. Chloe turned out to be the first bit of excitement he'd had in a long time. They'd had a brief but passionate affair. His head wasn't in the right place for anything more and she was only in town for a month, but it had been a bright point in an otherwise dark period of his life.

Their affair had burned bright. Their chemistry overshadowing conversation. Chloe was young, carefree, on a working holiday; she wasn't interested in anything deep and meaningful. He was jaded; he didn't want to dampen her enthusiasm for life with his tales of woe. That wasn't what she needed. It wasn't what *he* needed. He wanted to forget about his troubles and she allowed him to do that.

She was addictive.

Restorative.

And then she was gone.

CHAPTER THREE

CHLOE FOLDED HERSELF into a seat on the Tube. She was tired—it had been a long day and a busy shift—but her mind was buzzing. Memories of Xander, snippets of the past, filled her thoughts.

The subway tiles whizzed past as the train zipped through the stations. The press of bodies, the fluorescent lighting and the blackness of the tunnels suffocated her. She closed her eyes against the glare of the lights and let her mind drift back to four years ago.

The London Underground couldn't be further from the Australian outback. The close confines of the flying doctor plane had been replaced by the trains on the underground and the occasional helicopter flight. Going to the pub in Broken Hill or the races had been replaced with an occasional girls' night out and trips to the park with Lily. The feel of the sunlight on her skin and the smell of the eucalyptus trees and dirt had been replaced with the hospital air-conditioning and the polluted air of London.

Even in the outback there had never been complete darkness but instead of artificial lighting it had been the stars overhead. Instead of the press of bodies sometimes it was just her, Xander, the pilot and a patient. Four people in thousands of square kilometres.

Sometimes it had just been her and Xander under the night sky.

It had been such a short period in her life but she'd never forgotten it. How could she?

Her mind drifted back to the night she'd met Xander. To the night that changed her life.

She had just arrived in Broken Hill, in the Australian outback. It was her third and final month on a study exchange program with the flying doctor service. She'd already completed stints in Adelaide and Port Augusta and had loved every minute of it but she was hugely excited about being in the real outback. Broken Hill was what she'd pictured when she'd applied for the exchange. It was so totally different to anything she would ever experience back home and she couldn't wait.

Jane, one of the flight nurses, had taken her to drinks at the Palace Hotel. It was tradition for any newcomers to the service. The imposing two-storey redbrick hotel with its unusual internal artwork—murals that covered not only the walls but the ceilings too—had featured in several popular Australian movies and Chloe had been keen to visit the iconic hotel. But when they'd walked into the bar her attention had been captured, not by the architecture or artwork, but by a man sitting alone at the bar.

She couldn't remember anything else.

Tall, blond, long, lean and tanned. He was physically perfect. In Chloe's opinion he had not even one flaw.

He was wearing pale cotton trousers that moulded to his backside and a dark T-shirt that clung to his chest and showed off muscular arms. Every blond hair on his head was perfectly in place.

His skin was flawless, not a freckle to distract attention. His nose was straight, his jaw square, his shoulders broad. His eyebrows, a slightly darker blond than his hair, framed a pair of grey eyes. Physically he was perfect but there was something wounded in his expression. Something lost in his grey eyes. He cut a solitary, lonely figure and Chloe couldn't resist.

She'd always been drawn to the damaged, the wounded. She had seen the pain her father's treatment of her mother had caused. It had affected Chloe and her brothers too, and as the eldest child she had always felt a responsibility and desire to try to fix things for everyone. She wanted to make the world a better, happier place and she'd been fascinated by the solitary man at the bar, by his sense of loneliness and touch of despair. She'd been immediately interested and desperate to know more.

She couldn't remember whether Jane had led her to him or if she'd made a beeline herself. Either way, it didn't matter. She'd been captivated. She'd stayed long after Jane and the other flying doctor personnel had left. Talking to Xander.

She'd known instinctively that she would sleep with him. It wasn't a case of 'if' but 'when.'

It had been an amazing four weeks, a magical month, a pocket of time that she'd expected she would wrap up in her bank of memories. Something to be taken out and relived when she needed something to smile about. She hadn't expected to relive it every time she looked into her daughter's eyes.

But despite the way things had turned out she wouldn't

change anything. Well, maybe a few things. It had been a simple time in her life with no one to think about except for herself. That had certainly changed and she wouldn't go back to a time before Lily but that didn't mean there wasn't something to be said for an uncomplicated life.

Unfortunately, she felt in her bones that her life was about to become decidedly *more* complicated with Xander's unexpected appearance. And she needed time to work out what she was going to do about it.

'That's enough riding for now, Lily, why don't you go on the slide.' Chloe felt like a bad mother, cutting short Lily's ride on her new bike, but she was tired; she'd slept badly, and she needed a break from running after Lily to give her a little push every time she needed to restart her bike.

'Is everything all right?' her mother asked as Chloe wheeled the bike back to the park bench and Lily scampered off to the slide. 'You look tired.'

'I didn't sleep well,' Chloe admitted to her mother.

'Problems at work?' Susan was a nurse too; she was familiar with the pitfalls of the job, with those days that you couldn't leave behind at the hospital, with those patients who continued to live in your head even once your shift was finished.

'Sort of. We have a new doctor at the air ambulance.'

A doctor whose arrival meant that Chloe had tossed and turned all night but still hadn't been able to figure out what she was going to do about him.

'Was he or she difficult to work with?'

'No.' She needed her mother's advice. 'It's Xander.'

'Your Xander?'

Chloe nodded. Her mother and Chloe's brothers were

the only people who knew about him. 'He's not mine, but yes.'

'What is he doing here?'

'He's covering sick leave. He's only here for a few weeks.'

'So you think it's just a coincidence?'

'What?'

'That he's turned up here, working with the Air Ambulance Service?'

'It must be.' Chloe didn't believe in coincidences—she always thought things happened for a reason—but it had to be. He couldn't have come looking for her. She had only started working at the Queen Victoria Hospital after coming home from Australia. She'd applied to work there because it was the base for the Air Ambulance Service but Xander couldn't know that.

'Does he know about Lily?'

Chloe shook her head. 'How could he?' Chloe hadn't even put his name on Lily's birth certificate. She hadn't been able to without his consent.

'What are you going to do?'

'I'll have to tell him. I looked for him for six months.' She'd only stopped when Lily had been born—time and money had made it impractical to keep searching for someone who seemed to have completely disappeared. 'I just don't know when. That's why I'm tired. I've been awake all night thinking about what to do.'

Chloe had long since accepted that she would raise Lily as a single mother. Perhaps it wasn't ideal but it wasn't impossible and she was managing. What effect would Xander's reappearance have?

'It's been four years. How do you think he'll react to the news?' she asked her mother.

'I have no way of knowing. Some men will rise to the challenge, others may not—every one is different and so is every situation—and unfortunately, he's disappeared once before. But there's only one way to know for sure.'

Chloe sighed. 'He has never looked for me. He must have been happy to let me go.'

Her mother raised an eyebrow. 'You don't know that. And that doesn't mean he won't want to be a father. That's two very different relationships.'

'I don't think they're that easy to separate. My father couldn't do it.'

'Your father left me but he never intended to leave you children. Our marriage was over—his actions damaged it irreparably—but he didn't abandon you. He wasn't planning on dying.' Her mother looked over to where Lily slid happily down the slide. 'You owe it to Lily to tell Xander about her. You owe it to him too. There probably isn't going to be the perfect time. You're probably better off just getting it out in the open.'

'No.' Chloe shook her head. 'I need to find out more. I need to know why he's here. What's been going on in his life? What if he has a family of his own? He might not thank me for disrupting his life.'

She wondered if he'd changed that much. If he'd finally decided he wanted children. Or if he was still convinced he didn't. He might not want to know about Lily. Or worse, he might want Lily but not Chloe. 'There are far too many questions and you know how I hate asking a question that I don't know the answer to.'

Chloe didn't believe in coincidences and she didn't like surprises. She needed to collect the facts before she started disseminating information that could change everyone's lives.

She didn't really know him. She didn't know how he would react to this news. She hadn't known four years ago and she was no wiser now. The truth was, after Lily was born and she'd come to terms with the fact that Xander was gone, a part of her had been secretly relived that she hadn't been able to find him. It meant she didn't have to deal with any unpleasantness. Fantasy and reality were rarely the same thing.

She still needed to find out why he was here. What did his arrival mean for her? And for Lily?

Did he have a family? He wasn't wearing a wedding ring. What were his thoughts on fatherhood and commitment now? Four years was a long time. Things may have changed but she didn't want to tell him about Lily if he wasn't going to love her. Life was hard enough without being unloved or unwanted. She wouldn't expose her daughter to that.

'I think you're making excuses,' her mother told her.

Chloe knew she was but she was scared.

She knew she had to tell him about Lily, but when?

And what if someone else told him first? Shania had almost asked the question and her air ambulance colleagues knew she had a daughter. They never had a lot of time to chat about their personal lives when they were on a job; the flights were never more than eleven minutes in duration and they were either preparing for a job or often caring for a patient on a return. It wasn't often that they came back empty-handed. But what if one of her colleagues said something?

Thank God she wouldn't have to spend hours with Xander. Not that she'd minded four years ago but until she worked out what she was going to do about the situation she was better off keeping her distance. Luckily, she didn't spend her days in the air ambulance unit waiting for a call; she was only ever an additional team member, called in specially for certain jobs.

Her mother gave her a hug. 'There's only one way to know how this will turn out, Chloe, and that's to tell him the truth. You'll soon find out what he thinks then.'

Her mind and the discussion went around in a never-ending circle and by the time Lily got bored with the playground Chloe was no closer to a decision about what to do. No closer to figuring out how to deal with Xander's unexpected appearance.

Xander was edgy. It was a busy shift, most of them were. On average the air ambulance attended five call-outs each day but it wasn't the caseload that had him unsettled. Each time they received a call he was on tenterhooks, waiting to see if they would need a midwife, waiting to find out if he would see Chloe. He felt like he'd thought of nothing and no one but her for the past three days and he was determined to ask her out next time he saw her. Nothing ventured, nothing gained. But at the end of his shift he knew he couldn't continue just to wait for fate, or an emergency, to intervene. He was going quietly crazy. He'd have to go and find her.

He changed out of his orange flight overalls and headed down to A&E only to be told she was up in the maternity wards.

As he stepped out of the lift Chloe's golden curls caught his eye. Her back was to him as she pushed a wheelchair down the corridor. He could see she had a patient with her and he waited to see where she was going. He didn't want to have this conversation in public. She stopped at the door to the NICU, swiping her card and letting herself in. It was only a minute or so before she reappeared, by which time he was walking casually towards her.

'Xander! What are you doing here?'

'I thought I'd drop past and see how Shania was doing,' he said, improvising quickly to explain his presence.

'Physically she's doing well and she also had an interview with a social worker. She hasn't made any major decisions yet but at least she's looking at her options.'

'And the baby? Tonya?'

'She's doing brilliantly too. I've just taken Shania to the NICU to see her. They're both doing well.'

'In that case I won't interrupt,' he said as he fell into step beside her. 'Have you finished your shift?'

'No, not quite. Why?' she asked as she pressed the button to call the lift.

'I wondered if you'd like to have a drink with me? Tonight, after work?'

'Why?'

He hadn't expected her to question his reasons. 'To catch up,' he said simply. 'I wasn't expecting to see you. It was a nice surprise and I'd like to hear about what you've been up to.'

'I can't.'

'You can't tonight or can't full stop?' he asked as Chloe's phone buzzed in her pocket.

She took her phone out and looked at the screen as the lift arrived and the doors slid open. She stepped into the lift and turned to face him. She said, 'I'm sorry. I need to go,' but didn't answer his question.

The lift doors closed, leaving him standing in the corridor. Alone.

He was an idiot. Just because he was still single, confused by his feelings and out of his depth, didn't mean she was still in the same position. Of course she'd be busy. She had a life. He'd noticed she didn't wear a wedding ring but that didn't mean she didn't have a significant other. It had been four years.

Four years ago she'd brought light back into his life and he'd been searching for it again ever since. But that didn't mean she felt the same way. They'd had undeniable chemistry but that didn't mean to say she hadn't found that with somebody else.

He should leave her alone. He was old enough to know one shouldn't go back. But he didn't want to give up. Not yet.

He'd given her up once before.

Chloe tried to resist the temptation to look at her watch. Again. She couldn't believe she'd agreed to let Esther set her up on a date with one of Harry's friends. She had hoped that the date would help keep her mind off Xander's reappearance but it wasn't working.

She tried to be a bit more engaging. It wasn't Stephen's fault she wasn't giving this date her full attention. He was pleasant enough but he wasn't the one she wanted to spend an evening with. She should have cancelled the date or at least rescheduled—she knew she was wasting his time and hers—but it was too late now. She found herself constantly comparing Stephen to Xander and he was falling short.

She knew it wasn't Stephen per se. In the past four years no one had given her the same feeling of excitement and anticipation that she'd experienced with Xander and she was worried that her four weeks with

Xander had ruined her chances of finding someone else whom she could fall in love with.

Her thoughts drifted as Stephen tried gamely to engage her in conversation. She wondered what Xander was doing right now. She'd had to turn down his invitation, not only because she'd already agreed to this date but because she hadn't worked out what to tell him. She'd panicked when he invited her out. Her first thought had been, *Did he know about Lily?* Was that what he'd wanted to talk to her about? And despite telling herself there was no way he could know anything she'd gradually worked herself into a state.

She'd hoped her date with Stephen would be a good distraction, would give her something else to think about other than Xander, but it was *not* going well. If she was honest, it was a disaster. She wondered at what point it wouldn't be considered rude to make her excuses and leave.

'Harry said you work with him at the Queen Victoria. You're a nurse?'

'A midwife. In A&E.' Chloe made a concerted effort to tune back into the conversation. 'I work with the air ambulance service too,' she added. Most people found that aspect of her job interesting. Maybe Stephen would ask enough questions that she could focus on that.

'How did you get into that?' he asked, almost on cue.

'I spent some time in Australia on a study exchange working with their flying doctor service. I loved it so much that I applied for the air ambulance when I got back. It's the closest thing we have.'

'And what did you think of Australia?'

'I loved it. Have you been there?'

He nodded. 'I spent twelve months there as a Fellow. Couldn't stand it. The heat was terrible and those awful flies, not to mention the endless discussions about sport.'

Chloe had loved her time in Australia. Not the flies—she'd have to agree with him on that—but she'd loved everything else. She'd loved the relaxed lifestyle. She'd loved the weather. She'd loved the people. She'd loved Xander.

She sighed. Other than their careers as medical professionals she knew she and Stephen had nothing else in common and she figured there was absolutely no point in wasting any more of the evening for either of them. Thank God she hadn't agreed to dinner.

She excused herself from the table. She'd go to the ladies' and call her mum. She'd get her to text and say Lily was running a temperature and needed her. She knew a normal person would see that for the excuse it was but she didn't care. She'd be doing both of them a favour by cutting the night short.

Chloe slipped her phone back into her bag as she left the toilets and returned to the table telling herself she could manage another five minutes until her mum called with a reprieve.

She had taken two steps in that direction when she heard her name.

'Chloe!'

She closed her handbag and looked up into a pair of familiar grey eyes.

Xander.

She stopped in her tracks, incapable of moving. She could feel her heart racing in her chest and wondered if he could see it beating beneath her shirt.

Why was he here? Was he meeting someone? Had he invited someone else for a drink when she'd turned him down or was this just a coincidence?

'What are you doing here?' he continued. 'Did you change your mind about that drink?'

Chloe shook her head. 'No. I'm on a date.'

'Oh. Of course.'

Chloe tried to read his expression, to decipher his tone. Was he disappointed? And what did he mean by 'of course'? She hardly ever went on dates; this was the first one this year, the second one in four months. But she couldn't explain her reluctance to date and the reason why her opportunities were limited without divulging her secret. Or should that be secrets, plural? That no one measured up to her memory of him and that she was a single mother.

'Are you meeting someone here?' she asked.

'No.'

Was his presence here just a coincidence?

'It's good to see you but don't let me keep you,' he said, leaving her free to go.

Maybe she would have to start believing in coincidences, she thought as she reluctantly returned to her table and her date.

If she could get rid of Stephen perhaps she could salvage her evening?

He watched her walk away before taking a seat at the bar.

What was it about Chloe? he thought as he nodded to the barman and held up one finger, indicating his usual, as he took a seat. He was a sensible, intelligent man but whenever he saw her, whenever she was near, all logical thoughts seemed to evaporate. Of course, she wouldn't have known he would be at that pub. It was close to the Queen Victoria Hospital but it wasn't the closest and it wasn't the local for the hospital staff. It was, however, near the short-term rental apartment where he was staying and he'd got into the habit of stopping in for a beer and something to eat. It was simpler to be fed than to cook and it gave him some company.

He'd just swallowed the first mouthful of his beer when Chloe reappeared.

'Is this seat taken?'

She was smiling and his heart leapt. Had she ditched her date? For him? He couldn't help the feeling of excitement as she sat on the bar stool next to him. The anticipation was familiar. *She* was familiar.

'What happened to your date?'

'He left.'

'What?'

She laughed and the sound was so familiar, so comforting, that it lifted his spirits even when he hadn't realised his spirits needing lifting. He hadn't realised a lot of things. Once again, Chloe brought light into his life, only this time he hadn't been aware of the darkness. Four years ago he'd known he was in a dark place and Chloe had got him out of it. He slipped back after she'd left and despite his concerted efforts to find happiness and make peace with the world he knew now he hadn't been successful.

'I told him that it wasn't working for me and I didn't want to waste more of his time.'

'Are you leaving too?'

'No,' she replied as she shook her head. Her bright

golden curls glowed in the light as she shook her head. She was striking, vivacious, a beacon.

'Good. Will you have that drink with me now?'

'Are you sure you're not meeting friends?'

'No.' He had a few friends in London—acquaintances, really, all in the medical field—but most were now married with children and they didn't have the flexibility or luxury of being able to meet for a midweek dinner. He'd caught up with a few for a drink or two on occasion but, ultimately, they all had to go home to their wives and families. 'And even if I was, you'd still be welcome to join us. But I'm here because I'm staying just around the corner. I'm just grabbing some dinner and a beer,' he said as the barman handed him a wooden board with a burger and a side of fries on it. 'Have you eaten?'

'No. I'm not hungry but I'll stay for a drink.'

'A gin and tonic?'

'Yes. Thank you,' she said as she reached over and pinched a chip off his plate. That was familiar too. He remembered she would order own her meal and then prefer to eat his.

'So the date went badly.'

'It wasn't the worst one I've ever had but it was close.' She was grinning. She didn't look too upset. In fact, she didn't look upset at all—she looked amazing.

'What seemed to be the problem?'

'He wasn't my type.'

'You have a type?'

'I guess so.'

The barman served Chloe's gin, placing it on the bar. She couldn't believe Xander had remembered her favourite drink and the idea that he had pleased her.

She was glad she'd come back to find him after making her excuses to Stephen. She'd put Lily to bed before heading out and her mum wasn't expecting her home anytime soon. She had plenty of time to have one drink with Xander. Just to catch up on what he'd been doing.

He picked up her drink and put it in front of her. His leg brushed against hers and the contact made her jump. It was nothing, really—his knee brushed the outside of her thigh—but she could feel his body heat even through her trousers and her body responded to his touch.

'So, your type,' he said as she stirred her drink, 'describe him to me.'

She took a sip of her drink, taking a moment to gather her thoughts. 'Someone with a bit more energy. Someone who makes me feel excited. Filled with possibility. Someone who makes me wonder what happens next.'

Someone who made her feel like Xander did.

'You're talking about chemistry,' he said.

She nodded and put her glass back on the bar and tried to ignore the fact that his leg was still resting against hers.

Sitting at the bar with Xander felt the same but different.

Familiar but strange.

Things had changed. At least for Chloe. She was no longer young and carefree. She was a single mother with responsibilities. But the chemistry was still there. She was still drawn to him. She longed to touch him properly, to see if her memories were real.

He was still gorgeous. Still a Norse god. His grey eyes still held a trace of melancholy. She'd always at-

tributed that to his divorce but surely that couldn't still
be the case. He'd been divorced almost five years now.
He must have put that behind him?

She forced herself to focus on the present. She
couldn't dwell in the past.

'How long have you been living in Wales?' she asked
when she recovered her power of speech. She was desperate to know where he'd been and what he'd been
doing for the past four years but she couldn't ask such
a direct question.

He frowned, his grey eyes cloudy. 'I don't live in
Wales.'

'Oh, I thought Rick said you had come down from
Wales to cover Eloise's sick leave.'

'I've been working in Wales with their air ambulance
unit but it wasn't permanent. It was a six-month rota-
tion. I was glad to get out of there, to be honest. I didn't
mind Wales but it wasn't the smartest move, spending
winter there. I should have timed it better.'

'And what are your plans when you finish with us?'
she asked. She needed to find out where he was going
next. Did she need to tell him about Lily if he had no
plans to stay in England? Was there any point in disrupting everyone's lives? She and Lily were fine—they'd
been fine for years on their own. They didn't need Xander and he might not need them.

He might not *want* them.

He might not want her.

The drink he had bought her could be for old times'
sake. He wasn't wearing a wedding ring but that didn't
mean he didn't have a wife or significant other waiting
for him somewhere.

'I haven't worked it out yet.'

'Are you travelling with family?' she asked as the barman cleared the remnants of Xander's dinner away.

'No. We're both still single. What are the chances?'

'Coincidence?' she said with a smile.

'I don't believe in coincidences.'

'Me either.'

He was holding her gaze and she was lost. She couldn't think. She could only feel.

He reached for her and the clocks stopped.

He tucked a stray curl behind her ear and Chloe's knees trembled. 'It's been a long time,' he said as she held her breath. 'It's good to see you. Did I mention I'm staying just around the corner?'

The invitation was unspoken but there was no mistaking it. But she couldn't accept. She had to get home. To her daughter. Their daughter.

'You did.'

'Would you like to come back for a coffee?'

Chloe smiled. 'You know I don't drink coffee at night.' She wondered if he remembered that too.

'I do.'

Her smile got wider. 'Will you take a rain check? I'm on an early tomorrow.'

'I will.'

She slid off the bar stool and picked up her coat. She needed to get out of here while she still could. Before she made a hasty, hormonal decision that she would more than likely regret when her head overtook her heart again.

'I'll walk you out to a cab.'

'It's okay, I'm taking the Tube.'

Xander shook his head. 'No, it's late. That doesn't sound safe.'

'I do it all the time after work.'

'Really?'

She nodded as he held the door for her.

She stopped on the footpath, reluctant to walk away but knowing she had to go. A cab pulled up on the street beside them.

'Please, let me pay for a cab,' Xander offered. 'I'll feel better.' He reached out and opened the door, ensuring the cabbie couldn't drive away, but then he took her hand, holding her back before she could step inside.

She turned to him. Instinctively. Her breath caught in her throat as he stroked the palm of her hand with his thumb. She was pinned by the force of his grey eyes. Held immobile by the intensity of his gaze. She couldn't breathe. The air was thick with tension. Her mouth was dry, her skin warm, her cheeks flushed. Her heart was beating quickly and her stomach was fluttering.

'Are you sure you have to go?'

She nodded.

He bent his head until his mouth was next to her ear. His breath was warm on her cheek as he repeated her earlier words back to her. 'Are you sure you don't want to find out what happens next?'

She knew what was coming and she was powerless to resist. She didn't want to resist. She turned her face towards him and whispered, 'I know what happens next.' And then his lips were on hers. Warm, soft. Then harder.

She parted her lips and tasted him. He tasted familiar. He tasted sweet.

Her body remembered his touch. Her skin remembered the softness of his mouth. Her tongue remembered his taste.

The years fell away as the memory of him returned.

Xander's fingers were on her face, on her bare arms. Her skin was on fire and she melted against him as her body responded to his touch. She was aware of nothing else except the sensation of being fully alive. She wanted for nothing except Xander.

One hand was pressed to her spine, holding her close, and she could feel the heat of his palm through the thin fabric of her shirt. She felt her nipples harden as she pressed herself against his chest instead as she kissed him back. All her senses came to life and a line of fire spread from her stomach to her groin. She deepened the kiss, wanting to lose herself in Xander.

'Do you want the cab or not?'

She jumped as the cab driver's voice interrupted their moment. Her eyes flew open as Xander straightened up. He was studying her face as if committing each of her features to memory.

He smiled as his fingers trailed down the side of her cheek, sending a shiver of desire through her. Her heart was racing in her chest and her breaths were shallow.

'Are you sure you don't want to come back to my apartment?'

She hesitated. The kiss was wonderful. Magical. She felt as if time had stood still and brought her back to Xander, back into his arms, but she couldn't stay with him. She had responsibilities.

'I can't,' she said as she stepped back, breaking their connection. 'You promised me a rain check, remember?'

She waited for him to agree before she made herself get into the taxi. Made herself leave him.

He closed the door and blew her a kiss.

Chloe gave the driver her address but scarcely re-called getting home. Her world suddenly felt full of possibility but she needed to be sensible. She needed to be careful not to get carried away.

CHAPTER FOUR

CHLOE JOGGED ACROSS the helipad. This time she could see Xander's familiar figure in the chopper. She was looking for him and her heart rate increased. The memory of his kiss was still fresh in her mind. She could almost feel the imprint of his lips on hers still.

She smiled in greeting as she climbed aboard. Was it only a few days ago that he'd re-entered her life? She felt lighter. Happier. Full of hope.

Since he kissed her some of her doubts had vanished. She knew she was being fanciful; just because he made her toes tingle and her pulse race didn't mean he'd want to be a part of her life. It didn't mean he'd want to be a father but she couldn't help the lifting of her spirits. It was amazing what a good kiss had done for her frame of mind. The dark clouds had lightened a little.

She was remembering how she'd felt all those years ago. How *he* made her feel. It was a long time since she'd been kissed senseless. Since she'd felt as if she could lose control.

But she needed to be careful. Last time she lost control she wound up pregnant.

But that thought still couldn't wipe the smile from

her face as she fastened her harness and strapped herself into her seat as she listened to the situation report.

He smiled back at her and she imagined the shadows in his eyes had eased a little.

She blushed and looked away, focusing on the information being dispersed.

'We're attending a two-car MVA,' Rick said. 'Paramedics and fire service are at the scene. There are four patients. Two victims trapped and unconscious, a third with minor injuries and a fourth is a pregnant woman, thirty-six weeks' gestation, in cardiac arrest. Paramedics are giving ALS.'

Chloe translated the report in her head. Four victims of a motor vehicle accident: two status unknown, one conscious and mobile, one in a critical condition receiving advanced life support.

'We'll need to triage on arrival,' Xander instructed. He was back to business.

Chloe knew the order of treatment would be determined by a few things. Whether or not the fire crew had managed to extricate the trapped victims and what injuries they had sustained. Whether or not the paramedics had managed to resuscitate the woman and, if they hadn't, were they still trying or was she deceased. There were a lot of unknowns but this wasn't unusual. The job this time though was complicated by the number of victims. They'd been told four but, in Chloe's head, she was counting five. At thirty-six weeks' gestation the baby was potentially a fifth casualty.

Nine minutes after take-off Simon banked the helicopter over the M25. Beneath them Chloe could see the accident site on one of the approach roads. Flashing lights of the emergency vehicles lit up the grey and drizzly day and bounced off the reflective panels on the uniforms of the emergency teams. Debris was strewn across the road and she could see the fire service still working on one of the crumpled cars, trying to free the victims.

Police had cordoned off the road and Simon brought the chopper down on the bitumen as Chloe pulled on a pair of gloves. Rick had the door open as soon as they touched down and Chloe, Rick and Xander grabbed their kits and sprinted to the scene.

A woman lay on a spinal board on a stretcher, two paramedics in attendance. Between them Chloe could see the mound of her pregnancy. The woman had been intubated and was being manually ventilated by one of the paramedics.

A pair of ambulances had stopped on the hard shoulder. In the back of one sat an older woman. She had a blanket wrapped around her shoulders as a third paramedic cleaned her head wound. Chloe wondered if she was related to the pregnant woman. Someone must have given the first responders some background information.

Xander paused beside the stretcher and Chloe heard him introduce himself.

'What's the situation?'

'Thirty-year-old woman, thirty-six weeks' gestation, suffered a cardiac arrest, non-responsive. I've administered three milligrams of atropine and eight milligrams of epinephrine via IV. Intubated on the first attempt and manual ventilation continuing. She has a head trauma, most likely the cause of the cardiac arrest, a facial cyanosis and an abdominal seat-belt hematoma. I'm concerned about an abdominal haemorrhage.'

'We can do an abdominal ultrasound on board the chopper if she can be moved.'

The paramedics nodded and the woman was transferred to the helicopter. It took all of the first responders working in unison. Four to lift the spinal board while Chloe held the drip.

Xander cut through the woman's clothing while resuscitation attempts continued around him. Her exposed belly was tight and drum-like. Chloe had the ultrasound ready. She handed Xander the transducer and squeezed the aqueous gel onto the patient's abdomen.

There was a heartbeat but it belonged to the foetus.

'There are signs of an abdominal haemorrhage but the bleeding has slowed.'

'How long since ALS commenced?' Xander asked as he wiped off the ultrasound gel.

'Fourteen minutes.'

'And the delay between the cardiac arrest and treatment?'

'Several minutes.'

'We could lose them both at this rate.' Xander looked at Chloe. 'Do we try to save one?'

She knew he was talking about saving the baby.

She nodded.

'What are you going to do?' Rick asked.

'If you can continue ventilation, we can perform a C-section to deliver the baby.'

'Here?'

It was Xander's turn to nod.

'Have you done this before?'

'Once.'

Xander's grey eyes were dark. Chloe suspected from

his expression that the last time didn't go so well. She hoped he'd learnt from the experience.

'Are you okay to help me?' he asked her.

She nodded. She was prepared to support him in this decision. She knew he wouldn't be suggesting this option if he thought the baby would survive any other way. They may even be able to save both patients.

They pulled a fresh pair of surgical gloves on over the first.

Chloe tore open sterile packages containing surgical instruments and laid them on the seat beside her. She poured disinfectant liberally over the woman's abdomen, spreading it across her skin.

Xander picked up a scalpel and made a deep incision, slicing through the woman's abdomen from her umbilicus to her pubic bone. Blood was pooled in her abdominal cavity obstructing their vision. Chloe packed gauze into the abdomen, soaking up the blood, as Xander tied off an artery.

The blood was dealt with quickly and no more appeared. The woman remained unresponsive. Without a pulse she wasn't able to bleed.

Xander had his hands inside the woman's abdomen. He palpated her uterus, looking and feeling for signs of trauma.

Chloe knew he was making the right decision. If they didn't deliver this baby they would have two fatalities.

'The uterus is intact,' he said but it didn't remain that way for long.

Xander cut the uterus open and swiftly lifted the baby from the womb.

A boy.

He handed him to Chloe.

The whole procedure had taken less than four minutes.

'No meconium, cord intact and free, placenta intact,' Xander recounted while Chloe focused on her patient.

The baby was pink but flaccid. He wasn't crying. Or breathing. He had no reflexes on stimulus and his heart rate was well below ideal at just sixty beats per minute. He had a one-minute Apgar score of three out of ten. He was not out of danger yet.

Chloe dried the baby, rubbing him vigorously to warm him up and hopefully stimulate respiration. When that didn't work she wrapped him to keep him warm and prepared to suction his airway.

Xander was stitching the woman's abdomen but she saw him glance over at her.

'Do you need help?'

She nodded. 'He's not breathing. Pulse only sixty. Can you get ready to bag him?'

Xander ripped off his gloves before pulling on another clean pair. He grabbed a mask and attached the bag, placing the tiny mask over the baby's face when Chloe removed the suction tube.

The baby's heart rate remained low, despite the oxygen that was now being pumped into him.

'Swap places with me,' Xander instructed.

'What are you going to do?'

'Administer epinephrine.'

Xander didn't bother looking for a vein on the tiny struggling baby. He used an intraosseous needle, injecting the drug directly into the bone marrow in the tibia in an attempt to stimulate his heart.

Chloe kept bagging the newborn, holding her own breath as she waited for signs of improvement.

The five-minute Apgar score was three points better. The heart rate was above one hundred and the skin was pink-coloured. The reflexes were still absent and there was no grimace but there was spontaneous, albeit irregular, respiratory drive.

Chloe relaxed slightly but monitored the baby closely as Simon flew them to the hospital.

It was a flurry of activity from the moment they touched down on the helipad. The neonatal team whisked the baby away to the neonatal intensive care unit and Chloe followed. He wasn't her patient any longer but she needed to know he was going to be okay.

She waited while the neonatal team assessed the baby. It seemed wrong to leave him alone with no one to watch over him. His mother hadn't made it—she'd been declared deceased on arrival—and Chloe's heart went out to the tiny newborn who'd had such a traumatic introduction to the world.

Who was going to be responsible for this baby?

Her mind returned to the older woman she'd seen sitting in the back of the ambulance at the scene of the accident. She wondered where she was. Who she was. The grandmother? Had anyone told her what had happened to her family?

Chloe's mind drifted to her own daughter. Who would be there for Lily if something happened to her? Her mother? Her brothers?

Her mother was a young grandmother but raising another child on her own at her age? Chloe knew she'd do it but it wasn't right. And her brothers had their own lives to live.

Lily had a father. Chloe had Xander listed in her will. If anything should happen to her, she'd asked that he be found. But four years ago he hadn't wanted a family. Had things changed? Would he want Lily now?

Her thoughts were maudlin. Triggered by the day's events.

One life taken, one life saved. Chloe didn't know whether it had been a good day or a bad day.

It could have been better.

It could have been worse.

By the time the baby had been checked and given a relatively good prognosis her shift had ended and she could go home. She was surprised to find she was still wearing her flight overalls. They were covered in blood—she must look a complete mess. She couldn't leave the hospital like that.

She went upstairs to the air ambulance unit to change. Her hands were shaking as she stripped off the jumpsuit and tossed it into the laundry hamper. She stood still, gathering her thoughts, searching for the energy to turn around and go home.

She made it outside but couldn't make it much further than a bench overlooking the river. Her vision was blurry and her legs were weak.

She sat, letting the London commuters flow around her as they made their way home. She needed to give her wobbly knees a chance to rest and her brain a chance to reset. Her thoughts were disturbed, her mind circling. She couldn't seem to separate the baby's fate from her own past.

'Chloe, are you okay?'

She turned at the sound of his voice. Xander was standing beside the bench, his grey eyes shadowed, his brow furrowed with concern.

'Not really.' Her voice wobbled and her eyes filled with tears.

'Is it the baby?'

She shook her head. 'No, he's okay, but the mother didn't make it.'

'I heard.'

Chloe wiped her cheeks with the back of her hand. Her face was wet with tears. 'I'm sorry. I don't know why I'm upset.' But she did know. She was finding it hard to separate her life from their patients' today. She wasn't usually so affected by her work. By the tragedies. Normally she could compartmentalise.

Perhaps it had something to do with Xander's reappearance. She'd found herself unsettled, off-kilter, for the past few days. Her personal and professional lives were colliding. And today's events reminded her that she'd grown up without a parent and she'd put her daughter, Lily, in the same position.

'Don't apologise,' Xander said as he sat down next to her. 'Some jobs just get to us more than others.' He wrapped his arm around her, completely unaware of the direction of her thoughts.

Chloe leaned into him. She fitted perfectly into his side.

'You're freezing. Come on, you need to get out of the cold.'

Despite Xander's body heat she wasn't warming up. There was a breeze coming off the river and the spring evening was getting chilly now that the sun was setting.

He pulled her to her feet but kept his arm wrapped around her.

'Where are we going?'

'To get you warmed up. My flat is about five hundred metres along the river.'

She didn't argue. Her brain was too cold to stage a protest.

He walked on the river side of her along the Albert Embankment, keeping her sheltered from the wind, and guided her into a large, modern building overlooking the Thames. He kept her tucked against his side as they went up in the lift, almost as if he was afraid she would vanish if he let her go. He had no idea she was incapable of making any decisions at the moment. She had her eyes closed as she rested her head against his chest and listened to the sound of his heartbeat. Its steady rhythm was soothing, helping to settle her anxious mind.

She matched her steps to his, the thick carpet muffling their footsteps, as they crossed the corridor to his apartment. He swiped his card and held the door for her. A small entry foyer led into an open-plan living, dining, kitchen area on the left with, she assumed, a bedroom and bathroom to the right.

Xander switched on the lights and steered her towards a small couch. It was the only seating option aside from the dining chairs. She heard Xander flick the heating on and fill the kettle but her gaze was drawn to the bank of floor-to-ceiling windows. The apartment was modern, generic, impersonal but the view over the river was spectacular. She curled up on the couch and let her gaze wander over the London skyline. The Houses of Parliament, Big Ben and the London Eye were spread out before her as the city lights began to glow as dusk deepened.

Xander placed a mug of coffee on the table in front of her but poured a nip of brandy into it before he passed it to her. He placed a plate of sweet biscuits on the table and sat beside her.

The couch seemed even smaller once Xander was sharing it with her. His thigh brushed against hers as he sat down and Chloe was tempted to climb into his lap. She made conversation to fill the silence, which she felt was becoming a little awkward.

'Did you notice the older lady at the scene of the accident?' she asked as she wrapped her hands around the mug to stop the shaking. Her hands felt like blocks of ice and she wondered if she'd ever feel warm again. 'The one who was in the back of the ambulance? Do you know who she was?'

'She was the baby's grandmother.'

'I wonder if she knows what has happened.'

'Is that what's bothering you?'

'Not just that.' Chloe shook her head. 'I've been wondering who is going to look after the baby. Does he have a father somewhere? Family. What if his grandmother is all he has?'

'At least he'll have someone.'

'He should have a mother. Better yet, he should have two parents.'

'We did everything possible, Chloe.'

'I know that. I'm not blaming anyone. It's just not the way things are meant to be.'

'There's absolutely no point worrying about things you can't change. I learnt that lesson a long time ago.'

'And I learnt the hard way that it's better to have two parents.'

'You did?'

Chloe nodded. 'I grew up without my father. He died when I was seven.'

Xander wrapped one arm around her shoulders and pulled her against his side. He held her quietly and his touch was reassuring. 'Do you want to tell me what happened?'

'He was a policeman, killed while on duty.'

'Oh, Chloe, that must have been tough.'

'It was.' She'd been angry at her father. He'd had an affair and had left her mother and his children. Chloe hadn't been able to understand how he could leave them all, how he could abandon her, and she hadn't forgiven him. And then he'd been killed responding to an armed robbery and she'd never had the chance to forgive him. She couldn't bring herself to tell Xander the full story right now; she still felt guilty about her anger. She didn't mention that he'd already abandoned them, had already walked out on them all to move in with his girlfriend, when he was killed. She tried not to think about that. She tried to forget that he'd chosen to leave them. She didn't subscribe to her mother's theory that he had left her but not his children. Her father had made a choice and she'd been left behind. 'Mum has raised us on her own.'

She had never told him any of this and talking about it now reminded her of how little they knew of each other. She had based her memories on a man who she'd possibly created in her imagination.

She went to sip her coffee and realised she'd finished it. She stared into her empty cup.

She was warming up but now she was restless. She jiggled her feet, making her knees jump up and down. She didn't like talking about her past. She should go home but she was reluctant to leave just yet.

Xander reached over and took the mug from her

hands, placing it on the coffee table. 'You're still cold.' There was a small throw rug draped over the end of the couch. He pulled it towards him and wrapped it around her shoulders. She leant into him as he draped the blanket over her. She couldn't help it. She was drawn to him. She'd always been drawn to him.

'It's the one thing I can't get used to,' he continued as he held her hands. 'The cold. And the sense of space.'

'That's two things.'

'So it is.' He smiled and her feeling of hopelessness lifted.

'How long have you been away for?' she asked.

'Four years. On and off. Before Wales I was in Canada and in South Africa before that. I've been home on a couple of occasions but I've been gone for over twelve months this time. I was thinking about heading home once I finished here but...'

'But?'

He was rubbing her hands between his, warming them up. He stopped rubbing when she asked the question but he didn't let go of her.

'Now I'm not sure.' He was looking at her intently, his grey eyes serious and considerate. 'I don't believe in coincidences but I do believe in fate.'

She believed in fate too but she knew it could bring both good and bad fortune. Fate had introduced her to Xander and then taken her away from him.

Fate had given her Lily when she'd needed someone to love.

'I'm wondering if there's a reason we've found ourselves here together again,' he said.

Chloe was convinced there was a reason that Xander was back in her life. She just wasn't sure if he was going to *like* the reason. She had no idea if he was going to want to be a father. She knew this was an opportunity to tell him about Lily but she couldn't bring herself to start that discussion. She was exhausted, emotionally worn out, and she didn't think she could do justice to this conversation tonight. Xander seemed happy to talk so she stayed silent. She knew she was being a coward but it was the easier option.

He lifted her legs and rested them in his lap. He picked up her hand and kissed her fingertips. 'I've missed you.'

She wanted to tell him she'd missed him too. That she'd thought of him every day. But her voice caught in her throat. She was too afraid.

Her eyes filled with tears.

Had they wasted four years? Could they still be together? Could they have lasted?

He misunderstood her tears but she didn't care as he gathered her into his arms and stroked her hair. 'It's okay. It's just been a bad day. Everything will look better in the morning.'

It's the sort of thing she would say to Lily. The sort of thing her mother would say to her. The sort of thing a father might say.

But he didn't want children.

She let him comfort her anyway.

'Would you like to stay for dinner?' he asked. 'I'll order something in.'

She shook her head. 'I can't.' She couldn't stay. She couldn't risk it. There was too much at stake now.

She hadn't told her mother she'd be late and both Susan and Lily would be expecting her home soon if she didn't call. She wanted to be home in time to put Lily to bed. Lily was her priority. As much as she wanted to stay, Lily came first.

She had a daughter to get home to. Their daughter.

She was going to have to figure out how to tell him he was a father. She couldn't let this attraction go any further without telling him first. And she wanted to take this further. She knew it would happen. It was inevitable. Just like four years ago. Was her memory distorted by rose-tinted glasses? Tainted by her feelings for him as Lily's father? She didn't know but she knew she couldn't resist him. She didn't *want* to resist him.

'Can I see you over the weekend, then?' Xander's question jolted her out of her thoughts.

'One of my girlfriends is getting married in a couple of weeks. I'm a bridesmaid and we've a full day of preparations planned for tomorrow.'

'How about on Sunday?'

'I have a family thing.' But she couldn't leave without knowing that she'd see him again. 'I'd love to make plans—can I call you later and we'll sort something out?'

He nodded and said, 'Pass me your phone. I'll put my number in it.'

He stored his number in her phone and walked her out to hail a cab.

'I'll sit by the phone,' he said as he kissed her goodbye, 'waiting for your call.'

'You have a mobile. You can keep it with you.'

He grinned as she climbed into the cab. 'I'll still be waiting.'

Xander watched the tail lights of the cab fade into the distance, taking Chloe away. The ball was in her court now. Would she call him? Their chemistry hadn't faded; the spark between them was still bright. She had to feel it too. Would he get another chance?

He wanted a chance to get to know her again but this time he knew it would be different. Four years ago he hadn't been prepared for a serious relationship. He'd been emotionally, mentally and physically battered and bruised. A bit of a mess. She had been a bright light… one he hadn't wanted to dim by subjecting her to his tales of woe. She had lifted him out of his funk.

She'd changed his life in the short time that he'd known her. She'd brightened up his life, but he hadn't expected her to take some of that hope and light with her when she'd left. He'd expected that they'd have a brief affair and they would both move on with their lives. He hadn't been looking for anything more than what they'd shared. A brief physical encounter. It hadn't been until she'd gone that he'd realised how much he missed her. But he still hadn't been in a position to offer her anything.

She had changed him. But not enough.

He wished he hadn't let her go but, even now, he knew that had been the right thing to do.

Four years ago he hadn't been capable of getting into something where there would be an expectation of a long life. A family. All the things that normal people dreamt of. He had been looking short term then. Five years ahead. Not fifty.

But what about now? His life was different now. *He* was different.

He knew he had changed. He was in a better place emotionally. Not as wrung out. He'd recuperated and he was able to look to the future again. He was five years post-chemotherapy, four years divorced. He'd made peace with what had happened to him.

But peace was not happiness and he wanted to be happy again. The last time he'd been happy had been with Chloe.

He'd travelled the world since then searching for something. Searching for something to replace what she'd given him.

Happiness and hope.

He didn't have either of those things any more but was he expecting too much to hope that Chloe could or would give them back to him?

'How did your date go?'

Chloe pushed open the door to the bridal salon and was immediately accosted by Carly. For a moment she thought Carly was asking about Xander. She could still feel the imprint of Xander's hands on her skin, his lips on hers, and she could feel herself blushing before realising Carly was talking about Stephen. 'Are you bringing him to Esther's wedding?'

Chloe glanced at Esther. She had texted her to tell her that the date was a disaster. She mustn't have shared that information with Carly.

'I've given Esther the sack as a matchmaker.'

'Oh. What was the problem?'

She was blaming Esther, although she knew it wasn't her friend's fault. Stephen had been pleasant enough but he hadn't set her world on fire. In short, he hadn't made her feel like Xander did. 'We weren't compatible and I didn't want to waste his time, or mine.'

'You don't think you were being hasty?' Carly asked.

'No.' She shook her head. 'But it wasn't all bad,' she

said as the shop assistant brought out armfuls of bridesmaid's dresses and arranged them on a rack.

The girls moved into one large change room and continued their conversation while they tried on the dresses, attempting to find something in a colour that suited them both and a style that flattered their figures.

'I actually ended up having a good night,' Chloe said as she stripped off her jeans and T-shirt.

'What? You went home alone. Has that become your definition of a good night?'

'I didn't go straight home.' She could see Carly's raised eyebrows as Esther zipped her into a pink dress. This was news to her.

'You didn't tell me that!'

'I figured you deserved to be fed information in small doses after the date you subjected me to,' Chloe told her. 'But then a guy at the bar offered to buy me a drink and I said yes.'

Chloe stepped into a bias cut, emerald green silk dress. Esther zipped up the dress. 'That colour isn't bad and the cut is flattering,' she said as Carly asked, 'Did you get his number? Will you see him again?'

Chloe nodded. 'Yes. He's just started work with the air ambulance. He's a doctor.' She didn't mention that he was from Australia. That she knew him before. That he was Lily's father. She wasn't ready for that conversation.

'I don't think I like the pink,' Esther said as she flicked through the racks and discarded anything floral or lace. 'I don't want anything that bright.' She turned back to Chloe. 'So, apart from work, will you see him again?'

'Yes.'

'When?'

'I'm not sure. I've got his number. I have to work out a time.'

'I'm organising drinks for Harry's birthday this Thursday,' Esther said. 'Why don't you invite him to that? I'll make sure *not* to invite Stephen.'

Chloe had planned on having a date, just the two of them, but perhaps a social event was a good idea. She could get to know him again a little better first, have a casual conversation, and she wouldn't feel pressured to mention Lily.

'I'll think about it,' she said before she turned her attention back to the task at hand. 'Now, what are we going to wear?'

'How about this?' Carly pulled a navy dress off the rack and held it up.

Esther smiled. 'Yes, that's perfect. I love it. Try it on.'

CHAPTER FIVE

'HAVING FUN?' ASKED Chloe's brother as he came to stand beside her.

Chloe was aware of some sideways glances from the other mums who had brought their children to the fire station open day as Guy stopped to talk to her. There was something about a man in uniform and Guy was tall, dark and handsome but Chloe knew he was also oblivious to the attention, totally besotted with his girlfriend of eighteen months.

'Lily is having an absolute blast,' she replied as she looked over to where Lily, wearing wellies, was stomping around in the puddles of water that had been left on the ground after the fire hose demonstration.

'I'm glad,' Guy told her, 'but I asked if *you* were having fun. This invitation was for you as well. I thought it would be a good way to introduce you to some of my single friends without it feeling like a set-up.'

Chloe was horrified. 'Why would you do that?'

'I've been wondering what your plans are. You're in danger of becoming an old lady before your time, staying home with Mum. You can't live with her for ever. You need some company your own age.'

'Don't you start!'

'What do you mean?'

'Everyone I know seems to be pushing me to date just because they've all found "the one." Carly and Adem, Esther and Harry, you and Hannah. You know I love the idea of being in love but I'm not like the rest of you. I'm not sure that I believe it can last for ever. It's hard to trust enough to give my heart away.' Especially when she'd done it once and it hadn't ended as she would have liked.

She hadn't planned to fall in love and it scared her how quickly she'd fallen for Xander. Her family thought she mistrusted men and was scared to love because of what happened with her father, but it was more than that. She'd been fearful to trust before meeting Xander and then when she met him all her defences were lowered. She'd fallen hard and fast. She had thought it was just a fling, an infatuation, and only later did she realise how serious she had been and how that fling tainted all other attempted relationships afterwards. Her reticence had less to do with her father and everything to do with Xander.

'Well, even if you don't want to date, what if Mum does? What if you're cramping her style?'

Chloe was aghast. She'd never even considered that she might be hindering her mother's social life. 'Has she said something to you?'

'No.' Guy laughed. 'I'm just stirring you up. But seriously, you can't stay tucked away with your mother and your daughter for the rest of your life.'

'I'm a bit preoccupied at the moment.'

'With what?'

She hesitated fractionally before deciding she could use his advice. Despite being four years younger than her Guy had an old head on his shoulders and he'd always had an emotional intelligence that she had sometimes envied. 'Xander is in London,' she told him. 'Working with the air ambulance team.'

'Xander? Australian Xander? As in...' Guy looked over to one of the fire engines where Lily was now sitting in the front seat beside her granny with a huge smile on her face.

'Yep.'

'Does he know?'

'Not yet.'

'You *are* going to tell him?'

'Of course I am. I'm just working out when.'

'What's the hold-up?'

'I don't want to spring it on him. It feels very sudden and abrupt to tell him when he's just arrived here.'

'What if Lily was the result of a one-night stand? Would you feel the same then? That you'd need to get to know the father better in that situation before you told him what had happened?'

'That's different.'

'Why?'

'Well, for one, I've never had a one-night stand so I can't imagine myself in that situation.' Even though she knew, the moment she met Xander, that she would sleep with him she waited until she knew it would be more than one night. She needed to get to know him first. She needed reassurance that he wasn't just going to sleep with her and run. 'And two, I'm not sure that I would tell them anything.'

'Really?'

'Would you want to know?' she asked.

'Of course. I have a responsibility. But I guess if

Xander is in London, you've got some time to think about it but he has a right to know. If I were you I wouldn't wait too long. He'll wonder why you haven't told him and I can't say I'd blame him.'

'I don't have all that long actually. He's only here for six weeks.'

And three of those weeks had already passed.

'You'd better spend some time with him, then. And quickly. If you like, why don't the four of us have dinner together?'

'Me, Xander, you and Hannah?' She assumed Guy was including his girlfriend in the group of four. 'Why?'

'I'd like to meet him and that gives you a reason to invite him out. Although Hannah is flat out with her final placement and studying for her final exams. Maybe we should ask Tom instead.'

'No!' Chloe panicked at the thought of *both* her brothers quizzing Xander. 'He'd feel like he was at the Spanish Inquisition. Hannah has to eat—maybe we could have a quick dinner one night. How is she feeling about her exams?'

'I'm actually a bit worried about her. She seems unusually uptight. She's very tired and not sleeping well. She seems a bit under the weather generally but I'm not sure what I can do to help.'

'Has she been to the doctor? It could be a virus, glandular fever.'

'She says it's just stress.'

'Is she eating properly?'

'I think so. Her mum does most of the cooking so I know she at least has one proper meal a day because it's made for her.'

'Maybe we *should* organise dinner,' she said as she

saw her mum returning with Lily. 'I can have a chat to her then if you like and see if I can't persuade her to see a doctor.'

'That would be good. I'm looking forward to the next few months being over. Hopefully things will go back to normal.'

Xander was pleased to get to work. He wanted to be busy. It stopped him thinking about Chloe. About how many hours had passed since he'd seen her. About how she'd said she would call but he still hadn't heard from her. He had her number but he didn't want to pressure her, although he was running out of time. He was already halfway through his stint in London. Granted, he could extend his stay—he had a working visa—but he knew the only reason he would stay was for Chloe.

His plan had been to go home once he finished up in London; he'd been away from home long enough. He hadn't found what he was looking for until now. And if Chloe didn't want to pursue things further with him there was no reason for him to stay.

He strapped himself into the chopper and concentrated on the job, listening as Jeff relayed the scant information they had received.

'Unconscious twenty-two-year-old female. Mother found her seizing on the bathroom floor. No history of epilepsy.'

Xander looked down at the city. He loved the view from the air. Loved taking a moment to relax. He took a deep breath as he mentally prepared for whatever came next. That was the thing with this job—he never really knew what he was about to encounter. The flight to the emergency always offered a moment of peace and calm.

The River Thames shone silver in the pale morning sun, lines of white disturbing the surface as the wakes of the boats disrupted the water. The commuting traffic was at a standstill below them as they banked right and he knew the commuters were probably feeling anything but calm and peaceful. Flying over the city was so different to the flights he'd taken with the flying doctor back home. The grey and green and silver of London contrasted sharply with the ochre, brown and turquoise of the Australian outback.

The chopper started circling and Xander switched back into the present, knowing they were about to land.

'She's in here.'

Their patient was lying on the bathroom floor. She was unconscious but someone—Xander assumed her mother—had put her into the coma position. She had been bleeding from a cut on her head and the blood had dried on her cheek and stuck in her dark hair.

She was dressed in track pants and a loose T-shirt. She looked cold but when Xander placed his hand on her bare arm he could feel heat radiating from her even through his gloves. Her face was flushed. Feverish.

He could see her chest rising and falling so, although unconscious, she was at least still breathing.

He turned to the woman's mother as Rick knelt beside the patient and started checking her vital signs.

'Can you tell me what happened?' he asked as Rick wrapped a cuff around the woman's arm to check her blood pressure.

The mother stood in the doorway of the bathroom, wringing her hands. 'When she went to bed last night she said she wasn't feeling well. I checked her later and she was sleeping and then this morning I heard her fall. When I came into the bathroom she was having a seizure. I haven't been able to wake her.'

Her eyes filled with tears and she looked worried. Xander could understand her concern; he was worried too, but he tried not to show it.

Xander squatted down and lifted one of the woman's eyelids. He shone a torch into her eye and her pupil contracted. He repeated the process on the other eye with the same result. He breathed out and relaxed slightly. She didn't appear to have sustained a head injury.

'She's never had a seizure before?' he asked. 'No family history of epilepsy?'

The mother shook her head.

'BP one-five-four over ninety-nine,' Rick reported as he clipped an oximeter onto the patient's finger before taking her temperature.

Damn. Her blood pressure was dangerously high.

'Not feeling well, how?' Xander asked the woman's mother. 'Nausea? Vomiting? Headaches?'

'A headache and a stomach ache. I'm not sure if she was nauseous but she hasn't vomited.'

'Heart rate ninety-two BPM; oxygen sats ninety-seven per cent.' Rick passed on more information.

'Had she been drinking?' Xander queried.

The mother shook her head. 'No. She's been studying for final exams. I thought it was stress but then I heard her get up before I heard a crash. When I went into the bathroom it looked like she was fitting.'

Xander continued his assessment as he listened to the mother. There was oedema in the woman's hands and feet, the swelling very obvious, given how thin her limbs were. He slid a stethoscope under her T-shirt and listened to her chest. Her breathing was irregular, her heartbeat rapid.

Rick was holding leads in his hand. He was looking at Xander, ready to attach them to their patient. Xander nodded and Rick proceeded to stick the ECG leads on.

Despite the woman's slim build her abdomen was distended.

Xander palpated her abdomen as he waited for the ECG to record the heart rhythm. It was round and tight with noticeable firmness in the right upper quadrant over the liver. The patient's temperature was elevated; she had no history of seizures and hadn't been drinking. He paused, considering the signs.

'Could she be pregnant?' he asked.

'Pregnant? No.'

'Are you sure?' The patient was the right age and the signs all fitted. She could be suffering from pre-eclampsia, but *only* if she was pregnant.

'Yes. She's been having her period as far as I know.'

'ECG is normal,' Rick said.

Had Xander made the signs fit his diagnosis? He didn't think so. It made sense.

He still had one hand resting on the woman's abdomen. He felt something move under his palm and he was almost certain it was a foot or elbow. Which would mean that, despite the mother's conviction, their patient *was* pregnant.

He slipped the stethoscope back into his ears and held it to the woman's abdomen, listening this time for a foetal heartbeat.

He found a heartbeat and counted the beats.

One hundred and thirty-five BPM.

He double-checked the woman's heart rate.

It was still ninety-two.

He was sure he was right.

'Can you set up IV glucose?' he asked Rick. 'And I'll also administer precautionary antibiotics. We need to take bloods for liver function and kidney function testing and then I want her in the chopper. She needs an ultrasound and we need to get her to the hospital.'

'What's going on?' the patient's mother asked.

Xander tightened the tourniquet around the woman's arm, ready to draw blood, as he spoke to the mother. 'I think there's a high possibility that your daughter is pregnant.' He realised he may be breaking confidentiality but, if he was correct, her condition was life-threatening. 'It's probable that she has a condition called pre-eclampsia. If I'm right the only way to resolve it is to deliver the baby. Which means performing an emergency Caesarean. We need to get her to hospital and I need to know, do I have your permission to provide whatever treatment we deem necessary to save her life?' He saw the colour drain from the mother's face as she digested his words. She nodded, numbly, as he said, 'I realise this is a shock and this is all extremely overwhelming but time is of the essence.'

Chloe stood on the helipad, surrounded by colleagues from the A&E. She heard the thump of the chopper blades and shaded her eyes, watching it approach above the city skyline.

The fire crew slid the door open as it touched down and Chloe's heart rate accelerated when Xander jumped out. Even though she'd been expecting to see him she couldn't control her reaction. Every time the sight of him made her buzz with anticipation.

Rick followed Xander out of the chopper and Chloe moved forward with everyone else who had been waiting, and met Xander and Rick halfway.

Xander handed a cooler bag to one of the nurses. 'I need kidney and liver function tests, please—stat,' he said before relaying the information he had to the rest of the medical team. Chloe had heard some of it before but the information was limited at best.

'We have a twenty-two-year-old female. She had a seizure and is now unconscious. BP one-fifty over ninety, but it was higher. Febrile. We've administered IV antibiotics.'

An oxygen mask covered the patient's face and an IV line snaked into her left arm.

'She's pregnant,' Xander continued, 'and I'm betting on the problem being pre-eclampsia. I think she's close to term.'

'You *think*?'

Xander nodded. 'Her mother had no knowledge of a pregnancy. We have no antenatal history and an unconscious patient. I did a fundal measurement and the baby seems a healthy size and certainly past thirty-four weeks.'

Chloe was standing at the patient's feet. From that angle she could see a slightly rounded abdomen, very slight. She certainly didn't look full term but she looked tall and she was young. Chloe knew strong abdominal muscles could keep a pregnancy disguised for some time, especially a first pregnancy. If Xander was right the baby's lung development wouldn't be a concern. But what if he was wrong?

'She needs an ultrasound scan. We didn't have time

on board, and we need those blood test results. If she's pregnant you'll need to deliver the baby.'

'Raphael Dubois is waiting. He's one of our obstetricians,' Chloe told Xander as they pushed the stretcher into the hospital and into the lift that would take them straight to the theatres. 'Have we got consent to operate?' she asked as the lift doors closed.

'Yes. From the mother.'

The doors slid open and Chloe stepped out, pulling the foot of the stretcher with her. Theatre staff crowded around them and the patient was quickly transferred.

The team rapidly disconnected and reconnected monitors and equipment. As the oxygen masks were swapped over Chloe did a double take.

'Oh, my God. Hannah!'

'You know her?' Raphael asked.

Chloe nodded.

'Are you all right to be the attending midwife?'

'Yes, I'll be fine,' she said. She'd be okay. She could do this. There was no reason why she couldn't be the attending midwife. She just needed to focus.

Anyway, surely Hannah wasn't really pregnant? Surely she and Guy would have shared that news with the family. Xander must have made a mistake.

Unless Guy didn't know?

Maybe it wasn't his?

No. She blocked that thought out. If Hannah was pregnant there had to be a logical explanation.

She had no more time to think. She had a job to do.

But although Xander had vanished in the ensuing chaos he hadn't made a mistake. Hannah was pregnant and close to full term.

'Liver enzymes are elevated and platelet count is

low.' Hannah's blood work was back and apparently Xander hadn't made *any* mistakes. His diagnosis was spot on. Hannah was suffering from pre-eclampsia and the only way to resolve this condition was to deliver the baby.

Hannah was prepped for surgery and sedated for Raphael to perform a Caesarean section. Within minutes he had delivered a healthy baby boy.

The baby was passed to Chloe to be cleaned and weighed and checked before the paediatrician gave him a more thorough examination.

His one-minute Apgar score was an eight and he weighed six pounds and ten ounces. He certainly looked close to full term, Chloe thought as she wiped him over with warm water.

She searched his face as she gently wiped around his eyes and nose, looking for any trace of her brother in the baby's features. She knew she was being silly. All babies looked the same. It was an old midwives' tale that they all looked like their fathers in order to persuade the fathers to bond with them. But was this baby her nephew?

If so, why hadn't Guy said anything?

The question nagged at her, refusing to go away as she waited for the paediatrician to finish her checks.

She took the baby back, swaddled him and placed him in a crib to be taken to the neonatal ICU for monitoring. The moment she handed over his care to the neonatal team she headed for her locker and pulled out her phone. She left a message for her brother. Regardless of her concerns someone needed to let Guy know where Hannah was.

Chloe had been pacing the floors in A&E since the

end of her shift, waiting for Guy. He eventually burst through the automatic doors, still in his fireman's uniform, his brow furrowed with concern. She saw him scan the waiting area, looking for her, and she walked towards him.

She wrapped her arms around him in a tight hug as he said, 'What's happened? Is Hannah all right?'

Chloe's message had just told him that Hannah had been brought into hospital but that she would be okay, and she asked him to meet her here as soon as possible. She hadn't mentioned the baby. That information wasn't something she was comfortable putting into a message.

'She will be.'

'Where is she?' His eyes continued to scan the waiting area as if he thought his girlfriend might be sitting in a chair.

Chloe steered him into a side room, one of the rooms they used when they needed to have a private conversation in A&E. Often those conversations did not go well and she could see Guy looking around nervously. She sat him down. 'She's in ICU. She needed surgery.'

'Surgery? What happened?' he repeated.

There was no easy way to approach this. Chloe had been racking her brain all afternoon trying to work out how to start this conversation but hadn't come up with anything subtle or gentle. 'Did you know she was pregnant?'

'What? Pregnant? No? Is that why she's been feeling unwell?' He paused and then added in a quieter voice, 'Has she had a miscarriage?'

'No. She's had a baby.'

'What? A baby?' Guy stared at her. 'Are you sure?'

'I'm positive. I was there at the delivery.' She paused

but continued when Guy didn't ask any further questions. She assumed shock was setting in. 'Hannah collapsed at home. She had a seizure and was unconscious. She was brought in with the air ambulance. Xander suspected that she was pregnant and suffering from pre-eclampsia. The baby was delivered via C-section.'

'A baby.' He sounded incredulous. Not that Chloe could blame him. 'Is it okay?'

'He's perfect.'

'It's a boy?'

'Yes.'

'And Hannah is okay too?'

Chloe nodded.

She saw Guy's shoulders relax and he smiled before asking, 'Can I see them?'

His request surprised her and she wondered why he hadn't asked any more questions. Perhaps the shock was numbing his brain. He certainly wasn't questioning the baby's parentage.

Her mind wandered and her silence obviously had Guy worried. He looked as though he was expecting her to say no.

She nodded again as she handed him a pair of clean scrubs. 'You can but you need to wash your hands and face first and put these on. You can't go into the nursery or into ICU covered in dirt. You can leave your uniform in a locker and pick it up later.'

She waited for him to change and then took him to the nursery. The baby was healthy and hadn't needed to go into the neonatal unit but, even so, she couldn't let Guy go alone—she needed to vouch for him. She needed to tell the nurses on duty that Guy was the baby's father, even if she wasn't certain of that herself.

The nurse congratulated Guy and led them to a row of cribs.

'This one?' Guy asked as he gazed down at the baby. He seemed happy if somewhat quiet and stunned.

Chloe nodded.

'He doesn't look like a premmie.'

'He's not,' Chloe replied. 'We think Hannah must have been at least thirty-seven weeks.'

Guy was staring at her. *Thirty-seven weeks?* How is that possible? I didn't even know she was pregnant.'

'Apparently Hannah's mother didn't know either. And when I last saw Hannah—what, a month ago?—I didn't notice anything and she must have been at least seven months pregnant then.'

'Why would she keep it a secret?'

There was only one reason Chloe could think of and her silence obviously led Guy to the same conclusion but he wasn't having a bar of it. 'Don't say it. He's definitely mine. Hannah wouldn't cheat on me.'

Chloe held her tongue. It wasn't any of her business. If Guy trusted Hannah, if he believed the baby was his—and at this stage Chloe had no reason to think he wasn't—then that was all that mattered. Which meant there was one other possible explanation.

'Maybe she didn't know either,' Chloe said.

'How could *she* not know she was pregnant?'

'It does happen.' She thought that was unlikely but not impossible. 'She's tall, fit, with good abdominal tone. The baby had room to hide in her abdominal cavity. And,' she continued, 'some women continue to experience light bleeding throughout pregnancy, which is a bit of a red herring. Obviously it's unexpected, so even though Hannah hadn't been feeling well lately she might not have considered pregnancy as the reason behind it.'

'You think *that's* why she's been under the weather? Not stress.'

'I don't know but it's possible.' Unusual but still possible, Chloe thought as she let herself relax. She might have jumped to all the wrong conclusions. The easiest explanation wasn't always the right one.

'Do you want to hold him?' she asked.

'Can I?'

'Of course.' Chloe picked up the baby and handed him to Guy.

'He's beautiful.'

Chloe had to agree. He was a gorgeous baby. Not red or wrinkled, not overcooked or underweight. Chloe was sure he was close to full term but his head must not have engaged in Hannah's pelvis as it was perfectly shaped and had stayed that way because he was delivered via Caesarean section.

Chloe remembered how it felt to hold your own child for the first time. The weight of your own flesh and blood in your arms, the amazing, overwhelming sense of love and awe. The realisation that you would do anything you had to to protect them from harm.

Guy had that same look of wonder on his face. He looked so young but at twenty-three he was about the same age as Chloe had been when she'd unexpectedly found herself a parent and she had managed. And she knew Guy would be a good father.

'Can I see Hannah now?'

Chloe nodded. 'You go up to ICU. I'll take care of this little one,' she said as she held her arms out to take the baby. 'Hannah's mum should be there. She will have to wait outside and give you permission to see her. It's only one family member at a time.'

'You're not coming?'

Chloe shook her head. 'I need to go home. Mum's got Lily. Will you come past later? Stay for dinner? I think you should have company tonight.'

'Okay. Thanks. For everything.'

Guy hugged her and headed for the stairwell. Chloe cuddled the baby for a while longer before returning him to his crib and heading for the lift. It had been a long and taxing day and she was looking forward to getting home.

The lift doors opened, revealing one occupant.

Xander.

The sight of him brought her close to tears. She'd had a stressful day and her emotions were running high.

'Are you okay?'

'Not really. It's been a crazy day.'

Her voice wobbled with exhaustion and she really needed a hug. She was tempted to step into his arms but instead she leaned back on the wall of the lift, out of reach of temptation.

'What's going on?' he asked.

'It turned out that the woman you brought in earlier is my brother's girlfriend.'

'The pregnant one?'

Chloe nodded.

'Did you know she was pregnant?' Xander asked.

'No. And neither did Guy.'

'So is it his baby?'

'He says it must be.'

'Do you believe him?'

She knew what he was thinking even though his thoughts remained unspoken. She squashed her sense of slight irritation; she couldn't get cross with him as she'd had the same thought. 'It's not my place not to,' she said.

'How is the baby?'

'He's fine. Perfect.'

'It was a boy?'

'Yes.'

'And the mother? Your brother's girlfriend?'

'She's in ICU but she's stable. You saved two lives today.' She smiled. 'Thank you.'

'It's what we do,' he replied. 'How is Guy coping?'

Chloe shrugged. 'He's in shock. Stunned. We all are.'

'It's not every day you discover you're an instant father.'

'No.' Chloe was quiet, wondering if she should tell him her news now.

No.

Now was not the time. She didn't have the energy for that discussion. That wouldn't be fair on either of them. Now was not the time *or* the place. She was beginning to wonder if there really wasn't ever going to be the perfect time. Maybe she'd just have to bite the bullet and have the conversation. Get it over and done with.

'Will he do a DNA test?' Xander asked.

'I have no idea. I don't think that's even crossed his mind. Is that what you would do?' Chloe's heart was beating rapidly and she was having difficulty breathing as she waited for his answer.

'Maybe. Probably.'

His answer wasn't unreasonable but it wasn't the answer she wanted to hear.

A shadow passed behind his grey eyes and she wondered if he'd been in the same position. Was that why his marriage broke up? She couldn't help but feel sympathy for him based on nothing but his expression and the sadness in his eyes. That troubled look in his eyes was so familiar. She hadn't noticed it as much over the last week but it was back again now, that slightly haunted look that never failed to draw her in.

The lift doors opened at the ground floor. She couldn't believe no one else had got in.

'Would you like to go for that drink now?' he asked as they stepped out.

'I can't.'

'I know I said I'd leave it up to you but we're running out of time and you look like you could really use a drink.'

'I have to go home. Mum and my other brother are waiting. I need to let them know what's been happening. But if you're free on Thursday I'm going out with some friends from here—just a small group, my best friends, really—and they've asked me to bring you.' She knew she should stay away but she couldn't.

'Really?'

She nodded. It was safer than having drinks with him alone. It gave her an excuse to see him without giving her the opportunity to divulge her secret. She knew she couldn't avoid that discussion for ever but maybe this could buy her a few more days. She was terrified of what might happen next.

'Shall I pick you up?' he offered.

'No!' There was no way she was having him turn up at her house. 'We're going to a pub for birthday drinks. The pub is closer to you. I'll meet you at your place.'

* * *

'Chloe?' Shirley stuck her head into a treatment cubicle where Chloe was giving her patient her discharge instructions. 'Do you think you could take your break when you're finished here? Hannah is asking to see you.'

'She's conscious?'

Shirley nodded. 'She's been moved to the maternity ward.'

Everyone in the hospital had heard Hannah's story, patient confidentiality didn't seem to extend to surprise births.

As Chloe made her way upstairs she wondered if Guy knew Hannah had woken up. He'd been into the hospital first thing today to see the baby and Hannah but she'd still been in high dependency then.

She could see Hannah's mother pacing the corridor outside her daughter's room. She held a baby in her arms.

'Chloe. Thank you for coming,' Pam said.

'Hey, little man,' Chloe said as she reached out and stroked her nephew's cheek. He was sleeping, blissfully unaware of all the drama surrounding his birth. She lifted her head and looked at Hannah's mum. 'How is Hannah doing, Pam?'

'Physically okay, the doctors tell me, but she's very agitated. The nurses brought the baby in to her and she got very distressed. She's insisting he isn't hers.'

'What?' Chloe had thought of a dozen different explanations for this surprise baby but she hadn't expected Hannah to deny the baby was hers.

'I don't know what to do.' Pam's face was lined with worry. 'She seems very confused but the doctors have said she's recovering well. I wondered if you might be able to have a chat with her. I thought seeing as she knows you, and Guy told me you were there for the delivery, Hannah might listen to you.'

'Okay, I'll see how I go.' She stroked the baby's cheek one more time, then went into Hannah's room.

'Chloe! Thank God,' Hannah greeted her.

She looked pale but otherwise okay. She was still connected to various monitors and an IV line ran into her arm but she was obviously coherent enough to recognise Chloe.

'Can you tell me what's happening, Chloe?'

'Of course. What do you remember?'

'I remember going to bed and then I woke up here, in hospital. I've got stitches in my stomach but no one will tell me what happened. Was I in an accident?'

What did she mean no one would tell her what happened? Was Hannah confused? Did she have short-term memory loss? Did she even remember being told she'd had a baby?

'You collapsed at home yesterday.'

Hannah frowned. 'Yesterday? What day is it?'

'Monday,' said Chloe gently. 'You'd been complaining of headaches but you had a seizure and your blood pressure was dangerously high. You were brought into hospital by the ambulance. You had pre-eclampsia.'

'Pre-what?'

'It's a condition associated with pregnancy. We had to deliver your baby.'

Hannah shook her head. 'Why does everyone keep talking about a baby? I don't have a baby!'

'Hannah.' Chloe sat in the chair beside the bed. 'I was there when you were brought into the hospital. I was there in the operating room. I was there when you had a Caesarean section.'

'A Caesarean section?'

'Yes. That's why you have stitches in your stomach.'

'But I wasn't pregnant!'

Chloe took her hand. 'Hannah, I promise, you've had a baby. I was there when the surgeon delivered him.'

'No.' Hannah shook her head again and Chloe could tell she was close to tears. 'I must be dreaming. Surely I'd know if I was pregnant. I'm not stupid.'

Chloe knew it was possible that Hannah hadn't known. She needed to give her the benefit of the doubt. In her distressed state she didn't need any other pressure. She sat on the bed and gently wrapped her arms around Hannah. 'Shh. You need to relax. Your body and your mind need time to recover. It will take time to get your head around this but it will be okay. Everything will be all right.'

'How can you say that?' Hannah's shoulders shook as she cried. 'This doesn't make any sense.'

'I know,' Chloe reassured her. 'I know it sounds crazy but I promise I'm telling you the truth. You have a healthy baby boy.'

She felt Hannah take a deep breath and her sobs stilled. 'You're telling me the truth? I really have a son?'

'You do. You have a beautiful, healthy baby boy. Would you like to see him?'

Chloe stepped out of the room when Hannah nodded and spoke to Pam. She took the baby from his grandmother's arms and carried him in to Hannah. He was tiny but perfect and Chloe's heart swelled with love. There was something so precious about newborn babies and, when they were family too, it didn't get better than that. Chloe would love more children of her own but, for now, she'd enjoy her nephew.

'Do you want to hold him?' Chloe asked as she held him out to Hannah, but Hannah shook her head and kept her arms folded across her chest, refusing to take him.

'I don't know what to do with a baby.'

Chloe cuddled the baby back into her chest. She was convinced that once Hannah held him she'd sense he belonged to her and would be as besotted as everyone else was. But she couldn't force her to take him.

'I know this is scary,' Chloe said. She knew Hannah would still be in shock and Chloe couldn't imagine how she must be feeling. To have no idea she was pregnant and to wake up being told she was a mum would floor anyone. Hannah had also missed out on all the joy and wonder of a pregnancy. Expectant mums usually had months to get used to the idea, months to make plans, months for the excitement to build and months of anticipation of holding their baby for the first time. Hannah had none of that. She must be feeling overwhelmed. 'But you have our support. You and this little fellow are Guy's family now. Our family.'

'Does Guy know where I am?' Hannah asked.

Chloe nodded. 'He's been in to see you. He was here last night and again this morning.'

'He knows about the baby?' Hannah looked worried.

'Yes.'

'What did he say?'

Chloe realised that was what she was concerned about. She was worried that Guy wouldn't want the baby.

'He thinks his son is amazing. He thinks you're

amazing,' Chloe reassured her. 'It'll be okay. Guy isn't going anywhere.'

'Are you sure?'

Chloe nodded. 'Do you want to hold him now? See how he feels. Smell him. There's nothing like the smell of a newborn baby.'

Hannah nodded this time and held out her arms, cradling him against her. 'He's really mine?'

'Yes.'

She stared down at the sleeping bundle.

'How could I not know that I was pregnant?'

'Some women have very straightforward, uncomplicated pregnancies. It's not an illness. But you would have had some changes to your body. Do you think you might have noticed some and attributed them to something else?' Chloe knew Hannah would be feeling foolish and she tried to give her a reasonable explanation.

'Like what?'

'Weight gain? Tiredness? Irritability?'

'I'd put on a little bit of weight but I haven't been exercising as much lately and I had a headache for the past week but I put that down to stress over my exams. Oh, my God!' Hannah looked up at Chloe. 'My exams! What will I do about those?'

Chloe thought that was probably the least of Hannah's concerns at the moment but she realised it was something she'd been working towards for months and it would seem like a big deal. 'I'll organise for a counsellor to come and speak to you. I'm sure there's a way of rescheduling or postponing your exams,' Chloe said as she saw Guy arrive. She kissed Hannah goodbye and left the room, allowing Guy and Hannah some privacy.

Hannah needed to spend time with him and their son. She needed to know that everything would be okay.

Guy had looked happy as he'd traded places with Chloe. He'd missed out on the excitement of the pregnancy too. Chloe knew from her own experience dealing with expectant fathers that many of them enjoyed the excitement and anticipation of a pregnancy as much as the mothers.

She wondered if Xander would have enjoyed the experience. Would he have changed his mind about having children if he was presented with a done deal? Would he have been excited? Would he have wanted to be involved? To experience it all or would he have remained distant? Surely he would have changed his mind? She hoped he would have. Surely he would have wanted to share the experience? Surely he would have wanted his daughter?

CHAPTER SIX

CHLOE PRESSED THE doorbell for Xander's apartment and checked her outfit in the mirror in the building's hallway. She fluffed her hair out over her shoulders as she waited for him to answer. She'd washed it and let it air dry, deliberately allowing it to curl wildly, knowing he loved her to wear it down.

She'd had the day off work but had spent it with Hannah, who had been discharged from hospital and was now home and trying to adjust in to her new role as a mother to baby Jonas. The week had been crazy and Chloe was looking forward to tonight. She was looking forward to talking and thinking about something else other than babies. She was looking forward to seeing Xander and pretending that she was four years younger, with no responsibilities and nothing better to do than go out for a drink with a handsome man.

His door swung open and he stood before her. He was still tugging his grey T-shirt down over his chest, obviously still getting ready, and she caught a glimpse of his belly button and taut abdominals. She swallowed; suddenly she was nervous. 'Am I early?'

'No.' His eyes travelled the length of her body and she was rewarded with a large smile. 'You're perfect.'

She had dressed carefully, choosing white jeans and a gauzy, pink and white floral, off-the-shoulder top. She knew she was tempting fate but she was excited about tonight and wanted to make an impression.

He didn't invite her in. He stepped into the hall and cupped her face in his hands, bending his head to hers, and greeted her with a kiss.

Her body felt as if it was exploding into a thousand tiny pieces. He just had to look at her to set her heart racing and once his lips met hers she could barely stand. Her toes tingled and her legs felt like jelly. She was immediately transported back four years. To when they couldn't keep their hands off each other. To when she had nothing to worry about—other than not getting pregnant.

That hadn't worked out so well.

She pulled back as that thought made its way out of her subconscious. She couldn't afford to get carried away. She couldn't afford to get too involved. Things were not so simple any more.

'Have we got time for a drink here before we go?' Xander asked. If he noticed her withdrawal, he didn't mention it. She nodded and he held the door for her as they stepped inside.

'Gin and tonic?'

'Thanks.' Chloe leant on the kitchen bench as he mixed her drink. This felt normal, comfortable, and she was able to relax a little.

'How has your week been? How are Hannah and your new nephew doing?' he asked as he handed her a glass. She hadn't seen him for three days. There had been no emergencies that had involved her on Tuesday and she'd had the past two days rostered off. It felt far longer than three days though; it felt like a lifetime.

She took her drink and followed Xander to the small couch. 'It's been absolutely crazy. But Hannah is doing well all things considered. I can't imagine having no warning that you're going to have a baby.' Chloe had found it hard enough to cope with a surprise pregnancy; she couldn't imagine having to cope with a surprise baby.

'Lucky for them you've got some experience with babies.'

'Mmm-hmm, I guess it is.' She had more experience than he knew but she wasn't ready to talk about Lily yet.

'And Hannah really had no idea she was pregnant?'

'Apparently. She'd had headaches and a few warning signs for pre-eclampsia but she was studying for her final exams and she put it down to stress. She said she never skipped a period and didn't have any morning sickness.'

'And what about your brother? How is he coping?'

'They have a lot to sort out but luckily there doesn't seem to be any issue over paternity. Their situation is stressful enough without any of those questions. They trust each other and they've been in a relationship for a while, even though this is a bit more serious than they had planned at this stage.'

'How old is your brother?'

'Twenty-three.'

'Is he ready for this?'

'I don't know if anyone is ever really ready. I see so many first-time parents—most of them have no idea. Age is just a number and I know Guy would never, ever, walk away from his child.'

'How can you be so sure?'

'Guy was only three when our father died and Tom was just a baby. The boys don't remember him and I know that has affected Guy. He would want his child to know him and even if he and Hannah weren't so solid I know he'd always make his child a priority.' She very nearly said, *He's so good with Lily*, but she stopped herself just before she could say something she couldn't take back.

'You have two brothers? Guy and…'

'Tom.' She nodded. 'What about you? Who's in your family?'

'Both my parents are still alive—they'll celebrate their fortieth wedding anniversary this year.'

Forty years! She wondered if they were happily married. If they'd had their share of ups and downs.

'And I have three older sisters,' Xander added. 'And four nieces and nephews.'

Lily had cousins on Xander's side as well. It was strange… Chloe hadn't imagined that. Lily had a whole other family. 'And one ex-wife.'

'Yes.'

'Would you get ever get married again?'

'I'd like to think so. I don't want to imagine spending the rest of my life alone. I always saw myself as a husband and father.'

'You want children?'

'Definitely.'

'Oh.' Chloe stood up and took her empty glass to Xander's compact kitchen as she digested that information. Somewhere along the line she'd got her wires crossed. He wanted kids. That changed everything.

'You seem surprised,' he said.

'I thought you said you and your wife split up because she wanted kids. I guess I assumed that meant you didn't.'

'It was a bit more complicated than that.' He glanced at his watch but not before Chloe saw the shadow pass across his eyes again. 'Should we go?' He stood up and grabbed his keys and it was clear that conversation was over.

Chloe nodded, happy to change tack. She needed a few moments to get her head straight.

'Just remind me who's going to be at the pub,' he said as he locked his front door behind them.

'It's Harry's birthday—he's marrying my friend Esther—and Carly, my other best friend, and her fiancé, Adem, will be there too. Harry and Adem are both doctors. I guess there will be a few doctors there so you'll have plenty to talk about besides weddings.'

'Your two best friends are both engaged? What about you? No serious relationships in the past four years?'

She shook her head. 'I've been too busy.'

'Doing what?'

'Doing everything I needed to get into the air ambulance service. I've been working at the Queen Victoria since I got back from Australia with the goal of becoming one of the midwives for the air ambulance. It took me a few years but I've been working with them now for the past twelve months. I love it but that has been my focus.'

That, and raising a child.

She was slightly relieved to see the pub ahead of them; intimate conversations were unlikely to be had once they were amongst her friends. She had almost mentioned Lily twice. She was such a big part of her life—she *was* her life—and outside of work Lily was her number one focus and, she realised, her number one topic of conversation. She'd have to be careful or she'd need to avoid Xander until she worked out what to say and how to tell him or, alternatively, she'd need to tell him about Lily pronto.

She didn't want to avoid him—she longed to spend more time with him—but that meant she would have to tell him her news. She couldn't, in good conscience, keep it from him any longer. She'd tell him tonight, she decided, after the drinks. She'd delayed the inevitable long enough and all this secrecy was becoming stressful. She'd go with him back to his flat after drinks and talk to him then.

She breathed out and relaxed, relieved to have made the decision.

'Is everything all right?' Xander asked as they reached the pub. 'You've gone very quiet.'

She looked up at him, into his grey eyes that were a reflection of Lily's. 'Yes.' She nodded. He wanted children. She had to believe that everything would be all right. She needed to stop worrying about things that were out of her control.

She stepped inside, followed by Xander. She could see her friends standing together near the fireplace at the far end of the bar. Harry, Esther, Raphael and Adem were chatting. Carly was on the phone. Chloe made the introductions while Carly finished her conversation.

Carly was buzzing with excitement when she ended her call and, while she let Chloe introduce her to Xander, Chloe could tell she had other things on her mind.

'Guess who's coming back in time for my wedding?' Carly said.

'Whose wedding?' Adem teased her.

'*Our* wedding,' Carly said as she tucked her arm through the crook of his elbow and beamed at him, placating him.

'Who?'

'Izzy!'

'Really! That's brilliant,' Chloe said.

'I wish she could be here for ours,' Esther chimed in, 'but this is the next best thing.'

'You've just gone from triple trouble to quadruple trouble, my friend,' Harry said to Adem.

Chloe noticed that Raphael, who was also a close friend of Izzy's, was the only one in the group who didn't seem surprised. 'Izzy is the fourth musketeer,' Chloe explained to Xander. 'Carly, Esther, Izzy and I all studied midwifery together but Izzy has been gone for a while. She's a Kiwi originally but her father was in the diplomatic core so she grew up all around the world.'

'Is her husband coming too?' Esther asked.

'I'm not sure.' Carly frowned. 'It didn't sound like it but I didn't specifically ask that. I was too excited. I said I'll call her tomorrow so I'll get some more details.'

'It will be so good to see her again. I hope she can stay for a while.' Chloe missed having all four of them together. They had been such a tight unit and it had been hard to get used to being one friend short.

'And I hope she makes it in time for some of the pre-wedding celebrations,' Carly said.

'If she misses too many we'll just have to have more.' Esther laughed.

'That's our cue, gentlemen,' Harry interrupted. 'I feel wedding talk coming on. Let's organise some drinks.'

'A G&T?' Xander asked Chloe.

'Thanks.' She smiled. 'Are you okay with the men?'

'No worries.' He winked at her. 'Ladies.' He nodded towards Esther and Carly as he excused himself.

'Oh, my,' Carly said with a wicked grin as she fanned herself with her hand. 'He's seriously sexy. If only I wasn't engaged.'

'And pregnant,' Esther said.

'Maybe I can blame those pregnancy hormones.'

Chloe looked at Xander. He was wearing dark indigo jeans, black Australian stockman's boots and a plain grey T-shirt. A simple enough outfit, but when the T-shirt hugged his chest and hinted at the taut abdominals she'd glimpsed earlier and his jeans showcased his firm behind and the whole outfit was further highlighted by his blond Norse-god features she had to agree he looked good.

In Xander's case it wasn't so much the clothes making the man as the man making the clothes.

'You never said he was Australian,' Esther said.

'Didn't I?'

'No. You didn't. You said he was from Wales.'

'I might have said he came here from Wales.'

'What else haven't you told us?'

'What do you mean?'

'You seem very comfortable together considering you've only just met—' Carly paused when Xander returned with Chloe's drink and turned to question him instead. 'You're Australian?'

'You're not going to hold that against me, are you? I have an English grandmother if that helps.'

'And you're here working with the air ambulance?'

'I'm on a sort of sabbatical.'

'A sabbatical?'

Xander nodded. 'I've been in Wales, Canada and South Africa working with their first response teams, their air ambulance services, which is their version of our flying doctor.'

'You're a flying doctor?'

'I am.'

'That job sounds amazing. The outback sounds so romantic.' Carly sighed.

'Is it like the movies, full of gorgeous men?' Esther wanted to know.

'Who ride horses and wrestle crocodiles?' Chloe laughed. 'Don't believe everything you see in the movies. There weren't that many gorgeous men.'

'Hey, I'm right here and I can hear you,' Xander protested. 'Should I be offended?' he asked, but he was smiling, clearly not offended.

'No, there were a few exceptions.' Chloe smiled back at him. His smile was impossible for her to resist. 'You were one.' She put her hand on his arm. It was a reflex and when she realised what she'd done she got flustered but she couldn't take it back, not immediately—that would just draw everyone's attention.

'Thank you.' Xander grinned and then answered Esther. 'Chloe's right, it's not exactly like the movies. Nothing ever is. But the landscape can be incredible if you can ignore the heat and the dust and the flies.'

'It must be exciting though? Flying around the country saving lives.'

'It's not like the air ambulance, it's not all emergencies. It can be routine. We do a lot of clinic runs, normal general practice type work.'

'Chloe did a study exchange with the flying doctor,

didn't you, Chloe?' Esther said. 'The two of you didn't happen to meet while she was there?'

'We did. In Broken Hill.'

'Is that where you grew up?'

'No. I'm a city boy. But I love the flying doctor work. I'll be back in Adelaide when I go home.'

'When is that?'

'Soon, I think. I'm starting to miss the sun and the space. It's nearly time to go home.'

He looked at Chloe and she grew nervous. Not about him going but she knew she'd miss him. It would take her some time to adjust again to him not being part of her life.

But that wasn't going to be the case this time, was it? It was likely that he would be, if not a part of her life, of Lily's. She really did need to have those conversations. She needed to start making plans and she needed to know his position before she could move forward.

'Xander!' Harry called to him from the other side of the room. 'How are you at pool? We need a fourth.'

'What are the stakes?' he asked before he raised one eyebrow and winked at Chloe.

'Don't embarrass them,' she said. She recalled one evening around the billiard table in the Palace Hotel in Broken Hill when Xander had thoroughly trounced all challengers.

'I promise to miss a few,' he told her before excusing himself.

'You already knew him!' Carly accused Chloe once Xander had left them to join the men.

'The question is how well?' Esther said.

'Pretty well, judging by the heat between you,' Carly added.

'What do you mean?'

'He looks at you like it's Christmas Eve and you're his present under the tree, just waiting to be unwrapped.'

'And you kept touching his arm and every time you did he'd look at you like he just wanted to throw you over his shoulder and carry you out of here.'

'My God, Carly, your hormones really are addling your senses. Not everything is about sex.'

'I think Xander might disagree with me there.' Carly laughed. 'The sparks were flying.'

'There's something familiar about him.' Esther was looking at him.

'Stop staring!' Chloe hissed.

'Oh, my God.'

'What?'

'It's his eyes.'

Chloe panicked. 'Esther! Stop!' She hadn't even *considered* that her girlfriends would figure it out. She couldn't believe she'd been so stupid. Even if they hadn't put two and two together what if they'd said something about Lily in front of Xander?

'What is it?' Carly repeated.

'I've just figured it out.'

Chloe interrupted. She knew she had to say something and at least if she admitted the truth she could choose the decibel level. She was about to admit to something she did not want the whole world to hear. At least not yet.

'You have to promise me you won't say anything.' She eyeballed her girlfriends and waited until they kept quiet and nodded.

'Xander is Lily's father,' Chloe admitted in a whisper.

'He's your mystery man? Your wild weekend of hot Australian sex was with Xander?'

'Keep your voice down, Carly!'

Chloe had never pretended she didn't know who Lily's father was; she'd just chosen not to share the information. She'd told her girlfriends she'd had a brief fling and had never expected it to have any consequences.

'Wow.' Esther was looking in Xander's direction. 'Lily's father.'

'You can't say anything,' Chloe insisted. 'He doesn't know.'

'What do you mean he doesn't know?'

'I tried to find him when I found out I was pregnant but he'd left the flying doctor service and no one would tell me where he'd gone. Our relationship hadn't been serious—we hadn't made any promises about keeping in touch when I left. It was simply a holiday romance.'

'I thought you said it was one weekend?'

'It was a bit longer than a weekend,' she admitted now.

'How much longer?'

'Four weeks.'

'That sounds a bit more serious than a couple of nights?'

'It was never serious.' It wasn't *meant* to be serious but it couldn't be helped that she'd fallen for him anyway.

'Is that why you've never told us who Lily's father is? Because it wasn't serious?'

'No. Because I couldn't find him and I didn't think I should tell the world until I'd told him.'

'But you still haven't told him.'

She shook her head. 'I was waiting for the right time.'

'I don't think there is such a thing when the news is as big as this.'

'I know.' Chloe sighed. She had no choice now; she would definitely have to tell him tonight. It was going to be impossible to keep Lily a secret any longer. 'I've already decided I need to tell him tonight. I nearly mentioned Lily twice before we got here. I can't keep her a secret.'

Carly clapped her hands together. 'This is fabulous. You'll get your happily ever after as well.'

'I don't know about that. I have no idea how he feels about fatherhood, commitment, any of those things. He might want nothing to do with Lily. Or me.' Despite the brief conversations where he'd implied he wanted those things Chloe knew that talking the talk was very different to discovering that he was already a father.

'The way he was looking at you just before I don't think you have any worries there,' Carly said.

'You make such a cute couple,' Esther added. 'I'm going to invite him to my wedding.'

'You don't need to do that! I'm not even sure if he'll still be in London.'

'We'll see. I want things to work out for you.'

'I get that and I appreciate it. I'd like things to work out for me too.' But she still wasn't sure exactly what that would look like.

Xander lined up the number thirteen ball, sinking it into the corner pocket. He missed his next shot but he and Adem only had two balls left to pot compared to Harry and Raphael's five, before they would win their second game. He stepped back, allowing Raphael to take his turn.

'Chloe tells me you and Carly are expecting a baby,' he said to Adem as he watched Raphael's ball hit the cushion and ricochet away from the pocket.

'Yes. I'm getting used to the idea,' he replied as Raphael's ball spun away and dropped into a pocket on the opposite side of the table. A lucky shot.

'It wasn't planned?'

'No. It was definitely a surprise but it's turned out to be a good one.'

Xander had always been slightly envious both of people who had children and of those for whom it happened so easily. His own plans for a family had derailed six years ago and he wondered now if he'd missed his opportunity.

Adem lined up to take his shot after Raphael missed the next ball. 'Have you got kids?' he asked.

'No.'

'Pity. I could use some advice,' Adem replied as the twelve ball dropped into a pocket.

'Don't you deal with babies all the time? You're an obstetrician, aren't you?'

'No, not me. Rafe is the obstetrician. I'm a neurosurgeon. I'm completely clueless when it comes to kids.' He potted the black ball, ending the game. 'Drinks on you,' he said to Harry and Raphael as they shook hands. 'Carly tells me we should be ready to be completely out of our depths, which I must say I don't find very reassuring,' he said as Raphael and Harry headed to the bar. 'I guess we'll be asking Chloe for a lot of advice.'

'Chloe? Why Chloe?' Xander wasn't following.

'She's the only one who's done this before.'

'What do you mean?'

'She's got a daughter.'

Xander's jaw fell open and he could feel the surprise written in his expression.

'You didn't know?' Adem asked.

Xander shook his head. He was at a complete loss, unable to think straight. He was glad the game was over. His head was full of white noise. Adem sounded as though he was talking under water.

Xander could feel himself sweating but he felt hot and cold at the same time.

'How old is she? The daughter.'

'I'm not sure. Little. Maybe two?'

Somehow he managed to get through one more drink before he escaped. He knew he was behaving badly but his head was reeling and he couldn't continue to stand at the bar and make polite conversation. He had to leave.

He ducked into the men's toilets and, from there, headed home. He didn't say goodnight to anyone. He sent Chloe a brief text with an excuse he suspected wouldn't hold up under examination but he couldn't think of anything substantial. He imagined she'd be upset but so was he. He'd deal with any repercussions of his early departure later. Right now he had other things on his mind.

Starting with, why hadn't Chloe said anything to him about her daughter? Lord knows, she'd had plenty of opportunity. Just a couple of hours ago they were talking about her experience with babies and she *still* didn't mention she had one of her own.

Why not?

It was only in hindsight as he marched along the footpath, constantly dodging and weaving to avoid other pedestrians—why couldn't these people stay out of his way?—that he realised he should have asked Adem some questions. Any information might have been useful.

He wondered who the father was. *Where* the father was? Was he still involved with Chloe?

Of course he'd have to be. They had a child together.

Did this complicate things between them?

He suspected it would. It changed the dynamics of getting to know her again. She was part of a package now.

Was that something he was prepared for?

He didn't know. It was certainly not something he'd anticipated having to deal with.

Was that why she'd been quiet, introspective? Had she been worried he would find out? Concerned about what he'd think? How he'd feel? What he'd say?

She had reason to be, although at this stage he wasn't entirely sure how he felt.

He knew he didn't want to think of her with another man. He didn't want to think that she would be tied to someone else for ever through a child. That connection would continue and there was no way he could compete with that.

He realised then that he wanted to at least have a chance, an opportunity, to be important to Chloe. To pursue a relationship with her. But now he would have to get in line. Behind a child. Behind an ex.

He needed time to think. About how he felt. About what this meant.

He had always wanted kids of his own. But did he want someone else's?

It wasn't a deal breaker, not with Chloe, but he did

wish she'd told him. He wished he hadn't heard the news from a third party.

Why hadn't she said anything?

He'd turned the key in his front door and stepped inside. He pulled his boots off and stripped off his clothes, thinking of the high hopes he'd had for this evening when he'd got dressed just a few hours ago. This had not been how he'd thought his night would end.

He'd sleep on it, he decided, even though he suspected sleep might elude him, and ask her about it tomorrow.

CHAPTER SEVEN

Something's come up.

CHLOE DROPPED HER phone on the kitchen table after checking it for the tenth time since dropping Lily off at nursery that morning. But Xander's message from the night before still made no sense and she'd heard nothing further. She'd phoned him three times before giving up. He was either very busy or ignoring her calls. Given that he wasn't part of the overnight air ambulance team and he had no family in England that she knew of she couldn't imagine what had 'come up' and had required his immediate attention. Which really only left one possibility. That he was ignoring her.

She was annoyed that he'd disappeared last night without a decent explanation and was also slightly concerned that something had happened but there was nothing she could do about it at the moment. He would be back at work now, and while she could call the department, what would she say? He didn't really owe her anything. She just had to hope that he'd get in touch eventually and meanwhile she had plenty to keep her occupied for the morning while she waited. It was just unfortunate that it was only household chores.

She sighed as she dumped a load of wet laundry into a washing basket. There was no point trying to guess why he'd left. She'd drive herself mad. She just had to assume he had a reason and he'd explain it to her when she next saw him.

She was hanging the last item of washing on the line when she heard a siren wailing in the distance. It got louder. It was joined by another. A third. A fourth. She could hear ambulances, fire engines and police cars. Their different sirens colliding with each other at an ever-increasing volume.

She paused, resting the empty washing basket on her hip. Could she smell smoke?

She turned around in a circle, her face tilted up to the sky. There was a column of smoke to the west.

She hurried inside, dropping the basket on the floor as she flicked on the radio and the television, searching for news.

It didn't take long to hear. There was a fire in a shopping centre. She knew the centre. It was only a few streets away.

It was a sprawling building with a supermarket as an anchor tenant, a gym, numerous restaurants, cafés and smaller speciality stores. It was a busy centre and Chloe knew it would have been bustling at ten o'clock in the morning. She could imagine the chaos of the evacuation.

She listened to the report. The origin of the fire was thought to be a café. The cause of the blaze as yet unknown. The list of casualties undetermined. The fire brigade, police and paramedics were all in attendance. Chloe's throat tightened in fear. Xander and both her brothers were working today. Were they there?

Her heart was pounding as she ran back outside. The column of smoke was thicker now, menacing and black. It was spreading across the sky. She heard the familiar sound of chopper blades and saw a news helicopter flying overhead. Followed by the air ambulance.

Xander.

She grabbed her keys and her phone and left the house. She sprinted west along the footpath. She knew there would be a crowd—disaster scenes were a magnet for the curious—but perhaps she could help.

She turned the final corner and was confronted by a wall of people. The noise was deafening—sirens, flames and voices all seemed to be at full volume. Soot fell from the sky and smoke was thick in the air. Chloe's eyes were stinging and her throat was dry.

Through the crowd she could see dozens of emergency vehicles filling the street. Police cars and ambulances but mostly fire engines.

The police were trying to clear the area of spectators, advising them to leave, but no one appeared to be listening. They held back the crowds but Chloe pushed her way through. She slid past some and ducked around others until she was close to the front. She looked for familiar faces. Guy. Tom. Xander. There were way too many paramedics and firefighters. She wasn't going to be able to identify her brothers so she looked instead for the orange jumpsuits of the air ambulance crew.

People were still running from the building, hurrying to escape, to get clear. It was pandemonium with the first responders doing their best to evacuate the building and get people triaged and treated. She wanted to offer to help but she knew she couldn't just speak to the first person she saw. Everyone was busy. No one had time to stop to talk to her.

If she wanted to help she needed to speak to whoever was in charge of coordinating the units, although it was difficult to tell who that might be. She doubted she'd be allowed to help. She wasn't on duty and she had no identification with her, but she had to do something.

She scanned the area but the crowds of people, the poor visibility due to the smoke and the incessant noise made it hard to pick out who was in charge. She needed to be up close to make herself heard. She didn't want to yell and add to the noise of the fire and of the emergency crews. The victims of the fire seemed mostly silent. In shock. A few were calling out, a few were in tears, but most were mute.

Chloe jumped as an explosion rent the air, adding to the noise and confusion. She turned back towards the building and saw a ball of flame shoot into the sky. A gas pipe must have exploded.

Movement on the periphery of her vision caught her eye. A woman, dazed and disoriented, was heading for the complex, heading back towards the fire, but it was the flash of orange that captured her attention. Someone was running towards the woman. Someone in an orange jumpsuit.

Xander.

He reached the woman just as Chloe thought she couldn't get any closer to the fire without being burnt. Her heart was in her mouth as Xander reached out his hand to stop her from walking any further. They were only metres from the burning building.

A second explosion ripped through the air, tearing a massive hole in the side of the building.

Xander was in the path of the explosion.

Glass and bricks rained down on him. Chloe heard herself screaming a warning but of course he couldn't hear her. He disappeared in a cloud of dust and debris.

The dust cleared and Chloe could see him on the ground. He was lying over the woman, shielding her with his body, surrounded by flaming rubble.

Chloe waited for him to get up.

He didn't move.

Fire hoses were aimed at Xander and the woman. Showering them with water, dousing the flames.

He still didn't move.

Chloe tried desperately to push through the last row of people blocking her path but they were too tightly packed. She was stuck but she knew the police would stop her from reaching Xander even if she could get through the crowd. She peered over shoulders and saw paramedics hurrying towards them. One of them knelt beside Xander. She was sure it was Tom.

She watched as Xander was lifted onto a stretcher, an oxygen mask strapped over his face. Tom raised the stretcher and moved away from the building.

Chloe pushed back through the spectators, not towards the fire, not towards the police, but behind the crowd. She moved parallel to Tom, heading for the ambulances. Her eyes tracked Tom's movements and she was able to occasionally make him out between the heads of the onlookers.

He was almost at the ambulance. She picked up her pace; she needed to get to him before he left the scene. She drew level with the ambulance and pushed her way to the front again.

'*Tom.*' She called to him but he couldn't hear her.

'Tom!' she yelled again as she got past the crowd.

'You can't come through here.' A policewoman barred her way.

'Tom!' She was getting desperate.

Finally, Tom heard her and she saw him turn in her direction.

'Tom. That's Xander.' Her voice was hoarse. Her throat was sore from screaming and her face was wet with tears she hadn't been aware of.

She saw Tom look to the stretcher where Xander lay and then back to her.

'It's okay. She's with the air ambulance.' He called out to the policewoman. 'Let her through.'

Chloe didn't give the policewoman time to argue. She ran to Tom. To Xander. All her earlier irritation over his disappearance last night forgotten. All she felt now was concern.

She put her hand on Xander's leg. His eyes were closed. His blond hair dirty with soot and ash. 'Xander? Can you hear me?'

There was no reply.

'Is he breathing?' she asked her brother, even as she realised he must be. They weren't trying to resuscitate him. He had an oxygen mask over his nose and mouth.

'Yes,' Tom said as he pushed the stretcher into the ambulance, 'but he's non-responsive.'

Xander's uniform was scorched. It was flame retardant but hadn't completely withstood the direct heat. She could see marks on his neck and wrists. Were they burns or just dirt? How badly was he injured?

Chloe put her hand on Tom's arm, stopping him from climbing into the ambulance. 'Can I come with you?'

He nodded. 'Ride in the front with Diane. There's no room in the back.'

Chloe didn't want to leave Xander but she didn't argue. She jumped into the front of the ambulance as Diane slammed the rear doors shut before climbing into the driver's seat.

'Where are we headed?' Chloe asked.

'St Barbara's Hospital.'

'But the Queen Victoria is closer,' she argued.

'I know,' Diane said. 'But the category one cases are being sent there. The less urgent ones have been directed to other hospitals.'

Chloe bit back a cry of frustration. She knew it wasn't Diane's fault but if they'd been able to go to the Queen Victoria Chloe would have some influence. She tried to console herself with the knowledge that they didn't think Xander was critically injured.

Chloe was out of the ambulance almost before Diane had pulled to a stop in the emergency bay of St Barbara's. She waited impatiently for Diane to open the rear doors as it wasn't Chloe's job, and once they got inside she wouldn't have a job to do either. It wasn't her hospital. She'd be helpless, useless. She'd have nothing to do except wait.

Diane and Tom pulled Xander's stretcher out. He still hadn't regained consciousness.

They pushed him inside. The hospital was busy but Xander was given priority. His airway, lungs and other injuries needed urgent assessment. He was whisked away and she knew she wouldn't be allowed to go with him. She would have to wait.

She had never been on the other side of an Accident and Emergency department. She'd never been one of the anxious family or friends waiting for news.

She wished she knew someone on staff but she had to sit and wait like everyone else. The television in the waiting area had been tuned into the news channel, which was still showing footage of the burning building. Chloe knew there would be fatalities.

She was worried about her brothers. Tom had gone back to the scene and she knew Guy would still be there too.

She was worried about Xander.

She didn't want to harass the staff. She knew what it was like to have patients' relatives asking for updates every few minutes, but the delay seemed interminable. She had to know if he was all right. She had to see him.

She waited as long as she could bear before approaching the unit manager. 'Can you tell me if there's any news on Xander Jameson. He was brought in from the fire.'

'Are you family?'

'No. I'm a friend and a midwife at the Queen Victoria. I work with Xander at the air ambulance.'

'Do you have some ID?'

She shook her head. She'd dashed out of the house with only her keys and her phone. She hadn't thought to grab her bag or her wallet.

'Then I'll have to ask you to wait.'

Chloe was prepared to wait. She'd known it was unlikely that she'd be given any information just on her say-so but she wasn't leaving until she had some news. She would wait until Xander could vouch for her. 'Can you ask him if I can see him?' she said as she took a seat.

'When I can.'

Chloe had no idea if that meant Xander had regained

consciousness and the manager would ask when she had a minute or if it meant Xander was still out cold.

She nodded. She couldn't complain. She knew there was a protocol to follow and she didn't want to cause a scene.

But what if something serious had happened to him?

What if she lost him all over again?

Why had she been hesitating to talk to him? To tell him what had happened. She should have told him about Lily. She should have told him how she felt. He deserved to know the truth.

'You have a visitor.'

Xander turned his head to look at the nurse and winced as pain shot behind one eye.

'Who is it?' he asked. He couldn't imagine too many people who would be visiting him.

'I don't know,' she replied. 'Shall I ask?' The nurse was young, a student, and she looked nervous. Xander assumed she was aware he was a doctor and that was putting her on edge.

That would probably be a good idea, he felt like saying, but it wouldn't serve any purpose to snap at her. He was still groggy. And sore. He'd been surprised to find himself in hospital. He remembered chasing after a woman at the fire but had no memory of anything after that.

'Male or female?' he asked.

'Female.'

'What does she look like?'

'Young. Blond curly hair. She said she's a midwife.'

Chloe.

'You can send her in.'

Chloe came into his room. Her face was pale, her normal happy expression overshadowed by a crease between her brows. She looked worried.

She came straight to his bed but hesitated a step away. She stopped and he wondered what she'd wanted to do. 'You're okay?' she said.

He nodded. 'Is the fire out?'

Chloe shook her head. 'What were you thinking?' She sounded cross. 'Running after that woman.'

He hadn't been thinking; he'd simply reacted when he saw the woman heading towards the fire. 'Is she okay?'

'I don't know. I think so. You know that going into burning buildings isn't your job.'

'I didn't go inside,' he argued. 'She was walking straight into the fire. Someone had to stop her and there was no one else nearby.'

'But you could have been killed!'

Was she worried about *him*? Afraid for his safety? Afraid that he had been injured?

He didn't want her to worry about him. 'I'm sorry if I scared you,' he said, hoping to reassure her. 'But, as you can see, I'm fine.'

'Are you sure?'

'I'm positive.'

'You were knocked unconscious,' she argued.

'Only briefly.' He tried a self-deprecating smile for good measure.

'Promise you won't do that again.'

'I'll try not to make a habit of it.'

She smiled and he saw her shoulders visibly relax.

She reached out and held his fingers. 'What happened to your arm?'

His left arm was wrapped in gauze bandages. 'The doctors picked some glass fragments out. They've cleaned and dressed it. That's all. Nothing major.'

She put her hand to his chin and turned his head slightly. 'And what about this?' she asked.

He had a dressing on his neck and he felt it pull tight, resisting the movement. He tried not to wince. 'A minor burn.'

He had a dull headache and suspected he had sustained a mild concussion but he expected the pain relief would take care of the ache. There was something niggling at the back of his mind and he concentrated hard to bring it to the forefront. He felt it was important. Something to do with Chloe.

A conversation.

He closed his eyes as the memory returned.

A conversation not with Chloe but with Adem.

'Are you all right? Can I get you something?' Chloe's voice broke into his reverie.

He opened his eyes. 'I'm fine,' he reiterated as he fought down a wave of nausea. He knew he wasn't physically sick. It was emotional. 'But there's something I need to ask you.'

Now that he'd remembered the conversation, he knew it would eat away at him until he raised the subject with Chloe. He was tired and sore but he needed some answers. They needed to have a conversation and while the emergency department wasn't the ideal place it would have to do. The sooner he heard her side of the story, the sooner he would know where he stood.

'Adem told me you have a daughter.'

The colour that had been beginning to return to her

face drained away completely, leaving her ashen. She froze.

'When did he tell you that?'

'Last night. At the bar.'

'That's why you left,' she said as she collapsed onto the chair next to his bed.

'Is it true?'

She nodded.

'Why haven't you said anything?'

'I was waiting for the right time.'

'We were talking about your nephew, about babies, just yesterday. Why didn't you tell me then?'

'Are you upset?'

'Damn right I am.' Her brown eyes were wide, worried, but he wasn't going to pretend everything was fine. 'I'm upset that you haven't shared this with me. We were talking about what you've been doing for the past four years. You told me about your plan to work for the air ambulance. You didn't think to mention you'd had a baby in that time?'

'Are you angry?'

'Angry? No.' He was but he couldn't share that he was mostly jealous that she had this history, a child, with someone who wasn't him. He thought that would make him sound petty. 'I'm frustrated that you kept this from me. That you didn't trust me.'

'It wasn't that I didn't trust you. I didn't know how you'd feel but I was going to tell you about her last night. I had planned to tell you after drinks but you'd already left.'

'That's a convenient story.'

'It's the truth. I'm sorry. I should have told you about her. You should meet her.'

She looked close to tears and Xander moderated his tone. He didn't want to argue. He didn't have the energy. 'I'm not saying I have to meet her. I just wish you'd mentioned her.'

'I think you should meet her. Lily has just turned three.' Chloe was looking at him as if she expected him to say something. His head was hurting and he couldn't figure out what response she expected him to make. In his silence, she continued. 'She's your daughter.'

CHAPTER EIGHT

XANDER FELT THE world stop.

'What did you say?'

'Lily is your daughter. You're her father.'

He shook his head as the nausea burnt his oesophagus. 'She can't be mine.'

An alarm was beeping.

He had forgotten that he was connected to monitors and the rapid acceleration of his heart rate triggered a warning. The young nurse came back into his room.

'Is everything all right? Do you need to rest?'

'No. I'm fine. Just switch the damn machine off.'

He saw the young girl glance at Chloe and he wondered if she was going to ask Chloe to leave but she just raised an eyebrow and Chloe nodded once, as if giving her permission to do as Xander said. She didn't need Chloe's permission but Xander knew he'd frightened her, given her a story to tell about how doctors made terrible patients, but he didn't care. The nurse pressed some buttons, resetting the machine, and scurried off.

He stared at Chloe. Waiting for her to speak. Waiting for the truth.

'I promise you, Lily is your child.'

There was no way Chloe was telling the truth but

she couldn't know how her words pierced his heart. She couldn't know how he'd wished for a child but knew that wish would be denied him.

There had to be another explanation. He'd known last night that another man had fathered a child with Chloe and he knew that was still the case today. There was another man somewhere in this story.

The question was—who was that man, because he was certain it wasn't him.

'She can't be mine,' he repeated.

Chloe listened to Xander repeat his words. Did he think that the more he said it, the truer it would become? Did he think she'd change her mind in the face of his denial?

It was her turn now to be frustrated.

She was annoyed with herself. She hadn't anticipated the conversation happening like this at all. She'd thought she'd be able to control it. To direct the conversation. To break the news to him gently.

She should have realised he wouldn't believe her. She remembered his reaction to Hannah and Guy's situation. He'd felt Hannah was tricking Guy. She should have expected this reaction but she'd been lulled into a false sense of security by Guy and Hannah's experience. They trusted one another but she and Xander didn't have that same level of trust. She wished they did but she knew that required a strong foundation to a relationship and she wasn't even sure they *had* a relationship.

She'd handled it badly but she wasn't expecting to have to defend herself.

She needed to stay calm. She needed to see things from his perspective.

No one deserved to find out about parenthood this

way. He was experiencing the same shock that Hannah and Guy must have felt and she'd empathised with them over that.

She closed her eyes and counted to ten.

But Xander wasn't giving her any leeway.

'You've made a mistake, Chloe,' he continued. 'I'm not her father.'

'Why not?'

'Because I can't have children.'

'What? Why would you say that? Are you accusing me of lying?'

'No. I'm saying you've made a mistake.'

'Why would you think that? I know how a pregnancy happens.'

'There must be someone else.'

'There was no one else.' Her voice was tight with anger and she fought hard to try to keep her tone level. 'I know how a pregnancy happens and I know how long it lasts. I *know* who I was sleeping with when I fell pregnant and that was you.'

'It can't have been me.'

'I promise you. It was.'

'Chloe, I can't have children.'

'Why would you say that? Lily is your daughter.'

'She can't be. I can't have children,' he repeated. 'That's why my wife left me.'

'What?' She didn't understand what he was telling her. She *knew* Lily was his. There was no doubt about that.

'My wife, ex-wife, wanted to have children. We tried naturally and when nothing happened we tried IVF. We had four cycles.'

'Four? And then you gave up? Surely that's not enough attempts to decide you can't have kids.'

'We gave up because, in the middle of all of that, my wife had an affair. That's why we split up.'

'But if you'd kept going you might have been successful. Maybe it was a problem with your wife? Sometimes a different partner makes a difference.'

'The problem was with me,' he said. His grey eyes were dark as he asked, 'If you think I'm the father why didn't you tell me you were pregnant when you found out?'

'I didn't know I was pregnant until after I got home. I tried to find you but you'd disappeared. I got in touch with the flying doctor service in Broken Hill but I was told you weren't working there any more. I contacted the headquarters in Adelaide but HR wouldn't pass on your information. No one would tell me anything and I started to wonder if you'd instructed them not to pass on your details. If you thought I'd become a crazy stalker.

'You weren't on social media,' she continued. 'I didn't know where you were living, where you'd gone. I called Jane, you remember Jane, the flight nurse, but she also said you'd left and she didn't know where you were. I couldn't afford to hire anyone to look for you and then, when Lily was born, I didn't have time to keep looking.'

'So instead you kept her a secret.'

'Not intentionally! I tried to find you.'

'Why didn't you send a letter to the flying doctor base and ask them to forward it to me?'

'I did. I sent a letter by registered mail. I wanted you to sign for it. I wanted to make sure it got to you. I thought it was all too easy for the letter to get lost, or for you to say you never received it, especially if you didn't like what it said, and I would never know the truth, but it came back unopened.'

'Do you have any proof she's mine?'

'How could I? Won't you take my word for it?'

He shook his head, wincing with the movement. 'I can't.'

Chloe wondered whether she should show him photos of Lily on her phone. She had hundreds. But Lily looked so much like her that she doubted he'd be able to see any resemblance to himself in his current state of mind. Would he see himself in Lily's grey eyes?

Only if he wanted to.

'How old is she?' he asked.

'She turned three on the tenth of March. She was due in April but she was born six weeks premature. I was in Australia from May to July,' she said. 'I only slept with you. You do the maths.'

'It's not a question of maths. It's a question of probability.'

'Last time I checked, that was maths.'

Xander sighed and rubbed his head. Chloe felt slightly guilty that they were arguing about Lily while he was in his current state but she was upset too. This was not going the way she'd hoped but it was exactly what she'd been afraid of—not knowing how he would react.

It wasn't ideal having this conversation while he was sore, and medicated, and judging by the look of him, nursing a cracking headache but he'd raised the subject.

'I'm not sure that now is the right time to be having this discussion,' she said, knowing they hadn't finished but they both needed some time to calm down.

'You're right,' he replied. 'I think you should go.'

* * *

Xander stared out of the window of his rental accommodation. The sky outside was grey and heavy and the weather was dismal, like his mood. Five days after the fire, almost six since Adem had given him the news, and he still wasn't sure how he felt. He wanted to believe Chloe but how could it be true?

How could Chloe's daughter be his?

Could he really be a father?

He wanted it to be true but he knew the chances were slim. But why would she lie? What did she hope to gain from this? And if she was telling the truth, then he'd missed out on three years of his daughter's life. How could she do that to him?

His mind continued in a never-ending circle, hour upon hour, day after day.

When he'd confronted her about her child he'd assumed another man was the father. He'd anticipated feeling self-righteous, upset that she hadn't shared her story with him. He hadn't expected it to become *his* story.

In the five days since the fire he was no closer to figuring it out. He had taken sick leave from the air ambulance but was due back at work tomorrow. He had used the downtime to do some things he should have done years ago. He'd called in some favours. Had some tests.

He scrolled through his emails, looking for the one he had forwarded to his oncologist in Australia. He checked the time and read through the scanned report as he waited for a phone call.

His phone vibrated on the table and the sudden noise in the silence of the room startled him. His hands shook with nerves as he read the number on the screen. An international code. He hesitated before accepting the call. It was the one he'd been waiting for but now he wasn't sure if he was ready for an answer.

'You got my email?' he asked, barely managing to get the pleasantries out of the way first. 'Is it possible for me to have children?'

'Yes, is the short answer. Your sperm count and motility is normal. On the low side of normal, which means you'd probably have more chance of having children with a young woman, but it's completely possible. Have you met someone?'

'Sort of.' How did he explain Chloe? 'There's a woman claiming I'm the father of her child,' he said, realising he didn't need to explain the situation more specifically than that.

'So your question is retrospective? You're not planning for the future?'

'No, this has already happened.'

'And you didn't know?'

'I've just found out.'

'How old is the child?'

'Three.'

'So, the pregnancy would have occurred almost four years ago?'

'Yes. Two years post-chemo,' Xander said.

'Your sperm could have recovered by then. Did you not test a sample after you finished treatment?'

'No.' Xander shook his head. 'There wasn't any need. We had embryos frozen at the time I was diagnosed so I started treatment immediately and then Heather and I separated after the last lot of embryos failed to implant. After that it didn't matter to me. I wasn't worried about whether or not I could father children. It wasn't something I was thinking about at that point.'

'Without a comparison sample I can't tell you what the situation was four years ago. There's a chance that the child is yours but it would be a slight chance. DNA would be the only way to know for sure.'

Could it be true? Could he have a daughter?

Lily. He hung up the phone and said her name out loud for the first time.

Lily Jameson. It was a pretty name, although it was more likely to be Lily Larson.

Regardless of what her full name was or whether or not Lily was his he needed to apologise to Chloe. He'd handled the discussion badly, although he didn't feel he was completely to blame. She'd blindsided him. He knew he'd brought up the subject but if he'd anticipated how the conversation would go, he would have waited until the painkillers had worn off. Until his head, and his mind, were clear. And no matter what condition he was in, no matter that he had raised the topic, she'd had ample opportunity to tell him about this child, his child, before then and she hadn't. But still, he needed to clear the air.

Chloe was surprised to run into Xander when she walked out of the hospital. It was almost a week since the fire. Almost a week since she'd told him about Lily. Since he'd asked her to leave him be and she hadn't heard from him since. She'd been going crazy, running through different scenarios in her head, trying to guess what he was thinking. What he was planning.

He was leaning against the wall outside the A&E

and he straightened up when he saw her and stepped forward. She knew he was waiting for her.

As she got closer she could see he was tired and his grey eyes were full of shadows.

'What are you doing here?'

'I thought we needed to talk.' He was holding a bunch of flowers and he held them out to her. 'These are for you. I owe you an apology.'

No one had ever given her flowers before, Chloe thought as she took them from him. It was an enormous bouquet of lilies. Had he chosen lilies deliberately? She was scared to ask him. Scared of what it might mean.

'Have you got time to take a walk with me?' he asked.

She nodded and fell into step beside him. She was pleased to have the lilies to hold. It gave her something to do with her hands and made her keep a little bit of distance from him. She needed to know what he wanted but she was terrified of what she might hear.

'I reacted badly,' he said, 'and I'm sorry. Your news took me by surprise, but still, I should have handled it better.'

'Are you saying you believe me now?'

'I'm still not sure.'

Chloe stopped in her tracks and turned to face him. 'What exactly are you saying, then? What exactly are you apologising for?'

'Let me explain.' He leant on the embankment railing and stared across the river, avoiding eye contact. 'I told you my wife and I got divorced because we couldn't conceive. That is true but it's not the whole truth. We'd tried for a year to conceive naturally and then started

IVF. We'd gone through two cycles unsuccessfully when I was diagnosed with testicular cancer.'

'What?' She couldn't believe he'd dropped that into the conversation as if it was of no consequence. 'You had cancer? You accused *me* of keeping things from you. At least I *tried* to find you. I *tried* to tell you I was pregnant. Why didn't you tell me about the cancer?'

He shrugged. 'We didn't talk much about anything personal. And I was angry. There was a lot of stuff happening in my life when we met. I was grieving. I'd lost my marriage, my health and potentially my chance of having a family of my own. I was in a dark place and you were the one bright light, the one good thing, but you were fleeting. I didn't want to sully things by talking about what I'd been going through—it wasn't important when I was with you. You gave me a chance to focus on something else and I was grateful for that. You were the one thing that gave me hope that I would get through that period of time and come out the other side.'

Chloe thought back to when they'd met. She knew he'd been unhappy and she'd taken pleasure in the knowledge that she had been able to make him laugh and smile. That she'd been able to lift those shadows from his eyes even though it had only been temporary. She'd attributed his sadness to his divorce. She'd never imagined there was more to his despair. He was right— they hadn't talked much.

'Heather, my ex-wife, is a couple of years older than me and her biological clock was working overtime. When I was diagnosed I wanted to start chemotherapy immediately. We had some frozen embryos in reserve so we continued with IVF while I started treatment. I assumed we'd get lucky with IVF—after all, how much bad luck can two people have—but when none of those embryos implanted successfully either Heather started to consider her options.

'I was told it could take two years before my sperm was viable again and, worst case, it may never recover. I guess Heather figured I was a bad bet and she couldn't wait—she didn't *want* to wait—for me to recover. I never really found out where her head was at. We were both stressed for different reasons.

'I foolishly expected her to stick by me, for better or worse. She could only see the worse. She had an affair and fell pregnant. I still wonder if it was deliberate. It was one way to make sure I'd let her go. Loyalty and honesty are really important to me and she betrayed me. Betrayed my trust.

'So yes, when I met you I was angry and the last thing I wanted to talk about was my divorce or my diagnosis because they were interrelated. One had led to the other and I really just wanted to pretend none of it had happened. Heather had just remarried. She'd wanted to make things official with her new partner before the baby was born so I agreed to the divorce. My whole life had come crashing down and I was living one day at a time. I was too scared to look too far into the future. I didn't know what sort of future I was going to have.'

'That's a lot to get my head around.'

'I know. Can you understand why I didn't want to talk about it four years ago? I just needed to forget.'

Chloe nodded. She could understand. But that didn't mean she had to like it. 'How long ago were you diagnosed?'

'Six years.'

'Are you okay now?'

'I'd say I'm fine.'

'*You'd* say. What do your specialists say?'

'That I'm cancer-free.'

'Did you have a sperm count done after you finished chemo?'

'No.'

'So you don't *know* that you can't have children.'

'No. Not definitively.'

She withdrew her phone and turned it on, opening her photos. She held it out to him.

'This is Lily. She has your eyes.' She'd taken it yesterday, deliberately making sure she got Lily's eyes to their best advantage. 'I'd like you to meet her. Do you think that's something you could do?'

He nodded but without any excitement. Without any anticipation. His eyes were dark with shadows back and she knew she'd put them there. She wanted the other Xander back, the one who looked like he wanted to love her. She wondered if he was gone for good.

CHAPTER NINE

XANDER WAS NERVOUS when he knocked on Chloe's door. He had agreed to meet her at her house. She'd felt Lily would be more comfortable in a familiar environment and he hadn't argued. It wasn't every day you got to meet a potential offspring and he wanted to make a good impression. He wanted Lily to like him.

He wiped his palms over the seat of his jeans, making sure they weren't clammy.

'Hi.' Chloe was smiling when she opened the door. She was wearing a pink T-shirt with cut-off denim shorts and canvas trainers. She looked good, she looked relaxed, and Xander felt some of his nervous tension dissipate.

'Hi.'

'I thought we'd take Lily to the park. She's learning to ride her bike—it will be better for all of us if she has an activity to focus on. Is that okay?'

'Of course.'

'Great. I'll get her. Do you want to wait here?'

She left him on the doorstep and his nerves returned.

'Lily, this is my friend from work, Xander. Xander, this is Lily.'

They were back.

He looked down into a face that was a miniature version of Chloe's, albeit with strawberry blond curls and grey eyes.

Chloe was right. She did have his eyes.

He tried not to stare.

Could she really be his?

'Hello, Lily.'

'Hello.'

'Xander is a doctor. He works in the helicopter.'

'Do you fly the helichopper?' she asked, and her expression was so like one of his sister's that it made him do a double take. She was definitely a Jameson around the eyes but the rest of her was Chloe.

He shook his head. 'No. That's Simon's job.'

'Uncle Tom drives an ambliance and Uncle Guy drives a fire engine.'

'That sounds very exciting.'

'Uncle Guy took me in the fire engine. Do you want to see my bike? Uncle Guy bought it for me.'

'I'd love to see your bike.'

Xander walked behind Lily and watched her wobble along on her bike as Chloe occasionally gave her a little push to get her moving or a steadying hand to keep her balance. His heart swelled with pride at the idea that this gorgeous, bubbly little girl could be his.

His daughter.

But that in itself was a dilemma.

He was due to go home soon. But he knew he wouldn't leave if it meant leaving his daughter behind. There was no way he was going to give her up. He needed to get to know her. He needed her to know him. He couldn't believe he'd missed three years of her life already. He wasn't going to miss any more.

Chloe had explained that she'd tried to find him and he had to believe her. He knew he'd been virtually untraceable for the better part of four years. That had been what he'd wanted. To disappear. He couldn't blame Chloe. It was *his* fault his daughter didn't know him. But he couldn't help but wonder if Chloe could have tried harder.

He had a daughter.

Was she really his? Could it be true?

He didn't care if it wasn't, he realised. He wanted it to be true.

'Why didn't you try harder to find me?' he asked as Lily rode ahead of them. 'Why didn't you try again?'

'I didn't stop completely. I searched the internet every year around Lily's birthday. I found a couple of articles about you on a Canadian website about a year ago but when I called the ambulance service there you had already moved on and once again the service wouldn't provide me with any details.' She shrugged. 'So I gave up again. I'm sorry. I don't know what else I could have done.'

'What have you told Lily about her father?' he asked as Lily abandoned her bicycle in favour of the slide.

'That he lives in Australia, which is a very long way away, but that he loves her very much. Now that we've found you I need to know if that is true before we tell her who you are. If you don't want to be a part of her life, I'm not going to tell her any more about you but when she is older I won't stop her from contacting you. What happens next is up to you.'

Lily was running towards them and Chloe stood up, wrapped up the conversation. 'We need to go home now. Lily needs her afternoon nap.'

Chloe sent Lily inside to wash her hands when they got home. And Xander knew it was time for him to take his leave. The Larson family had their lives to lead and he wasn't part of it yet.

Chloe handed him a large envelope as she walked with him to the front gate.

'What is this?'

'It's our DNA samples. Mine and Lily's.'

'You've done a test?' He was surprised.

Chloe nodded.

'Why?'

'I've thought about what you said and I decided your concerns were valid. I shouldn't have dismissed them. There was no reason for you to believe me, even without your history. The tests were non-invasive. Lily was quite happy to copy me when I did my cheek swab. It wasn't difficult and I thought it was only fair to you. I'm claiming that you are Lily's father and I'm happy to prove it to you. I know what the tests results will show. It's only fair that you have the confirmation you wanted.'

Xander took the envelope.

'And if you are free tomorrow,' Chloe said, 'I thought we could spend the day together again? Just the three of us?'

'I'd like that,' he said as he bent and kissed her on the cheek. He'd take whatever she offered him at the moment. She'd turned his world upside down but he had to hope it would be in a positive way.

'Where would you like to go first?' Chloe asked as she reversed her car into a parking space near the Brighton pier. The forecast was for a beautiful day and she had decided to take Xander out of the city and Brighton had numerous attractions that would keep Lily entertained and give them all a chance to spend some time together away from her family.

'What are the options?'

'The Pier, the aquarium, the beach, the Tower.'

'What would Lily like?'

'Probably the Pier.'

Xander had charmed everyone today when he'd met her family. He had the advantage—her family knew this situation was a shock for him and they were taking it easy on him. They hadn't bombarded him with questions; instead they were giving him time to slowly acclimatise to the idea of being a father and gaining an instant family in the Larsons. He'd handled it well, meeting everyone, but Chloe still didn't know how he was feeling about the instant fatherhood. Was he accepting the situation or was he still wary, unsure, uncertain?

She hoped he would do his DNA test soon. She knew the results would corroborate her claims and, in her opinion, the sooner that happened, the better. They couldn't really move forward until Lily's parentage was confirmed and they needed to work out where they went from here. There were a lot of unknowns in this new situation she found herself in.

They walked past the Royal Pavilion as they made their way to the pier.

'A palace!' Lily cried. 'Is there a princess in there? Can we visit her? I'd like to be a princess,' she continued without pausing for breath. 'I'd like to live in a palace and wear pretty dresses every day.'

'Do all three-year-olds talk this much?' Xander wanted to know.

'She does have good language skills. I think it's because she spends so much time around adults. Me, my mum, my brothers. There's always someone to talk to or a conversation to listen in on. Her ears are almost as big as her vocabulary.'

'Who is your favourite princess, Lily?'

'Anna.'

Xander looked at Chloe and she knew he had no idea who Lily was talking about. She figured he would know the traditional fairy-tale princesses but Anna and her sister, Elsa, were far from traditional.

'Anna looks a bit like Lily,' she said, explaining the attraction.

Lily nodded and said, 'She has hair like mine.'

'Can you show me a picture on my phone?' Xander asked as he squatted down beside Lily and opened a browser on his phone.

He admired several photos of Anna, Elsa and even Olaf as they waited for their turn on the carousel and kept up a conversation with Lily, which was not an easy thing to do. She chattered non-stop and changed topics rapidly, making it difficult to keep up with her train of thought, but Xander seemed to take it all in his stride. Was he warming to the idea of being a father?

Chloe listened as Lily giggled in response to Xander's questions about the characters. He had an affinity with Lily. Did he feel a connection with her or was Chloe making more out of this than it really was? Was she hoping for more?

She knew she was.

'Can I go on the trampoline, Mummy?' Lily asked as Xander lifted her off the carousel horse at the end of the ride.

'Not yet, baby girl. You have to be a bit taller.'

Lily started to pout and Chloe expected an argument but Xander jumped in. 'I'll bring you back when you're taller, Lily, but why don't you choose something else for now.'

'You shouldn't make those promises,' Chloe said quietly. 'You might not be able to keep them.'

'I always keep my promises,' he insisted. 'I am a man of my word. Honesty and loyalty are really important to me.'

Chloe let it slide. She wasn't going to get into a debate about that in the middle of an amusement park.

'Which ride would you like, Lily?'

'I'll sit this one out,' Chloe said when Lily insisted on a turn on the spinning cups and saucers.

'Really? What happened to your adventurous spirit?'

Four years ago she had wanted to try everything in the outback. She'd been young, full of adventure and full of joy. Sometimes it seemed like a lifetime ago. 'I can't handle the spinning motion,' she said honestly as she handed over two tickets for the ride.

'Time for one last ride,' Chloe said as her daughter and Xander climbed out of the cups. 'Which one would you like?'

'That one.' Lily pointed at a brightly lit ride that had miniature vehicles 'driving' around a track. Chloe could see an ambulance, a fire engine, a racing car and a rocket. 'I want to sit in the fire engine like Uncle Guy.'

Chloe stood at the barrier, watching Lily on the ride. She felt Xander stand behind her but when he put his hands on her hips she jumped at his touch. She hadn't been expecting that. He'd kissed her on the cheek yesterday, chaste, distracted, leaving her worried about what damage she'd done to their relationship. She wondered if the news about Lily had overshadowed their chemistry. Had it changed Xander's view of her, and of their relationship? Was it more serious? Different? Would Lily become his priority and would Chloe be pushed aside?

She didn't know where they were at. She had no idea how he was feeling.

'Is that okay?' he asked.

She hesitated.

It felt nice. She leant back into him, very slightly, and nodded. She actually wouldn't mind if he wrapped his arms around her but Lily would be sure to notice and would be bound to ask why. Most of her questions at the moment started with that word.

Xander stood behind Chloe and watched Lily. He had his hands on Chloe's hips but he'd felt her stiffen at his touch.

'Is that okay?' he asked, and then she relaxed into him. He was close enough to smell her hair. She smelt like shampoo and sunshine. He felt her apprehension, her worry, and he tried to reassure her. 'It will be all right,' he said. 'We'll figure it all out.'

He was feeling positive about the future. It had taken him a long time but he was certain things would work out. He didn't believe in coincidences but he believed in fate. In things that were meant to be.

'I'm hungry.' The ride had finished and Lily was standing in front of them again.

'How about we get some hot chips for lunch?' he suggested.

Lily clapped her hands. 'I love hot chippies.'

'So does your mum. Especially when they're somebody else's,' he said with a wink in Chloe's direction.

She laughed, as he'd intended her to, and said, 'They taste better off someone else's plate.'

'So I've noticed.'

They sat in the sunshine outside the fish and chip shop and watched as Lily threw almost as many chips to the seagulls as she ate. She climbed off the bench to chase the birds as Chloe cautioned her. 'Be careful, Lily.'

Xander was watching Lily and saw her trip and, almost in slow motion, fall and land awkwardly, her arms outstretched.

Chloe was up out of her seat but Xander was faster. Three strides and he was beside her.

He and Chloe knelt on the ground but the moment Chloe touched Lily, her daughter screamed.

'Hang on, Chloe, let me have a look at her.'

Lily was as white as a ghost and her left wrist was swelling already. She cradled it protectively against her body.

'Chloe. Look at me.' She was agitated and he waited for her to focus. 'I think she may have a greenstick fracture. She needs to go to hospital. Do you know where the closest one is?'

Chloe didn't answer and Xander realised she was in shock.

'Do you need some help?' A lady pushing a pram stopped beside them.

'Do you know if there's a hospital near here?' Xander asked.

'The children's hospital is about a mile from here,' she said as she pointed to their right.

'Chloe, give me your scarf. I'll immobilise her arm as best as I can.'

He wanted to be able to help. He wanted to be useful. He wound the scarf over one shoulder and behind Lily's back holding her arm against her chest to stop it from bouncing around as he explained what he was doing. 'We need to take you to the hospital. We're going to take a picture of your arm and see what you've done.'

He scooped her up in his arms and headed for the car.

Xander parked the car in a doctor's bay in front of the hospital. He didn't care for procedure. His priority was getting Lily into the A&E. He carried her inside as Chloe walked beside them. He spied a wheelchair just inside the door and gently lowered Lily into it as he heard someone exclaim.

'Chloe? What are you doing here?'

'Joanna!'

Xander looked up to see Chloe being greeted by a woman in a nurse's uniform. He listened while Chloe explained what had happened. She seemed to have recovered her wits. She was still pale but the shock seemed to have eased.

'I didn't know you worked here,' she was saying before she glanced his way. 'Xander is a doctor. He thinks she has a greenstick fracture of her wrist.'

Lily was still pale and teary but she sat silently in the chair.

Joanna glanced at her quickly and nodded. 'Give me a second and I'll organise an X-ray,' she said as she gathered some forms. 'Can you fill these out?'

Xander took the forms. 'I'll do it,' he said to Chloe. 'You go with Lily.'

Chloe didn't argue. She followed behind Joanna as

she pushed Lily's wheelchair through the next set of doors, whisking her away and leaving Xander alone. He sat in the waiting room and read through the forms. He filled in Lily's birthday and her address but that was as much as he knew. There was no way he could complete the form without Chloe's help. He knew so little about the girl who was supposedly his daughter. He didn't know her middle name or even her surname. If she had allergies. He knew almost nothing about her and only a bit more about her mother. But he could feel himself being drawn in. He didn't want to let Chloe go. Not this time. Not again. She came as a package deal now but that was okay.

Joanna reappeared and Xander stood up, waiting for news.

'You were right. It looks like a greenstick fracture. I've left them in a treatment bay—they're just waiting for a doctor's consult. Have you finished with the forms?'

Xander shook his head. 'No. I need Chloe to fill out some of the detail.'

Joanna looked sideways at him, obviously assuming he was Lily's father and then assuming he was an idiot. He didn't correct her, on either assumption. 'Come with me, you can wait with them.'

She took him in to Chloe and Lily.

'I need your help with the forms,' Xander said to Chloe. 'I've got her birthday as March the tenth. Does she have a middle name?'

'Alexandra.'

'Alexandra?'

Chloe nodded. 'I wanted to give her something of yours. That was the closest I could manage.'

'Thank you.' It was an unexpected gift and the small gesture gave him an extraordinary amount of pleasure. 'And her surname.'

'Larson.'

Chloe's name. Not his.

The doctor on duty came into the bay, putting an end to that conversation. He engaged Lily in a discussion about the plaster he was about to apply as Chloe took the clipboard and forms from Xander and swiftly completed them.

'What colour would you like your plaster to be?' the doctor was asking. 'Would you like pink?'

Lily shook her head. 'Green.'

Like Anna's dress, Xander thought. He may not know everything about Lily but he knew her favourite colour. And the more time he spent with her, the better he would know her. He just hoped he would have as much time as he wanted.

Lily was asleep in the car, her green, plastered arm cradled in her lap. Xander was driving but Chloe noticed that he was constantly glancing in the rearview mirror, checking on Lily.

'I felt so useless today when I couldn't fill out those forms,' he said as he returned his gaze to the road. 'It made me realise how much I've missed, how little I know about her.'

'She's only young,' Chloe said. 'There's plenty of time if you want to be involved in her life.'

'She's taken her first step, got her first tooth, said her first word. You got to see her first smile. She's had her first day at nursery. There's a lot to make up.'

Chloe didn't want to argue; this day had been stressful enough, and she knew he was right. She tried to placate him. 'She still has to have her first day at school, lose her first tooth, have her first boyfriend. She'll need someone to teach her how to drive a car.'

'Those things are all in the future. I've missed her past. I've missed three birthdays, three Christmases, three father's days. I missed her birth.'

'Xander, I said I'm sorry. I *did* try.'

'I know. I'm not blaming you for that.'

Was he blaming her for everything that came after that though?

'She was born at 6:52 in the morning,' Chloe told him. She didn't know if he wanted a description of the day Lily was born but perhaps it would help him. 'She was six weeks premature. I was terrified when I went into labour. Despite my training I had no idea how it would end. I'd had none of the risk factors for early delivery and my mother had had no problems with any of her pregnancies either. I was worried that something was wrong with Lily. With me.

'She spent a week in the NICU and three weeks in hospital. But she's a fighter, a survivor. She progressed really well and she's meeting all her milestones but it was a scary time. I think partly because I knew all the things that could go wrong and I worried about every last one of them. I wish you'd been there. I could have used your calm head.'

'I don't know how calm I would have been.'

'Are you kidding? You're so good in a crisis.'

'It's always different when it's personal.'

'You were good today. I don't know what I would have done without you. She is everything to me,' Chloe said as Xander turned the car into her street.

She unlocked the front door and let Xander carry Lily inside and she felt the tears well in her eyes as she looked at Xander with the tiny, precious bundle in his arms.

Her mother met them in the hall, alerted to their arrival by the sound of Chloe's key in the lock.

'Oh, the poor darling.'

'She's okay, Mum, but I'm going to put her straight to bed.' She looked at Xander. 'Can you give me a few minutes?' She needed some time to compose herself.

Chloe took Lily from his arms, dismissing him, and the loss of her weight felt like an ache in his heart.

He could feel Chloe's mother watching him and he tried to keep his expression neutral. It had been a stressful day and he could feel his emotions bubbling close to the surface. He needed to hold it together. He needed to stay strong.

'Come and wait with me, Xander,' Susan offered. 'I'll put the kettle on.'

He could use something stronger, he thought as he waited for the water to boil while he filled Susan in on the details of Lily's accident.

'How was your day until then?' she asked.

'I'm not sure,' he admitted. There had been patches where he'd felt they were both relaxed and shared some easy conversation, a few connected moments, but there'd been times he thought that Chloe was holding something back too. 'Chloe says you raised her and her brothers on your own. I don't know if she thinks I'm needed.' That was his main concern. That Chloe didn't need him.

'I'm not sure I'm the one you should be having this

conversation with,' Susan said as she warmed the tea-pot. 'I didn't choose to raise my kids by myself but I managed. I raised them on my own because my husband left me with no choice.'

He thought that was an odd turn of phrase.

'Has Chloe told you anything about him?' Susan continued.

'She said he was a policeman and that he was killed in the line of duty.'

'That's true, but there's more to the reason why I raised my kids alone. Grant had an affair and left me. I struggled for a while before I pulled myself together for the sake of the kids. My mum came and stayed. Chloe was seven, old enough to remember, and she's never forgiven her father. She finds it difficult to put her trust in people.'

'In me.'

'Not just you,' Susan said as she poured the tea.

'I feel like she's giving me small bits of information, not the whole story.'

'It hasn't helped that she couldn't ever find you. It made her second-guess everything. She wondered if you knew she was looking for you, if anyone she spoke to who had worked with you ever passed on a message to you and if you just ignored that.'

Xander shook his head. 'I never knew.'

'You need to make that clear to her. You need to figure out what you want to do.'

'What do you mean?'

'You have lots of options. I'm not someone who thinks every child needs two parents. Every circumstance is different and if you've got a parent who isn't invested in their child, then that's no better than only having one. Children need as much love as they can get. If you love them, you'll do your best by them and that's all anyone can expect. Chloe loves Lily. Adores her. She has been her world for the past three years. Longer, really. From the moment Chloe realised she was pregnant Lily has been her priority.

'She and Lily have my support and the support of Chloe's brothers but I know Chloe's choice would be for Lily to have two parents who love her equally. But there is nothing to say you have to be involved in Lily's life or that you have to do things Chloe's way but I will ask you this—please think very carefully before you disrupt their lives. Chloe's or Lily's. And you need to expect that it will take time for her to adjust to sharing Lily. If that's what you want.'

Xander was still mulling over Susan's advice when Chloe reappeared.

'How is she?' Susan asked.

'She's okay. She woke up but she's gone back to sleep now. I expect we'll have a restless night.'

'You already look exhausted,' Xander said.

'Thank you.' She gave him a tired smile. 'Always nice to hear I look as bad as I feel.'

'I didn't mean that.' In his opinion she still looked beautiful but her skin was so pale it was almost translucent and there were dark purple shadows under her eyes. The day had taken its toll on all of them. It had been stressful, emotionally charged, and it hadn't ended the way any of them had expected.

Chloe collapsed onto a chair as Susan excused herself. Leaving them alone.

'Lily didn't ask for me when she woke up?' Xander asked as he picked up the teapot and poured Chloe a cup.

Chloe sighed. 'She's met you twice, Xander. She doesn't know you yet. Give her time.'

She was right. It was going to take more than a weekend for Lily to bond with him. For her to get used to him being around. And it wasn't only Lily who needed to learn he could be trusted. Who needed time. Chloe needed that too.

He wanted to be part of her life. Their lives. Chloe's and Lily's.

It didn't matter if Lily was his biological child or not.

She might be the only child he ever had and Chloe's word was good enough for him. He didn't want to muck things up.

Mindful of Susan's words, he knew he needed to find out what Chloe wanted. What she needed. He couldn't afford to make a mistake.

'I want to be part of Lily's life. I want her to know who I am. But I also need to know what you want. We're in this together. We need to work out how we do this going forward.' He needed a plan. He needed to prove to Chloe that his intentions were true. That he wasn't going to disappear again. He needed to make plans to stay. 'Tell me what you want.'

'I'm not sure.'

'What did you want when you found out you were pregnant? What did you want when you looked for me?'

'I dreamt of a life with you but that was a fantasy. It wasn't reality. I thought you didn't want children so I convinced myself that it was better that I couldn't find you. Then I didn't have to listen to your side of the argument.'

'But I do want children and if I am Lily's father I want to be part of her life. And yours. I think we both need some time to work out what that means.'

Even before he saw Chloe unsuccessfully try to stifle a yawn he knew they weren't going to solve their issues tonight. The conversation needed fresh heads and clear minds.

'We can talk about this later. It looks like you need to go to bed. Will you let me know how Lily is in the morning?'

'Of course.'

She walked with him to the front door.

He kissed her on the forehead and wondered where they would go from here as he said goodnight.

Chloe watched him walk away.

He wanted to be part of her life but what did that mean exactly? He was Lily's father and nothing would take that away from him but how did she fit in? What did their future look like in his eyes? Did he want her?

He had said he would like to get married again. What if he married someone else? Lily would spend half the time with him and a stepmother. That wasn't the life she wanted for her daughter.

That wasn't the life she wanted for herself.

She wanted to share her life with someone too.

She wanted Lily to have her father. She wanted someone to love Lily.

She wanted someone to love her.

She wanted Xander.

She sighed and wiped a stray tear from her eye as she closed the door. She still loved him.

Had he ever loved her?

CHAPTER TEN

'Hi. This is a nice surprise.' Xander answered his door to find Chloe outside. He had spoken to her but hadn't seen her for a couple of days. She had taken time off work so she could keep Lily at home and keep her quiet for forty-eight hours following her accident. 'Come in. How are you? How's Lily?'

'She's perfectly fine. She's home with my mum today but she's not complaining of any pain.' She stepped inside but stopped beside the small table in his entryway. 'Are these the DNA tests?' she asked.

Xander had left the addressed envelope lying on the table. He nodded.

'Have you done your test?'

He nodded again.

'But you haven't sent it off?'

'No.' He walked past the table and Chloe followed him into the lounge.

'Why not?' she asked as she sat down.

'Because I don't need to know the results. I don't care. I want her to be mine.'

'She is yours.'

But he'd been afraid of what might happen if the results said otherwise. That was why the envelope remained unsent. He wanted Lily to be his daughter so badly. Chloe had sworn she was and his fertility tests confirmed she could be. That was enough for him.

Chloe was holding out her hand. She held a USB stick between her thumb and forefinger. 'I brought you something. A peace offering. It's some photos of Lily. Of some of the moments you've missed.'

'Thank you.' He had missed so much, he thought as he took the gift. Three years. He wondered if Lily would feel the same sense of loss. 'Do you think she's missed having me in her life?' he asked as he led her into the living room.

'I've tried to do my best.'

'You've done a brilliant job,' he said. 'She's gorgeous, bright, inquisitive, friendly and confident.'

'I honestly think that if you're prepared to be part of her life from now on that will be enough. She's young. She's not going to remember these years. They're formative but she's had good role models, lots of love. That's what she's needed. I don't think she's missed out.'

'But I feel like I have.'

'I know. And I'm sorry. I really did try to find you but when I couldn't I started to worry. I didn't really know you. I had no idea how you felt about kids. All I knew was that your divorce had knocked you for six. I wasn't sure if you'd want anything to do with us and I started to think you were avoiding my attempts to get in touch. Maybe I should have tried harder.' Chloe sat on the couch, her arms crossed defensively over her chest.

'I wasn't avoiding you,' he said as he put the USB stick down and reached for Chloe's hands, trying to encourage her to relax. 'I didn't know you were trying to find me. When you left I was miserable. Everywhere I looked, everywhere I went, I was reminded of you and it was horrible. I was happy while you were there and then you were gone. I didn't want to be there any more so I left. I needed to get away from all the memories.'

'You didn't think to come to find *me*? Why spend all that time travelling the world and not come here?'

'You were young and gorgeous, happy to have a working holiday romance. What could you possibly want with a grumpy old man?'

'You weren't old.' Chloe smiled. 'And you weren't always grumpy.'

'I was a miserable old man.' He could smile about it now. That man was gone, thanks to Chloe. His future was full of possibility. 'You had your whole life ahead of you. I had a broken marriage and health issues. We had four weeks together. I didn't know how you felt and I didn't know what my future held. I didn't know what my prognosis was at that stage and it wasn't fair to think you might want to take a chance on a man who may have only a few years left. I figured eventually I'd find a place where I was happy again. I couldn't come for you. I had nothing to offer you then.'

'And now?'

'Now I'm thinking what an idiot I was and how much time I've wasted. But hindsight is a wonderful thing. I should have listened to my heart four years ago but I listened to my head instead and I've been searching for happiness ever since. I've found it again. With you. We can make this work.'

'Make what work?'

'You. Me. Lily.'

'How?'

'I could stay here,' he said. 'I've had a long journey

to get here but I feel like this is where I am meant to be. With you. We will figure this out.'

He'd given this a lot of thought over the past few days but he needed to know where Chloe stood.

Xander reached one hand towards her and Chloe could feel herself being seduced by his words. By the picture he was painting. By the earnestness she could see in his grey eyes.

Did he really want to be with her?

Would he stay?

Could she trust him?

His fingers skimmed her jaw and slid into her hair. His thumb stroked her skin. Waves of desire washed over her and she forgot about his promises. It took all her concentration to remember just to breathe. Her life might have changed—her life was no longer simple and carefree—but her reaction to Xander remained constant.

The touch of his fingertips on her bare skin sent a buzz of anticipation straight to her groin and she felt as though she was on fire. She rested her head back on the couch, relishing the sensation as his touch brought her body to life.

He leant towards her. He was inches from her, his lips close enough to kiss, his neck close enough to nestle into. She breathed in deeply, savouring his smell.

She met him halfway, closing her eyes as his lips touched hers. She heard her soft moan as he kissed her. She parted her lips, welcoming his tongue into her mouth. Letting him explore her and taste her as she tasted him.

His hand was on her hip and he lifted her easily and

pulled her onto his lap. She felt his hand slide up under her shirt, warm against her back, but his lips didn't leave hers. Her hands wound around his neck as he undid her bra with a flick of his fingers.

She arched her back as his fingers traced her ribcage. She gasped as his fingers cupped the underside of her breast and her nipple hardened in expectation as his thumb stroked her flesh. He found her nipple, stopping to tease it, running his thumb over and around it, sending electric shocks through her body.

His hands moved to her waist and Chloe lifted her arms above her head as he removed her clothes. He trailed a line of kisses down her neck to her breasts and ran his tongue across one nipple, turning her dizzy with desire before he took her other breast into his mouth, sucking it and making her writhe in ecstasy. She pushed her hips towards him, unable to keep still.

She needed him to touch her. She needed to feel his hands on her. She couldn't think beyond where his fingers might land next. Where she might next feel his mouth on her skin. She was consumed by need. By passion.

She reached for him now, her hands reading her mind. Reaching for his shirt she pulled it free from his pants, running her fingers over his skin, feeling the heat radiating from him. She undid his belt and her fingers fumbled with the button on his waistband. He lifted his hips and, with one hand, pushed his trousers down without moving her off his lap.

Chloe knew where this night would end—there was no denying that, just as there was no denying she wanted it as badly as she'd wanted anything in her entire life. As far as she was concerned, she was his for the taking. She knew she'd wanted this since the moment he'd reappeared in her life. She didn't care that her life had moved on. She no longer cared where he'd been for the last few years. All she cared about was feeling his hands on her again, his lips on hers, having him inside her once again. She'd worry about what happened next another time. There was no room in her head for anything else.

His hand was on her belly and then his fingers slid beneath, under the elastic of her underwear, and rested between her thighs, covering her most sensitive spot. A place that felt like the centre of the universe. He slid one finger inside her and Chloe closed her eyes, almost unable to bear the waves of desire crashing through her. Heat flooded through her and she tore open the buttons on his shirt and pushed it aside, pressing herself against him, chest to chest, skin to skin, as his fingers continued to work their magic, bringing her to a peak of pleasure. She threw her head back as she thrust her hips towards him and just when she thought she was about to explode he paused.

She opened her eyes and she saw the question in his face. She didn't want him to stop; there was only one conclusion she could bear to have.

She wanted him unable to resist, she wanted him at her mercy and she wanted him inside her. She pulled his head down to her and kissed him hard, wondering at what point she had become the leader. She broke away, biting his lip gently between her teeth before lifting her head. She wanted to watch him, wanted to see his expression as she took control.

She pushed his boxer shorts down over his hips, freeing him, and closed her hand around his shaft. He was fully aroused, firm and warm in her hand, and as she ran her fingers up his shaft and across the sensitive tip she heard him gasp with pleasure. His lips were parted, his grey eyes dark, his breathing rapid.

'Wait.' His voice was deep and hoarse, as if he could barely summon the energy to speak. He gave her a half-smile. 'I guess we need some protection.'

Her bag lay on the floor beside the couch and she reached for it, opening her purse and finding a condom.

'You carry them with you?'

'Perks of the job.' She smiled as she tore open the packet and rolled the condom onto him.

She pushed him backwards slightly, adjusting her hips before she brought him back to her and guided him inside. She welcomed him in and wrapped her legs around him to keep him close. He closed his eyes and a sigh of pleasure escaped his lips. She lifted her hips, pushing him deeper inside her, and closed her eyes too as she listened to him moan in delight. She concentrated on the rhythm of movement, the sensation of their bodies joined together as he thrust into her.

But he wasn't to be outdone. He found a gap between their hips and with one hand he stroked the source of her pleasure. His fingers moved in small, soft circles that almost brought her undone.

She heard his name on her lips as he thrust inside her, as his fingers continued their magic, bringing her to a peak of excitement.

'Now, please,' she begged for release. She couldn't hold on any longer. Her head was thrown back and Xander dropped his head to her breast, sucking on a nipple. She lifted her hands to his head, holding on to his hair, keeping his head down as he brought her to a climax.

Her entire body shuddered and, as she felt her orgasm peak, she felt Xander's release too.

They collapsed in each other's arms, spent and satisfied.

It felt as though it had been only days since their bodies had known each other. The memory of their time together imprinted on every nerve ending, every cell, coming back without hesitation. But Chloe knew time had taken its toll. No matter how she felt. No matter how intense their chemistry was, nothing about this situation was simple.

Chloe stepped out of the shower, dried herself off and reluctantly got dressed. Xander had gone back to work for a training session and she needed to get home.

Her whole body still tingled. Their chemistry was still amazing. It hadn't diminished and the more she learned about him, the closer she felt, and that added another layer, another dimension, to their lovemaking.

But amazing chemistry wasn't the solution to their issues. They really needed to have a discussion about what happened next. He was insistent that they could make things work but he didn't live here. His time in London was drawing to a close and then what would happen? She didn't know if his comment about staying in London was serious. Was that really his plan? And what would that mean for Lily going forward?

They hadn't even told Lily who he was yet. She had argued that Lily was young and it would confuse her. She'd wanted Lily to have time with Xander, a chance to get to know him before they thrust big changes on her. But she knew it was more about her resistance. Her own hesitance. She'd wanted more time herself. She didn't know what changes she could cope with.

She'd had three years to work out what she would do if, when, she found Xander and still she didn't know. The reality was that three years wasn't long enough to figure it out and six weeks definitely wasn't long enough.

Could they have a future? she wondered as she picked up her bag. He certainly seemed to think so but she was more pessimistic. She didn't believe in everlasting love. But she was willing to see where this would go. For Lily's sake.

For hers.

No one had ever made her feel like Xander had and she didn't want to regret letting him go again.

She opened his front door, noticing again the envelope sitting on the hall table. She slipped it into her bag. She would post it. She wanted him to see the results for himself. She thought it was important.

Chloe lay curled against Xander's side revelling in the fact that she could stay the night. Lily wouldn't miss her. She was used to Chloe working night shifts and leaving her in Susan's care and Chloe had no idea how many more opportunities she'd get to lie in Xander's arms. She didn't want to miss any of them.

She lay with her head against his chest and listened to the rhythm of his heart and let the waves of contentment wash over her. She closed her eyes and relaxed into the peace and comfort of his embrace.

'What are you thinking about?' His voice rumbled under her ear.

'About one of the last times I spent the night with you. How peaceful I felt. I feel like that now.'

'Which night was it?'

'Your thirtieth birthday. Do you remember where we were?'

'At Uluru.'

Chloe nodded. It had been their last weekend together before she had left Australia. 'I think that was the most peaceful place I've ever been.' They had walked around the base of the massive red rock and watched the colours change as the sun set over the ancient land. They had made love under the stars and had walked through Kata Tjuta the next morning. The weekend was everything she'd imagined it to be but a hundred times better because she was spending it with him. She had known her time was ending, that she would soon be leaving, so she made sure to savour every detail, making memories she could take home with her. 'There was something special about that country. Something more than the space and the colours and the stars. It was spiritual. Did you feel it? Something was at work there. Something bigger than us. Something powerful.'

Xander looked sideways at her. 'Why do you say that?'

'I think that's when I fell pregnant.'

'I still can't get my head around the idea that my ex-wife and I had trouble conceiving *before* I had cancer but after my treatment, when I had all but given up on the idea, you fell pregnant in the blink of an eye.'

'I think it was meant to be.'

'Fate?'

Chloe shook her head. 'It was more than that. I felt spirits.' Walking through Kata Tjuta she had felt that they weren't alone. That they were being watched. There hadn't been a breath of wind, nor a sound. There had been not another soul in sight but she hadn't been able to shake the feeling that they were not alone. 'I'm not a religious person by any means but I can only describe what I felt as something spiritual and extraordinarily peaceful.'

'Spirits?'

She nodded, waiting to see if he was going to laugh at her idea but he surprised her when he asked, 'Why would they give us a baby?'

She'd thought a lot about this over the past four years.

'I think I needed someone to love. I think you did too. But fate, or the spirits, forgot to factor in that I was leaving soon. Maybe it was just science. Maybe it was as simple as the pill I forgot to take and the fact that you recovered quickly, but I still feel there was more at play. I thought there was a reason it had happened.'

'You missed a pill?'

She nodded. 'I always take one in the morning, but when I went to get it out of my bag, I found I forgot to pack them. We were literally in the middle of the desert, so there was nothing I could do about it. I didn't think it would matter—we were using protection as well but I guess condoms really are only ninety-nine per cent effective. I think someone, somewhere, really wanted me pregnant.'

'You can thank the spirits,' Xander said, 'but I call it fate. And now fate has brought us together again. I just wish we'd had the last four years as well.'

'Do you think we would have lasted if we'd spent every day together?'

'I do.' He smiled and flipped her onto her back. He

lifted her into the centre of the bed and spread her legs before running his fingers up the inside of her thigh. 'Let me show you why,' he said as he pulled her hips towards him.

Chloe sighed and arched her back as she felt his warm breath between her thighs.

Right now, she would believe anything he told her. She didn't even care if they didn't have for ever. She'd got over him once before and she knew she could do it again if she had to.

CHAPTER ELEVEN

THE WEDDING HAD been beautiful and Chloe hoped that Esther and Harry would prove her wrong. She really hoped they would get their happily ever after. She realised there were no guarantees but she'd be happy to bet on Esther and Harry making the distance.

She'd enjoyed the day. The weather had been glorious, perfect for a wedding in an historic mansion, and their vows had been genuine and heartfelt and had made plenty of the guests emotional. And dinner had been divine, the speeches both entertaining and moving, and the bride looked stunning.

Chloe was already looking forward to the next wedding, to Carly and Adem's special day, not least because it would mean Izzy was back as well. She was excited to think that the four of them—Carly, Esther, Izzy and herself—would be able to spend time together. She knew things were different now—Esther was married and Carly would soon be a wife *and* a mother—but even though their focus had shifted Chloe knew the four of them would always be in each other's lives. She could count on them.

She let her gaze wander across the room, towards Xander. She had tried to concentrate on being a good bridesmaid, and she hoped she'd done her duty, but she'd been constantly on the lookout for Xander. Always aware of where he was. And whenever she looked in his direction she found he was watching her. He would wink or smile at her and she glowed in the attention.

The wedding had been fabulous but she was ready to leave now. She was ready to go home with Xander. Her mum was looking after Lily and Chloe wasn't expected home until tomorrow.

He looked handsome in a dark, charcoal grey suit, with a fine white stripe. The colour highlighted both his tan and his grey eyes. She still got goosebumps when she looked at him and his touch continued to make her heart beat faster and her breath catch.

Could she count on him?

Could Lily?

They really needed to have a discussion about what happened next. He had mentioned leaving and he had mentioned staying but he'd said nothing about either option lately and she didn't know what he was planning on doing next. She had no idea but she couldn't continue to ignore the fact that he didn't live here and his six weeks were almost at an end.

He was walking towards her. His eyes did not leave hers as he crossed the room. She waited for him. Knowing he was coming for her. His gaze pinning her to the spot.

'Can I drag you away from your bridesmaid's duties for a moment?'

He took her hand and she couldn't think. She couldn't speak. All she could do was follow him outside onto the terrace.

'There's something I need to ask you,' he said.

Fairy lights glowed in the garden around them as he sat her down and then sat beside her.

'Chloe?'

It was a magical, romantic setting and Chloe's breath caught in her throat. 'Yes.'

'I want to tell Lily that I am her father,' he said. 'It's time.'

'Have you got the DNA results back?'

He nodded and withdrew an envelope from his jacket pocket.

Chloe swallowed, suddenly nervous, even though she knew what the results would show.

'And? What do they say?'

'I don't know. I haven't opened them.'

Chloe stared at the envelope that Xander held between his fingers as if she could see through it and read the writing inside. 'Why not?'

'Because I don't need to. Because in my heart I know she's mine,' he said as he tore the envelope in two and put it back in his pocket.

'What are you doing?'

'Lily is our daughter, Chloe. I don't need a piece of paper to tell me that. I trust you and I believe you. I know she's mine and now I want to tell her who I am.'

She nodded. He was right. It was time. She couldn't deny him this any longer. Lily deserved to know the truth too and then they'd have to work out what happened next. 'When do you want to tell her?'

'I want to come home with you tomorrow. I'm going back to Australia next week. My parents are celebrating their fortieth wedding anniversary and my sisters want me there. They've insisted. I want to take Lily with me.'

'You want to do what?' Chloe felt her surroundings

sway. She had spots in her peripheral vision and Xander faded in and out of focus. She wasn't sure if she was going to faint or vomit. He *couldn't* take her. 'You want to take her away?'

This was *not* part of the plan.

'I'm not taking her away but I want her to meet my side of the family—'

'Chloe! There you are.' Carly stepped onto the deck and spotted Chloe and Xander. 'I've been looking everywhere for you. Esther and Harry are leaving and I thought you'd want to say goodbye.' She was greeted with silence and stony expressions. She looked from Chloe to Xander and back again. 'Am I interrupting?'

'No,' Chloe said. She'd heard enough. 'We're finished.' She stood up and followed Carly back inside, ready to farewell the bride and groom.

Chloe stood with Carly as they waved Esther and Harry off. The minute the newlyweds had departed Adem came and claimed Carly for one last dance, leaving Chloe on the sidelines. She had never felt more alone than she did right now.

'Chloe.' Xander materialised beside her. 'Please, you need to listen to me. There's more to explain.' His grey eyes were dark, anxious. What more could he have to say? Was that why he'd gone quiet about his plans recently? Because he'd been intending to take Lily away? She never should have trusted him.

'I'm tired. It's been a long day and I want to go home.' She was close to tears and she really didn't think she had the energy to deal with anything unpleasant.

'Please. Just give me ten minutes. It's important.'

She sighed. She could tell from the set of his shoulders, from the shadows in his eyes, that he wasn't going to let this go. 'Ten minutes,' she replied, and let him guide her back out to the terrace, away from the other guests.

'I don't want to take Lily to Australia by herself,' he said when they were outside again. 'She is still getting to know me. I want you to come too.'

'Me?'

'Of course. I couldn't take Lily to the other side of the world without her mum. I thought we could make it a family trip.'

'But we're not a family,' she argued.

'Not yet,' he said as he got her to sit down, 'but I'd like us to be. People have told me you don't miss what you've never had but I never believed that. I missed being a father but missing fatherhood was nothing compared to finding out I have a daughter and knowing that I could miss out on her life, on watching her grow up. There is no way I'm walking away from Lily. Or from you. I want us to be a family.'

He knelt down beside her and said, 'I want you to marry me.'

'What?'

'Marry me. Make us a family.'

She was shaking as she said, 'I can't marry you.'

'Why not?'

'It's too soon.' Her heart was racing. It was too fast, one beat merging with the next. She couldn't breathe. Couldn't think. Couldn't see.

'How do you figure that?'

She swallowed and took several deep breaths as she tried to slow her heart rate. Tried to stop her hands from shaking. 'We've known each other for eight weeks and half of those weeks were four years ago. We know nothing about each other. Not really.'

'I know we have amazing chemistry.'

Chloe shook her head. 'Passion like that isn't sustainable. It would burn out and then what would we be left with? We'd be two strangers who had a child together.'

'You can't believe that.' He held her hands in his and finally the shakes subsided. 'We are so much more than two people. We are two halves. We're meant to be together. I know you feel it too.' He lifted her hands to his mouth and kissed her fingers. 'I should have asked you to stay all those years ago. We could have avoided all of this. We could have been together.'

'But you didn't.' She had waited for him to ask. She would have stayed if he had asked her to. But he'd said nothing. Done nothing and so she'd left. Nursing her heart. Carrying her secret.

'I couldn't. I had nothing to offer you. My life had not gone in the direction I had hoped and I was struggling to process all of that. I was recently divorced and waiting for that magical five years post-diagnosis. I was damaged. Hurting. I was angry.'

'Were you still in love with your wife? Did she break your heart?'

'No. She didn't break my heart. My ego was bruised. I was disappointed and damaged. I grew up in a close-knit family and I always imagined I would have that too. That was how I pictured my life. A wife and kids. I know I rushed into my first marriage. I was caught up in living my dream and when it came crashing down, instead of turning to my family for support I turned away. I couldn't handle watching their happy lives. I had a lot of soul searching to do. I've spent years trying to find meaning in my life, trying to tell myself that I loved my job and that was enough for me. That it was fulfilling. And it is, in its way, but it's not enough. I need more. I need you.

'I didn't fall in love with my first wife across a crowded room but you took my breath away the moment I saw you. I felt an instant connection. I was sad when my marriage ended. I was disappointed, lost, but I was adrift when you left me.

'She bruised my heart, you repaired it. She damaged my spirit and you healed it but then I let you go. I'm not going to make the same mistake twice. I want to spend the rest of my life with you. I love you. Marry me, Chloe. Be my wife.'

This was what she wanted but she couldn't let herself believe that it could be her life. That she could be happy. That she could get the ending she had dreamt of. 'We don't have to get married.'

'I want to.'

'Marriage is just a piece of paper.'

'Not to me,' he said.

'How can you say that? You've already been divorced once.'

'That wasn't my doing. I took my marriage vows seriously but I couldn't stay married. Her affair was a deal breaker. But I'm not sorry that I got divorced. It left me free to meet you. I didn't think I'd be lucky enough to find another person I could love and then I didn't realise it was you until you'd gone. I let you go once and I'm not going to let you go a second time. I couldn't be lucky enough to find you a third time. I don't believe in coincidences but there's a higher power working for us. We'd be silly to ignore it. I love you, Chloe. Do you love me?'

'I'm scared.'

'Of what?'

'Of giving you my heart and it not working out. Of you making promises that you might not be able to keep. Of you feeling like you have to marry me because we have a child together. I've seen it all before. It doesn't work.'

'Is this about your parents?'

She nodded. 'They got married because of me. And they shouldn't have.'

'What happened between them?'

She took a deep breath. It was time to tell him everything. Time to expose all the secrets. Maybe then she could move forward.

'My father had just broken up with his girlfriend when he started dating my mother. She fell pregnant unexpectedly and my father did the "right thing" and married her. In hindsight that was a mistake. A pretty big one. They stayed together for a few years, long enough to have my brothers as well. Long enough to make things really difficult for Mum when Dad left.

'He moved out just after Tom was born. Apparently he'd started seeing his old girlfriend again, the one he'd broken up with before he met Mum. He said he'd never got over her and if Mum hadn't got pregnant he would never have married her but would probably have patched things up with his ex. I don't understand why he waited so long to call it quits. I get that he thought he was doing the right thing, but he shouldn't have made a life with Mum, shouldn't have spent all those years with us, only to leave. He left us all. Just walked out. And then he was killed before they got divorced but I can't forgive him for leaving us in the first place.

'And so, you see, I don't believe people are truly capable of making a commitment to each other and keeping it. I think we're setting ourselves up to fail. Even if one person is committed, it takes two. Even if they're in love it isn't always enough to keep a marriage going and a child is no guarantee either. When I found out I was pregnant I dreamt of finding you and of us being able to work it all out but I never really believed it. I would never have pressured you into anything but I must admit I did, briefly, imagine a happy family situation, but I realised there are no guarantees of that. We had insane chemistry but I knew that wasn't enough.'

'I promise you, I'm not going anywhere. I won't leave you.'

'You're going home,' she said.

'Home?'

'To Australia.'

He shook his head. 'That's just for a visit. I want to introduce my family to you and Lily. Home is where you are. My two girls. I've applied for a permanent position here, with the air ambulance service. Eloise has resigned. She and her husband are moving to Spain. My maternal grandmother was English. I can stay here. With you. I want us to be a family. You, me, Lily. From the moment I saw her I knew she was mine. She's a miracle. My miracle. The child I thought I'd never have. But even if she wasn't biologically mine I wouldn't care. She's a part of you and that's enough for me. I'm not asking you to marry me out of obligation. I'm asking because I love you.'

He placed her hand on her chest, over her own heart

and wrapped his arms around her. 'Close your eyes and tell me how you feel.'

She had fallen hard for him four years ago but she'd convinced herself that such powerful feelings couldn't last. They would have to burn out. People fell in love all the time but obviously those feelings didn't last, otherwise there wouldn't be divorces. But Xander had already been divorced—if he still believed in love and marriage maybe she could too. She closed her eyes and listened to his heartbeat keeping time with her own. 'I feel safe,' she said. 'I feel like I'm where I'm supposed to be.'

'Trust your heart,' he said as she opened her eyes.

'It's not my heart that's the problem. It's my head. I have spent years believing that true love can't last but you make me want to change my mind.'

'What do you mean?'

'I fell in love with you all those years ago but I talked myself out of it.'

'You loved me?' he asked. 'Could you love me again?' he asked when she nodded.

'I never stopped loving you,' she told him. 'But I don't know if love is enough.'

'Of course it is. What else is there? What we have is special. I can't compare it to anything else I've known. Trust me on this. We can make this work. I haven't felt like this in four years. Maybe ever. I feel at peace. It's not a coincidence that you fell pregnant. It's not a co-incidence that we found each other again. It's fate. We are meant to be together. I love you. I love our daughter and I want us to be a family. Please believe in me. Believe in us. Will you be my wife? Will you marry me?'

She loved him. She knew that much.

She'd been waiting for him all her life.

This was her chance. She had to take it. She had to trust him. She had to trust in them.

'Yes,' she said as she kissed him. 'I love you and I will marry you.'

EPILOGUE

CHLOE SAT IN an upholstered tub chair and gazed out of the window. She felt as if she was living in a dream. This morning she had woken up in London, and now here she was, fourteen hours later, sitting in a hotel room in France looking out at the lights and turrets of a make-believe castle.

They were fifty kilometres east of Paris but she felt as though she'd been transported into her own personal fairy tale. It felt like a dream and she knew that was what the creators of this fantasyland were trying to achieve; she just hadn't expected it to be so effective.

She watched as Xander opened the doors onto the Juliet balcony and the curtains billowed in the spring evening breeze, bringing in the scent of jasmine.

She jumped, startled out of her reverie, as Xander popped the cork on a bottle of champagne.

'I don't have any gin but I thought champagne was a more fitting way to celebrate our engagement,' he said as he poured two glasses and handed her one just as the first firework burst in the sky above the iconic castle.

Chloe gasped. 'I had no idea we'd be able to see the fireworks from our room. Did you book this especially?'

He nodded. 'Do you like it?' He looked well pleased with himself, as he should—the view was spectacular.

'I love it! Lily would too.'

'Shall we wake her up?'

Chloe shook her head. Lily was fast asleep in an adjoining bedroom. She was exhausted from the travel today and then an afternoon spent exploring the theme park and racing from one magical princess-themed ride to another. Although admittedly she had barely walked—Xander, a devoted father, had carried her on his shoulders for most of the day—but Chloe didn't want to spoil tomorrow by having an overwrought three-year-old to deal with. 'No. She can watch them tomorrow. She'll be unbearable then if she gets up now and I want her, want *all* of us, to enjoy the princess breakfast you've booked.'

'To tomorrow.' Xander tapped his champagne flute against Chloe's and reached for her hand. He pulled her off her seat and into his lap. She nestled against him and sipped her champagne as the last fireworks lit up the sky and the clock edged towards tomorrow.

'Good morning, Your Royal Highnesses. Sleeping Beauty. Anna.'

Chloe sat up to find Xander standing at the foot of her bed, which she'd climbed into in the early hours of the morning so that Lily didn't find her in the bed next door, with Xander. There was time enough for that once they were married.

In the bed beside her Lily sat up, rubbing her eyes. 'Who's Anna?'

'You, of course, Your Majesty,' Xander replied as Lily giggled.

'Why are you dressed like that?' she asked.

He was wearing a pair of black trousers with a white shirt. There was nothing startling about that, but over the top he had a jacket in a royal blue fabric with gold buttons and heavy gold embroidery. He had a frilled collar placed over the front of his shirt. He looked like a footman from any number of Disney movies.

He placed a tray on the bedside table as he said, 'Every princess gets a hot drink brought to them in the morning by the royal tea maker. A cup of tea for you, Sleeping Beauty, and a hot chocolate for Princess Anna,' he said as he handed out mugs. 'And then it's time to get ready for breakfast.'

'Is the princess breakfast today?' Lily squealed.

'It is. We have forty minutes to get dressed and be downstairs. Drink your hot chocolate and I will see to your clothes.'

'Where on earth did you get that jacket?' Chloe asked.

'Some mice made it for me in the night,' he replied with a wink before he spun around and left, going back through the door into the adjoining room. Chloe frowned—what was he up to? Lily's clothes were in the wardrobe in their room.

He returned seconds later and laid a garment bag across the foot of Lily's bed.

'What's in there?'

'If I told you that I'd ruin the surprise. All the princesses will be in their best dresses this morning and I thought Lily should have something new to wear too.'

'Is it for me?' she asked as Chloe reached over and took Lily's hot chocolate from her before her bouncing emptied the contents of the mug all over the bed, Lily and the bag.

'Can I open it?' Lily was clapping her hands with excitement.

Chloe nodded and Lily slid the zip down to reveal a dress with a dark green velvet bodice, soft cap sleeves and a pleated cream and green embroidered skirt.

'It's beautiful, Xander.'

Lily leapt up from the bed and threw her arms around Xander's neck. 'Thank you, Daddy, thank you!'

'You're welcome. I'll leave you to get ready,' he said, and as he turned for the door Chloe was almost certain she saw tears in his eyes.

Lily could barely stand still. Dressed in her costume she couldn't stop twirling around in circles as they waited in the line for breakfast. She had insisted on walking to the restaurant between Chloe and Xander, holding their hands, but the minute they got to the queue she had let go and Xander had slipped Chloe's hand into his instead.

The line moved forward, bringing them level with two thrones, a pink and gold one on their left and a red one to the right. A photographer was taking pictures, filling up time while people waited to be greeted by the hostess, who was dressed as Belle.

'Bonjour!' The photographer welcomed them and led them to a throne. *'Une famille très belle.'*

'Merci,' Xander said as Chloe beamed.

They were a family.

And their family was about to get bigger.

She smiled as the camera flashed, thinking of the news she planned to share with Xander tonight.

She kissed Xander's cheek as the camera flashed again, capturing the moment. She was getting her fairy-tale ending. Her own happily ever after.

She had everything she wished for.

*   *   *   *   *

A FLING TO
STEAL HER HEART

SUE MacKAY

MILLS & BOON

CHAPTER ONE

'ARE YOU CERTAIN you aren't still in love with him?'

'Couldn't be more certain.'

Isabella Nicholson held back on saying more. Admitting the truth that she doubted she'd really loved her ex enough in the first place would be embarrassing, even if Raphael Dubois was her best friend.

Best as in she'd usually tell him everything, whenever the urge took her, even in the early hours of Sunday morning, which it was right now. Four a.m. here in Wellington, four p.m. Saturday in London, where Raphael worked at his dream job in obstetrics and gynaecology at the Queen Victoria Hospital.

Wait a minute. He'd texted to see if *she* was awake, and knowing she currently suffered insomnia it was a no-brainer.

'Hey, why did you call? Not to ask about Darren, surely?'

'Izzy, is that the absolute truth or are you afraid of the answer?'

Typical. The man never missed a beat when it came to asking the hard questions, whether of her or his patients. Yet he always ignored *her* questions whenever it suited him.

Two could play that game. Though she'd try once more to shut him down. 'Don't I always tell you the truth?' Minus some niggling details in this instance.

'You're good at leaving out the specifics when it suits,' he confirmed, chuckling so she knew he was letting go the subject of her failed marriage.

'So what brings you to call in the middle of Saturday afternoon? I'd have thought you'd be at a rugby game with the guys.' One of them had found the niche they were looking for—and it wasn't her. Two years ago she'd returned home to New Zealand with her new husband, full of hope and excitement based around Darren's promises for what lay ahead, and with the intention of finally stopping in one place and surrounding herself with family and friends. Instead, twelve months later, her marriage had crashed badly, leaving her dreams up in the air. The friends had been all his, and her parents were always busy with their own lives. Since then she'd gone back to what she was good at—moving around the world from job to country to anywhere enticing, only for a lot shorter periods than previously. A fortnight ago she'd finished a volunteers' job in Cambodia and returned to visit her parents while deciding where next. Only she couldn't bring herself to go just anywhere this time.

Find something more permanent kept popping into her head. *Go solo on that dream of settling down.*

'I've been delivering triplets,' Rafe replied. He'd settled in London, been there nearly three years, bought a house, was keeping some distance from his claustrophobic family at home in Avignon as he grappled with his own demons. He seemed content in a quiet way, which was not the Raphael she'd known most of her life.

Please be her turn next. Even if it meant remaining single, which wasn't so bad. She was used to it. Nursing and midwifery jobs were fairly easy to come by, but after a childhood of moving around with her parents in the Foreign Service she'd hankered after settling back in New Zealand for ever when she'd married. Maybe that's where she'd gone wrong, put too much emphasis on where she lived and not who with. So here she was, minus the husband, ignoring the hole inside that needed filling with something unrecognisable, and which she suspected had to do with love. 'Triplets. Hard to imagine how parents cope with that many babies all at once.'

'This couple would've been grateful for quads if it meant becoming parents.' His voice fell into sentimental mode. 'You should see these little guys. So cute, looking tiny in their incubators hooked up to monitors, giving their parents heart failure already.'

'But they'll be fine, right?' He'd hate for anything to go wrong. When a baby in his care had difficulties that couldn't be fixed he'd get upset for days, distraught for the parents, blaming himself while knowing it wasn't his fault. She'd never been able to find out what was behind his extreme reaction that had only started over the last few years. Seemed they both kept secrets from each other.

'For triplets they're in good shape, though one of them is smaller than his brothers so I'll be keeping a closer eye on him. They made it to thirty-four weeks' gestation before the Caesarean, which means everything's on their side. The parents had fertility issues so we did artificial insemination and, *voilà*, the best of results.' Raphael's accent thickened when he became emotional.

'Great outcome for all of you.' Because he would've been almost as invested as the expectant parents. 'You should go out and celebrate.'

'I'm meeting up with a couple of the guys and their better halves as soon as I've talked with you. What did you get up to last night?'

Huh? Her social life had never been of much interest to him before. There again, recently he had taken to expressing concern about how she was coping with getting over Darren. Worried she'd go back to the cheat?

'I went out for a meal and a couple of drinks at the local with a neighbour.' She hadn't stayed out late, preferring to head back to her parents' place rather than being eyed up by men obviously wanting one thing only.

Getting old, girl.

Or jaded.

'Beats staying inside the four walls feeling sorry for yourself.'

Again, huh? What was this all about? 'That's harsh, Rafe.' She preferred it when Raphael went all sentimental over the babies he delivered, not digging deeper into her messed-up life. 'I'll say it one more time. I do not love Darren. Any feelings I had for him died when I found Gaylene Abernethy's naked body wrapped around him in our bed.' If only it was that easy: blame Darren for everything and feel superior. But it wasn't. She'd taken his promises about their life together at face value, colouring in the gaps with what she wanted and not seeing that he'd never aspired to the same. Though the affairs were a different story. Her husband had gone too far there.

'That's positive. I had to ask.' That couldn't be relief

in Raphael's voice. Then again, why not? The two men had never got on, were summer to winter.

'Sure you did.'

Naturally he hadn't finished. 'Love doesn't always stop the moment there's a reason to.' He spoke from firsthand experience. Was that what this was about? Would he finally tell her what had happened six years ago when his heart was torn out of his chest?

'I did love Darren, though not as much as I should've if I was committing to "until death us do part."'

'Does anyone say that any more? What if you both lived till you were ninety-five? That's a lot of marriage. At fifty who's the same person they were at thirty, let alone in their nineties?' asked the guy who'd signed up for ever with Cassie, only to get the boot within two years. Failed marriages were another thing they had in common.

'Typical of you to come up with that question.' If she fed him a little bit more about her relationship would he let it go? Not likely. This was Rafe. Neither did admitting how she'd failed come easily. She'd made a mistake marrying Darren. His promises of buying a house and having children didn't eventuate. Instead the parties, going to the rugby games with the mates and leaving her behind, the late nights at the office not working—found that out later—the weekends away with the boys... None of it ever stopped, actually became more intense, as though he was afraid to face what he'd agreed to do with her. She'd got more morose and by the time their first wedding anniversary came around she was blaming him for everything that went wrong in her life. Not accepting that she'd rushed in on those promises without asking herself if she really loved

Darren as much as she'd believed. 'I'm fine. I made a mistake, and now I've put it behind me.'

'As long as you're sure,' Raphael muttered. 'I don't want you regretting leaving him further down the track.'

'Drop it, Rafe. We are not getting back together. It's over.' How many times did she have to say it?

'Right. Tell me about Phnom Penh, then. What made you stay on an extra month?'

She'd rather talk about her ex. 'A tragic case that I got too close to.'

'We're not meant to do that, Izzy.'

Tell her something she didn't know. 'It's different over there. When someone's sick or seriously injured the whole family's involved, from great-gran to baby brother, and I got swept up in it all.' To the point where she'd put the brakes on racing around chasing happiness while she thought about what she really wanted for the future. 'Can we change the subject?'

'Fine. So what's next? A summer at the Antarctic with the New Zealand science contingent? Or a month on one of the charity ships in Africa?'

There seemed to be another question behind Raphael's queries, but Isabella couldn't hear what it was. Strange, given how well they knew each other—apart from those secrets. 'Come on. I'm not that restless.' Though the past year said otherwise. Auckland, Melbourne, Cambodia. Maybe she was more like her parents than she cared to admit, and therefore she was never going to find that permanent happy place. Nothing wrong with Mum and Dad's thirty-two-year marriage despite rarely stopping in one place for more than three years at a time though. They just shouldn't have brought her into the mix. 'I spent six years in Wellington training and working as a nurse. Four more in London doing midwifery before—'

'*Oui*, I get it. But right now you'll be overthinking what you're going to do next. Stay in Wellington, move to Africa or America.' He paused. Then on a deep breath, he continued. 'With your attitude about failing, this breakup will still be winding you into a tight ball of conjecture. "Where shall I live? What's the next project to undertake? Am I more Kiwi or English?"' He sighed, then said, 'Tell me I'm wrong, Izzy.'

She couldn't. That was exactly who she was. Except that family in Cambodia had changed her in some indefinable way. But she wasn't ready to talk about it yet. Might never be. Isabella stretched the length of her bed, and tucked the thick woollen duvet around herself. 'You'll be pleased to know I can't imagine being stuck on an iceberg for months on end having to rely on in-depth conversations with penguins.' She pulled her pillow down around her neck. Autumn had thrown a curve ball today, sending a reminder of what winter would have in store in a few weeks.

'Penguins are probably more interesting than half the people you get to meet every day.' His laughter was usually infectious, but tonight it was sounding a little tired, fed up even.

'Something wrong at your end of the world?'

'No more than the usual. We're short-staffed and it seems every female in London over twenty is pregnant at the moment.'

'What about life outside the Queen Victoria? Love, life, laughter, those things?' Raphael was one of the most good-looking men she knew. Women fawned over him, fell in love with him without him having said *bon-*

jour. Yet, since Cassie, he'd not had one serious relationship, preferring the love 'em and leave 'em approach
to relationships—when he found time for one. At least
he didn't promise anything else and always warned the
women he wasn't looking for a partner. In fact, he was
so kind and careful about his approach they all still
thought he was wonderful long after he'd said *au revoir*.

'Don't know what you're talking about.' At least his
laughter was genuine now. 'Haven't got time for much
than work and study.'

'That sounds as pathetic as my life right now.' What
a scintillating pair they made.

'You think?' Raphael took a long, slow breath.
'Crunch time, huh, Midwife Nicholson? For you, not
me,' he clarified.

'You sure about that?' she grumped, hating him for
making her face up to what was bothering her.

'It's not me lying awake for hours every night trying
to put the pieces of the puzzle back together.'

'You're right, and don't you dare gloat,' she added in
a hurry. 'I do have some decisions to make.'

'Starting with?'

That was the problem. She didn't know where to
start. 'Where to live?'

'What's wrong with where you are?' Straight to the
point, as always.

'If I'm staying here I need to buy a property and
get stuck in making it mine.' Isabella sighed. It was
the truth, just not all of it. Try again. 'Funny how I always thought of Wellington as home and yet it doesn't
feel like that.'

'You haven't exactly been happy there in the past. We
all need some place to call home, but it doesn't mean

we have to settle there if we're not getting what we require from it. Like me and Avignon.'

Yeah, where he got too much of what he wanted. 'Now there's an interesting city.' The ancient wall surrounding the city centre, the old fort on the other side of the river, the famous Pont d'Avignon. The history had drawn her, made her yearn to belong somewhere, to feel a part of something—and so when Darren came along she'd moved back to Wellington with him. Except now she'd probably leave again. Something was missing. With the city? Or inside her? 'I think I want to get back to friends who *know* me and where I've come from.' Maybe even *where* she was headed.

Raphael should understand. They'd met on trips with their respective schools to a ski field in the Swiss Alps. Out of control on a snow board, she'd crashed into him, and nursing bruises over hot chocolate in the café they'd instantly bonded. His father worked in a bank in Geneva while her dad was working at the New Zealand consulate in the same city. She'd been used to making friends quickly, aware how fast three years passed when she'd have to move and start all over again. Raphael had been homesick for his grandmother and cousins back in Avignon, and resented his parents for taking him away from them all. She'd wanted her parents to return home and stop moving. Instead, when her mother obtained a position in an international accounting company that had her travelling a lot, Isabella had been sent to boarding school in England, leaving her feeling unconnected, abandoned. Even when she returned to the family fold, that disconnect remained. She'd done too much growing up in the interim and had changed for ever.

Despite being two years older than her, Raphael had

gone out of his way to keep in touch, and they had remained close, despite living in different countries for most of their friendship. She'd briefly worked with him once in Tours, which had been great. Since then? Modern communications systems were the best thing to ever be invented.

Raphael asked, 'You're still coming over here for Carly's wedding, right?'

'Wouldn't miss it for anything. It was bad enough not making it to Esther and Harry's.' She'd been supposed to fly to London for that, but when the Medical Volunteers Charity asked her to stay on another month because the traumatised Khy family she'd been working closely with still needed her there as stability, she hadn't been able to say no. They'd needed her, and she'd wanted to be needed. Still did. 'Flights are booked.'

'Why not make it a one-way trip? Your girlfriends from midwifery training days are here and all working in the Queen Victoria, although for how long is anyone's guess with all these weddings going down. Then there's *moi*.'

Her laugh was brittle. 'You make it sound so easy.' It was. With an English mother getting a work visa for the UK was straightforward. But did she want to go there and be watched over like she was going to come out in a rash for being on her own again? Or questioned about every move she made? Every decision she arrived at? Because Raphael had changed. Since she'd left Darren, come to think of it. He was always questioning what she did, the jobs she chose, the countries they were in. No way did she want put up with any more of that, and living on his back doorstep wouldn't help. At least she wouldn't be *in* his house.

He continued in a coaxing voice. 'Okay, why I really rang. There is a nurse's position coming up on my ward if you're interested. With your midwifery qualifications as well as nursing you're ideal for the job. The girl who's leaving hasn't told anyone other than me yet, and she's agreed to keep quiet till I talk to you. What do you think?'

'How soon would I have to start?' She was stalling, not feeling the excitement that usually stirred when she had an offer on the table to do something new. Weighing up the pros and cons? Unlike her.

'Jasmine wants to be gone within three weeks. Something about a boyfriend in Canada and a road trip they've been planning to do over summer.'

Did she want to return to London? As in *really* want to? Or should she be staying put, making more of an effort to integrate into Wellington and stop blaming Darren for feeling confused? Making this the home base she'd always wanted?

'And…ta da, the best bit.' He paused for effect. Typical Raphael. 'Don't forget who's the charge obstetrician on the ward. Your call, but remember, we work well together.'

That they did. Working as a midwife for those few months in Tours just after she'd finished her midwifery training had been the best job she'd ever had; having her closest friend in the same hospital added to the pluses. He'd shown her the French lifestyle, taken her to Avignon to meet his maternal grandmother and his cousins, tripped all over the country on their days off to show her castles, cities, mountains. Then he'd taken up his current position in London, and she'd met Darren in France while watching a rugby game between the All Blacks and Les Bleus, and the rest was history. A rocky, sorry history, but what didn't kill her was going to make her stronger. Just not certain when. Not to mention how persuasive Raphael could be when he put his mind to it. 'You know what?'

'You're on your way.'

'I might be.'

'Hello? Where's strong, do-it-her-way-or-bust Isabella gone? You're coming or you're not. Which, Izzy?'

She had to make her mind up now? Why not? Raphael was right. She'd always approached life head-on, didn't usually waste time dithering over decisions, and accepted that when she'd got it wrong it was part of the gamble. Her marriage failure had set her off kilter, made her worry and fuss too much about getting things right or wrong, made her wary of trusting people. Then watching the closeness of the Khys as they struggled to keep their son alive and how they coped after it all went wrong had blitzed her completely.

'Izzy?'

If taking up a new position back in the city where her nursing friends and Raphael lived turned out to be a mistake, then she'd survive. If Rafe became too bossy she'd tell him what to do with that. But at least they were all there, the people who mattered the most to her. 'Got to go. Have to pack my bag.'

CHAPTER TWO

TWO WEEKS LATER, as Raphael paced the arrivals hall at
Heathrow, Isabella's text pinged on his phone.

Landed.

About time. Something settled in his gut. Relief?
No, this sensation felt stronger, not that he recognised
it, but it did make him wary and happy all in one hit.
He'd felt this way when Izzy said she was coming to
London. His fingers flew over his phone.

I'm waiting in arrivals hall.

The flight was an hour late. Serve him right for getting here early, but he'd been ready to pick up Izzy since
crawling out of bed first light that morning. Not even
doing a round of his patients and checking on the triplets
had quelled the need to get to Heathrow on time, which
in his book meant early. Very early. He'd given his regular visit to the market a miss, cursed the traffic holdups
all the way to the airport and ranted at the arrivals notice board every time it brought up a new flight arrival
that wasn't Izzy's. Damn it, he even checked his phone

app every time to make sure the board and the app were on the same page. *Oui*, of course they were. But this hanging around for Isabella was doing his head in.

He couldn't wait to see her. It seemed ages since she'd married Darren, who in his book was a complete idiot, and left London for what she euphemistically—in his mind, desperately—called home. It had been as though she'd been on a mission to prove something to herself, and she hadn't told him what it was, which worried him. Yet when Isabella suggested he pay them a visit in Wellington during his leave last year he'd pleaded prior commitments so as to avoid her husband. Unfair, but he and Darren had never seen eye to eye about anything, and especially about the woman they both cared about. Her husband could not get his head around the fact that Raphael and Isabella were close friends, not lovers and never had been, and he kept making digs about how she was *his*. Yeah, right. Look where that had got the guy. Single again, and still missing the whole point about commitment.

His phone pinged again.

Bring a trailer?

You've brought that much gear?

Yep.

Really? Isabella travelled light. Something she'd learned as a Foreign Service brat. While her parents had a container-load of gear follow them wherever they went, Izzy never packed much at all, said carrying only her regular gear around kept her grounded in reality.

Did this mean she'd come to London with the idea of staying long term?

Calmes-toi.

There was long term and then there was Izzy's ingrained version of staying put. They did not match. There'd been nothing to stop her settling in London permanently last time she lived here. But he wasn't being fair. She had decided to stay here and then along came the husband offering all sorts of carrots in Wellington. She'd always had a thing about returning to the city where she'd been born and partially brought up in, so Darren's promises raised her hopes of a life there. The failure of said marriage seemed to have screwed with that idea, and stalled her about making any serious decisions over what to do next. Odd, because Isabella was no stranger to being strong and getting what she wanted. But on the other side of that argument, she *didn't* always know exactly what she wanted. Hence fast-track midwifery training.

He texted back.

Great.

It was, actually. Could be she'd finally figured out what she was looking for. Given half a chance he'd go back to Avignon and the family tomorrow. But it wasn't happening any time soon. He'd return there only when he'd got over the guilt for the way Cassie had treated his nearest and dearest. And stopped feeling angry for the cruel blow she'd hit him with. His son, his parents' only grandson, dead at eight days from SIDS, and he hadn't even known he was a father. The pregnancy one more of Cassie's ways of paying him back for not falling into line with all her outrageous demands.

The doors from the other side swished open as a small group of people towing cases on wheels came through. Swallowing the familiar bitterness and hauling his concentration to what was important today, Raphael craned his neck trying to see around them. No sign of Isabella. Nothing on his phone. 'Come on. Where are you?' he ground out. No doubt dealing with the inevitable questions from immigration. He'd take another turn of the hall to fill in some minutes.

Except Raphael remained glued to the spot, his eyes never leaving the doors now that his phone had gone quiet. Hopefully that meant she'd soon burst through the doors like the hurricane she could be. Not that she sounded as revved up these days whenever he talked to her. Her ex had dealt some harsh blows to her confidence. Though there could be more to it than Izzy was telling him.

The doors opened again and more exhausted people spilled through, followed by a laden trolley being pushed by... 'Raphael.' The shout was accompanied by a small body hurtling through the crowd, aimed directly for him.

'Izzy.'

Oof. *Oui*. Definitely tornado.

His lungs huffed out every last molecule of oxygen they were holding as Isabella plastered herself against him. His arms wound around her like they never intended letting go. She smelt of travel and tiredness and excitement and—

Mais oui, Isabella. Soft, tough.

Careful. Friends, nothing else.

'Hello, Rafe. Good to see you.'

The relief expanded. Isabella *was* here. Izzy. He inhaled deeper, hugged harder and kissed her on both cheeks French style. Friendly style. Then, without letting go of her, he leaned back to gaze down at her fine features with dark shadows staining her upper cheeks. There was strain in her eyes, negating her usual go-get-'em attitude. Anger lodged behind his ribs. This was Darren's fault. The man had hurt her. But apparently it took two to tango, so had Isabella done something wrong too? He'd leave off the big questions until she'd got some sleep and was looking more like her normal self. Since the flat she'd arranged had fallen through she was staying with him for a little while—until they had their first row at least. Something not uncommon between them. 'Great to see you, *mon amie.*'

The familiar cheeky twinkle was back in her gaze, though the corners of her mouth were still drawn. 'You see me every other week.'

He relaxed enough to go with the change. 'Usually your chin is huge and your eyes somewhere above the screen. This way I get to see you properly. I can read your expressions,' he added to wind her up for the hell of it. Because that's how they'd always been with each other, and until now he hadn't realised how important it was. It kept him on track, especially at the times Cassie's betrayal got to him too much. He hadn't shared the details, but Izzy had always been at the end of a phone. They knew each other better than anyone, and had often relied on that to get through the upheavals life threw at them, yet there'd been apprehension in his veins since Isabella had agreed to come to London and take up the job he'd suggested. He didn't understand his apprehension, unless it was to do with the uncomfort-able, almost painful, feeling that overcame him at her marriage ceremony where he'd stood beside her as she said her vows to Darren. A sense that he'd found out something important when it was too late.

'Next time I'll focus the camera on my slipper-covered feet.'

'Not the ones the neighbour's dog chewed.' Next time. Reality check. This wasn't a long-term move. Was that disappointment rapping his knuckles? And if so, why? He was used to her coming and going as it suited, or, when they were young, as her parents had decreed. Could be that his need to see her happy wasn't going to be satisfied. Could also be that his hope of spend-ing more time with her wasn't going to be fulfilled. He looked around. 'We'd better rescue that trolley be-fore someone crashes into it and the bags topple off.' This was going to be interesting. His car wasn't made for organising a complete house move. 'Did you leave anything behind?'

Her tight laugh had him wondering just what was going on. 'This is only the beginning. I'm shipping more belongings across. The container's due to arrive sometime in May.'

Raphael dived right in. 'So you're looking for somewhere to unpack properly? As in lock, stock and clothes?' This was nothing like her usual style of one backpack and the laptop.

Her laughter died. 'Don't be so shocked. Just because it didn't work in Wellington doesn't mean it won't here with all my friends around me.'

He reached for her, needing to hug a smile back onto her face. 'You're right, and I'm one of them.'

'I hope so,' she murmured against his chest before pulling away, still without a smile. She'd never doubted him before. But before he could question her, she continued. 'There's a couple of pieces of furniture, some kitchenware and lots of books coming.'

He stared at her, a knot of unease tightening in his belly. She was serious about this move. He was thrilled for her, and him, and would help make it work, but… But he'd have to be careful about keeping his distance. Risking their friendship was not happening over some out of kilter emotions he'd felt on and off since her marriage. 'Truly?'

She nodded, her mouth twisted into a wry smile. 'Truly.' A sigh trickled over her lips. 'I'll add to them as soon as I find my own place.'

'Your own place?' The relief should be flooding in. It wasn't.

'A place to rent for a start.'

He sighed. *Stop being disgruntled.* His friend was back in town. Someone to talk the talk with, have a beer at the pub or take a ride out in the countryside. One day at a time and see how they went getting back to that easy relationship they'd always shared until she'd got married.

It goes back further than that, mon ami. *You've never shared much about your time with Cassie. Or the devastation she caused.*

'Thanks for putting a roof over my head until I find somewhere.'

'It'll be better than squatting under London Bridge.' Suddenly there was a bounce in his step. He'd been looking forward to this moment, and now Izzy was here. Right beside him. Recently his life had become all about work, and very little play. All too often he cancelled going to rugby with the guys, the only excuse being his patients needed him. But he needed to be more rounded, balance his lifestyle. Izzy was good at shaking him up, would take no nonsense about how he was a doctor before all else. Well, he was, but she always reckoned that didn't mean his work should fill twenty-four hours every day of the week. 'Let's get out of here.'

'Let's.' Isabella smothered a yawn with her hand. 'That was one hell of a trip. Crying babies, and an enormous man in the seat next to me who kept falling asleep and sprawling in every direction, mostly mine.'

'Sounds fairly normal.' Long-haul flights were hell on wings.

'One day I'm going to fly first class just to see what it's like. I did get some sleep though, which is a change. Probably because I had so little in the nights leading up to getting on the plane.'

'You done anything about that insomnia?'

Untidy auburn hair flicked across her shoulders as she shook her head. 'What's the point? I've tried everything except sleeping pills and I'm never resorting to them. Seen too many patients who've become addicted, and then any gains in the sleep department are lost. Besides, I'm used to getting by on a couple of hours at a time.'

This had gone on for almost as long as he'd known her, sometimes minor sleep deprivation, sometimes quite major, and in recent years it had cranked up a few more notches. Guess a person could get used to anything given enough time, though it wasn't good for her. 'Still, I think you should see one of my colleagues. He's good at helping people get to the bottom of what's causing the problem and might even be able to give you some practical advice.'

'Let me get unpacked before you start organising my life.' Isabella gave him a lopsided smile, with a warning behind it. 'Okay, what've you got planned for tonight?'

Whatever she was trying to tell him, he'd leave it for now. 'Running three laps of the neighbourhood before digging up the back garden and putting in some plants.'

'Cool. Nothing for me to worry about. I can sit down and watch a movie on my phone, dial out for pizza.'

Raphael laughed, and it was like pushing Play on an old CD player, bringing back memories of fun times when his heart hadn't been ripped out of his chest. He halted the trolley to sling an arm over Isabella's shoulders and hug her against him again. 'You're on to it.' This was more like it. Cheeky Izzy not taking any of his nonsense seriously. It was one of the things he missed the most. Not even the overloaded, heavy trolley could put a dent in the sense of fun ahead now spreading through him. A familiar feeling he'd known the very first time they'd met, stronger than the pain in his thigh where her snowboard had struck hard. She'd been embarrassed at losing control, and tried blaming him for being in the way. They'd argued and laughed and shared hot chocolates and swapped phone numbers, and afterwards met up every weekend in Geneva when they could get away from school activities. 'I've missed you.' It hadn't been so easy to have two-hour conversations when there was a husband in the background, and he'd been very aware of how he might've felt if the situation had been reversed. He mightn't have liked Darren, but he understood the boundaries. And afterwards, Izzy had been a bit withdrawn with him.

'Same.'

'I would've headed down under for a week this past year to support you, cheer you up, get you back on track, but you were never there.' Her phone calls over the last twelve months had been quiet, and filled with sadness and, at times, something like despair that she'd never explained.

Again those auburn locks swished back and forth across her shoulders. 'You didn't have to do that. I'm a big girl. Anyway, I managed, and you were always at the other end of the phone when I needed to talk. You'd have been fed up with me by the end of the first day and champing to get away. I had to do it my way, and having you rant in my ear about my future when I couldn't hang up on you wouldn't have worked, for either of us.'

'You're probably right, but still…' He'd let her down. And himself. Again he wasn't sure why he thought that.

Raphael began pushing his friend's worldly goods towards the lift that'd take them to the car park. 'Bumped into Carly on Wednesday. She's pretty excited about you returning to the Queen Victoria.'

'She's more excited about her wedding. We've already got a night out planned with the other two from our training days' group. Funny how we're again all here at the same time. I wonder if that means everyone's settling down, becoming responsible adults, or is this just another stop along the way? Seems London's our place. My place?'

This sounded more like the Isabella he'd known for so long: always confident and putting it out there about how she wanted to live, and yet being gnawed at on the inside with her insecurities over people sticking by her, not breaking the bonds she desperately needed. Her parents had put her into boarding school when they felt she'd have better support and company than at home with them. They hadn't known a thing. He'd held her while she'd cried over being sent away. But after falling heavily for Cassie, and having her treat him so badly, he knew what a shattered heart felt like—and wasn't risking going there again. Nor hurting someone else similarly when he wasn't able to give enough of himself to her.

He said, 'Stop trying to second-guess everything, and enjoy being back amongst us all.' He would never desert her; he needed her friendship as much as she needed his. She understood him like no one else. If only he could stick with friendship, not let other emotions get in the way. 'You can do it. You have to believe in yourself.'

Then Isabella flicked him a look he couldn't interpret. 'Like you?' Her eyes were locked on his. 'I can follow your example? Work non-stop, get a home that I won't get to spend much time in?'

His happiness slipped. 'Is that what I've become? A workaholic?'

'It's what you told me only weeks ago.'

'I was probably trying to deflect you from your problems.' He'd been voicing his concerns about how everyone around him seemed to be finding love and making babies, while he was getting further tied up with work. What he hadn't said was how he wished he could find what it would take to try again, to finally put his past to rest. But he couldn't. Because of Cassie's selfishness, he'd lost a son and still wasn't able to make peace with himself about that.

'About those problems, will you always be here for me on the bad days?'

Where did that come from? '*Oui*, you can count on me.' She already knew it.

'Thanks. I can't tell you how good it is to spend time with you. It's been a while since anyone told me what to do.'

'Most people are too scared to.' He laughed. 'Let's get this load home and go have a drink and a pub meal to celebrate your arrival in London.' Better out somewhere surrounded by people than stuck in his kitchen together. Only now was he beginning to understand the coming weeks sharing his house might not be as comfortable as he'd thought. Which was so far left field it was crazy. Izzy would get busy beginning her new life, and he'd be hanging on to the dull but predictable one he'd made for himself.

'Sounds good to me. I loved the pub food when I lived here last time.' Isabella's hand tapped her stomach, then a hip. 'Not that it ever did me a lot of good. But I'm in for tonight anyway.' She threaded her arm through his, ignoring how the trolley aimed sideways and caused him to put more pressure on to controlling it with the other arm. 'Honestly, Rafe, I keep wanting to pinch myself. It's been for ever since we last saw each other. Talking on the phone or through the internet doesn't quite cut it. I like to know you're within reaching distance.' She gulped, tripped, righted herself and stared straight ahead. 'Talking too much. Put it down to jet lag, if that happens so soon after a flight.'

This was different. He hauled the brakes on the hope beginning to unfold deep inside. In the long run he wouldn't be enough for Izzy. She needed someone to love her unconditionally. That wouldn't be him after the way Cassie had blown his trust out of the water because Izzy had her own issues about believing anyone would love her enough to stay around. Anyway, give her a few days to settle in at work and catch up with the girls and she'd be off doing all sorts of random things, and then he could relax around her. 'You don't suffer from jet lag.' He'd always been envious when he'd had to grapple with debilitating exhaustion for days after a long-haul flight, while this woman usually bounced off the plane ready to party.

'Always a first time.' Isabella remained quiet until they reached his car. More unusual behaviour.

Something was up, and finding out what was imperative if he was to be onside as she settled into London for good, but best left alone today. He tipped his head sideways to stare at Isabella. Naturally he always wanted to help her when she was in difficulty, but normally he'd accept it if she refused to talk. But today he wanted to get behind the pain in the back of her eyes, see her achieve genuine happiness. Opening the car boot, he said, 'Let me do this. You get comfortable inside.'

'Like I'm your grandmother?' She smiled. 'How is Grand'mère, by the way? Fully recovered from her hip replacement?'

'Chasing the great grandkids with her crutch, apparently. Being her, she'll be back cycling around the city before she should,' he said with a smile. He adored Grand'mère. She was the only other person besides Izzy to support him in all his endeavours without criticism. His family loved him but always wanted to tell him what they believed he was doing wrong with his decisions. 'I was talking to her last night and she said whenever you need a change of scenery, pop over and spend time with her.' What she'd really said was, when Isabella was fed up with him, go pay her a visit and she'd sort her out. Grand'mère had a soft spot for the lost Kiwi girl who'd often hopped a train to go spend a day with her when she was working in Tours.

'Cool. I'll do that sooner than later. I love your grand-mother, and Avignon's one of my favourite cities.' She handed him one of the smaller cases.

He shook his head. 'That big sucker first.'

'She might be just what I need on the days when you're not available for chewing your ear off.' Fixing a smile on her face she made to shift the bags. 'The family still as smothering as ever?'

Typical Izzy. Here he was holding back on the big questions and she just leapt in. 'Out of the way. This is man's work.'

'Whatever.' Her eye roll made him laugh. At least she backed away from the stack of cases.

'What have you got in here?' he groaned. 'You must've paid a small fortune in excess baggage costs.'

'You avoiding my question?'

'You know I am. Now, get in the car before I put a bag on your seat and leave you to catch the train.'

Isabella snuggled into the soft leather seat and tugged her crumpled denim jacket across her chest to keep out the chill. From what she'd seen coming in to land, London had not turned on the sunshine in welcome, and the air out here was proving it. But Raphael had more than made up for the chilly welcome, hugging her tight as though he never wanted to let her go. There'd been relief in his gaze as she raced to him, as though he hadn't really believed she'd turn up.

Well, she was here, and right now she needed friends who didn't ask awkward questions. Count Raphael out, then. She sighed. He never let her get away with anything. There again, he knew how to help her without seeming too intense. Demanding an instant decision about the job in the Queen Victoria had been unusual for him but just what she needed to get out of the blues she'd dumped herself into. Since his phone call determination to get on with consolidating her life had started growing, begun to fill the empty place deep inside, even excited her. There was a long way to go, but a start was way better than nothing at all.

The car rocked as Raphael clambered in beside her. 'Ready?'

She nodded. Fingers crossed, for everything. 'I sure am. What's Richmond like?' It was the suburb where he'd bought his house. 'I hear it's very pretty.'

'It is. There're plenty of fabulous cafés, and I enjoy walking or cycling along the river when I've had a rubbish day and need to put things into perspective.'

'That would be often.' He gave his all to patients. Studying him as he drove out of the airport, shock hit her.

He's changed.

His face was drawn, his movements heavier, his words spoken more thoughtfully. Why? Another sigh. He wouldn't thank her for asking so she changed the subject. 'How's Pierre?' His cousin's son held a special place in Raphael's heart.

'In love with the girl next door. Apparently he's going

to die if she doesn't kiss him soon.' Raphael chuckled. 'Everything's so intense at his age.'

'Too much so sometimes.'

Rafe had been seventeen when he'd helped Adele during the birth of her son. He'd been driving her through the country lanes headed for the birthing centre when her well-spaced labour pains went out of control. He'd told Isabella there'd been no time for embarrassment with Adele gripping his arm and screaming to do something about the baby. The first birth he'd seen and aided, and from that day on he'd known what he wanted to do with his future career in medicine. 'Pierre's now a robust fifteen-year-old, and also thinking of going into medicine. Though not obstetrics. He's keen on cardiology, though that might have something to do with his heart being in torment at the moment.'

'You think?' Shuffling down further in her seat, Isabella stared out the window as they followed the main road leading into the city. 'This is familiar. I like familiar. It makes me feel I might be doing the right thing coming back.' She did feel connected to London, something she didn't get often. Wellington had been the only other place, and Darren's infidelity had altered that. Sure, he hadn't been the only one to get things wrong with their marriage, but he had broken her heart by seeking solace in other women's arms, and wrecked her trust in people.

'Papa and Maman have returned to live in the family home in Avignon. Dad's left the bank. It was getting too stressful so now he's working part time with a importing company and aiming to enjoy time out with the family.'

'That's huge.' Monsieur Dubois had worked long and

hard most of his life. 'It's great news, isn't it?' Then her heart stuttered. Would Raphael move home now? Just when she'd returned to London? When she wanted to spend time with him?

Rafe was leaning forward, his concentration fixed on the road and cars ahead. His tight grip on the steering wheel was another giveaway he was rattled. *'Oui.'*

'But?' she dared to ask.

His fingers loosened their grip, tightened again. 'I'm still not ready,' he said in a 'don't go there' voice she knew not to ignore.

She closed her eyes and tipped her head back, let the silence take over. Better than saying anything to upset her friend. Apart from his parents almost suffocating him in love she had no idea what was behind his refusal to return home. He seemed more content than in those dark days after he and Cassie broke up, but there were times Isabella wondered how happy he really was with his lot.

The silence became uncomfortable. 'We had such plans growing up, didn't we? Nothing turned out anything like them.' There'd never been any doubt Raphael was going into medicine. He had intended setting up a private practice in his home city, while she'd thought she'd go into marketing, then car sales so she could drive to-die-for vehicles. Running a bar came into the plans somewhere around that time. But nothing had felt right, like something was missing as it was in her family. Then hearing Raphael talking about working with patients and the pain and fear and love that surrounded people when they were sick, she understood she wanted to work with people too. Not by handing them a full glass over a counter, but soothing their fears when they were injured, caring that they got through whatever was frightening them. So she applied to start training as a nurse, and had been the most at ease in her life for the next four years. Until she was qualified, and once again restlessness overtook her so finally, in desperation, she came to London and signed up for the midwifery course. Being there for those babies, and sharing—albeit on the periphery—the love and excitement every baby brought its parents, had made her happier than she'd ever believed possible. Having two options to her career was a bonus, and she had no intention of doing anything else career-wise. It was the one thing she was absolutely certain about.

'I am so glad you're here, Izzy.' Rafe sank back against the seat, and flicked her a quick smile, his knuckles no longer white and tight. Then he stiffened again. 'Not that I'll have a lot of free time to spend with you.'

It sounded like a warning of some sort. He wasn't available for friend time? Again, her heart stuttered. Which frightened her. *Raphael was a friend.* Couldn't be anything else. Of course they were never going to be anything else. These oddball jitters just went to show how far out of sync she'd become with what she needed from life. 'I'll be busy too,' she told him with a dollop of self-preservation for her pride. 'Finding a flat to rent, catching up with the girls, starting my new job.' A yawn caught her. Bed would be good right now. Damn but she needed some sleep, although past experience told her she was best to stay up till a reasonable hour, and eat a decent meal. Even then, there'd only be intermittent hours of unconsciousness. Glancing over to Rafe, for the first time in ages, pure happiness surged through her.

It was as though she had come home, not left it. And she suspected she wasn't only thinking about London and friends, but Raphael in particular. Whatever that meant, she was too tired to worry about it. She let the silence return. Until again she couldn't stand it. 'I can't wait to see your house.'

He sucked in a breath. 'You're going to be disappointed. I'd be lying if I said it's a work in progress. I haven't done anything about the paintwork or getting the kitchen altered and the bathrooms modernised. I never seem able to find the enthusiasm or time.'

'Maybe I can help.'

His eyebrows rose in shock. 'I'm not talking a small job here.'

'Have to start somewhere, and if I'm going to get my own place eventually I might as well practise on yours first.'

'You think?' He grinned. 'Afraid I'm going to have to turn your offer—' he flicked a finger in the air '—down.'

'Coward.'

'Pink walls and floral curtains are so not my thing.'

'Mine either.' Her tastes were more along the lines of pale colours—more white than anything, lots of natural light, big empty spaces. That came from the real estate programs she'd watched avidly back in Wellington when she'd begun collecting furniture for the future house she and Darren were going to buy. 'Dark blue walls and carpets, a dash of white in the curtains, lime green furniture should do it.'

'Excellent. We have a plan.'

Isabella smiled. It was great how he said 'we.' As if she had a place in his life. But then she always had. Did that mean she'd be looking for a home in his neighbourhood? Doubt she could afford a dog kennel in Richmond. The idea of moving too far from Raphael suddenly irked, when it shouldn't. Friends moved around, came back together, moved on. At the moment they were in the coming back together phase. Who knew for how long?

'Here we are.' Raphael parked outside a brick row house. 'Welcome home.'

It wasn't her home, only a stop gap while she found somewhere for herself, but she'd take the warmth that went with his words and enjoy. Shoving the door wide, she clambered out on tired legs and looked around. Trees lined the street, a dog barked from behind a house next door and puddles glistened in the sun that was making its way out from behind the clouds. Home. Yes, it felt exactly like what she'd dreamed of having in Wellington. A house in a quiet neighbourhood. Throw in friends nearby, and Rafe had got it right when he chose this place. It was perfect.

Nothing's perfect. There're always faults.

The warning didn't dampen the warmth pushing aside her exhaustion.

Following Raphael inside, she stopped and stared at the hallway walls. Eek. 'Magenta? This is so dark it feels like it's falling in on us.' Definitely a fault.

'Wait until you see the kitchen.'

That colour had to go. Sooner than later. It was hideous. She shivered and traipsed behind Raphael up the stairs with the smallest of her cases in hand. It soon became obvious nothing had been done to spruce up the house for a long time, probably well before he moved in. Every room she peered into was in need of a coat of paint, preferably a very pale, neutral shade to lighten them, and new curtains to match. At the top of the stairs on the third floor he dumped the heaviest of her cases. 'This is your room for as long as you want it. It's the best of the two spares, and anyway I use the smallest for an office,' he told her before heading back down to get the next bag.

Isabella looked around the neat but bland room, and shrugged. No magenta in here, thank goodness, but the pale mauve reminded her of an old lady's room. Still, it was somewhere to put her head down, and give her time to find somewhere to rent. So why the flicker of excitement? Sinking onto the edge of the bed she rubbed her arms through her jacket, and said aloud to prove she wasn't dreaming it, 'I'm back in London, in the other country I call home.' Her mother came from the Lake District and she'd only visited her relatives once last time she lived here. The welcome mat had been in storage that day, something to do with her mother marrying a New Zealander instead of the lord of whatever they'd planned on having as a son-in-law, and Isabella being the offspring of someone less desirable, despite her father's mega career in the Foreign Service, hadn't changed their attitude. They should've got over it by now, but it seemed some things weren't meant to be, and she'd quietly headed away, deflated but resolute she wasn't going to beg for recognition.

'I'm glad. For both of us.'

Hadn't heard Raphael returning with another case, had she? Blinking, she looked up into the steady but shocked gaze coming her way. Why shocked? He hadn't expected to feel glad she was staying with him? No. He wouldn't have offered if he didn't want her here.

Or would he these days? 'I made the right call. Thanks for letting me know about the job.' She couldn't wait to start. It would be a bonus working alongside Raphael. Another was the girls were also all working at the same hospital.

'*Aucun problème.* Now, there's a bathroom on the floor below. It's all yours as I've got an en suite bathroom attached to my bedroom. Help yourself to anything you want. The kitchen pantry's full and the freezer's holding some of your favourite fish.'

'A shower's what I need. And some clean clothes.' She sniffed her jacket and grimaced. 'Yuck. Long-haul travel has its own peculiar smell.'

He flinched, looked away. 'Take as long as you need. We're only going along the road for a drink and a bite to eat.'

Despite his reaction, that sounded so normal she laughed. This was what she'd come for. Normal. Whatever that was. At the moment everything felt right. Especially being with Raphael, knowing he'd never hurt her, no matter how far either of them pushed the boundaries of their friendship. Yes, packing up and coming here was a good move. Better than good; it was great, and filled with promise.

Believe it.

Yet she didn't feel quite normal with him. Yet. Still to come?

CHAPTER THREE

'HERE'S TO LONDON and your new job, and catching up with special friends.' Raphael held up his glass to tap Isabella's, just as loud laughter broke out further along the bar. 'Also to sorting out what's putting that sad look in your eyes whenever you think I'm not looking.'

Ignoring that last comment, Isabella tapped back. 'To spending time with you.' Except he'd already warned her he wouldn't be on tap all the time. They'd both opted to stick to soft drinks. She was wired. And exhausted. Even a little excited. Throw in worry about a whole heap of things she couldn't deal with right now, and she had the whole picture really. The trip in from the airport had touched her in an unexpected way. While it *had* felt like coming home, maybe being with Raphael was the reason. They understood each other so well, despite the awkward subjects they hadn't shared over the years. Cassie, the love of his life; and her truth about her marriage. She hadn't realised how much she'd missed his sharp remarks, though lately they seemed too sharp.

'Good luck with that. I struggle to find time to spend with myself.' His grin was lopsided and a little tight.

'Sounds like you need to find a life.' What was wrong? He wasn't known to forego having fun during his downtime, despite the serious side to the man who cared deeply for people worse off than himself.

'I bet you're about to sort me out,' he grumped. Then his grin became genuine. 'This could be a win-win for both of us. I could do with a kick up the backside.'

'Thanks for putting me up at short notice. I'll get on to other rental agencies ASAP.'

If I can't stay with you long term.

She choked. Stay with Raphael permanently? Where had that come from? So what was wrong with the idea? How about because they were friends? Sure, friends often shared accommodation, but she and Raphael had never lived in each other's pockets. Not even that time they'd worked together in Tours.

'No problem.' Raphael was suddenly intensely focused on the bar counter, his hands twirling his glass back and forth.

'I'll be out of your hair as soon as possible.'

I've only just got here, and I want to spend time with you. Need to, if I'm being honest, so that I can untangle the mess I've made of things by talking it out and then get on with living in London.

So she could get over this sensation of wanting more with him. Raphael usually kept her grounded. Today she was confused. Here was the reliable, helpful, caring Raphael she knew, and yet there was more. A deeper feeling that wanted to push hard at the walls, let him in in a new way. Into her heart. Her glass banged down on the counter. No. No way. She'd only let him down, and hurting him was not happening on her watch. Grabbing her glass again, she gulped down her drink.

Raphael had returned to watching her. 'Take your time. You've only just arrived.' His hand covered hers.

Whipping her hand away, she looked around the pub, frantically trying to still the wild thudding behind her ribs. 'Sure,' she muttered. This was not them. Glancing back at him, her heart did a funny little dance, while her eyes began tearing up. Rafe looked beyond stunning. He always had, yet she'd never really seen him as other women did. He was her friend. Nothing had changed. So why notice the stubble on his chin? Stubble was stubble, right? Or was it? Her palm itched. Reality check. Something had changed. Now she needed to focus on putting things back the way they used to be or move out of his house tomorrow. London Bridge was looking good.

'You cooked any French cuisine lately?' The question wasn't light-hearted. Was Rafe feeling her tension?

'Not really.' Darren had refused to eat anything he thought remotely French, all because of Raphael. So childish, but to keep the peace she'd thrown out the French recipe books and stuck with the boring basics: roasts, steak, sausages.

'We'll have to remedy that. Can't have you forgetting how to make a good béarnaise sauce.'

When she looked at Raphael she found a smile that held nothing back coming her way. Her stomach squeezed, while her heart filled with relief, returned to normal. See? Everything was fine. Time apart hadn't affected her perception of their friendship. It was the tiredness tripping her up, making her look at things differently. Today they were a little off centre, but that could be because she was now an ex-married woman he didn't know as well as he used to when she was single. 'Last time I saw you was in the bar further down this road. You'd put an offer in on a house and we were celebrating early because I wouldn't be around when the sale went through.' They'd also been toasting her moving back to New Zealand with her husband, though thinking back she remembered Raphael hadn't been too enthused about that. What she hadn't realised at the time: she was probably as much at fault as Darren. Which went to show she was utterly hopeless at relationships, not having had much experience other than snatching at friendships as and when they presented, because who knew how long she'd be staying around. Better keep that in mind if those odd feelings for Raphael returned.

'*Oui.*'

'You got drunk, and I had to get you home in a cab before you passed out.'

He winced. 'Sometimes your memory's too good.'

'What was that about anyway?' Rafe didn't do drunk, or drinking less than sensibly. Or very rarely and then only when something had gone horribly wrong for him.

'Can't remember.' He was looking everywhere but at her. 'Ah, here come the chips I ordered.'

Okay, the avoidance game. She should demand to know what he wasn't telling her, but she didn't want to spoil the rest of the evening. Past experience told her she'd eventually win, but she didn't have it in her tonight to do the hard grind to get there. Then she got a whiff of hot chips and relaxed. 'Yum. It's great to be catching up.'

That was the truth, no matter what else she might be feeling. Her legs were aching and her head filling with wool. But then she was starting over on the other side of the world to where she'd been two days ago, and for the first time ever, it was scary. Until now everything had been about making sure she had people with her, by her, there for her. After impulsively accepting the job at the Queen Victoria she'd then sat down and thought it through, and realised how tired of moving from one opportunity to the next she was. The Cambodian experience had shaken her, made her see how strong and enduring families could be for each other. It had made her understand she had to believe in herself before asking anyone else to. She couldn't keep winging it with any relationships. This move had to have a finality about it, *and* she'd go it alone so that eventually she might find herself equipped to give as much back as she needed for herself. More, in fact.

'Want another drink?' Rafe had the barman's attention. 'Izzy?'

Shaking away the questions filtering through the fog in her head, she pushed her drink aside. 'Can I have a water, please?' She studied Raphael for a moment. The gangly teen she'd first met had grown into a lean, muscular man with a face that said *Trust me.* A striking face that other women said made them think bed every time. Her stomach squeezed again, harder this time, showing how concerned she was becoming about him. Something wasn't adding up. Nothing to do with bed.

'You seeing anyone at the moment?' The question was out before she thought it through, but since when did she have to hesitate over asking him anything? He mightn't always be happy with her nosiness, or even give her an answer, but never had he made her uncomfortable over voicing what she wanted to find out. No idea why it felt so important to know where he was at with women, but it did, and she'd acted on those feelings. Being left in the dark was never an option. Knowing what was going on around her meant always being on top of problems before they erupted. Except when it came to her marriage. Then she'd been scared to face the truth, to accept she'd made a monumental mistake.

'*Moi?*' He tapped his chest, mock shock on his face. 'This is Raphael Dubois you are asking.'

'Yes, you, Rafe.' Good-looking men didn't hang around being single for ever, especially doctors in a hospital filled with females of all ages. He'd had his share of women. She knew because he'd talked about them sometimes. Never a derogatory word, always admiration, along with the old wariness about relationships and not trusting they'd last for ever.

His shock was replaced with genuine resignation. 'No. Nobody serious and usually nobody at all.'

She sat up straighter and reached for her glass, took a mouthful. Definitely something out of whack. She'd give him a break from the quiz. 'Tell me about my new job. Anyone I might know on the ward?'

'Not that I'm aware of. Your girlfriends work in different areas, none on the maternity ward, but I guess you know that.'

'The emails have been flying back and forth. Carly's wedding is so close. Everyone's excited about that.' Now she had something genuine to grin about. 'Which reminds me. Do you want to come with me? The invitation is for Isabella and partner. You'll have to sit alone during the ceremony since I'm going to be a bridesmaid.' Once it was definite she'd be here for the wedding, Carly had insisted.

'No one else to invite?' He was smiling at her but there was a slight hitch in his voice.

'I want you to come. Otherwise I'll go on my own,'

she added for good measure. Could be sounding pushy, because she didn't want to turn up at her friend's wedding without someone at her side. The other three girls were all loved up, and she'd only feel lonelier than ever. The odd one out. Unless Raphael was with her.

'Count me in, unless I'm on call that weekend. What's the date?' When she told him he scrolled through his diary. 'Free all weekend.'

'Great. You still happy with your position at the Queen Victoria?'

'Can't complain. It's turned out to be everything I wanted, and some.' He smiled. 'Perfect, really.'

What about Avignon? Returning there was always in the back of his mind. 'I'm glad. You deserve it.' Hopefully she'd be able to say the same about her new job. That would help steady her path to getting this move right.

'Same goes for you. You've just got to believe it.' His gaze was steady—and serious. He believed her, though maybe not fully *in* her. But then he did know her as well as she did herself.

'I will.'

'Say it again. This time with more determination.'

Heck, she'd missed that accent. Talking on the Net it didn't sound quite so deep and so French, more of a garbled mix. Oh, hell. This was weird. Rafe was a friend. 'I will,' she growled through her confusion.

'Isabella,' he growled back.

'So when I suddenly go into a tailspin and make a beeline for the airport with my passport, you'll stop me and tell me to think about what I'm going to do?'

'It won't come to that.' He smiled at her, deep and true.

Suddenly she wanted to cry, and laugh. Coming over

to join Raphael was *the* right thing to do. Which brought up more questions than answers. Thank goodness his phone rang then.

'Please be the ward,' Raphael muttered to himself as he tugged his phone out of his pocket. He needed to put space between Izzy's questions and himself. He'd gone from excited to see her to wary about spending too much time with her. Looking at the phone his heart sank. No reprieve coming.

'Hello, Cooper. How was the game?'

'Get your sorry butt up here now. Haley's in labour and you promised you'd be with us for the delivery.'

Okay, it was a reprieve. Haley was almost three weeks early, nothing to be concerned about. He stood and slipped his jacket on, the phone held between his ear and his shoulder. 'How far along is she?'

'The midwife said she's dilated four centimetres,' Cooper snapped. 'That was ten minutes ago.'

'Take it easy. There's a way to go yet,' Raphael told his friend. Fingers crossed the baby didn't suddenly decide to rush out. 'I'm on my way.'

Izzy stood up, drained her glass of water and slipped her bag over her shoulder.

Damn. Isabella.

'I'll come with you,' she said, solving his dilemma about taking her home and earning more wrath from his friend.

'Faster than fast,' Cooper growled, the stress growing every time he said anything. Fathers and their babies.

'See you shortly.' He nodded to the exit and followed Izzy outside. 'You could catch a taxi back to the house.' Give him some time away from those sad eyes. 'You're exhausted.'

'True, but it's still early and I always try to stay up until my normal bedtime when I've come off a long flight.'

He didn't have time to argue, and a minute later he was driving down the street away from the pub and heading to the Queen Victoria faster than fast. 'I met Cooper and Haley at the hospital. He's a general surgeon and she's a radiologist. This is their first baby,' he explained.

'Exciting.'

That wasn't how Cooper had sounded on the phone. Raphael pressed the accelerator harder, and concentrated on getting to the hospital as quickly as possible.

'Which birthing suite is Haley in?' he asked Claudia as he charged on to the ward.

'Four,' the midwife replied. 'She's reached six centimetres and stopped. Baby seems in two minds about coming out.' Then she glanced past him to Izzy, charging along with them.

'Claudia, meet Isabella Nicholson. She's starting here next week.'

'Hi, Claudia.' Isabella smiled. 'Great to meet you.'

'And you.' Claudia laughed. 'We are having the night from hell, more babies than beds.'

Raphael slowed before he entered the suite, turned to Isabella. 'You want to sit in the office for a while?'

She pulled up short. 'Of course.'

A bell sounded throughout the ward. Claudia muttered, 'I've got to see to that. I'll be back as quickly as possible.'

'There you are.' Cooper stood in the doorway. 'The

contractions have slowed. Probably to give you time to get here.'

Raphael gripped his shoulder. 'There are a few speeding tickets coming my way you can pay for.'

'Who's this?'

'This is my friend I picked up from the airport this afternoon. Isabella, meet Cooper.'

As Cooper reached out to shake her hand, he asked, 'You're a nurse, aren't you?'

'Yes, and a midwife.' She never let that one go by.

'Come and meet Haley. She could do with a distraction.'

Isabella glanced at him. 'Okay?'

'Of course.' Raphael headed towards Haley, his teeth grinding. So much for putting distance between him and Isabella. 'Hi, Haley. I hear things have slowed down since Cooper phoned me.'

Haley grabbed his hand and burst into tears. 'I'm glad you're here. I thought I was going to have the baby without your help.'

'Not a lot I'll be doing other than monitoring the progress. You'll still be doing all the work.' He leaned down to kiss her cheeks just as a contraction tightened her body. His hand was in a vice. 'Breathe out slowly. That's it.'

'Easy for you to say,' Haley muttered as the tension let go. 'You're not the one going through hell here.'

'True. How far apart was that contraction from the previous one?'

'Five minutes,' Cooper answered for her.

'Five minutes, four, six. Who cares?' Haley began tensing again. 'Bet you haven't timed this one, huh? Standing around talking to your buddy like all is well in your world. Which it is. You're not the one going through this agony.'

Raphael struggled not to laugh. He'd heard it all before but to hear Haley talk so much was a surprise. 'And I thought you were shy.' She'd become a radiologist since they didn't have to talk to patients very often, mostly spent their days reading X-rays and MRIs.

'You can shut up too. Get on with making this baby come out.' Then she stared behind him. 'Who are you?'

Izzy stepped forward. 'Hello, Haley. I'm Isabella, Rafe's friend.'

'You made it, then. Raphael was unsure whether you'd turn up.'

I was? 'Hardly. When Isabella says she's going to do something, then there's no changing her mind.' She just didn't always last the distance.

Haley tilted her head at him. 'You've been on tenterhooks ever since she accepted the job here.'

'Lie still. I'm going to listen to baby.'

And shut you down before Isabella starts getting the wrong idea.

'Ah!' Haley cried. 'Here we go again.'

Cooper took her hand, held tight.

Raphael moved to the end of the bed, and gently lifted the sheet covering Haley.

'Are you comfortable lying down through the contractions?' Isabella asked when the current one was over.

'I prefer standing, but when one starts I can't get off the bed quick enough to see it through. I know I should sit on the side, ready to be hauled to my feet by Cooper. It's just that every way I sit or lie it's uncomfortable.'

'Want to try standing next time? I'll help you.' Isabella began rubbing Haley's back, easing out the knots that were no doubt in her muscles, and she started relaxing.

'All right.' Haley was surprisingly acquiescing.

Raphael made the most of Izzy's distraction to examine Haley. 'Eight centimetres. You're back in business.'

'Knew the little blighter was waiting for you to get here. Now there'll be no stopping him.' Cooper's tension had backed off some since he and Izzy had arrived.

Isabella was still rubbing Haley's back. 'Walking around the room might help too, could ease the pain some and get the labour moving along faster. What do you think?'

'I'll try anything. I just want this over.' Haley sat up and slowly slid her legs over the side of the bed. Then another contraction gripped her and Raphael and Cooper took an arm each and hauled her to her feet.

Cooper held her against him, whispering sweet nothings in her ear and rubbing up and down her sides. 'You can do this, darling.'

'Not a lot of choice,' she groaned through clenched teeth. She'd barely got through the contraction and another came. As it finished, she growled, 'Don't think I'll be walking anywhere at this rate.'

'Let's give it a go,' Izzy encouraged. 'Anything's worth a try.'

Raphael watched her with Haley. She had a way about her that made Haley relax. She was going to be an asset on the ward. And when the next contraction came she was right there, encouraging her while Cooper held his wife and murmured in her ear.

'I'm feeling pressure, like I need to push. That's supposed to happen, isn't it?' Haley said some time later.

'Back on the bed,' Raphael told her. 'I'll take another look at what's going on.'

Izzy stood beside him. 'Looking good.'

'It sure is.' Raphael grinned. 'Baby's crowned. Let's get him out here so we can all met the little man.'

Cooper took Haley's hand. 'Come on, darling, give it everything you've got.'

'What do you think I've been doing?' This time there was no anger, only exhaustion, in her voice, and she gave her husband a smile before drawing in a breath and beginning to push.

Raphael glanced across to Izzy, who was back to rubbing Haley's tense back muscles. 'That's it. You're doing great.' She looked up at him and smiled as though to say, 'I love this job.'

He grinned. So did he. Bringing babies into the world had to be the best experience he could have. And when the baby was his friends' he couldn't be happier. 'And again,' he told Haley. 'The shoulders are out.' Then, 'One more push.' Moments later he held a tiny, new human being in his large hands, quickly checking him over before gently laying the baby on Haley's stomach. 'Haley, Cooper, meet your son.' Blink, blink. Damn it, he wasn't supposed to get emotional over this, but these two deserved this moment. 'Izzy, Cooper wants to cut the cord. Could you assist, please?'

'Sure.' She found gloves on the trolley to pull on and helped Cooper cut the cord when it had stopped pulsing.

Raphael watched as Izzy carefully wiped the baby with a towel. She looked so right doing that. What would she be like with her own baby? Besotted, no doubt. But like all midwives she'd probably be a nervous wreck over doing something wrong when she knew exactly how to look after a newborn. Now she carefully lifted the baby and wrapped him in a clean towel before handing him back to his mother, a look of awe on her tired face.

Raphael tapped her on the shoulder, nodded towards the door. 'We'll give you time to bond. Just holler if you want anything.'

For once Cooper was silent, and Haley seemed to have returned to her normal quiet self.

Outside the suite, Izzy leaned against the wall, and grinned. 'Wow. It never changes, does it? The thrill that comes with a baby arriving in our hands?'

'It certainly doesn't.' Not caring who saw him, he pulled her into a hug. 'Welcome home, Izzy.'

Her body tensed. Then relaxed. 'Yes, at last.'

Late the next morning Raphael nudged the shower off and reached for his towel. The tension in his legs put there by a harder than usual run had at last diminished under the onslaught of hot water. Outrunning the images of Izzy rushing at him in the arrival terminal, her wide-eyed gaze as she explored his house and yawning into her chips at the pub hadn't worked. Then there was the one after where they'd returned from the hospital and he'd helped her up the stairs to the third floor and the bedroom that was temporarily hers, her body struggling to put one foot in front of the other as exhaustion outdid everything else. He'd nearly swung her up into his arms to carry her up there, but common sense had stepped in just in the nick of time, forcing him to take her arm instead. Once he'd not have hesitated, but now the very thought of getting close to her and then letting her down was frightening.

After pulling on knee-length shorts and an open-necked shirt he tidied up his room, and made the bed. Earlier, when he'd popped into the kitchen to grab his keys on the way out for his run, he'd been saddened by the empty water bottles on the bench, evidence that Isabella had been downstairs during the night. The way she'd been all but comatose when they'd got home she should've slept right through the night without once opening her eyes. Something needed doing pronto about her insomnia. That sort of tiredness undermined everything a person did if left too long.

He hadn't reckoned on being quite so rattled on seeing her yesterday, and hearing her laugh and talk. Except it'd been Izzy with a difference. The laughter was strained, the conversations awkward. His heart had stirred at the sight of her, which once he'd have said was because of their friendship, yet now felt it might be about something more intense. They loved each other, platonically. But no denying that since the day he'd had to watch her marry Darren he'd felt he'd lost something, that he loved her in a way he shouldn't. Not that he trusted his feelings. Look where love had got him last time. He'd fallen fast and hard, and gave Cassie everything, only to have her continually complaining it wasn't enough. And that was before her final treachery.

When Isabella first told him she and Darren were splitting his heart had soared with selfish relief. Then, as the sordid details of their marriage registered, he'd been angry and distressed for her. Since then his emotions had run the gamut from hope to despair and everything in between for her. And for himself. Something he only admitted at four in the morning when sleep was elusive.

Now he had to cope with Izzy living in his own space, however temporarily. A space she'd slotted into last night as easily as he'd seen her shrug into a puffer jacket in midwinter on the Rhône years ago. Nothing unusual in that. Except he also had to ignore how his heart was involved. Cassie had finally taken a back seat. But not the loss of his child. He'd never forgive her for that, which meant his heart wasn't ready for anyone else.

Goosebumps lifted on his forearms. Rubbing hard did nothing to knock them down. Nor did the light woollen jersey he pulled over his head in the bedroom. His nose twitched. Coffee vapour was filtering up the stairs. Coffee. Had to be the answer. Obviously Izzy was in the kitchen. Damn, no dashing into the hospital for a bit of time out.

She was leaning one hip against the bench, a full mug wrapped in her hands, and a bewildered smile lifting her lips as she glanced down at the creature rubbing against her legs. 'You've got a cat.'

'I rescued her from the RSPCA.'

'Yeah, but you and a pet?'

'Since I was a little guy I've wanted a dog. Now that I'm settled it was time to do something about it.'

Isabella blinked, then laughed. 'Do I need to point out this is a cat?'

'Her name's Chienne.'

'Dog? You are so mean.' She put her mug aside and picked up the cat to snuggle against her breast. Ah, chest. Nope, definitely breasts, the rounded shape filling her T-shirt perfectly.

'That's me,' he muttered, and reached for a mug.

She rubbed her chin on Chienne's head. 'What was your real name before this mean guy got hold of you?'

'According to the RSPCA, Waster was on the tag around her collar. I was not going to keep calling her that.'

'So you came up with something even more original.' Izzy blinked and looked down at her furry bundle. 'I bet you're spoilt rotten. Raphael has never been mean.'

A band of warmth wrapped around him. It felt good to hear that, and while nothing was wrong in his life, who couldn't do with the odd compliment or two? 'Cover her ears while I say that I'd prefer a dog but they need so much attention and given my erratic and long hours it wouldn't have been fair to get one.'

Izzy began nibbling her bottom lip, which was new to him.

'What's up? You look like you're not sure where you are.'

She blinked and reached for her mug to sip the steaming liquid. 'I know exactly where I am, yet I feel kind of lost. Could be my brain hasn't kept up with the rest of me and will be arriving later.'

'Or it might be because this is the final move of your life.' That'd be confronting for her. If she meant it. Except she'd tried that once before and look where that got her. Back here. Though not alone. *I'm here.* 'I remember feeling a little bewildered the day I moved in here and dumped my few possessions on the table I'd ordered from the local furniture store, along with a lounge suite and a bed.' The second bed in the room Isabella was using had arrived on Friday after a frantic phone call to organise that and a chest of drawers for her. 'I struggled to believe this was *my* home.' He tapped his chest with his knuckles. 'And that I got to stay here until *I* decided otherwise.'

'It's real, isn't it?' Isabella seemed to be holding her breath.

Expecting the right answer from him?

Sorry, Izzy, but I only know what's right for me, and I'm not sure I've got that right yet.

'It's as real as you want it to be.'

Her mouth quirked. 'Back at me, huh?' Then she hit the serious button. 'No regrets?'

'Honestly? No. Sometimes I think about how my life might have turned out if I'd let Cassie talk me into moving to Paris, but…' He shrugged.

Izzy's eyes widened at the mention of his ex, but she just stroked the cat.

Raphael filled his mug with coffee before topping up hers. Time to get on to something normal and ordinary. 'I'm going in to see Haley and baby as soon as I've had this. Want to come?' Gulp. That was not what he planned on saying.

'Give me ten to take a shower, and fix up the face.'

It was going to take a fair amount of make-up to hide the shadows under her eyes, but he wasn't saying. 'There's no hurry.' Tell that to his taut body. He wanted to be doing something other than standing in his kitchen drinking coffee and smelling Izzy's perfume instead of the coffee. But he'd have to be patient.

Oui.

'I'll introduce you to whoever's about. You can also meet the three little guys I told you about a couple of weeks ago. They're something else. Their mum wants a quick word with me too.'

She paused on her way out of the kitchen. 'They've got to you, haven't they?'

'Just a little.' He'd love to have a family of his own.

There'd be no replacing the son he lost but could it be time to think about moving on?

No. He wouldn't survive that sort of pain again.

CHAPTER FOUR

'HELLO, HALEY,' ISABELLA said to the happy woman cuddling her son in the single room where she'd been transferred after the birth. 'How're you feeling today?'

'Isn't Ryan the cutest baby ever?' Haley's eyes lit up. 'I can't believe I'm a mother.'

She'd soon get used to that with sleepless nights and nappies to deal with. 'Believe me, you are. I saw it happen.'

'So did I.' Raphael laughed from the other side of the bed. 'Can I have a hold?' He held out his arms.

Haley reluctantly handed him over. 'One minute.'

'Then it's my turn,' Isabella said. 'How are you doing with breastfeeding?'

'Eek. That's no fun. I can't quite manage it yet, but I've been told that's normal.'

'Certainly is. You'll soon get the hang of it. Don't stress though. That only makes matters worse.' She looked at Raphael. There was a look of relief in his expression. As though he didn't quite believe the outcome of Haley's labour would be so good. Which didn't add up considering there were no complications. Or was he thinking about children, as in his own? Why not? Could be his biological clock was ticking? That wouldn't be just a woman's prerogative. Deep in her tummy she felt a twinge, as though her clock had come to life. Her mouth dried. That was not part of the plan to settle here. Not yet, not until she'd got all the other factors right. In the meantime she'd get her fix holding other people's babies. 'Time's up.' She held out her arms for Ryan, and laughed at Rafe's reluctance to hand him over.

Haley was watching her son, hunger in her eyes, and Isabella couldn't not pass Ryan back to his mum. 'There you go. I'll have another turn before we leave.'

'Come and meet the triplets,' Rafe said as they left the room.

The moment they walked into the nursery Isabella felt the same awe she'd seen in Raphael's face when he talked about the three little boys. They lay in their cribs lined up side by side, blinking at any movement made by the two people leaning over them, smiling and chatting as though the boys understood. Raphael went straight across and gazed down at the babies too, warmth in his eyes. But also a shadow of something else. Anger? Pain?

'Hello, Raphael.' The mum turned to him. 'You didn't have to come in on your day off.' Her gaze shifted to Isabella. 'I know you don't get a lot of time to yourself as it is. Your partner must get fed up with you being called out all the time.'

He blinked and those emotions were gone. He was back to professional doctor mode. 'Melody, it's fine. I was coming to see another patient anyway. And this is Isabella Nicholson. She's a nurse and midwife, and will be starting on this ward later in the week.' Not his partner. Though he hadn't actually put it into words, it was there. Raphael nodded at the man gazing down at the boys with a besotted look. 'Isabella, this is Ollie, the doting dad.'

'Hello, Melody, Ollie. Your boys are gorgeous.' Isabella smiled. 'Look at them. They're so busy, moving their arms and kicking their little legs. You're going to have your hands full when you get them home.' Even the smallest boy, still attached to more monitors than his brothers, was staring up at everyone.

'Aren't we? And I can't wait.' Ollie grinned. 'Antony's taking a little longer to get up to speed, but really, we've been so lucky. These other two are already putting on weight. The sooner we're all at home, the better.'

'I don't want to rush things,' Melody said with a worried glance at Raphael. 'What if I can't cope?' She looked to Isabella. 'I've never had much to do with babies before. To have three at once is daunting. Not that I don't want them,' she added hastily. 'We've waited too long for this as it is.'

Ollie brushed a kiss across his wife's forehead. 'You'll be fine, sweetheart. With the folks dropping in to help and the daily visits from the district nurse, we'll manage.' He grinned. 'You'll soon be telling everyone to get out of the way and let you get on with looking after your boys.'

Raphael nodded. 'You'll be more tired than you've ever been, and there won't be enough hours in the day, but you'll manage. I promise. Even mothers with one baby for the first time go through the same concerns that you have. If you'd taken them home within a couple of days of them being born as usually happens when it's only one baby, you wouldn't have had time to think about all the things that need doing—you'd be doing them.'

'So everyone keeps telling me.' Melody sighed. 'But what if I'm useless as a mother?'

'Stop it,' Ollie growled softly. 'We're going to be the best parents ever. We're doing this together, remember?' He turned to Isabella. 'I've turned our back bedroom into an office so I can work from home for the foreseeable future. Whenever clients need to see me I can meet them there or at the company rooms in town.'

The worry in Melody's eyes only increased, as though nothing was registering except she had three babies to look after and all the things that could go wrong. Was she a candidate for postnatal depression? Isabella glanced at Raphael, and relaxed. He was on to it. Of course the same thought would've occurred to him.

He said, 'I'll arrange for you to talk to someone about how you're going to cope, Melody. Try not to get too wound up about everything. Make the most of this time in here where you can learn a lot about being a mum in preparation for going home. Enjoy your babies. They grow up so darned fast you'll soon be wondering where the time went.'

Ollie lifted one boy—Shaun, according to the card on his little cot—and held him out to his mother. 'Here you go, Mum.'

Melody immediately relaxed and placed her son against her breast, rubbing his back as though she'd always been doing that.

'See, just like a pro.' Isabella nodded. 'He's as happy as can be, snuggling against you.'

'He's hungry.' The father picked up Antony and held him in a similar position.

'Aren't they always?' she said, and leaned over the third crib. 'Hello, Morgan. Aren't you the cutest little guy?' He was blinking and moving one hand in the air. So innocent and trusting. What would his life be like? All their lives? Would the three of them watch out for each other? Or compete over everything? If she'd had a sibling she was certain her life of moving from country to country would've been different. There'd have been someone who was always there, a constant, someone of a similar age to understand what she'd longed for, to share the good and bad times, to love always. Not all siblings got along though. There was that. No point thinking about what couldn't be changed. She was grown up now, and making her own way without having to do as her parents demanded. Besides, she'd had Raphael in her life since she was a teen. Still did. As good as a brother. *Brother?* These feelings she was getting for him had nothing to do with a brother.

Behind her, he was talking to Melody. 'I hear you've got another infection in your Caesarean wound.'

'Yes, but why when I've been taking antibiotics? It's not fair.' Melody sounded close to tears.

'We'll try a different antibiotic. Mind if I have a look first?'

Melody shook her head.

'Isabella, do you want to get me some swabs?' Raphael asked when he saw Melody's inflamed wound. 'They're in the trolley outside the door.'

'Sure.' She pushed the trolley into the room and slipped gloves on before handing him the swabs. 'You want the antiseptic fluid?'

'Please.' He cleaned the area and dabbed the yellow liquid all over. 'There, that should help. I'll make sure someone does that regularly. And I'll sign a prescription for the nurses to collect. Any other worries?' When

Melody shook her head, Raphael said to Isabella, 'I'll go check on my other patients. You okay finding your way around?'

'You can introduce me to whoever's at the station and I'll go from there.' Though right now she'd be happy lying down for a nap. 'If you can't find me I'll be curled up somewhere out of the way.'

Raphael was quick to look at her, worry now in *his* eyes. 'Are you all right? This is so not like you.'

'The jet lag's new, I admit. But I haven't been sleeping well for so long I hardly notice.' Ever since she'd been forced to face up to the fact she hadn't married Darren purely for love but mostly for the security and one-stop life he'd promised. That had been as important to her as love. Maybe even more. It had taken her reaction to finding her husband in bed with another woman to bring her up sharp, and to start thinking about why she'd married in the first place. She hadn't liked the answers. They had her questioning her ability to have a loving, caring relationship. She'd been selfish in wanting the lifestyle Darren offered before anything else. Didn't mean he had to betray her though. How was she supposed to trust any man with her heart again?

'We'll talk some more about this when we're back home.'

'Ah, no, we won't.' She wasn't ready for that. It was history, and she was getting on with *now*. 'Come on, play nice and introduce me to whoever's here.'

Two nurses were sitting in front of computers in the work area, and looked up at the same time. 'We were wondering if you'd drop in, Raphael. Mrs Baxter has been seen by the duty specialist and has settled down again.'

'No one let me know that.' He didn't look happy. 'But since I'm here I'll talk to her.'

One of the nurses was on her feet instantly. 'I'll come with you.'

'First let me introduce Isabella Nicholson to you.'

The same nurse turned to her. 'You're starting here later this week, aren't you? I saw your name on the roster. Hi, I'm Annabel, and this is Mary. What are you doing in here today? Should be making the most of your days off.' Annabel's eyes flicked from her to Raphael, a question in her gaze.

'Hello. I came along for the ride.' Not going to explain why she was with the handsome doctor who obviously had one of the nurses in a bit of a lather. Which was odd, because she was usually quick to let women know she was his friend, not his lover.

'Can you show Izzy around, Mary?' Izzy, not Isabella. Rubbing it in how friendly he was with her?

'Sure.' The other nurse stood up. 'Anything would be better than doing the stock figures.' Then she grimaced. 'Sorry, Isabella. That sounded all wrong. Take no notice of me.'

Isabella laughed. 'Don't worry. I'll get over it.'

'Want a coffee first?'

It might help her stay awake. 'That'd be great.'

'Come through to the staff kitchen, then. The lockers are along here too, and uniforms are next door.'

'It's all coming back.' When Mary shot her a puzzled look she explained, 'I trained as a midwife in this hospital, and spent many nights on this ward.'

'In that case, shall we grab coffees and go back to the station so I can keep an eye on things while interrogating you?' It was said with a smile, and Isabella laughed.

'Not sure I've got anything interesting to say, but let's give it a go.' As long as she didn't want information on Rafe. That would not be happening. His details were not for her to share.

'Actually, I did hear you'd worked here before. It slipped my addled brain. Esther and I are friends.'

'How is she? I only got here yesterday so haven't had a chance to catch up with her or our other two friends. The four of us trained together, and now we're all back here again.'

'She's great. Totally in love with Harry with stars in her eyes all the time.'

'Isn't it awesome?'

Mary handed her a mug and pushed the coffee jar in her direction. 'Help yourself.' Leaning back against the bench she watched Isabella. 'You're close to Raphael? Since he brought you in I figured you must've been together when he got the call,' she added hurriedly when Isabella tightened her mouth.

'We're friends from way back.' That wasn't divulging anything that could be twisted into something more interesting. 'It's been a while since we had time together.'

And that's all I'm saying.

'Lots to catch up on, then.'

Time to change the subject. 'So do you do all shifts or weekends only?'

'I cover all the rosters just like you're going to do. Most of the staff do, apart from two nurses who work nights only, and one who only does weekends. Where were you last working?'

'Based in Wellington, New Zealand, but I volunteered in Cambodia recently.' When they were seated in the workstation sipping coffee, Isabella filled her in on her working background and avoided questions about her private life. She was here, that's all that mattered. In fact, that was a good line to follow herself. 'What's the social life like here? Does everyone get together for drinks at the end of the week?'

'Some of us do. You up for that?'

'Absolutely. It's the best way to get to know people.'

Her eyes were heavy, and her head thick with sleep. She shook herself and straightened up in the chair. Where was Raphael? He seemed to be taking a long time.

A phone rang and Mary reached for it, then brought up the computer screen. 'Here we go. Knew the quiet spell was too good to be true.'

Isabella looked around the work area, saw nothing unusual to ask about. All fairly standard. It wasn't going to be hard to slot in with everyone. A yawn slipped out and her eyes drooped.

'Wake up, sleepy head.' A firm hand shook her gently.

Isabella dragged her chin up off her sternum and blinked up at Raphael. 'Guess I didn't make the coffee strong enough.'

'Let's get out of here. You're giving everyone the wrong impression.' He winked.

All very well to make a joke of it, but she probably was. There seemed to be more people wandering around the area now. Saturday afternoon brought friends and family out in their droves. 'I'll be fine by the time I start work on Wednesday.'

Mary laughed. 'Seems I bored you to sleep talking about shifts and who's who on the roster.'

Didn't hear any of that. 'Sorry. I'll do better next time. I'm still getting over my flights.' She stood up slowly, picked up her bag from the floor where it had fallen. 'See you when we're on the same shift.'

Mary nodded. 'Or handing over.'

'Do people know I'm staying with you?' Isabella asked Raphael as they waited for the lift to take them down to the car park.

'I haven't mentioned it to anyone except Jacki, since she's the head nurse for the ward, and I figured she needed to know since I put such a good word in for you.' He grinned. 'It's none of anyone else's business though. Not that it's a secret, but I don't want someone saying I'm favouring you once you're working amongst us.' The lift rattled to a stop and the door cranked open. 'Come on, let's get out of here and go do something interesting.'

'Like what?'

'For you that means getting some sleep.'

'If I sleep during the day I won't get much during the night.'

'The problem with that theory is that you're already dropping off every opportunity you get. And you don't sleep at night anyway.'

Isabella grimaced. 'True. How about I have a snooze, then we go for a walk along the river?' The exercise would do her good.

They climbed into Raphael's car and started for home.

'Want to talk about why you're so tired?' he asked quietly as they waited at traffic lights.

'Not really.' It wouldn't change things. But this was the one person she used to tell everything.

'Don't blame the jet lag. This is worse than normal.'

'Didn't mention the jet lag.'

'It's to do with Darren, right?'

Just spill the beans, get it off your chest. What's Raphael going to say that you haven't already said to yourself?

'I stuffed up big-time.' She paused, stared out the window at the tail lights on the car in front. 'I'm talking about my marriage. Our bust-up wasn't all Darren's fault.'

'There're usually two sides to these things.'

Yeah, but she was uncomfortable with her contribution, or lack of. 'I didn't love him as much as I should've.'

'Then why did you marry him?' There was genuine confusion radiating from Raphael. Maybe a hint of disappointment.

Shouldn't have told him. But she'd started, so might as well get it over. 'Because I thought I did. I *believed* I did. Right up until it all began disintegrating.'

No, earlier than that. I stayed in denial for as long as I could.

'The pain wasn't as deep as you'd expect?' Forget disappointment. Raphael was looking confused. Which made no sense at all. More to think about when she wasn't so tired.

'Yes, it was, but for the wrong reasons. That took a bit to figure out but when I did it hurt more than ever.' She drew a deep breath and rushed on. 'Darren promised a home and family, and to live in the same city for the rest of our lives. I so desperately wanted that I didn't look beyond to anything else. By marrying him I let him down. Hell, I let myself down. And you know what's the worst? I don't know with complete certainty that I've learnt my lesson. What if I make the same mistake again? I was so intent on living the life my parents had denied me I got it all wrong, and it worries me.' What if she fell in love again, only to find she'd made another mistake?

They'd stopped at another set of lights and Raphael's fingers were playing a silent tune on the steering wheel. 'We all make mistakes, Izzy.'

'I got wrong the one dream I've had most of my life.' She swallowed a bitter mouthful of pain. 'Which is why in the meantime I'm sticking to running solo and making a home of my own, by me for me. I don't want to hurt someone else. Better to play safe.' Get it, Rafe? Actually, it was her she needed to remind of that.

'I think you're being hard on yourself.'

'Yeah, right,' she growled. 'Easy for you to say. Darren did some bad things like those affairs and spending more time with his mates than me, but if I'd loved him as much as I'd professed, then he wouldn't have had to. He might've stayed home more often, might've been happy to go house hunting instead of skirt chasing.' She was grasping at straws. According to the partner of one of his mates, Darren had always had a roving eye. Not that it was his eye doing most of the work. But apparently she wasn't the only partner he'd cheated on, just the first wife.

'He could've talked to you about it, not buried his head in the sand.'

'Like Cassie did with you?' Isabella snapped, and instantly regretted her words. This was about her and her messed-up relationship, had nothing to do with Raphael's history. But he didn't seem to accept she was at least trying to take some of the blame in an attempt to soften the hurt Darren had created and that riled her. As he said, she was usually so honest it could be awkward. 'I shouldn't have said that.'

'*Non*. You shouldn't have.'

Silence took over in the car, tense and uncomfortable. Isabella stared out at the passing buildings, not really noticing them, instead seeing Wellington on a bright summer's day with the harbour sparkling and the ferries passing further out. Her heart didn't flutter with longing, instead seemed to sigh with relief. Yes, she'd done the right thing in leaving there, as she had in walking away from her marriage. And from now on she was dropping the worry about that, looking forward, no more doubts. Hopefully then the trust issue would start to resolve itself, and she could consider a new relationship. She'd make herself get on with it. Now. Not tomorrow or next week. Now. 'So what did you have in mind for us to do this afternoon?'

Raphael drew in a lungful of air and sighed it back out. He could hear Izzy's distress, understand her fear of repeating her mistake—because he knew it all too well himself. Cassie had torn his heart to shreds, and he was reluctant to try again. Hell, in the beginning he'd given Cassie *everything*. His love, his life, his family, trust. He'd only put his foot down about living in Paris because he already had the job he needed to set up his career as he wanted. It had been the only thing he'd denied her, and it had backfired, brought out her fickleness. So no, he wasn't getting involved with anyone else. Certainly not the woman sitting beside him.

Then he went and messed with that idea. 'Thought we'd get the bikes out and go for a spin alongside the river.'

'We what?' Shock filled her face. 'Me? On a bike? Think you've got the wrong person in mind for that.'

He'd made her forget what she'd been gnawing her lip over though, hadn't he? Her lip was swollen. A kiss might help ease the soreness. Swearing under his breath, he scrabbled around for something inane to say. 'One of the doctors was selling her bike last week so I bought it for you.'

'Hope you got crash pads and a helmet and padded clothing to go with it. And a pair of those thick fancy shorts that make butts look bigger.'

Butts. Bigger. Fitted shorts. He swallowed hard. Sure. 'You forgot the steel-capped boots.' Even to his ears, his laugh sounded strained. But he was glad to have made her smile, though he was still sour about her snide remark over Cassie, even if it was true. That was just Isabella putting up the wall to keep him away. Though she had gone for the jugular, not something she usually did.

He'd never told her the whole story. Certainly hadn't mentioned the baby he'd only learned about when he'd tracked Cassie down a couple of years later. Nearly as bad was coming to terms with the fact Cassie should've been more upset, but relieved their baby hadn't suffered. Her new career in acting had been taking off and a baby would've been a hindrance. Later he learned the bit parts hadn't flowed into roles of any significance, had instead ebbed away to the point she now worked in a sleazy bar on the outskirts of Los Angeles, struggling to make ends meet. It was the last time he'd seen her, and he'd woken up. They had nothing in common, and he'd wondered how he could've loved her so much. They said love was blind, and he'd found out the hard way how true that could be. He didn't want to lose his sight ever again.

'Honestly, Rafe, I haven't ridden a bike since I was a teenager.'

'Which means your backside and legs will ache afterwards.' The way Izzy's backside filled out her shorts and trousers set his body aflame. 'No, you're right. Better I go alone and get home earlier.'

'You're backing out now?' She turned to face him.

There was no winning with Izzy. 'Let's stop somewhere for a late lunch instead.'

'Your shout for winding me up.' Her mouth spread into a cheeky smile and they were back on track, tension about their pasts forgiven.

But not forgotten. One day he'd find the courage to tell her the rest of the Cassie story. But not today. He'd hate to see pity in her eyes. 'Wouldn't have it any other way, *mon amie*.' Except friends didn't make his gut tighten over a smile. This was getting out of hand. He needed breathing space, which would be hard to find while they shared his house and worked on the same ward.

'How about we have a French week?' She'd know exactly what he meant. It wasn't the first time, and probably wouldn't be the last. 'Everywhere we go except at the hospital.' Probably get locked up for speaking nothing but French there.

'Je ne veau pas faire de vélo.'

'Dure.'

Too late he realised how intimate spending time talking in his native language might be. He grimaced, then went with cheeky. 'I don't need to teach you to ride. Your body will remember how to push the pedals even if you cry foul, so toughen up.'

'Does this mean you're cooking dinner tonight? I'd like coq au vin.'

'Say that in French and I might oblige,' he replied in French. Actually, she wasn't too rusty, but he'd keep at her as it'd been a while since she'd been submerged in the language and he intended taking her back to Avignon to visit Grand'mère in the next few weeks.

And that idea had nothing to do with the feelings he wasn't admitting even to himself.

Or did it?

CHAPTER FIVE

RAPHAEL SLIPPED INTO the seat opposite Isabella in the hospital cafeteria with a mug of coffee in one hand and a large egg mayo sandwich in the other. 'What are you doing here?'

'Initiation course.' At eight that morning Isabella had received a call from the head nurse of the maternity ward to come in and do the drill all newly signed-on employees had to partake in.

'Damn, sorry, I was meant to tell you about that.'

'Apparently.' Forcing a laugh, she tried not to notice how Raphael's shoulders shaped his suit to perfection. That *perfect* word again. It popped up a lot around Rafe. But how his body filled his clothes? This was Raphael. Seems when she got jet lag she got it bad. 'No problem. It's the same old, same old. Work in one large hospital and you know the routine for any others you go to.' She'd spent the last few hours learning the ropes of where fire extinguishers and staircases were, as well as all the safety rules involving staff. 'Lunch is the best bit so far, even if beyond late.' It was nearly two and she was starving.

He blinked. 'Not same old food, then?'

'Nothing different about that, but it's far more interesting being in here.' Her hand swept the room. 'There are real people in here, not sheep following Miss This-Way-Folks all over the hospital.'

Raphael's laugh sent ripples of warmth through her. He was watching her closely. Looking for what? 'You seem a lot more awake than I've seen since you arrived. The jet lag must be wearing off,' he said.

'How was surgery?' He'd left home before six as his surgical list had four ops, one of which he thought might throw up some complications, and he'd wanted to be prepared. Nothing unusual there.

Now he nodded once, a grim expression on his face as he glanced around them. 'The woman I told you about? The cancer has gone through to the uterus, as I'd suspected. Then when we had that sorted she haemorrhaged from the large bowel and we found another growth. I had to call in David Stokes, one of the general surgeons, to take over when I'd done all I could.' He shook his head. 'Some people get a raw deal.'

It wasn't sounding good for the woman. 'Take it easy. You've done all you can.' Isabella reached for his hand, squeezed it before letting go in a hurry. That wasn't a normal gesture from her to Raphael. But he was so distressed she could almost see anguish oozing out of his pores. It was also there in the tightness of his shoulders and the white lines around his mouth.

'I know. It's up to the oncologists now. She's only forty-one.' His frustrated sigh cut through her, had her wanting to take his pain for him.

One reason for preferring midwifery to nursing patients that specialists like Raphael dealt with was not having to face some of these grim cases. 'If you're not too late finishing tonight do you want to go out for a meal?' In her lap her fingers crossed of their own accord. Knowing doctors had little control over their private hours she didn't really expect an instant acceptance.

'Sounds like a plan.' Where was the enthusiasm?

'Look, we can give it a miss if you'd prefer.'

He looked straight at her. 'If I knock off about six will you hang around in town? I'm thinking we can go along the river to this bar everyone frequents. You'll like it.'

'That's a yes, then.' Raphael hadn't said no, or maybe; he'd said he'd be there. Yippee. Suddenly the ho-hum day had become bright and exciting.

Careful. This is your friend. He won't see it as a hot date.

Nor should she. Yeah, but it was growing on her that she'd come home, as in found her niche. Being with Raphael relaxed her in ways she hadn't known for a long time—for two years, really. Was that what close friends did? Or was there another reason for this deep sense of belonging whenever she was with him? If only she could sort out her mixed-up feelings for him. Slowing her breathing, she went for calm. 'Great, I'll be around here somewhere. Might see if Carly wants to go for a coffee and catch up while I wait for you. She's on days this week.'

'I need to tell you—you'll probably get a call asking if you mind starting on the ward tomorrow instead of Wednesday. We're three staff down and as busy as can be,' Raphael told her. 'Don't feel pressured to say yes. I know you're still tired and taking naps like a toddler.' His smile sent ripples throughout her body, which was frankly weird. He shouldn't make her feel like this. Except apparently he did.

'I'll be fine, might even be better for doing something. If not, there's the weekend to catch up on sleep.' Now she was becoming boring. Though it wasn't boredom rippling through her body as the impact of that smile continued blasting her. Since when did Raphael's smiles disturb her in any way? Isabella had no answer so went with devouring her now cold pie. Their relationship was changing. Hopefully for the better.

'Have you made appointments to look at flats yet?' No grin now. More of an intense scrutiny of the bottom of his empty mug.

So he wanted her gone sooner than later. Her shoulders slumped. She hauled them tight. She would not be upset. 'I've hardly had time,' she snapped. 'I didn't think there was that much of a hurry.'

'There isn't.' Now he locked eyes with her. 'I just thought you were in a hurry to get started on settling down.'

'Should've known.' She'd reacted too quickly and come up with the wrong answer. 'I'll get on to it shortly. I need to decide where to live that's not too far from the hospital and yet in a bit of a community. If that's possible close to the city centre. I do like the area you're in but rentals there are probably exorbitant. You wouldn't want me too close keeping an eye on what you get up to either.'

He stood and gathered his plate and mug. 'Not true, Izzy. I'm thrilled you're staying in my house, and about to start working on my ward. It's been too long since we spent time together, and we mustn't let that happen again.'

Quite the speech. One that sounded false. She didn't fully understand, and suspected there was something more behind the words. But thrilled? Really? Good. Great even. One thing she knew for certain. 'I agree. It's been for ever since we could sit and shoot the breeze.' For some reason the thought of not having Rafe nearby, if not right beside her, was beginning to feel wrong. As if they were meant to be together. The last crust of her pie fell to the plate. She and Raphael? Together? As in a couple? Come on. That's what she'd been avoiding admitting since arriving in London.

'I'll text you when I'm done tonight.' He was smiling, happiness shining out of his cerulean gaze. 'Want me to take your plate, or are you going to finish that pastry?'

Pushing the plate at him she shook her head, and tried to find something to say. But nothing sensible came up, so she remained quiet. She was off balance, and Raphael wasn't helping by looking at her like he wanted more from her. They knew each other inside out. Ah, not quite. See? She'd never have thought that before. Okay, but since when hadn't she been able to read whatever he wasn't saying? Usually she could do it with her eyes shut. Not today. 'I'll see you later,' she muttered. Yes, she still wanted to have dinner with him. More than before. Really? Yes, really. As in more than catching up. As in getting to know him when she already did. As in trying to understand why she was so off centre around him. Was she on the rebound from Darren? But if this was a rebound, why pick her friend?

Because he's safe and kind and I know where I stand with him.

Oh. That was a wet blanket smothering her. If she did fall in love again, it would be for the right reasons.

I never truly fell completely in love in the first place.

Anyway, no rebound in sight. She was totally over the man. He wasn't as sexy as Raphael, nor as kind and selfless, or as gorgeous.

Shoving upright, Isabella headed for the exit. The cafeteria had become too small and airless. A few minutes alone outdoors might help unscramble her mind. Might not, either, but she had to try.

'Where are you headed now?' Raphael stood beside her as she peered left, then right.

'Thought I might go introduce myself to the rest of the gang on the ward.' So much for heading outside. She turned in the direction of the lift bank, walked away.

'Isabella.'

She stopped, turned back slowly. 'Yes?'

'This is going to work out for you.' His smile was fleeting, as if not quite believing what he'd said, or not accepting she'd meant it about stopping moving around.

'I hope so.'

Doubtful he heard her quiet reply as he strode away, hands at his sides, back ramrod straight, head up. In Raphael coping mode. What was he coping with? Her decision to live in London? Did he want her here? Or gone by sunrise? He'd suggested she move across the world. Had he changed his mind now it was real? Who knew? She certainly didn't. She needed to get over herself. His mind was more likely to be on his patients, particularly the woman with secondary cancers.

Yet there was a nagging sensation going on at the back of her head saying there was more to this. Isabella slumped against the wall, out of the way of people charging in both directions like they were on missions she was not party to. What was happening to her and

Raphael? To their easy, accepting friendship? Never before had she felt awkward with him, yet right now she had no idea what he was thinking or wanting, and that'd happened a few times over the past couple of days.

Her phone rang as she reached the nurses' station on the maternity ward. 'Hello, this is Isabella Nicholson.'

'Jacki Jones, Isabella. I'm ringing to ask a favour.'

Isabella glanced around, saw a woman talking into a phone not more than two metres away. Holding the phone against her chest, she called, 'Jacki? I'm Isabella.'

The head nurse spun around on her chair. 'Oh, hi.' She shoved the phone on its stand and stood to meet her. 'Talk about timely.'

'I've finished the safety course and thought I'd drop by to introduce myself.'

'I was ringing to see if you'd mind starting earlier than first agreed. Tomorrow? We're down on staff and it's bedlam in here.' She had a strong Welsh accent, making Isabella smile. She also seemed to be holding her breath.

Glad of Raphael's warning, the answer came easily. 'Not a problem. Whichever shift you need me on.'

'Thank you.' Jacki's relief was loud and clear. 'Raphael said you probably wouldn't mind, but I still worried you'd say no. It's a bit desperate up here at the moment.'

'Do you want me to put in a few hours this afternoon? I'm signed off on the course and all set to go.'

'Thank you again, but we'll manage today. I know it's only been a couple of days since you arrived in town. Go home and make the most of your time off. You'll be busy enough tomorrow.'

Since her head was starting to pound, she agreed. 'You're probably right.'

A nurse stuck her head around a corner. 'Jacki, I need you in here with Rosalie.' She sounded desperate.

'Coming,' Jacki said calmly. 'A very prem birth, twelve weeks early,' she told Isabella before heading away. 'Raphael's on his way and everything's under control.'

And I'm in the way. Totally get it.

'I'll see you at seven tomorrow.'

'Thanks again, Isabella. I really appreciate it,' Jacki called over her shoulder.

Waiting for the lift again, Isabella texted Carly.

Want a coffee when you knock off?

Not expecting an immediate answer, since Carly was working, she headed for the main entrance and the fresh air. Talking with Carly and hearing more about the man she'd fallen in love with would put everything into perspective, and she'd be able to see Raphael as she'd always done. The best friend ever, who had her back, and had once told her they could rely on each other for anything any time.

Ping. A text landed in her phone.

Three-thirty at the café left of the hospital. Casper's.

Oh, yay. Awesome. Isabella's step picked up as she walked outside. Now what? Nearly an hour to fill in. She'd go for a walk along the Thames and soak up the atmosphere. Stop worrying about everything. Seemed lately she made problems out of anything. Especially her and Raphael. Like she was looking for trouble, when nothing had changed. But it had. She was different. She'd made a serious decision to move here.

You did it in a blink when Raphael made the suggestion.

Raphael. Everything came back to him. She needed to get to the bottom of these niggling concerns, and the sooner, the better. Needed to relax and be happy, more like.

The sun was weak but it didn't matter, the air so much better than the overheated hospital rooms and corridors. The sky was blue with a smattering of fluffy clouds, while boats of all shapes and sizes were making their way purposefully up and down the flowing waters of the Thames. Already there were lots of tourists on the pathways and bridges, cameras busy, selfies being snapped, excitement high, voices loud and excited. This was London. She recalled the first time she'd come here and feeling exactly the same. Hugging herself, she smiled widely at the scene before her and relaxed. The thumping in her head began quietening down.

Strolling along amongst the tourists, hearing a babble of languages and laughter, she let the city take over and push aside everything bothering her, and went with the flow of people all around her. For the first time since landing at Heathrow she didn't feel like falling asleep on her feet despite only a short time ago wanting to crawl into bed, and the tightness in her belly that had been plaguing her had taken a hike.

Isabella lost track of time and had to scramble to get back to the café before Carly gave up on her and headed away. If she hadn't already. Staring around the crowded café she couldn't see her friend.

'Isabella, Izzy, here.'

Relief and excitement had her charging through the spaces between the tables to where Carly stood waving from a table.

Laughing, she reached Carly and was instantly wrapped in a tight hug with a baby bump in the middle. 'It's been a long time.'

'Hello, you,' Carly murmured against her.

'Blimey, this is amazing. I've missed you guys so much.'

'Know what you mean.' Carly stepped back and sank onto a chair, her hand doing a loop of her belly. 'There's so much to talk about. First, go grab yourself a coffee. I had to get my mint tea when I got here so we could have this table.'

When Isabella returned, with an overfilled mug and a bottle of water, Carly was texting, but put her phone aside at once, her face all soft. 'Adem.'

'Look at you. All loved up. I'm so happy for you.' They should've been celebrating with wine, but with a baby in the mix this was the next best thing, as was the talk and laughter as they caught up on day-to-day news. Then Isabella said, 'Tell me all about Adem. When am I going to meet him?'

'Not telling all.' Carly chuckled. 'Izzy, he's everything I've ever wanted and more.'

'As is obvious from your face.' As her friend talked nonstop about her man and the baby they'd made, a mix of happiness for her and an unknown longing for herself rolled through her. 'I am so happy for you. Look at you. You're sparkling.'

'Isn't it great?' Then Carly's perpetual smile dipped. 'How are you now? Completely over that jerk?'

'Have been since the day I caught him out with one of his floozies.' Again, there were things that this close friend didn't have to know. She'd told Raphael in the end, because he was too perceptive for his own good, and she hadn't wanted it hanging between them. Didn't mean Carly needed to learn how stupid she'd been.

'Honestly?'

'Yeah, honestly.'

'Great.' Carly eyeballed her. 'You up for finding another man to have in your life yet? A hot doc, maybe?'

'You're rushing me.' Raphael was as hot as they came. And a doc. Her cup hit the table hard. Can't be. Other women said that about him, not her. Even thinking it was beyond weird.

'I know. I haven't forgotten what it's like to have the man you think you love turn out to be different to your expectations. But I've moved on, and definitely for the better. I only want the same for you.'

'Thanks.' It was a kind thing for Carly to say and it had the longing expanding, had her being truthful. 'Yes, I do eventually want to try again at marriage.' Despite trying to convince herself otherwise. She wanted to fall head over heels in love and not come up for air for a long time. 'This time with someone who doesn't stray.' Raphael would never do that. Gasp. The cup shook when she picked it up again. What was going on? Her head was all over the place. Couldn't blame this on the long-haul flight. She was the problem. Or Raphael.

'How's Raphael? It's cool that you're staying with him.' Then Carly took on a surprised look. 'Raphael's single. You get on brilliantly with him. Now there's a thought. I can see that working.'

'Carly,' Isabella snapped. 'Stop right there. We are

friends,' she ground out, not liking how Carly had come to a similar conclusion she was working her way towards. 'You know, as in talk, and laugh, and do things together, but not have sex or kiss. Or set up house and have babies.' Who was she trying to convince here?

Carly merely laughed. 'You think? He's hot, knows you inside out. Okay, not quite, but that can easily be fixed. Seriously, what's wrong with the idea?'

'Everything.' Nothing. Her fingers trembled, her head spun. No way. This conversation was not happening. 'You're doing what everyone who's just fallen in love does—trying to set up your single friends to have the same experience.'

'Too right. And Raphael's perfect for you. The whole situation's perfect. You're living in his house, spending lots of time with him. Make it happen, Izzy. Can you honestly say you haven't looked at him as other women do and gone, wow, he's gorgeous?'

That *perfect* word again. Better get on the phone to make appointments with the letting agents ASAP. Except when could she find time to go looking when she was starting a new job tomorrow, and needed to see the dressmaker for a fitting for her bridesmaid dress, and still got tired without trying? She refused to think about putting this other aberration to bed. Alone. 'I haven't,' she muttered. It used to be true. Not so long ago in the cafeteria she'd noted how well he filled out his suit. Friends didn't do that. Did they? She hadn't in the past. Damn, this was getting too complicated. So much for relaxing with Carly. Now she was wound up tighter than ever. 'Concentrate on Adem and leave my life to me.'

Carly's reply to that was to laugh.

'Thanks, friend.' After this conversation it was apparent she'd have to be wary about how often she mentioned Raphael. Couldn't have Carly keeping an eye on her and Rafe to see if there was anything growing between them. Oh, damn, he was going to the wedding with her.

The moment Isabella sat down beside Raphael in the pub she'd agreed to meet him at after she'd said goodbye to Carly, any thought of moving vamoosed. Only to return when she realised he was hardly talking. But why rush into any old flat just to put space between them when they got along so well? Except they weren't so easy with each other at the moment. Okay, she'd make time to visit the rental agencies. In the meantime staying with him might fix this strange idea he meant something else to her now from expanding further. They'd inevitably quarrel over the dishes left in the sink or about one of them emptying the milk and not replacing it. That's what flatmates did. It was normal. It would ground her in reality. Or it could grow, expand, take over her common sense.

'Here, you look like you need this.'

She grabbed the wineglass Raphael was holding out to her, took a mouthful. 'Thanks.' The wine was cold, and calming. She took a breath, had another mouthful, felt the tension begin to ebb away. 'I see you're on the lemonade.'

'The joys of being on call.' He settled more comfortably on his stool. A good sign. 'I hear you've agreed to start tomorrow.'

'Jacki talked to me briefly this afternoon—when she wasn't running round like a headless chook. The ward was frantic.'

'Don't call her that to her face, or she'll put you on cleaning bedpans for a week.'

'Not the nurse I saw talking about a woman who'd gone into labour twelve weeks early. She seemed so calm, while a few doors away the woman was crying loud enough to be heard all over the hospital.'

'The baby came in a hell of a hurry and is now in PICU, attached to every monitor ever invented. Joseph Raphael Gleeson. Fitted into my hand like a newborn puppy when I transferred him to the incubator.' Rafe held up his hand. 'Doesn't matter how often I deliver these prem babies, I never get used to that. If all goes well, one day he'll be an adult, working, playing, maybe having his own kids.'

'A puppy? You and your dogs. Better keep *that* to yourself or no one will want you near their babies.' Isabella laughed. Placing her hand on his, she squeezed gently, her eyes watering. 'They named him after you. That's cool. Bet it gave you hiccups when they told you.'

'It did. Apparently Joseph, his grandfather, is thrilled too.' Raphael turned his hand over and wound his fingers between hers.

Oops. Bad move. She carefully extracted her fingers. 'How many Raphaels are out there because of you?'

'Not too many, *merci*. Imagine if I'd been given a really horrible name. There'd be all these poor little blighters cowering at the school gates every day, waiting for the teasing to begin.'

She laughed again, and withdrew her hand. Reluctantly, she realised with a jolt. 'I can't think of any names that bad.' They'd briefly held hands. As in how friends didn't do. More laughter bubbled to the fore. She held it in, afraid Raphael would want to know what was funny. Happiness wasn't funny, and she'd swear she was very happy, happier than she'd been in ages. Did Carly have a point? More to think about. Later. When she was tucked up in bed—on her own. What? As if anyone would be with her. Her gaze flicked to the man sitting with her. This was becoming beyond bizarre. And yet the happiness still bubbled through her.

Raphael was doing that staring into the bottom of his drink trick again. It happened quite a lot. 'I'm attending a conference in Cardiff this weekend. Won't be around to take you shopping.'

'As if I need you for that. I do know my way around. I'm also hoping to look at a couple of flats on Saturday morning. The woman I dealt with from Wellington rang to say she had some places that might work for me.'

That could not be disappointment flickering across his face. 'That's quick.'

'Yes, well, don't want to hang around harassing you for too long. You might regret getting me the job and I need it.'

'Don't go making any decisions that you'll regret later.'

'I'll run everything by you if I find a place I like.'

'Do that.'

'I got a text from Jacki an hour ago, asking if I'd fill in on Saturday night. I said yes.'

'There's no holding you back, is there?' Raphael sipped his drink. 'Let's order. I've got some notes to go over when I get home.'

'For the conference?'

He nodded. 'On Sunday morning, along with the man who still mentors me, I'm speaking about two cases of early menopause we had this year.' A wry smile crossed his mouth. 'Not sure why he wanted me there, since most things that will come out of my mouth came from him in the first place.'

'Is that what you were doing in your office late last night? Working on your talk?' She'd gone downstairs for a glass of water and seen Raphael hunched over his computer, completely focused on the screen. 'You looked like nothing could interrupt you.'

'Obviously you didn't.' He grinned.

'You know me, quiet as a mouse.' Looking around, she noted the place was filling up. 'Want to share a pizza? I don't want to be out late either. Starting a new job in the morning, you know.'

Raphael couldn't forget that if he wanted to. He'd spent the night tossing and turning, thinking about Isabella and their relationship. So much for wishing for her to come to London, and to work with him. He'd got what he'd asked for all right, he groaned as he snapped off the vinyl gloves he wore and dropped them in the theatre's bin.

At 6:10 they'd caught the same train into the hospital, Izzy up early and ready to go long before he'd got his act together. She'd even looked more focused than he'd felt. But the usual evidence of her not getting through the night without going down to the kitchen had been there when he'd finally made it to the coffee machine—all primed and ready to share its life-saving liquid. Maybe she hadn't gone to bed at all.

His work phone buzzed. It was Jacki. Can you look in on Milly Frost sooner than later?

So he wasn't going to avoid seeing Izzy throughout the day. Not that he could avoid going on the ward for eight hours, but thankfully surgery had kept him busy until now. 'So much for lunch,' he muttered as he dried his hands and checked his tie in the mirror.

'Should've studied grass growing if you wanted meals at set hours,' one of the theatre nurses quipped.

'See you back here, hopefully on time,' he threw over his shoulder as he headed out of the theatre suite.

'Isabella noticed the foetal heart rate's stressed,' the head nurse explained when he strode into Milly's room. 'I've checked and agree.'

Jacki would've been keeping a close eye on everything Isabella did today. It was always a strain taking on new staff, no matter how highly recommended they came. Raphael nodded. 'I'll listen to the heartbeat as well.' Three heads were better than one. Finding a smile he turned to his patient. 'Hello, Milly. Aaron.' He nodded at the woman's husband. 'I understand your labour is going well, but baby might be distressed. I'm going to listen to the heart and watch the screen here to get a clear picture of what's happening.' If Isabella and Jacki were correct, he and Milly would be going to Theatre shortly, and as those two nurses were good at what they did, and wouldn't have made a mistake, he had an unexpected operation ahead of him. Nothing unusual in that, just meant he'd be later getting home. Again, nothing unusual, but for the first time in years, he regretted it.

Thought you were wanting time away from Izzy?

Face it. He didn't have a clue what he wanted.

'Is Evie going to be all right?' Fear darkened Milly's eyes as she scrabbled around for Aaron's hand.

Milly's question put him back on track. 'Let's see what's happening before I answer that.'

On the other side of the bed Isabella was lifting back

the sheet in preparation to pull Milly's gown up and expose her baby tummy. Then, 'Another contraction, Milly?' As their patient rocked forward, pain marring her face and tightening her grip on her husband's hand, Isabella rubbed her back and waited for the spasm to pass.

Raphael also waited, watching the screen on the foetal heart rate monitor. Thankfully baby's heart rate did not slow any further during the contraction so no recovery afterwards, but it was already too slow and the contraction had done nothing to alter what was going on with baby. Next he listened through his stethoscope. 'Has baby been moving as much as usual?'

'Not for the last little while,' Milly cried. 'I didn't say anything. I thought he was resting. We've been going at this for a few hours now. It's all my fault.'

'It's nobody's fault.' Had there been any indicators he should've seen earlier? Before labour started? No. He knew there weren't, and playing the blame game did no one any favours. 'I see Isabella's noted he slowed down very recently.' He straightened up and delivered the news Milly and Aaron would not want to hear. Even though saving their daughter's life was the priority this wasn't how they'd planned on welcoming their baby into the world. 'I'm going to do a C-section. Baby's distressed and it isn't safe to leave her in there.'

'Is Evie going to be all right?' Milly repeated, this time with fear echoing around the room.

'Is our daughter in danger?' Aaron shouted.

This never got any easier. 'Surgery is the safest option. There's some risk of meconium being in the amniotic fluid. I don't want her breathing that in, so urgency is required. Isabella will prepare you to go down to Theatre, while I go organise the emergency team and scrub up, Milly.' He paused for a moment, fully expecting a load of questions, but the parents were both stunned—gripping their joined hands and staring at each other in raw silence. 'Isabella—' he nodded '—stay with Milly and Aaron until they go into Theatre.' Then he was striding away, talking on his phone to the head theatre nurse. 'My next procedure has changed. Urgent C-section to save full-term baby.'

'Do you want to cancel any surgery on this afternoon's list?' Kelly was very matter of fact. No wasting time on trivia.

'Not at this point. Let's see how we go.' Which meant he'd do all the listed procedures. Cancelling an operation was hard on patients when they were mentally prepared to go under the knife. He reached the scrub room and began preparing, his mind busy with every step of the procedure he'd done innumerable times. Milly and Aaron's daughter was going to get every chance on offer and more.

Evie Frost was delivered within minutes of Milly reaching Theatre. Raphael checked her breathing for abnormalities, and gave the mother a smile. 'All good. No meconium in her lungs.' Relief thumped behind his ribs. 'Evie's heart rate's normal for all she's been through.' He watched as a nurse handed Milly her daughter, and felt the familiar lump of awe build in his throat. New parenthood was wonderful, special. There weren't enough words to describe the amazement covering mums' and dads' faces when they met their child for the first time. Aaron was looking gobsmacked. Love spilled out of his gaze as he stared at his wife and daughter.

Raphael moved away. Despite how often he'd witnessed that scene it never grew stale. The awe he'd known the day Pierre slid into his shaking hands had never left him. That tiny boy had grown into a wonderful, strong lad with a great enthusiasm for life and an abundance of confidence. Raphael felt proud for being a part of his arrival, although he'd actually done little more than make his cousin comfortable and catch Pierre as he shot out into the world.

'Well done.' Kelly walked alongside him.

'Thanks. He's a little beauty.' He'd done a good job for baby and parents. Then the usual flip side of the euphoria hit. Anger filled him. What about *his* baby? What had he looked like? Who did he follow? Blond or dark? Short or tall? Cassie had refused to tell him anything, saying it was best he didn't know. Best for who? She'd never answered that question. He spun away, headed for the lift. He needed air and no friendly faces while he swallowed this particular pill yet again.

Then he'd return to Theatre and lose himself in work.

When Raphael called in on Milly after his last operation for the day Isabella was there. 'Evie's so cute. But then I say that about them all.' She'd been keeping a close eye on mum and baby all afternoon.

Now she and Raphael moved out of the little room to stand in the corridor. 'You ever think about having your own brood?' It was one thing Izzy had never talked about. Probably because it hadn't been an issue until she'd married Darren and then he hadn't wanted to hear her say yes. As for him, yes, he'd wanted children. Still did, but... Joshua, his little boy he'd never met... How did he cope with getting someone pregnant and waiting out the nine months until he got to hold his child? He was watching Izzy, wondering what she would say even as he dealt with his own pain.

She blinked, appeared to think about it. 'I've always presumed I would one day, and thought it would come about when I married. Now, I can't say I've been planning on it happening any time soon, if at all. It's filed with other things I hope to get to do some time, and when I do, be grateful if all goes according to plan.'

In this job they saw enough times when people's dreams of having a family went horribly wrong to know there were no guarantees. But was she referring to that, or her expectations for her future? Not asking. Not here anyway. 'What will be, will be,' he quoted.

Isabella nodded. 'Everyone thinks it's a given we'll get pregnant when we want to, but working in this job I've learnt how wrong that assumption can be.' Then she shrugged and perked up. 'We're being glum when there's a very lucky little girl in there with two of the happiest people in the world.'

'True. Weren't you meant to knock off an hour ago?' He still had patients to see, but surgery was finished, and suddenly he was exhausted. That often happened after a big day in Theatre and on the ward. Especially after a sleepless night. Add in the confusion Izzy was causing him and he was screwed. 'Feel like picking up some Italian on the way home? I'll be at least another hour.'

'I'll get the take-out and see you at home.'

At home. A soft sigh escaped.

If only you knew, Isabella Nicholson.

Putting his hand in his pocket for his wallet, he smiled when she shook her head.

'My shout.'

'Fair enough.' He knew better than to argue. He wouldn't win. 'See you later.' The sooner he checked on his patients, the sooner he could go home. Home. The connotations of that word had never been so huge. So frightening. Yet the need to settle grew the more time he spent with Isabella. She wasn't the only one wanting to find that special place in life. At least she'd made a start at getting on with it. Wouldn't it be great if he and Izzy could get what they wanted—together?

Stop right there. She's been hurt once. You can't risk putting her through that again.

No, he couldn't. It was his role as a friend to keep her safe, which meant putting some barriers up between them.

CHAPTER SIX

'THANK GOODNESS FOR FRIDAYS.' Isabella slammed the front door shut and stared along the hallway.

'You didn't even do a full week,' Raphael called from the kitchen at the far end. 'Come on. I've been waiting for you to get home so we can have a drink.'

'Good idea.' She was entitled to one after the hectic few days she'd spent on the ward.

'Dinner's not far off.' Raphael's glass of red wine with dinner was a nightly ritual. Another French habit he'd picked up from his family back in Avignon.

At the door into the kitchen she paused, gazed at Rafe as he stirred a sauce in a pot while at the same time squeezing garlic into it. She hadn't seen him so relaxed. It suited him. 'That smells divine.' Beat take-out any night of the week.

'Boeuf Bordelaise.'

'Yum.' So was the sight before her. 'What happened to heading to Cardiff today? Isn't that why you took the afternoon off?'

His shrug was a little stiff. Not so relaxed now she was here? 'No rush. The conference proper doesn't start till nine tomorrow. I'll head away first in the morning. Won't miss much if I'm a bit late.'

Warmth filled her. It wouldn't be a night alone after all. 'Cool. I'll get changed.' That wine was sounding better and better. She'd spent an hour with Carly, discussing the wedding, and love. She'd mostly listened, trying to ignore the flare of sadness that she wouldn't be walking down another aisle any time soon. There'd also been her selfish wish that Carly didn't have a man to rush home to, could go out on the town with her. But deep down, she was more than happy for her friend, and got over her funk quickly.

Up three stairs and she hesitated. Again it felt as though the ceiling was coming down on top of her and the walls crowding in. 'That colour has got to go.' Or she was more tired than she'd realised. She headed upward again, in a hurry to get away from the darkness.

'Izzy?' Raphael had come along the hall and was looking up at her. 'What are you on about?'

'That magenta is hideous. It's so dark and brooding, makes the hall seem smaller than it really is.' Not even the cream paint of the stair rails softened the atmosphere, instead accentuated all that was wrong with the paintwork.

He shrugged. 'Like I said the other day, changing it is on the list. I just don't happen to have forty-eight hours in every day.'

'When you've poured that wine can you get out the colour schemes you said came with the place?' Not waiting for an answer, she continued upstairs.

'Oui, madame.'

They'd never got around to the French week, but it didn't really matter since they flipped from English to French and back again all the time.

Pausing, she looked back down at Raphael. 'I have

more free time than you, and I like redecorating.' She could help until she moved. When she found some free time that was. 'I'll wow you with my skills.'

'Oh, no. You are not going to paint my hallway.'

'Why not? It's not like I haven't done this sort of thing before.' Being useful, instead of feeling a bit redundant, might help her sleep at night, too. 'Find those charts.'

His mouth twitched. 'You know how to make a man feel guilty.'

He had to be pulling her leg. He'd be more than happy to have the *problem* taken out of his hands, and having her do that shouldn't be getting him in a twist. 'You can't come up with a reason for me not to do it, can you?' Fist pumping the air, she grinned. 'Love it when I win.'

Raphael shook his head at her before heading back down the hall.

There was a small pile of charts on the table when she returned showered and in clean clothes. 'What are these?' she asked, tapping some pages of notes.

'The interior design suggestions that came with the house. Like I said, I'm not the only one who hasn't got around to doing up this place.'

'It's not everyone's idea of fun,' she conceded, flicking through the pages and pausing at a design for a new kitchen layout. 'Wow, I like this.' Glancing around the kitchen, she nodded. 'Lighter for one. Far more functional for another. And modern.'

'That's not hard to achieve when you think how old this must be.' Raphael was also staring around, looking as though he'd never really seen it before. 'I wonder if the design company's still got the in-depth plans?'

Excitement was beginning to crowd his gaze. 'They're based on the other side of Richmond.'

'Only one way to find out,' she drawled.

He grinned and pushed her glass in front of her. 'Drink up and stop being annoying.'

'Why is wanting to help being annoying?' The wine was delicious, a perfect end to a busy day.

Ignoring her question, he went with some of his own. 'How do you feel after your first week on the maternity ward? Glad you joined us?' He gave the sauce a stir before leaning against the counter and stretching his legs before him. Legs that went on for ever.

Gulp. He'd always had those legs. Why were they any different tonight? Another gulp of wine. What was the question? Oh, right. 'I'm loving it. And yes, I believe it was the right move. Though only time will really be the judge of that.' Following his example, she perched on another chair and reached for the colour charts, noting the ones that had been circled with a marker pen.

'I'll add my bit to making it happen.'

'Tell me something I don't know. You'll be a dog with a bone.' Looking around she spied Chienne on her cushion. 'Sorry, not trying to insult you, Cat. You're too good for bones.' The cat was getting to her, making her feel more and more at ease. But then she did like to share the bed in the darkest hours of the night, or curl up on her lap when she came downstairs for a glass of water and some upright time in an attempt to get into a fall-asleep zone.

'Don't listen to her, Chienne. Izzy likes to con everyone round to her way of thinking.'

'Why not if it gets me what I want?' She grinned. Then focused on the colours that had been circled with a marker pen, rather than stare at those thighs filling his black jeans. 'Who suggested these colours?' They weren't bad. The colours? Or the thighs? She could live with them. Both of them. Gulp. Nice wine. Hope there was more in that bottle for after dinner.

'Believe it or not, in the first months when I was fired up to get on with fixing the place up I visited the paint shop and the woman I spoke to was very helpful with suggestions. Said these were the latest in colour schemes and if I want to sell the place would appeal to more buyers.'

'You're thinking of moving? Already?' First she'd heard of it. She didn't like it. She was getting used to Raphael being here and had hoped they'd live in the same vicinity long term. Was he really considering moving again? Of course she'd known he would eventually return to Avignon. That's why. He'd always felt a pull towards his family and hometown. As she had with Wellington. Look where that got her. It hadn't been Wellington at fault, more her and the man she'd returned there with. Whereas Avignon might very well be the best thing for Raphael. Her heart stuttered. Didn't she want him to be happy? Deep, deep breath. Yes, she did. More than anything. More than her own happiness. Truly? A sip of wine. Truly.

'Can't guarantee anything's for ever. But I'm here for the foreseeable future at least.' He spaced the words, loud and clear, as though it was important she believed him.

The relief was strong. 'Glad to hear it.'

'What are you looking for in a flat?' He sipped his drink as he waited for her reply.

'Two bedrooms, though I guess one would suffice.

Located near a train station, of course, and close to shops and food outlets.'

'Sounds ordinary.'

'I guess it is, but ordinary's fine for now.'

'As long as it doesn't bore you, Izzy.'

'I'm not about to dash away again. This is a permanent move. I'm determined to keep it that way.'

Raphael went back to stirring his sauce. 'You ever feel it's not working out please tell me.'

'Why?' The word shot out of her mouth.

Tipping his head back, he stared up at the ceiling.

And she waited, sensing if she uttered one word he'd not answer her.

Finally his head dropped forward, and he took a small mouthful of his merlot. 'I like having you back in London.'

So? She liked being here. But was that what this was about? She waited, breath caught in her throat.

His words were measured as he continued. 'I've lived here for two years, and when I say lived I mean I've come and gone, and not really noticed the place. It is four walls and shelter, comfortable in a less than desirable way. It's a house, not a home.'

What did that have to do with her?

'Since you arrived, it already feels different, more like the home I intended making it. *My* home. I think about coming back at the end of the day now, not just going somewhere to eat, shower, study and sleep.' He stopped.

What to say to that? Her mouth had dried, and there didn't seem to be any answers forthcoming to what Raphael had just said. Inside, that feeling of finally getting her life right expanded a wee bit more. They did fit well together, but how well? Were they becoming more than friends? Was that even wise given there'd been no attraction in the past? Could people suddenly want someone physically after spending most of their lives not noticing each other that way? 'I'm glad you're finally enjoying your home.'

Crass, Izzy, crass.

Totally. But she couldn't tell him what she'd been thinking. For one, she hadn't been here very long, and secondly, she had to haul on the brakes. She wasn't reliable in relationships, and Raphael was vulnerable after how Cassie dumped him.

'I've surprised you.' Raphael was studying her.

What was that about? 'A little.' It would be a relief to tell him how she felt, but then there'd be a whole other can of worms to deal with. Best shut up. She began flicking through paint charts, the colours one big blur as thoughts of holding Raphael, of kissing him, being kissed back, rose and heated her before she could squash them back in place.

At five next morning, fifteen minutes before the alarm was due to go off, Raphael dragged himself out of bed and into the shower, then stared at his puffy face in the mirror as he shaved.

'Don't lose any sleep over where I'll find a place to live,' Izzy had said over their beef dinner. How prophetic.

She'd blighted his night with thoughts of what it might be like if she didn't find a flat, and instead stayed on with him, moved down to the second floor and his bedroom. Of course none of that had been suggested, but he hadn't been able to think of anything else as he'd watched her swing her small but shapely legs while she sat on the stool. The relief had been immense when he'd put dinner on the table and she'd had to shift. But then he'd been subjected to seeing her fork food through those full lips, and conjuring up thoughts of her mouth on his skin.

The razor slipped. He swore. Dabbed the blood away. 'Concentrate, man.' Hell, now she had him talking to himself like some brain-dead moron on P.

It was far easier to blame Isabella than take a long, serious look at himself. If he did that, he'd have to admit he was floundering here, and hell, he didn't usually get into a quagmire over his own emotions when it came to women. Only Cassie had done that to him. Until now. Now Izzy was having a damned good go at tipping him upside down. At least she was on the good side of the barometer, not like the hellhole Cassie had shoved him into. But then it was not as though he was falling hard for Izzy like he had for Cassie. If anything he was getting there slowly, carefully, and with a whole heap of concerns to deal with.

Focusing entirely on removing the last of the growth on his face, he managed to quieten his thumping chest for a few minutes. No more nicks on his skin. Yet the moment he rinsed the shaver the thumping started up again. This strange sensation Izzy brought on threw him whenever he wasn't totally engrossed in work or study or any other blasted thing that didn't start with *I*. He couldn't go on ignoring his feelings for her. Nor could he do a thing about it until he returned from Cardiff. Taking a mug of coffee up to her room and saying, 'Oh, by the way, I think I might want to spend the rest of my life with you. Can't talk now. Lots to sort out first. See you tomorrow night,' wouldn't win him any favours. Not that he had worked out how to approach this yet, only understood the time was coming when he'd not be able to stay uninvolved. All he knew was if Izzy laughed at him, he'd die inside.

Now his alarm woke him up. As in out of his stupor and into getting ready for the trip to Wales. Swiping the screen of his phone to shut the infernal noise off, he tossed it into his overnight bag along with his shaving gear, and got dressed in his latest swanky suit and tie. Bag zipped shut, he headed downstairs for a quick coffee and toast before hitting the road. He was early due to that lack of sleep, but hopefully that meant the roads would have less traffic to contend with.

'Hey, coffee's ready and waiting. I put it on when I heard you moving around up there.' Izzy sat at the round table at the edge of the kitchen, a mug in one hand, and Chienne on her lap schmoozing against her other hand.

'Morning.' He hadn't smelt a thing. Too distracted. Then, 'Cheeky.' He nodded at the cat. 'You'll do anything to get attention.' He wouldn't ogle Isabella in her sleeveless top with no bra underneath. Was that a pyjama top? Guess so, if the matching loose shorts Chienne was stretched across were an indicator. So she—Izzy, not Chienne—still wore shapeless PJs. Or had she reverted to them once Darren had left the scene? He'd seen enough on washing lines throughout their lives to know she'd never been one for matching bras and knickers, let alone fancy lingerie of any kind, but who knew what being in a relationship might've done for her? Turning away, his mind filled with an image of her in black sexy lingerie. And he swore.

'Pardon?'

Did he say that out loud? Sloshing coffee into the mug waiting by the coffee machine, he drew a slow breath and looked over his shoulder. 'Sorry. I spilled coffee, that's all.' Grabbing a cloth he made a show of wiping down the bench, which was coffee-free. If this was what not sleeping did to him, then how did Izzy manage day to day on the little she got?

'I take it you didn't sleep again? Perhaps you should stop drinking coffee.'

'One step ahead of you.' She waved her mug at him. 'This is tea. Not that I'm giving up entirely on my caffeine fix.'

Then he noticed the paint charts once again spread over the table. Showed how much attention he'd been paying to Izzy and her PJs if he hadn't seen those. 'You are serious about getting the decorating under way, aren't you?'

A rare worry flickered through her eyes. 'Does that bother you?'

He shook his head. 'Not at all. I should've known you'd get stuck into sorting my mess out.' It was what she'd always done. Only difference was this was a large, hands-on job, not like making sure the rowdy guys in the room next door at university stopped banging on his door in the middle of the night when he was trying to study.

Her shoulders softened, and Chienne got another stroke. Lucky cat. 'It's okay. You'll recognise the house when you return tomorrow night. I've got too much else on today.'

'Thank goodness for that,' he retorted. 'Can't have you taking over completely.' The coffee was blistering hot and he needed to be on the road. 'I'll put this in a travel mug. Got to go.'

'Fine.' Izzy sipped her tea. When her tongue did a lap of her lips the thumping started up in his chest again, only harder and faster.

Just as well he was going away.

Except as Raphael and his colleague, Jeremy, stood on-stage receiving a hearty round of applause at the end of their talk on Sunday, he knew he wasn't hanging around for the afternoon's workshops. 'I'm out of here,' he muttered in an aside.

'I'm not surprised. You've been miles away since you got here. Except during our talk,' Jeremy added hastily.

'It's a miracle I managed to get through that without making stuff up.' Though he had concentrated hard, determined Isabella wasn't going to wreck everything about this weekend. He missed her. Had done from the moment he'd backed out onto the road in Richmond yesterday morning. It had taken strength not to text to see what she was up to. He just wanted to be with her, even when that twisted his gut and tightened muscles best ignored. Sure, he wouldn't be able to do what he really wanted to—kiss those tantalising lips and hold that soft, curvy body against him—but he could give her cheek and laugh, and make her a mug of tea.

'What's playing on your mind?' Jeremy asked as they stepped offstage.

'Nothing to do with work,' Raphael was quick to reassure his mentor.

'I didn't think so.'

Right. Now what? He hated lying to anyone, and particularly to this man who'd been nothing but kind and helpful to him from the day they met in the gynaecology department when he'd come on board as the newest specialist. 'Just some personal stuff.' Hopefully Jeremy would get the hint and drop the subject. Not that he'd ever done that if he really felt it important to get to the bottom of something. The man could be a hound when he put his mind to it.

'Woman trouble?'

Got that right. Now what? He wasn't talking about Izzy to anyone. He tried to laugh it off. 'Isn't it always about women?'

'Not with you, my friend. You make sure of that; no repercussions when a fling is over. Everyone comes out smiling. Even you.'

Yes, and could be that was the problem. He had got not getting involved down to a fine art. *Magnifique.* He was getting nowhere fast. Try the truth line again, diluted, of course.

'My close friend Isabella is staying with me at the moment.'

'And you want to get home to spend time with her. Why didn't you say so?' Then Jeremy's eyes widened. 'Oh, oh. I sense trouble.' He tapped Raphael's chest. 'In there.'

'Stick with gynaecology, will you? You're better at it.'

Jeremy didn't laugh. Not even a glimmer of amusement showed in his face. 'This Isabella, I've met her on the ward. She's a very competent midwife. So she's special? You've known her a long time?'

'Since I was an incompetent teen.'

'And now you're not incompetent. Nor do you want to remain just friends.'

Mon amie. Izzy. Special. More than a friend.

Jeremy gripped his arm. 'What are you going to miss by not being here for the rest of the day? Nothing you don't already know. It's time you put your personal life before your career. You need a balanced life, Raphael, one where you have someone to go home with at the end of the day.'

'Don't I know it.' Yet it was a new idea, one that began filling him with hope from the day he'd picked Izzy up at the airport. No, not new, because two years ago he'd seen what he wanted and had had to bury the longing, to focus on the other thing necessary to him— work. Not Isabella. 'Thanks, Jeremy. I'm out of here.'

Not that he was heading home to spill his heart. No way. There was a lot to work through before he was even close to admitting his love. Time spent with Izzy, laughing and talking, or more likely arguing over next to nothing, was always time well spent. Hopefully he'd be relaxed and she wouldn't pick up on these new feelings because he had to get them under control and back in the box.

The house was locked up when he arrived home. Inside, as he walked along the hall, he called out, 'Izzy? You about?'

Silence greeted him.

The vacuum cleaner stood against the wall, still plugged in, as if Isabella had been interrupted, and fully expected to come back to the job she'd started.

There was no note on the table explaining where she was. Nor on his phone. Not that there should be. She wouldn't have been expecting him home this early, but still. The anticipation that had been growing as he'd negotiated highways and roads filled with weekenders with nothing better to do than get in the way evaporated, leaving him feeling like an idiot. Of course Izzy would be out doing her thing, hadn't been sitting here pining the hours away. Why would she?

He'd text and see where she was. Might go join her for a drink or some shopping or whatever took her fancy. It was yesterday she'd gone to look at flats. Had she found one she liked and gone back for a second look? That could mean she'd be out of here soon and he could get back to his quiet life—which he didn't want any more. Truly? Yes. Didn't mean he knew what he was going to do about it though.

Raphael sighed, then reverted to normal and went in to the Queen Victoria to see how his patients were faring.

'I'll get you a new tumbler,' Isabella told Brooke. 'It's not a problem.' Her patient was stressing out over every little thing as the contractions got harder and closer together.

'You're so calm, it's annoying,' Brooke growled through gritted teeth.

Isabella chuckled. 'You're not the first to complain about that.'

'Wait until you have a baby and then see how composed you are.' The woman blinked. 'Or have you had children of your own?'

'Not yet.'

Not yet? Like there was a possibility in the near future? Raphael flashed across her mind. As he'd been doing all weekend. No wonder she'd agreed immediately when asked to come in and work the afternoon after one of the nurses had gone off with a stomach bug.

But Raphael and babies and her? All in the one sentence? As if that was happening. Although they were getting on in a closer way than ever before, and she had no idea where that was leading, there was always an air of uncertainty between them. Besides, her dream of babies with Darren had been stolen from her. She wasn't ready to be that vulnerable again.

'Got to get a man first,' she told Brooke.

But not before I get that tumbler.

Heading for the water dispenser and the stack of plastic mugs, she glanced at her watch. Less than an hour to go. It had been a frantic few hours, babies arriving in all directions.

Raphael had been quiet. No texts asking what she was doing, or telling her how the conference was going. He'd have finished his talk hours ago, could possibly be on the road by now. Wonder what he'd like for dinner?

After giving Brooke her water and checking how baby was doing, Isabella went to see Caitlin Simons, who had delivered an hour ago. Since the door was open she popped her head around the corner of Caitlin's room to make sure she wasn't interrupting anything, and stopped, a gasp whispering across her lips.

Raphael was sitting awkwardly on a narrow chair. Baby Simons swathed in light blankets was cradled in his arms. The usual look of relief was in his gaze as he looked down at the boy, but there was something else too. Something like—pain? But it couldn't be. What was there to be sad about here?

A sharp pain stabbed her chest. A lump blocked her throat. Breathing became difficult. Rafe would make a wonderful father. Despite that intense look there was something so tender about him that blindsided her. Shook her to the core.

She could never imagine Darren like this.

She stared at the beautiful man holding the tiny baby, and the floor moved beneath her feet. The air thickened, breathing became impossible.

This was Rafe, the man she'd known for so long. This was Raphael, a man she'd begun falling in love with. She couldn't do a thing about that because she wasn't settled, could not risk hurting him. Raphael was polar opposite to her ex. How could she have thought she loved Darren? This feeling she'd been denying since arriving in London was so different to anything she'd felt for him. Strong and soft, caring and gentle, hungry and fulfilling.

Isabella closed her eyes, counted to ten, opened them. Her eyes filled with tears. She and Raphael made great friends. What would they be like as lovers? He deserved someone who would stick by him through thick and thin, and she couldn't guarantee that was her, no matter how hard she was trying to settle here. The picture before her would've been perfect if that was their child. As she swiped at her cheeks her heart crashed against her ribs. Now what? How could she return to his house tonight as if nothing had changed? She had to get away. Turning around she froze when Raphael called out.

'Hey, Izzy, come and meet Fleur.' Raphael's eyes locked with hers, nailing her to the spot.

She took an unsteady step, then another, and another, until at last she stood before him and looked down, down at the baby but mostly at Raphael. Saw him as the man she wanted to spend her life with.

'Want a hold?' He lifted the child towards her.

'I've already had a hold.' She took a step back, afraid she'd drop Fleur. Which was plain stupid, considering how many babies she'd held during her career.

'Have another.'

'Okay,' she whispered.

'Come on. She's so cute.' Raphael stood up, held out the precious bundle.

Taking the baby, she stared down at the wrinkly, pink face of the girl she'd help deliver earlier, and who now opened her eyes wide. 'Hello, Fleur.' Then she couldn't say another word, fear of telling Raphael about the mass of emotions tying her in knots.

'Izzy?'

'Isabella, Brooke's asking for you,' Claudia called across the room. 'I don't think we've long to go now.'

'On my way.' Gently placing Fleur back in her bed, she turned to Caitlin. 'She's gorgeous. Well done, you. Anything I can get you?'

'My mum. She's gone for a coffee, and I need her here.' Caitlin was a solo mum, the father having done a bunk when he learned about the pregnancy.

'Not a problem. I'll dash down to the cafeteria right now.' Phew. That'd give her some space from Raphael. 'Make that after I've checked on my other patient.'

'I'll go see Mrs Johnson, Izzy,' Raphael said.

So much for getting away from him while she cleared her head. But what could she say? She might be one of the midwives on the case, but doctors came first. Always. Glancing across at him, she saw he was looking more like his normal self, the longing and awe now under control. 'Fine.'

'How long have you been on shift?' he asked as he made for the door.

'Started around lunchtime, and should be finished shortly.' Not regular shift hours but who cared? If she was needed here, then that was fine by her. Ignoring any further questions Raphael might come up with, she said to Caitlin, 'Fleur's lovely. Thank you for letting me hold her.' Then she shot away to find Mrs Simons, who'd hopefully put a smile back on her daughter's face. It was hard for the women who had to go through labour without their soul mate. A friend or family member was well and good, but not the same thing as a doting husband or partner.

'Isabella, wait.' Raphael was right behind her. 'Are you all right?'

'Yes,' she muttered. 'I got side tracked in there when I should've been with Brooke.' Not that she'd done anything wrong. Brooke had not been ready to give birth when she left the room.

'You find a flat?'

'Yes.' Her mouth was dry, her hands damp. Snatching a plastic cup at the water dispenser she filled it and turned to head for the lift only to come to an abrupt stop in front of Raphael. She couldn't read his expression at all. 'You came back early from Cardiff.'

'I'd had enough of being squashed into the hotel conference room.' His reply was terse.

'Thought you were meant to be getting a life outside these walls.' And who dropped the housework to come in here when Jacki called to say she was desperate for staff for the rest of the day shift? Who hadn't gone home when the next shift arrived?

'I won't hang around after I've seen Brooke. But

first, are you sure you're okay? You looked a tad pale, and are as jumpy as a frog on steroids.' Nothing but concern radiated out of those blue eyes.

Damn it. Think of something to say that'll keep him happy. Think, girl. 'Just didn't expect to see you holding Fleur like you never wanted to let her go, that's all.' Wrong. All wrong, and she couldn't take back a single word.

'What?' Raphael glanced at her. 'Never.'

Shrugging aside her mood, she asked lightly, 'Never want your own family? Or never like that with anyone else's child?'

'You know the answer to both those questions. Or I thought you did.'

She nodded. 'I suppose I do. Lack of sleep catching up.'

'I saw the crossword on the kitchen bench when I got in. How many hours did you get last night?' The concern had returned, but this time annoyance was in the mix.

And she owed him an apology. 'Actually, I did sleep quite well for me, and the crossword was breakfast entertainment.' Not saying she'd started it at three in the morning. 'Now, I'd better get cracking. It's busy in here.' She nudged past him, striding down the hall to the room she was needed in.

'For the record, in case you've forgotten, I do want children of my own with a woman whom I love, and no, I don't get all possessive over someone else's baby.' Raphael was right beside her, his mouth grim. This conversation wasn't over. It was going to be a barrel of laughs at home tonight.

Maybe she'd go to visit Carly. Except she and Adem

weren't going to be home tonight. Something about having a meal with family members. All part of the wedding build-up. Lucky girl. Isabella took a sideways look at the man who had her heart in a flutter. What was it like to be planning a wedding with the man of your dreams? Not once had the small celebration she and Darren had turned her heart into an out of control bongo drum. The planning had taken a few hours on the phone, and the dress had been in a sale in the local shop.

Damn it, Isabella, why did you not see how wrong that was at the time?

Because she'd been so desperate to have the life she'd been promised she hadn't seen past the hype. And if she had? Would she be feeling differently about Raphael now? No answer dropped into her head, nothing stopped the tailspin she was in.

Raphael tapped her on the shoulder. 'I'll wait and give you a lift when you're done.'

'That's not necessary.'

'Maybe, but I'll wait anyway.'

CHAPTER SEVEN

'RAPHAEL, CAN YOU take a look at Janice Crowe?' Jacki asked as he left his patient's room. 'Baby's breeched.'

There went any chance of snatching a coffee. 'Room?'

'Three. Janice is eighteen, hasn't been to antenatal classes or seen a doctor for three months.'

So she'd be terrified and blaming everyone else. Raphael sighed. Young women without family support always had a hard time of their pregnancies. 'Bloods?'

'Haemoglobin eighty-six, MCV and MCH indicate iron deficiency. Still waiting for the results on the blood group, iron and liver functions.'

He raised his eyebrow. 'Drugs?'

Jacki shook her head. 'There's a distinct yellow tinge to her skin and eyes.'

Inside room three Isabella was trying to calm the distraught girl. 'Janice, breathe deep. That's it. Keep at it, and you'll help baby.' She glanced up and relief flooded her face when she saw him. 'Here's Mr Dubois, the obstetrician. He's going to help you and baby.'

'Hello, Janice. Call me Raphael,' he said in an attempt to put her at ease. He had her notes in his hand but didn't look at them, instead kept eye contact with his patient. 'I hear your baby's turned the wrong way round.'

Janice nodded, her teeth biting deep into her bottom lip.

Izzy held her hand.

'I have to examine you. Is that all right?' It'd be a problem if she refused as there weren't any female doctors on duty today. 'Or would you prefer Isabella does it? Though I do like to see what's going on myself.'

Janice's mouth flattened, and she stared at him.

He held his breath as he waited for her approval. It went better when the patient was on the same page. This baby was going to be all right. It had to be.

'Okay.'

'Good.' Slipping gloves on, he watched as Izzy talked Janice into lying back and bending her legs, placing her feet apart.

'Now, I am going to lift the sheet up to your waist. At least the room is nice and warm.' She was good with the terrified girl. 'Hold on. That's another contraction, right?' Izzy immediately went to hold Janice's hands until it passed. 'Breathe. You're doing great. That's it.'

Tears spilled down Janice's face. 'It hurts so much.'

'Yes, but the painkiller should be working by now. You need to relax.' Izzy smiled. 'I know. Stupid thing to say, right? But believe me, if you can relax a bit the pain drug will work better. Now, lie back and let Raphael see what baby's up to.'

Raphael positioned himself for the examination. 'Do you know if you're having a boy or girl, Janice?' Chances were she hadn't had a scan, but keeping her talking would make what he was about to do go easier.

'No. When I had my scan it was too early to find out. I want a boy though.'

'Why a boy?' Isabella kept the conversation going, while ready to pass him anything he might require.

Janice shrugged. 'They seem easier.'

Raphael laughed. 'You think? My mother wouldn't agree with you.' His hand felt the baby. Definitely breech, and there was the umbilical cord below the presenting part of baby. His laugh snapped off. They had a problem. This had become urgent. Drawing a breath, he prepared to tell his patient what the next move was. 'Janice, baby is trying to come out feet first and that doesn't work. There's also a complication with the cord being flattened by baby so not enough blood is getting through. Do you understand?'

'I think so. Is my baby going to die?'

'No. I am going to do a C-section. Urgently.'

'You're going to cut it out?'

That was putting it bluntly. 'Yes, I am. It's best for baby, and for you. It doesn't take very long, and means no more contractions. You'll be sore for some days afterwards and need help with baby, but someone will talk to you about that later.'

Izzy pulled down the sheet to cover Janice. 'You're being very brave.'

'Can you stay with me when he takes the baby out?'

Izzy looked at Raphael, one perfectly shaped eyebrow lifted.

'As long as Jacki doesn't mind losing you for a while, it's fine with me.' He had to have a nurse there anyway, and why not Izzy? He liked working with her. 'Right, I'll get the ball rolling.'

'I'll get Janice ready.' Her smile warmed him right to his toes.

There were no hiccups with the C-section. The baby girl was healthy and Janice seemed to have forgotten she wanted a boy as she gazed down at her precious bundle.

Raphael felt the tension between his shoulder blades back off as he accepted that another baby had made its way into the world and was going to be all right. There were a lot of hurdles ahead for Janice and her daughter, but he'd done his bit for them and got it right.

He and Izzy. He watched as she tended to Janice, getting her a drink of water, wiping her face, constantly keeping an eye on the baby, showing Janice how to hold her, to rub her. Oh, yes, Izzy was good at this.

His mouth dried and his heart thumped. What was he going to do?

Just after midnight on Wednesday Isabella lifted the ward phone and speed-dialled Raphael. 'You're needed. Tania Newman's showing signs of puerperal sepsis.'

'I'm putting you on speaker phone so you can fill me in on the details while I dress.'

That she did not need to think about. 'Heart and resp rates are high, BP's down, and she's running a temperature. White count an hour ago was slightly elevated but no indicators of infection.'

'Any abdo pain that's nothing to do with contractions?'

'Yes, and she's started vomiting.'

'I'm heading out the door now. Take another blood for CBC, mark it urgent,' Raphael told her. 'Always happens at night time, doesn't it?' Click. He was gone.

Had he really had time to haul on some pants and a

shirt? Guess he was used to dressing in seconds. There was always a pile of clothes on his dresser, no doubt just for moments like this. Isabella rushed back to Tania's room with the phlebotomy kit in her hand. 'Mr Dubois's on his way. He wants another blood test done.'

Katie, the nurse on with her, nodded. 'You take the sample while I wipe Tania down again.'

Isabella set the kit on the bed beside the terrified woman. 'Tania, I know you don't like needles but this is really important.'

'Do whatever you have to,' the thirty-four-year-old woman grunted through her pain. 'Just save my baby.'

'We're doing everything we can, and like I said, Raphael is on his way. Pushing his speed to the limit, I bet.'

'Hope he's careful. We need him here,' Dominic Newman said as he held his wife's hand, looking lost and nothing like the notorious criminal lawyer he was. Babies were great levellers. 'What can I do? There's got to be something other than sitting here like a useless lump.'

'You're on keeping Tania calm duty.' It was a big ask. The woman was frantic with worry and fear.

'I read about puerperal sepsis on a website,' Tania cried. 'It's bad. Really bad. Baby might not make it.'

True, sepsis at this stage of pregnancy was not good. 'Sometimes I wish the internet had never been invented.' Isabella slid the tourniquet up Tania's arm. 'Tighten your hand into a fist. That's it. Now, a small prick.' She hit the vein immediately and released the tourniquet as the tube filled.

'Why do you always say that? It's not the first time I've had my blood taken,' Tania shouted.

'It's routine.' Isabella drew the blood, placed a cotton ball over the site and slid the needle out. 'There you go. All done.' She named the tube and filled out a form, marked it urgent. 'I'll get that up to the lab now. Hopefully we'll have the results by the time Mr Dubois gets here.' Hopefully the lab tech would make a film when he received the sample and not wait to find out what the white count was. The film would be required to do a white cell differential count to ascertain the number of neutrophil band forms which were indicative of infection. The more bands and even earlier forms of that particular white cell, the stronger the infection.

'Agh!' Tania cried, and straightened out on the bed, grabbing at Dominic and gripping his wrists like a vice.

His face paled, but he didn't budge, let his wife squeeze as though her life depended on it.

'Deep breaths,' Isabella said, and rubbed her shoulder constantly until the spasm passed. 'Well done.'

'Like I had any choice,' Tania snapped.

'Hey, steady, darling. Isabella and Katie are here to help us.'

'It's all right.' Katie grinned. 'We've heard worse.'

'I'm sorry.' Tania looked contrite. 'I really am. It's just so painful, and then this puerperal infection. I'm terrified.' She struggled upright and leaned her head in against Dominic, who took over the rubbing.

'Can I take a look at your cervix?' Isabella preferred asking rather than just saying that's what she had to do. A simple question gave her patient some sense of control over a situation where she had absolutely none. Especially in this case. As soon as Raphael got here there'd be a lot going on, and Tania wouldn't be given a chance to say anything. Urgency was now a major factor in this delivery. If this was PS, then the infection would run away on them if they weren't careful. Antibiotics had already been administered, but Rafe might up the dosage.

'Why have I got an infection down there?'

Katie answered, 'You said your breasts were sore when you first arrived, and I thought it looked as though you've got a small infection in your nipples.'

'The other doctor gave me antibiotics for it. She said it would be all right for baby to take them.'

'The infection could've already spread, and the symptoms have only just begun showing up in the last little while.'

Isabella waited until Tania gulped hard and nodded at her. 'Go for it. Hopefully baby's nearly here and we can get this nightmare over and done with. What if he gets the infection too?'

That was the problem. 'Mr Dubois will explain everything when he arrives.' Ducking for cover, but it wasn't her place to fill this couple in on what might happen. Times like this she was glad to be a nurse and midwife, and not a doctor. They could have handing out the grim news. She'd seen how much it upset Raphael. Tugging on gloves she positioned herself at the end of the bed and waited for Tania to lie back. 'Okay, try and relax.'

It didn't take long to get the measurement and Isabella felt relief. 'Nine centimetres. We're nearly there.'

'About time,' Tania grumped. 'I've had enough.'

There was still the pushing to undertake, but best keep that to herself for now. No point in upsetting her patient any more than she already was. Hopefully Raphael would be here before they started.

'Hello, Tania, Dominic.' The man himself strode into the room minutes later, looking beyond calm.

But Isabella knew better, saw the tell-tale sign where his mouth tightened in one corner. 'That was quick.'

'The roads were fairly quiet for a change. Right, let's see what's happening, shall we? Tania, tell me about the pain in your belly.'

From then on everything happened fast. A phone call came from the lab alerting them to the CBC results and the raised white cell and band form counts. Raphael administered another antibiotic intravenously. Tania began pushing before she was told to, and reluctantly stopped, only to have baby make her own mind up that it was time to come, and soon it was over. Baby Sophie met her parents, had a brief, safe cuddle from each before being whisked into the specialised cot and wiped over extra carefully because of the infection mum had.

'I'm going to give Sophie antibiotics too,' Raphael told the worried parents. 'We don't know yet if she'd caught the infection, but I prefer to be on the safe side. You have to understand what this means.' He ran through what could go wrong, then reassured them it was unlikely, but they had to know. 'Then she'll go to PICU where they'll monitor her continuously.'

Tania was crying. 'I want to hold her. I want her here, not on a different floor.' She hiccupped. 'I know what you're doing is the right thing, but it's so unfair. We've waited years for her and now we can't keep her with us.'

Dominic wrapped his wife in his arms, tears streaming down his face to mingle with hers. 'Shh, darling. It's going to be all right.'

Raphael talked to the couple some more, working at pacifying them.

When he'd finished, Isabella looked at him and Katie, and they nodded agreement, then left the room quietly, pushing Sophie's cot ahead of them.

'Phew,' Isabella sighed. 'It never gets any easier with distraught parents.'

'The day it does is the time for you to walk out of here and go work as an interior decorator.' Raphael chuckled. 'Me, I'll learn to play the banjo and sit on my back step all day.'

Katie agreed. 'I'll find a rich man and retire for good. Right, come on, Sophie, let's get you settled in PICU.'

As Katie headed down the corridor at a fast clip with her special cargo, Isabella's heart went with the wee tot. 'She's so vulnerable.'

Raphael moved closer. '*Oui*, they all are. I wonder how something so fragile and tiny can be so strong. It scares me sometimes.'

'Would we be worse parents because we know all the things that can go wrong?'

'I'd say so. I've seen it often enough with colleagues who've had babies on my watch. Their pregnancies are hard work.' He didn't blink at her use of 'we'.

But then she hadn't meant it as in we, us, together. Had she? Oh, hell. Get busy, find someone who needed her attention. Raphael would go home soon. Fingers crossed.

But now he looked worried. 'Who can tell with these things? Right, I'd better go interrupt the couple and do some more checks on Tania before I head away.'

'Hopefully you'll get home before it's time to get up and come to work.' She still had five hours to get through before knocking off at seven. By the time she reached home Raphael would be back here. Ships in the night. It should be ideal. No talking about things that got her in a knot, or brought that faraway look to his eyes when he was watching her. No wishing she could sit down and tell him the truth. To say out loud that she wanted more from their relationship but was afraid to act on it for fear of hurting both of them, especially Rafe. To explain she could not give him what he deserved after how Cassie treated him, and still she wanted to try.

'I'll do my best.' He shrugged. 'You got anything planned for the day once you've had some sleep?'

'A second inspection of the apartment I'm renting.'

His face dropped. Had he not believed she'd move out? She'd thought he'd be only too happy when that day came. Seemed it wasn't only her who was all over the place in what they wanted.

Friday and the end of a particularly drama-filled week with patients. Raphael felt his body come alive at the thought of a free weekend ahead. What would he do with it? Spend time with Izzy when she wasn't working? Go and see where she was intending to move to. Visit the shops. There was quite a bit of shopping for kitchenware and furniture going on at the moment, and the landing on his second floor was filling up with packages and small cartons. Every time he walked past to his bedroom his heart slowed. She was definitely setting up her own home. Getting on with her life. He could learn from her. Find the courage to do the same.

Raphael let himself into the house and stopped. Paint fumes hit him. A foreign lightness in the hall made him gape. Wow. What a difference. Should've done it years ago. Except there'd been no motivation before. Izzy had changed everything.

She stood at the bottom of the stairs, dressed in over-large paint-spattered overalls with a roller in one hand and a wide grin on her face. A paint smear streaked across her cheek. Cute. Sexy. 'What do you think?'

I think I want to kiss that spot.

His stomach crunched, his blood hummed.

I think I want to kiss your soft lips and taste you.

Forget humming. There was a torrent in his veins. He was over waiting, being patient, giving her time. He had to do something about his feelings for her.

Dragging his eyes away from the sight that had him in meltdown, he looked around at the white with a hint of grey walls, woodwork, ceiling, and felt his mouth lifting into a smile that grew and grew. 'Amazing. Who'd have believed getting rid of that magenta could make such a difference. This hall is twice the size it was when I went to work this morning.'

'That's a relief.' She placed the roller in the clean tray.

'You were worried I wouldn't like it?' He stepped closer, put his keys and phone on the bottom stair and stood there watching the varying emotions flitting through her beautiful old-wood-coloured eyes.

'Not really.' Her teeth nibbling her lip told him otherwise.

He had to force himself not to reach over and place a finger on her lips to stop her action. 'Why wouldn't I? It was me who bought the paint two years ago.'

Izzy shifted her weight from one foot to the other, then lifted her head enough to lock those eyes on his. 'I worried I've overstepped the mark by doing this without telling you what I was up to.'

Izzy never worried about upsetting him. Carrying on with whatever *she* thought best was a trademark of their friendship, always had been, and was one of the reasons he adored her. Something was off centre here, and it frustrated him not knowing what that was. 'Relax. I'm more than happy with what you've done. In fact, I'm blown away.' He waved a hand at his new hall. 'This is amazing. It fires me up to get on with doing up the rest of the house.'

He hadn't noticed the tension in her shoulders until they softened, and a smile touched those lips. 'Thank you, Isabella.'

Her eyes widened and she glanced away, came back to lock eyes with him again. The tip of her tongue appeared at the corner of her mouth. 'Phew.'

Raphael could not stop himself. He reached out, placed his hands on her arms and drew her closer. 'Again, thanks. By doing this you've starting turning my house into a home and up until now I hadn't realised how important it is if I'm to continue living here and become ensconced in a London lifestyle, not just working at the hospital every available hour.'

She was shaking under his hands.

His thumbs smoothed circles on her arms. 'Izzy.'

Her breasts rose, stilled, dropped again. 'Rafe.'

Afterwards he didn't remember moving, couldn't recall anything but his mouth on hers at last. Soft. Sweet. Isabella. Strong, tough Izzy. Returning his kiss. Returning his kiss! She tasted of promise, of fun and love, of life. And then her tongue nudged past his into his mouth and the world stood still. While his body fizzed, the thudding behind his ribs frantic, his groin tightening, and tightening further. It felt like an out-of-body experience, yet his feet were firmly planted on the stair below her. His hands were holding Izzy's arms, now sliding around to bring her in close, closer, up against his body, chest to breast, her thighs against his groin, mouth to mouth. Kiss for kiss.

Yes. This was what he'd been waiting for. Izzy. She'd always been there, in his blood, his heart, but not like this. Until that day she married someone else and he woke up.

She moved, slid her mouth away, leaned back to stare up at him.

She'd better not have read his mind right then.

Her tongue was licking her bottom lip. Tasting him? Her throat bobbed. Her eyes were saucers, big, golden globes of heat and desire. 'Oh, Rafe,' she whispered through what sounded like need—for him.

His own need was pulsing throughout his body. 'Izzy? You all right? With this?' *Please, please, please say yes.*

A slow nod.

'I...' He hesitated. Talk too much and kill the moment. Don't explain where he was coming from and risk having her change her mind, and running for the hills. 'I want to be more than friends. Have for a long time now.'

Another nod. This time with a hint of concern darkening that golden gaze.

'You don't agree? I should stick to being friends?'

Raphael wants me.

Isabella wanted to let go her grip on his shoulders,

to step back, take time to think this through. But if she removed her hands, couldn't feel him under her palms, she'd curl up and die. She wanted him. Yes, she was admitting it at last. She wanted Rafe. But that fear was still there, lurking at the edges of her mind. What if she failed him? What if it didn't work out? She'd lose the most important person in her life.

He was waiting. Patiently. Yet there was tension in his muscles. She felt it under her hands, saw it in his jaw, knew it in his eyes. Had he thought beyond this moment? Of course he would've. This was Raphael—not Mr Spontaneity, not Mr Take-What-I-Can-Get-and-to-Hell-with-the-Consequences. Friends or lovers? She could not continue being neutral. Had to stop playing safe. Digging deep, she found it wasn't so hard to ask, 'Want to go upstairs?'

He lifted her off the stairs, held her against him. 'Thought you'd never ask.'

Slipping her arms around his neck she gazed at this man she'd always known and was now going to learn about in an entirely different way, and let go all the hang-ups, the questions, the need to be someone, and went with being who she was, who she had. Raphael. Nuzzling his neck, she smiled when his arms tightened around her as he carried her up to his bedroom.

He lay her on the bed.

Oh, no, you don't.

She leapt up, stood in front of him and reached for the first button on his shirt, slowly slid it through the buttonhole and leaned close to kiss the spot she'd revealed. Then the next button, and licked his skin, smiling when he groaned. The third button, and Rafe's hands skimmed down her back to clasp her butt.

The fourth button and her head was spinning with need.

Those strong hands were lifting her up against his erection. His manhood pressing into her belly. OMG.

The fifth and— She had to stop or this would be over before it got any further. She couldn't stop. Her whole body was crying out for release, yet she wanted so much more, wanted to touch all of him, every inch of skin. Forget the buttons. She jerked the shirt out of his waistband and pushed it up.

Rafe lifted his head enough for her to tug the annoying shirt off. Then she went back to kissing and licking that smooth skin, and absorbing the hits of sharp desire stabbing her belly, her breasts, her centre. Hands on her waist, then she was wobbling on her feet as the domes of the overalls were pulled open. The oversized boiler suit fell to her hips, then to the floor, unaided by Rafe's hands now intent on lifting her T-shirt and touching her—everywhere.

A groan slid across her swollen lips as his thumbs rubbed her nipples, arousing them further, tightening them into painful knobs of pulsing need. Her own hands were claws against Raphael, trying to caress while tightening further as the need in her deepened to the point she lost all comprehension of what was happening. 'Rafe. Please,' she begged. 'I can't take any more.'

Her bra hit the floor, her panties slid down to her ankles with the help of one of those hot hands. He quickly grabbed a small packet from the drawer beside the bed, tore the packet open and rolled the condom on. Then he was lifting her to his waist, turning around to lean her against the wall as she wound her legs around him. 'Izzy,' he growled.

His hot tip touched her centre.

She tried to reach for him, to hold him intimately.

Another throaty growl. 'Not yet. Won't last.' And he was filling her, giving to her.

Her head tipped back against the wall and she rocked with the need exploding throughout her body. 'Rafe,' she screamed.

Then with a guttural roar he took her, his body tense as he came.

They lay on his bed, legs and arms tangled, lungs working hard, eyes closed.

Wow. Isabella sighed. Never would've thought she could feel like this. As if she'd found something so special it might break if she wasn't careful.

'Don't go there, Isabella.'

See? He knew her too well. Rolling onto her tummy and sprawling half across him she eyeballed him. 'It's hard not to.'

He winced.

Immediately she lifted up to kiss him. 'I am not sorry.' Kiss. 'I'm mind-blown.' There was no comparison between her feelings for Raphael and those she'd believed she had for Darren.

A return kiss that lasted longer than hers to him, and started clouding the subject. 'That's two of us.'

There was so much she wanted to tell him. How she loved him, wanted to always be with him. But what if she did let him down? That was too awful to contemplate. She still didn't know if she'd got it right. Look what happened last time she told a man she loved him. Not that she was ready to utter the L word. Afraid to, more likely. Rolling onto her back as he got up to dispose of the condom in his bathroom, she stared up at the ceiling that was desperately in need of a coat of paint. 'Pinch me.'

He came back into the bedroom and lay back down next to her. 'Please don't say you're already regretting this.'

Reaching for his hand, she held on tight. 'Not at all. Why would I?' Hell, what if Rafe only wanted sex, and had no wish for a future with her? Hadn't thought of that, had she?

Raphael rose onto his elbow and gazed down at her. If she didn't know better she'd say that was love coming her way. But it couldn't be. Not the 'this is for ever, sexy, everything together' kind of love.

When he remained quiet, she had to ask, 'What?' Her heart smashed against her ribs as she waited for him to reply.

At last, 'Nothing.' That was it? Then he kissed her and her muscles loosened a little.

Wrapping her arms around his strong, muscular body, she pulled him into her. She'd hopped off the fence on the side of go for it, and was ready to give this everything she had. But not ready to talk about it. That might ruin everything.

Raphael gathered her into his arms and began making love to her like he had no intention of ever stopping. She could live with this for as long as it was on offer. Reality would step in some time, but for now she was safe from the demons that liked to wreak havoc with her dreams.

Raphael yawned. It was his turn not to sleep. How could he with Izzy wrapped around him like a limpet? A warm, soft one. Okay, not a limpet, but the best damned thing to have happened to him in a long time, if not in for ever.

Sensationnelle.

He'd poured years of emotions into his lovemaking during the night. Had he always loved her?

But if that were true, then he wouldn't have been so devastated by what Cassie had done to him.

He shivered. Slow down. Think it through. Last night had been amazing, but it didn't change anything. He and Izzy were still friends, and despite being intimate, that hadn't changed. Other than to put pressure on him to get it right. Big pressure. Izzy was vulnerable, still coming to terms with Darren's treachery. She didn't need him trying to get too close, too fast, and then finding he wasn't ready to commit to her either. Because he was still struggling to accept the loss of his child, and why. Especially the why. If he told Izzy about Joshua it might free some of the knots holding him back, but he didn't want her to see his vulnerability. That was saying he wasn't as tough as she believed him to be.

His body tightened, and not in the way it had often during the night as they made love. He had to tell her. It would be a lie not to. She was entitled to know everything, otherwise he would never be able ask her to become a part of his life when he was ready. If he was ever ready. *Thump, thump* went his heavy heart.

'Rafe?' Izzy muttered.

'Oui, mon amie?' Stick to friend, keep this real.

Her reply was a small snore.

So, not ready to talk. Thank goodness. He could continue the dream by lying here, holding her warm, sexy body against him, feeling her hot breaths on his skin, knowing she was relaxed with him as she hadn't been since she arrived. But this was Isabella. There'd be questions and concerns scooting round her mind about whether they were doing the right thing, how long this could last, was it for ever or a rerun of her marriage. Knowing her meant he was forewarned.

And this *was* Izzy. He couldn't hurt her in any way. He had to back off until he sorted out his mess. Had to. No other way to go forward. But how, now that he knew Izzy intimately?

How, when she was living in his house for another few weeks?

When he was going to the wedding with her?

Damn, he'd made the situation between them worse, not better.

CHAPTER EIGHT

OUT ON THE DECK, Isabella stretched onto her toes, leaned back to ease the rest of the kinks out of her muscles that a long soak under a hot shower hadn't fixed. What a night. What a lover Rafe had turned out to be. She'd never known sex to be so wonderful.

And then she'd slept like she hadn't in for ever. Right through to ten in the morning. Why? She'd have thought the excitement of making love with Raphael would've kept her awake all night, not knocked her out. Had she found her safe place with Rafe? No, couldn't have. Must've been because he'd exhausted her with his love-making. But she did feel different. Relaxed and happy.

Why wasn't he here? It had stung a little to wake up and find herself alone in his bed. He hadn't been downstairs when she made her way to the kitchen. There'd been a note saying he'd gone for a run and might go into work afterwards. As though putting distance between them. Was he regretting last night already?

Her heart sank. He wouldn't. He might.

Then what? She'd have to suck it up and get on with her plans of setting up the flat she was about to rent. She had to do that anyway. Just because they'd become lovers didn't mean she would change everything. She still had to make her own life work for her. Preferably including Raphael. But she was not going to follow him or anyone to do what they wanted without keeping herself true to herself. She'd messed up once. It wasn't happening again, if she could help it.

Her phone rang.

Rafe.

She snatched it up. 'Hey, good morning. Where are you? I didn't wake up for hours. I feel so good.' Shut up, let the man say why he rang.

'Could've set a bomb off and you wouldn't have woken. Guess I've got my uses, then.' He laughed.

'Seems like it.'

'Feel like going to the movies and dinner tonight?'

Pardon? 'As in a date?'

Silence. Then, 'Yes, a date.'

He could sound more enthusiastic. 'You sure that's what you want to do? I mean, if last night was a one-night stand say so.' Get the pain over with now.

'Yes, Isabella, I do want to take you out. And…'

She gritted her teeth. 'Go on.' He was about to break her heart.

'I don't want it to be a one-night stand.'

Phew.

Then, 'But I admit I'm uncertain where we're going with this.'

How about into a relationship that would blossom into love? 'We don't have to rush it, Rafe.' Her heart was squeezing painfully. 'I've got things to think about too.'

'I know. That's also what's holding me back. So, you still want to go out tonight?'

Did she? 'Yes, I do.' She could be setting herself up for a fall, but sometimes she had to take a chance.

'See you about six, then.' And he was gone.

She stared at her phone. Did that just happen? He hadn't said where he was. It was the weekend and he wasn't rostered on the ward but bet that's where he was. It was his bolt hole, she realised. Put a bed in a corner, and fill a cupboard with his clothes and he'd never come home. No wonder he hadn't got around to redecorating.

Chienne rubbed against her leg.

'Hey, you. At least I know where I'm at with you.' She lifted the cat onto her shoulder for a cuddle. 'I've got a date with your dad.'

A date meant dressing up in something decent. And if she wanted a repeat of last night whatever she chose to wear had better be more interesting than jeans and a shirt.

Raphael stared at the apparition in red standing in his lounge. *Sacré bleu.* This was Izzy? He could feel his heart exploding against his ribs, while his groin was tightening. 'I want to rush upstairs and tear that dress off you.' It had to be the sexiest dress he'd ever seen, and yet he wanted to remove it?

'That bad, huh?' She grinned.

'Oh, yes.' This had to stop or they'd never make it to the restaurant and as much as he wanted to make love with Izzy he was taking her on a proper date so they could calm down after last night. Put some perspective on things. Except she'd gone and raised the bar to impossible heights. Somehow he had to be strong, stop being diverted by a red ball of sex on amazing legs and ladder-high shoes. Reaching for her hand, he tugged her close and began walking to the front door, past the stairs that'd take them up to his bedroom. 'Let's get out of here while we're still capable.' Except her hand was soft, small in his, and adding to the need clawing through his body. So much for pulling back.

Hopefully the movie would be scintillating and he'd forget all about his companion. As if.

A couple of hours later Raphael had to admit it hadn't been too bad. He had forgotten Izzy enough for his body to quieten down. 'What did you think?'

'That I prefer romance movies to fantasy.'

'Got that wrong, didn't I?' He looked around. 'Let's give that bar a go. Or do you want to choose since I got the movie wrong?'

'There's good.' She wasn't sounding as excited as she had earlier.

Which might be good since he was trying to slow things down. 'Wine?'

'Please.' She found them a table in the back of the room and shuffled her cute butt onto a stool.

And his body went back to tightening and wanting. While his mind tried to deny everything.

In his pocket his personal phone vibrated. He ignored it. He shouldn't have brought it with him, but who knew when it might be needed in an emergency. For the first time in ages his hospital call phone was on the table at home since he wasn't on call. There were other specialists to cover his patients if the need arose. No one was interrupting them tonight.

'How is Grand'mère?' Izzy asked. 'Back on her bike yet?'

'Not quite. Or she's not admitting it if she is. I'd have to tell her off.'

'Yes, and she'd laugh at you, so no problem.'

'She rang today. She wants me to go home for a visit sometime soon.' He paused.

Izzy sipped her drink, her gaze fixed on him over the rim of the glass. 'To spend time with her? Or is there something else happening?'

Was this Izzy's way of asking did he still intend moving home one day? 'Only that she wants to catch up and it's easier for me to make the trip at the moment. She suggested you tag along too.'

'I'd love to.' Izzy was still watching him like she was looking for something more. Of course she was. She'd be thinking that if he was over Cassie enough to have a fling with her, then he could very well be ready enough to move back to France. She might be right, and how would she feel about that? Her growing excitement and determination to make London home would come down in a rush, sending her back to wondering if she could ever settle anywhere and be happy. She could relax on that score. He wasn't going to wreck her new-found happiness, even if that meant ruining his own before he got started.

Raphael gazed at Isabella, his mind stumped with the way he'd been blindsided with their lovemaking. He'd felt as though he'd found something he'd been looking for all his life. Yet it scared the pants off him. He wasn't ready. Might never be. But to walk away without trying might be beyond him. It might be too soon for Isabella as well. Not to mention the Joshua hurdle for him to get over. He'd never thought it would be so hard to tell Izzy. Sure, no one else knew either, but this was so much more important. It scared him to reveal the depth of his pain and anger. Holding on to those emotions was the one grip on keeping himself complete he had. Airing it might undo him so much that he'd never be the same again.

'Earth to Raphael.' Her warm hand covered his. 'Where have you gone?'

Quick, come up with something. 'Thinking about when we can manage to go over to Avignon together.' Together? He really wasn't keeping back from this, was he?

'We'll have to pick a weekend we're both off.'

'Of course.'

Their pizzas arrived, looking and smelling delicious. And tasting just as good.

Izzy asked, 'I know Grand'mère says she's getting out and about as though the hip operation never happened, but do you think she might've slowed down? Might be starting to think about the future in a different light?'

'I do. She says she's not ready to move out of the family home, and is thrilled Maman and Papa have moved in. As soon as she's getting around properly she'll take the downstairs rooms and save herself those horrendous stairs now that she's had a fall.'

'Bet she already thinks she's capable,' Izzy said, those golden eyes focused entirely on him. 'It's your family tradition for someone from each generation to live in the family house at some stage, isn't it?'

'*Oui.* Though my parents have taken a while to get there.'

'You haven't thought of skipping a generation and moving in yourself?'

Damn. Should've kept his mouth shut. 'Izzy.' He reached for her hand. 'I live here. I'm still not ready to return to Avignon.' *Please believe me.* Why should she when he didn't?

Tipping her head to one side, she studied him so intently she must've been able to see everything he was striving to keep to himself. As bumps lifted on his skin, she said, 'As long as you're sure. And happy.' Then she picked up a slab of pizza and ate so calmly that he struggled to believe she'd been any different moments ago.

If Isabella remained determined to make London home, then he might have to factor that into any decisions he made about his future. His heart slowed. He did want to return home one day. He also wanted to have Izzy in his future once he'd laid everything else to rest.

As soon as the pizza was finished, Izzy pushed her plate away and stood up. 'I'm ready to go home.' The gold returned to her brown eyes. 'I'm whacked.'

'You and me both.' Physically and mentally.

Isabella could feel her heart pounding on the quiet drive home. She couldn't make Rafe out. He was on edge, like he didn't want to be with her while at the same time he enjoyed her company.

What had changed since last night? Had he got cold feet? Raphael, Mr Confident, running scared? Couldn't be. Was he going to let her down too? Hardly. He hadn't made any promises about anything. Could be it had been a one-night fling. Except she couldn't accept that. They were too close for that. Or was that the problem? They were close and he was afraid they'd lose it all? *That* she could understand.

Pulling into the drive, he said, 'Thanks for the night. I enjoyed it.'

That was it?

'Me too.'

She shoved the door open and clambered out in an ungainly fashion with her high heels. So not used to wearing anything so far off the ground. Making her way inside she waited by the front door until Raphael joined her.

'I might do some work on the computer,' he muttered, looking everywhere but at her.

Isabella placed her arms around his neck and leaned in against him, tipping back enough to look into his startled face. 'You really want to do that?'

'I think it's best.'

For who? She stretched up on her toes and placed her lips on his mouth.

His hands took her hips. To pull her forward? Or push her away?

She pressed her mouth over his, slid her tongue inside. Tasted him. Slipped out and back in.

'Izzy,' he groaned. 'Stop.' His hands tightened their hold of her, tugged gently so her stomach touched his need.

And he wanted her to stop? Try again, Rafe.

Now he was kissing her, possessing her, giving as much as she was offering him.

Pressing her peaked nipples against his chest sent ripples of desire racing through her, heating her body, fizzing her blood.

'Isabella.' Strong hands lifted her away, put space between them.

Isabella.

He was serious. 'Don't you dare say we can't do this. Not now,' she growled.

Not when I'm pulsing with need for you.

'You don't understand.'

'Damn right, I don't.'

'I can't promise you anything, Izzy.'

She relaxed at Izzy. 'I haven't asked you to.'

'I know.' He was still holding her. 'I might hurt you.'

True, and she might hurt him. 'I'm a big girl, Rafe. I'll take whatever happens on the chin.'

'Yes, but…'

She placed a finger over his mouth. 'But nothing, Raphael. Make love to me. Please.'

Those dark eyes locked on her, searching for what she had no idea. There was apprehension in his gaze, which was slowly replaced by excitement. 'If you're sure,' he said as he swung her up into his arms and carried her upstairs.

Very sure. If there were consequences, then she'd manage. It would hurt but she could not walk away from tonight.

Isabella looked through the window to the beautiful garden beyond where Carly and Adem's wedding ceremony would take place in a few minutes. She was so happy for her friend. She also couldn't help wondering if she and Raphael would ever get to this point. They'd had an amazing week, making love every night, but there was an obvious hesitation in his approach to her, as though he wasn't ready. Which he had kind of intimated on their date night. Well, she wasn't one hundred per cent ready either but she was up to giving it a chance by working hard to keep the doubt gremlins quiet, and believing in herself. The past was over, the doubts brought about by Darren finished with. But she wasn't here to think about that. This was Carly's day.

'Isn't this a gorgeous setting?' she said to Esther. The gardens were colourful with roses and peonies and other flowers bright in the sunshine.

'Magic. And don't we all look swish in our silk dresses?'

'Not bad at all.' Raphael was standing with her friends' men, looking completely at ease. The moment Carly knew he was accompanying her to the wedding, he'd been told he'd be Isabella's escort when they stood with Carly and Adem as they exchanged their vows. What was he thinking? Would he ever want to get married again?

'Lily, no.' Esther grabbed Lily's hand before Carly's bouquet of blue flowers was destroyed. 'Come on. We'd better get this show happening before little miss here does something we'll all regret.'

'Group hug first,' Carly said as she approached them. She looked beautiful in her dress with her hair falling free over her shoulders, and a small baby bump beginning to show.

Tears threatened to spurt down Isabella's face. 'You look stunning. And so happy.'

The four women gathered close to hug, tears on everyone's faces. 'So much for the make-up,' Chloe laughed.

'Me.' Lily pulled at her mother's skirt. 'I want a hug.'

She got four, then Isabella, Chloe and Esther gathered around Carly to lead her out to the garden to get married.

The ceremony was short, spoke of love and commitment and had every female in the garden in tears. Glancing sideways at Raphael, panic struck. Here was a man she truly loved, with everything she had. Yet she couldn't celebrate. He wasn't showing signs of loving her back. What if she was doomed to another broken heart? This time would be far harder to get over than her previous mistake. Swallowing hard, she dragged in air to calm the banging in her chest. She could not get upset or worried today. Not when her girlfriend was celebrating finding the love of her life, and *she* was standing beside Raphael.

'Knew I'd need this.' Rafe handed her a handkerchief. 'Brand new, just for you.' His smile was soppy, like he too was feeling the love going on. And why wouldn't he be? There wasn't a soul in the garden who didn't look the same.

'Ta,' she sniffed, dabbing her nose and eyes, and doing her best not to mess up her make-up. Mascara under the eyes was such a great look. Except by the time Carly and Adem slid rings onto each other's fingers the make-up was long gone, and Raphael had passed her a second handkerchief, pocketing the first one, sodden and stained blue-black. When Adem leaned in to kiss Carly, Isabella clapped, hiding the sudden spike of jealousy.

'You're such a softie.' Rafe grinned, then blinked, looking away.

'And you're not?'

'Un peu.'

'Sure.'

A little? Underneath that serious specialist façade was an emotional man who was good at hiding his feelings when he felt they'd be used against him. She gave a little gasp. Was that the cause of his hesitation to talk about the future? He had something to hide?

Not now, Isabella.

True. She was wasting a wonderful occasion worrying about herself. Today wasn't about her. Or Raphael. 'Weddings do that some people.'

'Not me usually. But for some reason today feels extra special.' He was looking into her eyes, right in, while smiling that sensitive, loving smile she adored.

What was he saying? 'It is.' She gave him back a smile. One that told him the words she hadn't managed to utter yet. *I love you.* 'There are weddings, and then there are other weddings. This is one of the best kind.'

Raphael's lips brushed her brow. 'You look beautiful, Izzy. Inside and out.'

'How many handkerchiefs did you bring?' she asked around a lump in her throat. Gone was her ability to fob off words she didn't know how to deal with by saying something witty or growly.

'It was a three-pack.' He stepped back and looked around the garden, suddenly very interested in the roses.

Great. She'd gone and lost him again. He was doing that more and more. She loved it when he kissed her. He made her feel cherished and at ease with her life. Yet all the time those doubts kept surfacing. How long was this going to last? Would they get more involved, or would he walk away? What did he want out of life?

An image of Raphael holding a baby in the maternity ward snapped into her head. Babies. He wanted a family. Still, there was a 'but' hanging around that he hadn't explained. And she still had to conquer her fear of letting him down. Drawing in a breath, she flipped from her worries to her friends. 'Right, I'm going to hug the bride.'

'I'm coming with you.'

Thought he might. 'Carly, I am so happy for you.' Isabella wound her arms around her friend.'

'You're next,' Carly whispered against her.

Her happiness plummeted. Don't say that. Might be tempting fate. 'Oh, that's a long way away off. I'm just enjoying the sex,' she whispered back.

Carly pulled back, stared at her in astonishment. 'You're not certain this will come to anything?'

'Just being cautious, that's all. Now I need to give Adem a hug.' And shut Carly down. She moved sideways to the bridegroom. 'Adem, congratulations. You look beyond happy.'

'I am, Isabella. Way beyond.' He wrapped her up in a hug, then turned to shake Raphael's hand. 'Right, can we get a drink now? Or do I have to abstain all afternoon?'

'Let's go inside. There's cocktails for everyone, and the dinner will also be in there.' Carly was waving to someone else, and when Isabella turned she saw Chloe and Esther coming their way.

'We're heading inside,' she told them.

'Good idea,' Esther said, nodding at the greying sky. 'It's chilled down a little out here, and doesn't look like improving. These dresses are amazing but they're not made for warmth.'

'Off the shoulder leaves a lot of bare skin,' Isabella agreed. Checking that Raphael was still talking to Adem, she saw that Xander and Harry had joined them, and more handshakes and stiff male hugs were going on. The four men got on very well, which made it easier for her and the other women. Nothing worse than a partner who didn't fit in with your circle of friends. Isabella spied Lily about to step into the garden and went to take her hand and head inside. 'Do you want something yummy to eat?'

'Chocolate?'

'Maybe later. How about some little cheese bickies first?'

'Will I like them?'

'We'll get some and find out.' All the other guests were now inside the understated room that spoke of class, and accepting the glasses of champagne being handed around. Izzy grinned. 'Just like old times.'

'What? Us together?' Chloe nodded. 'It is, isn't it?'

'I'm hungry,' Carly said. 'I was too nervous before the wedding, and the baby needs food.'

Isabella agreed. 'I'll bring one of those of hors-d'oeuvre plates over from the table.'

The day disappeared into evening while they ate dinner and drank toasts, and people made speeches, and had a wonderful time. Then Adem stood up and placed his hand on his wife's elbow to bring her up beside him. 'Thank you for sharing our special day, everyone. But now, we're going to leave you and head to our hotel.'

Everything wrapped quickly after the newlyweds left.

'Ready to hit the road?' Raphael asked.

'I guess. We're all done here.' Suddenly she didn't want to go back to the house and find out if Rafe was going to make love to her or if tonight was one he said he had work to do. Like he had twice last week. 'Or we could go clubbing.'

He shook his head. 'Not me. I'm more than ready to hit the sack.'

With or without me?

'Fine. Let's go.'

'Isabella, I'm sorry if I've let you down.'

She sighed. 'It's all right. Really. I'm feeling a little deflated after such a wonderful wedding, that's all.'

The ride was so slow and yet sped by. Isabella couldn't wait to get out of the car yet didn't want to stop. She couldn't face being turned down by Raphael heading to his office to work. As if he really had any that needed dealing with tonight. Was this when she stepped up? Put her feelings out there? Let him know she wanted more, not less? Her chest ached with the pounding going on behind her ribs. *Be strong, be brave.*

The moment Raphael shut them in the house she turned to him, reaching her arms up and around his neck.

He tensed. 'Isabella.' Never a good sign when he used her full name.

'You're not working tonight.' Then she stretched up to kiss him, long and hard, and he kissed her back, demanding, giving, sensual.

Yes. She smiled under his mouth, and ran her hands down his back and under his jacket. Tugged his shirt free, touched his skin with her fingertips, absorbed his groans through their kiss. Yes.

Raphael pulled away, stared down at her. 'Izzy.' Better than Isabella.

She put her finger on his mouth. 'Don't say a word.' Then she pushed his jacket down his arms and let it drop to the floor. The shirt was next, and then his belt and fly and his trousers landed around his feet.

Raphael stepped out of them, and waited, his reaction to her obvious and large in his boxers.

Afraid he might still change his mind, she kissed him, slowly, while she touched him, rubbed the head of his erection. Arousing him further. And then she was lifting her leg around his waist, trying to wrap herself around him. She wanted him. Now. Hard. Fast. Satisfying.

Raphael moved, took her around the waist, lifted her into his arms and charged upstairs to his bedroom, his manhood knocking against her butt.

What was wrong with where they were? She didn't ask. With her finger she teased his nipple, made it peak and him cry out. Then they were on the bed and she was tugging her panties off and tossing them aside. Raphael pulled her dress up to her waist and bent down to lick her.

'No. Now. You, me, together.'

He quickly sheathed himself, then rose above her and thrust into her. Hard and fast. She cried out and pushed up towards him to take him again.

It was over almost before they started. She'd been desperate to make love to him. To show him how she felt.

Isabella fell back against the pillow, her breast rising and falling rapidly.

Raphael sprawled out beside her, and draped an arm over her waist.

'Rafe.'

'Shh...don't say anything.'

She stared up at the ceiling, seeing nothing in the dark. He didn't want to talk. *She* wanted to tell him she loved him, but the words kept getting stuck in her throat. She still didn't quite trust herself to be one hundred per cent certain she loved him, and at the same time she did. That was the trouble. She knew, bone deep, he was the only man for her. But she still needed to know that these feelings weren't about settling down and making the life she'd craved since she was a kid. She'd done it once, had truly believed it was right, that her love had been for Darren and not just that picture, and she couldn't have been more wrong.

Raphael listened to Izzy's breathing as she slowly got her breath back. Did that really just happen? She'd been like a wildcat, taking him without preamble, turning him on so fast he'd hardly kept up. He'd tried to slow down, but she wasn't having it.

Hell, he'd tried to avoid going to bed with her altogether. After seeing the sadness lurking in her eyes as she witnessed her friend's betrothal he'd known he had to stop leading her on. Not that he was deliberately playing with her, but he didn't think he could promise her what she so desperately wanted—a for ever love, marriage and children. Yes, he had been moving on from Cassie a lot faster now, and believed she was history. She'd left him, and that was that.

As for Joshua, he had a way to go on that, and probably would never completely get over the pain. But before he could move forward he had to tell Isabella, and then his family. And he just wasn't sure how to do it. It meant exposing his heart, his vulnerabilities. Izzy knew him well, but still. It wasn't easy. He'd never talked much about the things that mattered, had kept them in wrappers so no one could use them against him.

Tell her now.

She wasn't sleeping. Her breathing had returned to normal, wide awake normal. He opened his mouth. Closed it. No. Not yet. He rolled away, stretched the length of the bed and prepared to wait the night out.

* * *

At last Raphael's breathing deepened.

Isabella carefully slid out of bed and crept out of the room. In the bathroom she took a short shower, then dressed in track pants and a sweatshirt before heading downstairs where the crossword book lay on the bench. She was done with trying to sleep, and with thinking about her and Raphael. There were no answers at the moment.

The sky was beginning to lighten and the birds were waking up, chirping happily, lucky things. Her body ached. Her heart was heavy. Her head pounded. Despite the number of times she'd not known what to do with her life, she'd never felt quite this bad.

A phone began ringing. Raphael's tune. Looking around, she couldn't see it. Listening harder, she followed the sound out to the hallway and his jacket. As she removed it from the pocket the ringing stopped.

At least it won't be work, she thought.

It rang again.

Raphael's mother's name showed on the screen.

'*Bonjour*, this is Isabella.'

'Is Raphael there?' Celeste sounded stressed.

'He's up in his bedroom. Hold on, and I'll run up there.'

'Izzy? Who is it?' Raphael appeared at the top of the stairs.

'Your mother.'

He jogged down and took the phone. 'Maman, what's happened?'

Izzy held her breath as she blatantly listened to Rafe's side of the conversation.

'When did that happen? During the night?' Rafe

looked to her and held the phone away from his ear.
'Grand'mère's in hospital. Fell down the stairs. Again.'
He put the phone back to his ear. 'Maman, what are her
injuries? Are they serious?'

Izzy reached for his free hand and gripped it. 'Is she
going to be all right?' Grateful she understood French,
Izzy stayed still, and waited. Fingers crossed nothing
too serious had happened.

'She broke her other hip? And her femur?' Raphael
looked shocked. 'And she's unconscious?'

This did not sound good. Raphael had to go home
and see his grandmother, as soon as possible. Isabella
headed for the kitchen and her phone, tugging Raphael
along with her. Typing in London to Avignon on her
airline app, she waited for the flights to come up.

'Being in a coma is worse than broken bones.' Raphael shoved a hand through his thick hair, his gaze
clouded with worry. '*Oui.* I'll come as soon as I can.
Yes, today if possible.'

Isabella tapped his shoulder, said, 'There's a flight
at 5:45 out of Heathrow.'

He raised his thumb. 'Maman, Izzy's on to it already.
I'll send the details as soon as I have them.' His phone
clattered onto the bench. He did the fingers through
his hair thing again, while reaching out to her with his
other hand. 'You heard? She's in a coma after falling
down the stairs going down to her room, which she's
not meant to be using yet. Stubborn old lady.'

'I know those steps. None too forgiving for old
bones. Or her head.' Grand'mère was strong but still.
Who knew what the outcome would be?

'I need to see for myself, find out all the details from
the doctors. Let me look at that flight.' Moments later,

'Yes, I'll take it. But I'd better talk to someone on the ward first, make sure they can cover for me for a couple of days at least. Not that I'm not going to Avignon.'

'You do that while I fill in your details here.' She paused, drew a breath. Now was not the time to be sulking over their relationship. 'Would you like me to come with you?'

He hesitated, locking his eyes with hers, then nodded. 'Yes. I would, very much. *Merci beaucoup*, Izzy.'

Raphael stood staring out the window, his shoulders tight, his back straight, as he talked to two different specialists about his patients. 'Thanks, Jerome. I'll call as soon as I know what's what over there. Won't be until tomorrow though, as I don't touch down until somewhere around ten tonight.'

'You wouldn't have your passport number on your phone by any chance?' Isabella asked as soon as he'd finished his calls.

Tap, tap. 'Here. And here's my bank card. Thanks, Izzy. You're a champ.' He was rubbing her neck as he watched over her shoulder as she finalised their bookings for one-way flights. 'Sorry about this.'

'Hey.' She twisted around on the stool. 'Don't apologise.' This could be good for them. Time together dealing with Grand'mère's accident and learning what the consequences would be. Serious compared to fun. Real life. And she'd be able to see for herself how determined he was to return to Avignon in the future, because not even Raphael would be able to hide the longing if it was what he wanted.

Leaning over, he brushed his lips across her brow. 'You're sure you don't mind coming?'

'Absolutely. That's what friends are for.'

He stared at her. 'Of course.' Then he turned away. 'I'll go and pack.'

CHAPTER NINE

'OH, GRAND'MÈRE, LOOK at you,' Rafe croaked around a throat full of tears the next day. 'Is she going to be all right?' he asked the hovering consultant.

Isabella reached for his hand, and held tight. She might be a nurse, but the sight of his grandmother's colourless face and her long, dark grey hair a knotted mess on the white pillow had shocked her.

'What to say? She's in a coma. Sadly.' The older man lifted a shoulder. 'There've been no signs of her coming out of it yet.'

'What about the fractures?' Raphael and the consultant got into a discussion about injuries and treatment.

Izzy extracted her hand and leaned over the rail that had been put up around the bed in case Grand'mère managed to move and fall off the bed. She reached for one of the cold, thin and wrinkled hands on top of the sheet. 'Hello, Grand'mère. It's Isabella.' Her heart sank. This accident could change Grand'mère's life for ever. But that was getting ahead of things. 'I haven't seen you for years. Raphael and I were talking about coming to see you as soon as we both had the same days off from the ward, but seems you beat us to it, got us hurrying across.'

Not a blink. No movement. The hand lay limp in hers. She rubbed her thumb back and forth over the cold skin on the back of Grand'mère's hand.

Rafe's hand gripped her shoulder. 'I'm staying here for a while. I don't want to leave her on her own. Silly, I know, but I can't help it.'

'Rafe, it's okay. You're only feeling what most people do in these situations. Useless, and worried. Your doctor hat is no help to you in this case. In fact, it's worse because you know all the things that can go wrong.' He'd have a mental list scrolling through his mind non-stop.

'Don't pull any punches, will you?' he grunted. 'But you're right. I'm a doctor with no role to play here.'

'Yes, you do. Grand'mère will want you giving her cheek and telling her to hurry and wake up. That's your job here. We can go back to the house for some sleep later.' They'd got very little last night by the time they'd landed in Avignon and then sat up talking with his parents. Nor had they the previous night, trying out that bed in various ways. At least when she went to bed to sleep she did actually sleep now. Had been since the first night with Rafe. It gave her a sense of knowing she was doing the right thing by staying with him, and believing they could make a go of this.

'Couldn't get two more different nights if I tried.' Seemed he could still read her mind even when distressed. Better remember that.

She glanced up at him. 'Know which one I'd prefer.'

Some of the gloom had lifted and he sounded a little more relaxed. 'Me too. Thanks for being here. It means everything. I don't feel so alone.'

Raphael wasn't alone. There was a large family in the city and surrounds. 'Don't get all sentimental on me, Rafe, or I'll have to paint your bedroom orange when I get back to London.' His least favourite colour by a long shot.

'Ha. When you've finished there you could come over here and do up the family house. Despite everything going on, I couldn't help but notice how tired and dated it is, and instantly I was thinking you would turn this into something special.'

Except I live in London. Not Avignon.

'What? Because I painted one hall, I'm a decorator extraordinaire now?' Was this where his thoughts were heading? Was he already considering moving back now that his grandmother might need him? Where would that leave her? Back in London where she had stated categorically her intention of living permanently, or moving to France on yet another attempt to stop and settle down? *Whoa. Slow down.* Just like the long-term future plans, she hadn't started on settling into her flat yet.

And don't forget you wanted to know what his thoughts were on moving.

'I've never seen her looking so frail and old, Izzy. It's a reality check. She's getting older by the week.'

Nothing to say to that, so Isabella reached for his hand again and held him.

'Even once she's out of the coma, it's going to take time and patience for her to get back on her feet. I'm not sure how well she'll cope either. Her bones are fragile, and healing takes so much longer at eighty-five.'

He wasn't even considering she might not regain consciousness. Isabella liked his determined positivity. 'Nor is she known for her patience.'

'True. But what worries me most is that her confidence will have been knocked badly. I've seen it happen often enough in the elderly to expect it, but this is Grand'mère. You know what I mean?'

'Yes, Rafe, I do. She's special to you, and this is the last thing you want for her.' He'd have pictured her always being there in his life, even when that wasn't possible. '*I'm* struggling with the idea of her not getting around, bossing everyone she meets, while listening to people when they needed an ear to bend.'

'It'll be a role reversal. Strange, but only a few weeks ago she was telling me that if anything happened to her she did not want to go into a rest home. Apparently those are for old people.'

'I'm surprised she was even thinking about it. Like she'd had a premonition.' Grand'mère was a person who knew exactly what she wanted and did everything to make it happen. 'Did she say where she'd like to go?'

'She'll stay downstairs as previous generations have, and if necessary we can employ full-time care, though that won't be fun for the nurses.'

'I see.'

They pulled up chairs and sat with his grandmother for another hour when Raphael suddenly stood up and stretched. 'Let's go for a walk through the city.'

'Some fresh air would be good.' She tapped the back of his grandmother's hand. 'We'll come back soon.'

Inside the wall the city was busy with locals and tourists crowding the streets and cafés. Isabella wandered beside Raphael, taking in the sights and scents, looking at the ancient stone walls. 'It's wonderful.'

'Coffee?' Raphael indicated a vacant table on the side of the street.

'Please. Then can we stroll through the market? I want to smell the spices.'

'I remember how you spent hours in there, buying spices that I bet you never used.' Rafe smiled and pulled out a chair for her before heading over to place their order. Then he took his phone out of his pocket and punched some numbers before wandering to the side of the café. Who was he talking to?

Isabella tried not to watch him, instead looking around at the people taking their time to walk the street, laughing, talking, pointing at buildings. Yes, she remembered that feeling of wonder the first time she visited Avignon. It was still there, making her happy when she should be worrying about Grand'mère, but there was nothing she could do for her, so might as well make the most of time spent in the city.

When Raphael finally returned he held two cups of coffee in one hand. 'I need to stay here for a few days at least, maybe more than this week.' He cleared his throat. 'I've just talked to my colleagues and they're more than happy to cover for me for as long as I need.'

Talked to them before her? She supposed it made sense to get his priorities right. But still. 'You have to do what you feel is right for Grand'mère. After all, she's always been there for you.'

'I'm glad you understand.'

That stung. 'Why wouldn't I?' Her voice was sharper than she intended.

'Izzy. Sorry. I don't want to upset you. I know you have to go back tomorrow, and I'll miss you. You're a great support.'

'You say the nicest things when you're trying to dig yourself out of a hole, Raphael Dubois.'

'Did it work?'

As quickly as that they were back on even ground.

The tension that had begun tightening her belly backed off. 'You know it did.' Being here, seeing Grand'mère, had created a new depth of understanding, sharing, helping one another. Rafe needed her to be strong and there for him. Not crashing at the first hurdle. If she got too lonely she'd get over herself, or come back here on her days off.

'Adele wants to discuss things with me tonight.'

'Things? Like what?'

'Family stuff.'

That was putting her in her place. Seemed she wasn't getting as close to him as she'd hoped. He was gazing round the area, smiling in a way she wasn't familiar with, almost as though he was at home. Guess he was. He knew these streets like the back of his hand, having spent most of his early childhood here before his family moved to Geneva.

That was what she wanted, only in London. With Raphael. Was she expecting too much? Draining her coffee, she stood up. 'I'm going to the market. I'm going to get some pastries and cheeses. Coming?'

'Yes.' He looked baffled. 'Why wouldn't I?'

She didn't have an answer. 'Tell me what I can get for your mother for tonight's dinner.' Adele wasn't the only one coming. All the Dubois family would be there.

'Maman will have everything sorted, believe me.'

'Then I'll buy flowers,' she said as they entered the Halles d'Avignon and breathed in spices and coffee and freshly baked bread.

'Leave those until we've finished wandering around or they'll be bruised from bumping into people by the time we're done in here.' There was a deep happiness in Raphael's voice that had been missing for a long time.

Isabella felt her heart drop. Not even their hot nights had brought that on so strongly. He really belonged here, and now he was starting to look around and see what he'd been missing out on all because he'd been so stubborn.

The buzz around the family dinner table later that night only increased Isabella's unease. Despite the reason for Raphael coming home everyone was laughing and talking non-stop and Rafe was right in the thick of it.

'Izzy, have some more beef. I know it's your favourite.' He didn't wait for her reply, just spooned more of the delicious stew onto her plate.

'Give her a break,' Adele laughed. 'You'll be frightening her away if you keep doing that.'

She wasn't staying long anyway. Swallowing hard, Isabella smiled and tried to relax. It wasn't easy when Raphael was enjoying himself so much. Of course she was happy for him, but with each passing hour she had to wonder if he'd ever get around to going back to London. He would. He had a job that he relished there, a home and a cat. But he belonged here too.

Raphael wound his arms around Izzy and cuddled her against his naked length as they lay in bed in his old bedroom from when he was a teen and where he stayed whenever in Avignon. It had been a bit awkward last night when they headed to bed. Maman had prepared another room for Izzy. He hadn't wanted that. He needed her with him at the moment. Selfish, maybe, but she'd come to support him, and he was grateful.

The sun was up, and he was ready to get out. 'Want to walk into the city and have breakfast by the bridge?'

She tossed the sheet aside and sat up, letting his arms slip away. 'Let's go.'

'Mind if we visit Grand'mère on the way?'

'Of course not. She's why we're here.'

Something wasn't right with Isabella, hadn't been since they arrived in Avignon on Sunday night. 'Talk to me.'

She sank her naked derriere onto the side of the bed and faced him. There was a sadness in her eyes he didn't like. 'Your family ties were strong, and couldn't be more different to mine. You are so lucky.'

Rafe nodded. 'I'm starting to think that.' Then he looked closer and felt like he'd been punched in the gut. 'You can be a part of it too, Izzy. They adore you.' Everyone had jostled for her attention last night at dinner. They'd never been like that with Cassie.

'I was made to feel special,' she admitted, still looking directly at him.

'Then what's the problem?'

'I don't know where we're going with our relationship.' She seemed to let go of some knot inside her as those words slid out of her mouth. 'Do you?'

Crunch time. He sat up fast. This wasn't how he wanted to tell her, nor where. But maybe he should just get it out of the way. Reaching for the water bottle by the bed, he tried to drink down some fluid and moisten his suddenly dry mouth, but his throat wasn't playing the game. His gut was churning. His head was banging. His heart had a whole new rhythm going on.

Izzy was watching him closely, concern filling her eyes. 'Rafe? You're frightening me.' Then she leapt up, strode across to stare out the window. 'Talk to me.'

If there was anyone he'd tell it would be Isabella. He

had to tell her. She knew so much about him, what was one more thing? Except this was huge. But if he wanted to banish that despair in her face he had no choice. Because he just couldn't put his story away and pretend nothing was wrong. For one, Izzy already knew there was something wrong, and for two, he had to be honest more than anything. Tell Izzy. Don't tell Izzy.

'I am a father.'

Her fingers tightened around her elbows as she turned to stare at him through wide-open eyes, but still she said nothing.

Am a father? Was a father? What was the protocol? Who cared? It was about his feelings. No one else's. 'Joshua. He died of SIDS at eight days old.'

Then she moved, came and sat beside him, reaching for his shaking hands. 'Oh, Rafe.' His name dragged across her shaky bottom lip. 'Raphael, I am so sorry.'

Don't show me pity. I'll fall apart.

And it would take for ever to get the pieces back together again. 'Cassie didn't tell me she was pregnant when she left me and returned to Los Angeles.'

'You didn't know?' Horror filled Izzy's face.

'No. All I knew was she went back for auditions in the movie industry. She was going to become the next big name in movies. Oh, and I was a stubborn bore who wouldn't move to Paris so she could have fun in the greatest city in the world.' Not that she'd ever shown any acting aptitude when he'd known her, except to pull off huge lies. And being pregnant hadn't helped her chances of getting her first break, something she'd told him was his fault.

'I didn't find out until two years later. We hadn't

communicated since she left France so I went over to
see her, wanting to find closure. I couldn't wrap it up.'

'And you got the opposite,' Izzy whispered.

'I never met my son. Didn't know he existed until it
was too late. Never held him, kissed him, hugged him.
He didn't know I existed.' Raphael stared down at the
floor. Hot tears slid down his face, dripped off his chin
onto his chest. He did nothing about them. 'How could
she do that to me?'

Warm arms wound around his back, tugged him
close to Isabella's soft body. Her hands rubbed slow
circles on his skin, her mouth brushed feather-light
kisses on his neck.

'Did she hate me that much?'

'Cassie was always very selfish.'

'True. But she went beyond the realm of selfish into
something so deep and hideous I can't believe it.'

Izzy tipped her head back to lock her troubled gaze
with his. 'Have you talked to your family about it?'

'You're the only person I've told. I have been arguing with myself for days now over whether to say anything or to carry on as though it hadn't happened. But
you deserve better than that.'

'Thank you.' With her thumb she wiped his damp
cheeks. 'Is this why you've stayed away from your family?'

He nodded abruptly. 'They already disliked Cassie,
they'd hate her if they knew this. And I'd always feel
their wrath. It's not something they'd let go in a hurry,
if at all. Also…' He breathed deep. 'I feel bad for the
things she used to say about them to their faces. I made
a monumental error when I fell in love with her, and

I don't like seeing that in their faces every time I'm with them.'

'I think you're overreacting. Your family loves you, and that's what matters. I doubt they judge you for making a mistake. Who doesn't at some time of their life? More often than once.'

'Hell, Izzy, you're amazing. I've been dreading telling you and here you are being sensible about it all.' He really did love her, and now he'd cleared the way to follow through with that. But not now. She might think he was using her sympathy.

She leaned in to kiss him. 'Tell your parents. They'll understand.'

'It'd be cruel to tell them they were grandparents and didn't get the opportunity to be a part of Joshua's short life.' He couldn't do that to them. It was still so painful for him.

'They're tougher than you're giving them credit for, Rafe.' Izzy stood up. 'I'm going for a quick shower and then let's go see Grand'mère. You could practise on her, since she won't hear you.'

'Oh, right.' From somewhere deep inside, he found her a smile. 'Should've told you a long time ago.'

'Yes, Rafe, you should've.'

He reached for her hands, was shocked to feel them shaking too. Anger? Sadness? Knowing Izzy, it would be a combination of a lot of emotions—all for him. 'I was afraid that if I opened up and told you I'd never be able to get myself under control again.'

'And now?'

His heart slowed, but a weight had gone from it. 'I think I'm going to make it.'

* * *

Isabella wandered through the old city centre to the Halles d'Avignon again, Raphael beside her deep in thought. Not surprising after what he'd revealed earlier. She was still trying to get her head around it. They passed people eating on the sidewalk and today her mouth didn't water as the smell of a fresh croissant and piping hot coffee reached her nose from the endless cafés.

How could Cassie have done something so cruel? Unbelievable. She'd stolen his chance of knowing his child, of knowing he had been a father. He still was a father. Along with that she'd turned him away from the very people who could've supported him through the pain and grief. Including her. He'd said he was afraid to let the pain out, for fear it would grow and spread. She understood that.

They reached the market and she hesitated. Not even the spices of every variety at the market could distract her. Glancing at Rafe she saw him smile ever so slightly, despite the heaviness on his heart. This was something he missed in London. But then he was French. And this was France. Home. He could live here all too easily. If he told his parents about Joshua. He had to. She knew that, probably better than he did, because until he did it would still be hanging over him, affecting everything he decided to do.

'Come on. I promised you breakfast and you can't back out on me now.' He leaned in to kiss her cheek.

She nodded, afraid to speak in case she told him that she understood him better than he realised, probably better than he did at the moment. He would front up to

his family with the truth, and then… Yeah, and then…
She couldn't put it into words. It hurt too much.

The pastry was dry on her tongue and the coffee ordinary. Finally she pushed her plate aside and watched
Raphael. She loved him so much, and still couldn't find
the courage to tell him.

'Come on, I'll buy you some Camembert and bleu
d'Auvergne to take when you go home.'

'My favourite cheeses,' she agreed. Hopefully her
appetite returned to enjoy them. 'Let's go.' Suddenly
impatient to be moving she leapt up. 'I'd like to visit
Grand'mère once more today.' Rafe's grandmother was
still in a coma, though when they called in before coming here the doctor said she was responding a little to
touch sometimes.

'I hope she has heard you talking to her. You hold a
special place in her heart, as her lost Kiwi.'

Isabella felt her eyes tearing up. 'She's always been
welcoming and kind to me. Even when I was a bumptious teen.'

'I think that's why she likes you. You don't take any
nonsense from anyone.' Raphael's arm wrapped around
her shoulders and he drew her against his side as they
ducked around people to reach the cheese stall. 'Let
loose, pick whatever you want.' He didn't let go of her
as she chattered away to the woman behind the counter,
nor when he handed over money to pay for her choices,
nor as they walked back to the hospital.

She was glad, needing him, wanting him to want her.

'No change,' a nurse told them as they walked past
the desk in Grand'mère's ward.

'To be expected,' Rafe said, though she could hear his despair.

'Gives you the opportunity to tell her what you don't want her to hear.'

Raphael stopped still, right in the middle of the corridor, and turned to face her. His gaze was serious and her heart lurched. She knew what was coming.

'You were right. I do need to tell the family about Joshua. I'll do it this afternoon.'

Reaching up on her toes, she brushed a kiss across his mouth. 'I'm proud of you.'

And I love you, but that's for another day.

The next morning Raphael bounced out of bed and into the shower at seven o'clock.

'Look at you, bouncing around like a kangaroo.' Izzy groaned. 'Some of us still need our sleep.'

'I had the best night in ages,' he told her. 'Slept right through. You were right. Telling Maman and Papa about Joshua was the right thing to do. I feel like a huge weight has been lifted from my heart.'

'Good. Sometimes I'm not so silly after all.'

'I'm going in to see Grand'mère and tell her, even if she is still unconscious. She'll probably wake up telling the world my story.'

'Then I'll stay here and have a lie-in.'

'See you later, then. I'll take you to the airport about two. How does that sound?'

'Awful. I don't want to go home yet.' What she really didn't want was to leave Raphael. It had been good spending time here with him, and joining his family.

'Sound like you mean it, will you?' Didn't he want her to go either?

She laughed. 'Say hello to Grand'mère for me.'

An hour later she rolled out of bed and into the shower before going to make a coffee and sit on the terrace overlooking the edge of the city and the Rhône beyond. It was beautiful with all the stonework and the wall that surrounded the city. But it wasn't home. That was London. She had to keep believing that or she'd be back at the beginning, not knowing where she was headed.

'Morning, Isabella.' Raphael's mother stepped onto the deck, a cup of coffee in hand. 'Beautiful morning, *oui*?'

'Stunning.'

'Where's Raphael?'

'He's gone into the hospital to see Grand'mère.'

'I can't believe what that woman did to him.' Celeste sat down beside her. 'It is cruel. He'll always wonder what his boy looked like.'

'Yes, he will.' It was the most hideous thing someone could do, and Cassie had once loved Raphael. Had that not counted for anything?

'It's good that he told us. We can understand why he's stayed away now. Not that he should've. We'd always support him.'

'I think he knows that.'

Celeste sipped her coffee and stared out over the balustrade. 'And what about you, Isabella? You're settling into London?'

'Yes, I am. I can't wait to move into my flat and start putting my own mark on it.'

'How long do you think you'll be there?'

Hello? What was this about? 'Long term.'

'I see.'

Isabella's stomach cramped. What did she see? 'Do you? It's been a long time since I've stopped in one place, and never for ever. I need to do this.'

'What about Raphael?'

'What about him?' The cramps turned to hard squeezing. Her heart began racing.

'He belongs here, Isabella. With his family. He misses Avignon and all of us, especially Grand'mère.'

She couldn't argue with that. 'He does.'

Now Celeste turned to face her. 'Thank you for understanding.' Then she got up and headed inside.

Leaving Isabella stunned. Of course his family would want him to return home. Face it, so did Raphael. It was her who had to either change her mind about where she'd live or give up on any thoughts of getting together with Rafe. Not that he was actively encouraging them. She was hanging her hope on the fact he hadn't stopped having sex with her. It had to mean something, didn't it? Or was she being naïve?

Damn it. She couldn't sit around here waiting for him to return from the hospital. She'd go for a walk.

But not even the stunning views of the river and city from the old fort could distract her. She felt as though she was walking in quicksand, getting deeper and deeper without any sign of a way out. She'd fallen for Raphael so hard she literally didn't know what to do with herself. To give up her own goals to follow him wherever he chose to live would be easier than fighting for what she wanted. But giving up her own dreams after finally starting to realise them was not being true to herself. But hey, she was getting way ahead of herself. He wasn't exactly reciprocating her love.

When Raphael stepped through the front door he heard voices coming from the lounge and headed towards them.

'Raphael, you remember Louis Fournier? From the hospital,' Papa said as he entered the room.

He put his hand out to shake the older man's. *'Bonjour, Docteur.'* From the smug look on his face, Papa was up to something. 'It's been a while since I talked to you.'

'It has. I've been keeping up with your career through your father though. You've done well.'

'Thank you. I've worked hard to get where I am, for sure. So what brings you out here?'

'Louis has some news for you.'

'I see,' said Rafe. But he didn't. Though he was beginning to suspect where this might be heading. 'Let's sit out in the conservatory.' There he'd be able to look out over the houses and the fort as he listened to what this man was about to say. He'd be able to see his hometown and think about a future here, compare it to what he had in London.

'I'll come straight to the point,' Louis said. 'There's a position for a gynaecologist coming up at the general hospital. I wondered if you might be interested.'

'Yes, definitely.' His heart rate sped up. Of course he was. His lifelong dream to practise medicine here was falling into place.

Izzy.

He couldn't walk away from her now. It was the only thing he was certain about. She'd been the one to convince him to talk about Joshua to his family. She'd come here with him when he was so worried about Grand'mère. She wasn't Cassie. He'd have to convince her she could start over—again—when he'd spent the last few weeks helping her realise she was where she really wanted to be. No, he couldn't do that to her.

Raphael closed his eyes, breathed deep, searching for answers. Found none. Or far too many. Look out for Izzy, the love of his heart? Or follow his own dreams and hope she'd tag along? No. He'd never ask that of her. Nor did he want to give up this opportunity in Avignon where his family was. For the first time in years he was ready to live where he belonged. If he could figure out a way to keep everyone happy.

'So? What do you think?' Papa was back. 'Couldn't be better timing, eh?'

Oh, yes, it could. Damn it. He wanted to take it up. Desperately. *So do it.* Inside, his heart was cracking. Half for Izzy, half for Avignon. This couldn't be happening. But it was. Yet he'd never felt quite so strongly about returning here until now. Grand'mère's accident had brought home to him that if he was to spend time with his family, now was it. 'How soon do you need a decision?'

'Why don't we go in now and I can show you around, introduce you to our team, give you a general idea of how we run things here?' Obviously Louis had no intention of letting him make up his mind slowly. At least, not without all barrels being fired first.

What did he have to lose? Though he already thought he knew his answer. He wasn't destined to fly solo when his heart belonged to Isabella. 'Sure. As long as I'm back in time to take Isabella to the airport.'

* * *

Isabella watched Raphael change into a suit and comb his hair. 'Something you want to tell me?'

'I'm popping out but I should be back in time to take you to the airport. If not, Maman will give you a lift.'

'You're going to the hospital to look at an opportunity of a position there.'

He stared at her as though she'd done something wrong.

'If you didn't want me to hear your conversation with Monsieur Fournier, then you should've stayed away from our bedroom window.'

He winced.

Her hands gripped her hips. 'So, Raphael, are you planning to move back here? Taking this job?'

'No… Yes… I don't know.'

'I see.' She didn't really. But she was angry. 'Thanks for not telling me about any of this. Was I supposed to wait and accept whatever you chose to do without hesitation? I know we've agreed to take our time working out where our relationship might lead, but not being open with me isn't going to help.'

'Izzy, we'll talk on the way to the airport.'

'No, thanks. I'll find my own way there. You go and see what's on offer at the hospital.' She turned her back on him and waited for him to leave the room.

'Isabella, I am sorry. I do need to make some decisions. I just don't know what they'll be.'

Less than an hour later Isabella paid off the taxi, slung her bag over her shoulder and went to check in. Her heart was numb.

Raphael had been offered a position at the hospital in Avignon. She should've expected it. He'd take it up.

When asked by Monsieur Fourier if he might be interested he'd said, 'Yes, definitely.'

She boarded her flight and sank into her seat, closed her eyes and pretended to be asleep.

For the first time since meeting Raphael she wanted to hate him. He'd lied by omission. They were better than that. He should have told her the truth. But instead of hating him, she loved him.

Which hurt like hell.

CHAPTER TEN

THE EXPECTANT MOTHER who'd been admitted an hour ago with early contractions was reading a book and quite comfortable with her lot—for now. Isabella's heart hadn't been in her work all day so when sign-off time came around she was out of the ward like a rabbit being chased by a hound.

Once she finally staggered into Raphael's house, exhausted from lack of sleep, she headed for the fridge and the wine, rubbing the small of her back where a persistent ache had started up hours ago. 'What a day. It couldn't have got any slower if it tried.'

Taking her glass with her, she wandered outside to the deck and slumped into the first chair. Chienne was quick to jump and spread herself across Izzy's thighs. 'Hey, you. Lonely too?'

Purr, purr.

'Okay, so you'll settle for anyone as long as you have food and cuddles.' Next week she'd be moving into the apartment she'd rented and beginning to unpack the mountain of kitchenware and other things she'd bought. It would be the start of everything she'd hoped for. Except a life with Raphael. He wouldn't leave his house to move into a tiny one-bed apartment. But he might—

make that probably would—leave this place for Avignon and the family he'd started getting back with.

A sharp breeze skipped across the yard, lifting leaves and chilling her skin. 'Guess we're going inside, Chienne. Wasn't enjoying it that much out here anyway.'

After making sure she was locked in, Isabella headed upstairs, not to Raphael's bedroom but to the third floor where she crawled under the covers on the bed, still in her clothes. Who cared? The cat followed, and quickly made herself comfortable curled up against Isabella's leg. Looking around, she sighed. The room she'd used for the first weeks was cold and uninviting, the bed not welcoming. No hints of Rafe. There again, not even his bedroom had been warm and inviting when she'd popped her head in earlier.

'At the end of the day, without Raphael this place is only a house, not a home.' She blinked hard. 'I love him.' So much it was unbearable. Did she really want to give him up to live in a one-bed downstairs apartment? After seeing Raphael's enjoyment as he wandered around Avignon the idea of living in London so she could have her own home was turning cold. What was the point if she wasn't with the love of her life? An old saying slipped into her head. 'Home is where the heart is.'

It was like someone had turned the lights on. Blink, blink. She couldn't leave Raphael. She'd go to the end of the earth if it meant being with him. And yes, she'd travel to different countries, other cities, if she had to. Though that was unlikely. If they settled in Avignon, it would be for a long time, probably for ever. She could do this. And be happy about it. She was in love. Nothing could be better than that. Could it? No, it couldn't.

* * *

From the hospital Raphael went into the city centre for a look around. He rolled his shoulders as he walked, trying to ease the tightness brought on by the dismay in Isabella's eyes as she told him he hadn't been honest with her. He breathed in the scent of the place, recalling other times he'd been here, with Grand'mère, his parents, his cousins. He knew most corners and streets, not much had changed. It was familiar in a comfortable way. Old yet pulsing with new energy. Tourists and locals alike sitting outside cafés enjoying the sun and coffee.

As he passed a bar the sounds of a rugby game on the television reached him and he paused to look in. The French were playing the Italians. If it had been the All Blacks playing Izzy might've been watching.

His heart lurched. She'd gone. In anger. And pain. He'd let her down. Badly. It was time to tell her how he felt.

Which was why he was walking around his beloved city, taking in everything, storing up new memories.

He tugged his phone out of his back pocket and pressed her number.

'Raphael.' Her voice was flat.

'Izzy, I'm sorry.'

'Sure.'

Right. 'Can you pick me up from Heathrow tonight?'

'You're returning home?'

What she was really asking was, *Are you coming home for good?* 'Of course I am.' Except there was no of course about it. In reply to her question about if he was moving home he'd answered no and yes. Home was a new word for him. It wasn't just a house with a bed in it any more. It was where his heart lay. Except his heart had been torn. London and Avignon. Izzy and his family. Would it have been greedy to want it all?

'Okay.'

He tried another tack. 'Grand'mère opened her eyes for a few minutes this afternoon.' It should've been the first thing he told Izzy, but he'd been overwhelmed with his love of his city and had to say something about it before it consumed him. Telling Izzy his dilemma should be a priority, but he was afraid to put it out there until he knew for sure what he would do. 'I was doing my talking thing, chatting about anything and everything, and looked over and there she was staring at me.' His heart had gone into overdrive as he'd reached for her wrist to check her pulse.

'Hey, that's great news.' Finally some enthusiasm. 'Give her another hug from me.'

'Already did.'

'What time do you get in?' Flat again.

He told her the fight number and arrival time. 'I'll see you later.'

'Okay.'

Who knew if she'd turn up to collect him, but he had to believe she would. Tossing the phone on the bed, he quickly shoved his clothes into the bag, for once not folding anything. He had a flight to catch and missing it was not an option.

His phone pinged as he paced the terminal, waiting to board his flight.

Get it right, my boy.

Grand'mère. Nothing wrong with her brain after the coma.

His gut churned. What if Isabella turned her back on him? What if she'd decided he wasn't worth the effort? Only one way to find out, and he had to endure two flights first.

Both flights were slower than a winter's day. At Heathrow Customs it took for ever just to reach the grumpy-looking woman behind the desk.

His phone pinged as he handed over his passport. Izzy.

I'm here.

'Excuse me, sir. I'm asking you to turn that off while you're here.' The grumpy official dragged out the questions like he was an illegal alien trying to get across the border. Finally his passport was approved and he was free to go.

Striding out into the arrivals hall he scanned the crowd, missed Izzy the first time. Then on a second sweep he saw her standing to one side, tired and sad. No human tornado tonight. His heart squeezed. 'Izzy,' he called as he crossed to stand in front of her. When he reached to hug her she stepped back.

'Did you take the job?'

'No. I didn't.'

'Why didn't you tell me that's what you were going into town for?'

Dropping his bag to the floor, he laid both hands on her shoulders. 'Because I didn't want to upset you when I had no idea if I'd take it or not. I wanted to be certain one way or the other before saying anything.'

She stared at him, her eyes wide and filled with a pain he'd never seen there before. 'Really?'

'Really. Really didn't know. And really turned it down. I live in London, Izzy.'

She blinked, bit her lip.

'I've come home to tell you I'm not moving away, that Avignon's a part of me but not all of me. I've finally come to my senses and see that returning there was a dream, and now that the opportunity has arisen to live and work there, it all feels wrong. I won't deny a part of my heart will always be there with my family, but…' He drew a breath. This was the moment he had to put himself out there. 'But really, my heart belongs with you. In London, in our house. I love you, Izzy.'

'Rafe? You do?' A tear snuck from the corner of her eye.

'Yes. I love you, Isabella Nicholson, with everything I have.'

'I love you, too,' she whispered. Then louder, 'I love you, Rafe, and it's been so hard thinking you wouldn't love me back.'

'Oh, Izzy.' He wrapped his arms around her familiar body and held on tight.

'I can't believe us.'

'Right pair, aren't we? Great friends, awesome lovers, and now for the future.' He pulled back enough to gaze down into her eyes, and he knew he couldn't wait until they got home. He dug into his pocket for the small box he'd put there hours ago, and dropped to one knee. 'Isabella Nicholson, will you do the honour of marrying me?'

She gasped. 'Raphael? Did I hear what I think I did?'

'Please marry me, Izzy? I love you so much I can't bear the thought of not being with you.'

She went quiet on him again, but he wasn't worried.

She wouldn't have lied about loving him. Just being typical Izzy, making him wait. 'Answer the question, will you, Izzy?' he pleaded.

Then her sweet, fierce voice whispered, 'I love you, Rafe, more than anything, but I am not asking you to give up your dreams for me.'

'I'm not. Yes, I adore my family and being back in Avignon has been wonderful, but I mean it. My heart is with you in London.'

'I can live anywhere if we're together,' she said. 'Yes, Rafe, I will marry you. Till death do us part in about sixty years' time.'

Phew. She was smiling right at him. Hadn't realised he was holding his breath.

'Are we seriously engaged?'

He slid Grand'mère's engagement ring onto her finger. 'As of now, yes.'

'Mummy, what's that man doing?'

'Asking the pretty lady to marry him.'

'Why?'

Raphael looked across to the little boy staring at him. 'Because I love this lady and want to be with her for the rest of my life.'

Loud cheers and lots of clapping drowned out anything else the child might have said. Raphael swung Izzy up in his arms and kissed her before he turned for the exit.

'Hey, mister, you've forgotten your bag.' A man ran after them, a silly grin on his face.

'Thanks.' He grinned back, happy as a man could get.

But at the car, his Isabella stood swinging the keys in her hand and looking slightly bemused. 'I can't promise you I'll settle easily, though I know it's you I want in my life more than a home in one place. If we move house every year I will be happy. And I certainly won't object to moving across to Avignon to be a part of your family.'

'*You* are my family, Izzy. I've got a home that as of now is ours. We both have jobs we love, though I'm going to look for something less time-consuming so I can have more time with you. There are our friends nearby we like to spend time with. We have everything that matters.'

A sob came across the rooftop of the car. 'You say the nicest things when you're not trying to annoy me.'

'Love you, sweetheart.'

EPILOGUE

Months later

HARRY TAPPED HIS glass with a knife from the dining table. 'Okay, everyone, please raise your glasses for a toast to the disgustingly happy couple.'

Isabella reached for Rafe's hand, and entwined her fingers between his. 'We did it.' It had taken time to organise a dinner in their London home with their friends. Everyone was so busy and a baby had been born, but eventually they'd managed it. If only they could get married now, but divorces took time, and she had to be patient.

'If you're half as happy as Esther and I, then well done.' Harry held his glass before him.

Raphael grinned. 'I reckon.'

'Cheers,' everyone shouted, before drinking to them.

Isabella felt the tears burning lines down her face, and grinned. They were happy tears. 'Thanks, everyone. I'm just glad we've joined you all in wedded bliss, or in our case, on the way to marriage.' This was the bliss, the wedded component to follow when she was single again. 'Less than nine months to go before the big day.'

At that, Raphael glanced at her, a question in his eye.

She nodded. They'd agreed about this before everyone got here.

His hand squeezed hers before he announced, 'We're going to join some of you in the parenting stakes too.'

The room erupted and Isabella found herself wrapped in Carly's arms. 'Go, girlfriend. That's awesome news.'

'Who'd have thought?'

'Everyone but you.' Carly smiled, and turned to Adem to scoop her daughter out of his arms and against her swollen breasts.

'She's gorgeous.' Izzy smiled.

'Here, have a hold. Derya Ann, this is your godmother.'

Izzy's heart swelled further as she took the warm bundle. 'She's so beautiful.' She sniffed. 'I'm so happy it's scary.'

'Not scary. Wonderful.' Carly grinned. 'Now, can I have my daughter back?'

Harry did his spoon-tapping-glass thing again. His smile was wider and softer as he focused on Esther, nothing but love in his eyes. 'We, too, are pregnant.' Once again the room exploded with joy and laughter and shouts.

Then Esther and Chloe were nudging Carly aside to give Isabella a hug. 'Go, you. A baby. No wonder you're looking so peachy.'

Peachy? Yuck. Isabella grinned and flapped her hand. 'I'm so glad Rafe suggested I come back to London.'

'The man had an ulterior motive,' Xander said.

'It worked, didn't it?' Rafe said.

Yes, it had. And she couldn't be happier. She had found her match, the man to go through life with, raise children with, laugh and love and do all the things she'd been hoping for. It didn't matter where, only that she was with Rafe. She took one more sip of her champagne and put the glass down. From now on water would suffice until their wedding day by which time junior would've put in an appearance.

Life couldn't be better.

* * * * *

COMING SOON!

We really hope you enjoyed reading this book. If you're looking for more romance, be sure to head to the shops when new books are available on

Thursday 20th March

To see which titles are coming soon, please visit

millsandboon.co.uk/nextmonth

MILLS & BOON

Coming next month

HEART SURGEON'S SECOND CHANCE
Allie Kincheloe

Dread pooled low in Rhiann's stomach as the door to the exam room opened with a slow and ominous creak. Broad shoulders in a white coat filled the space and her eyes roamed the doctor's familiar form, taking in the subtle changes time had wrought. Three years ago, he hadn't had those deep lines etched into his face. His dark hair had a little more silver at the temple than she remembered, but he was as lean and handsome as ever.

Dr. Patrick Scott stepped into the room, his eyes looking down at the screen of the silver laptop in his hand. His movements carried the spicy aroma of his cologne into the small room, those pleasing notes covering the harsh antiseptic and teasing a part of her that had gone dormant since her divorce. But on top of the overtly masculine scent, he brought with him a wave of sadness that hinted at tragedy.

"Hello, Mrs. ... Masters, um..."

His deep gravelly voice trailed off and his sky-blue eyes jerked up to meet hers when he recognized her name. The slight fake smile he'd had on his lips when he opened the door faded fast. From the ice that frosted over his gaze, the animosity he held for her hadn't eased since she'd last seen him.

The exam room door shut behind him with an audible click and the laptop clattered slightly as he set it roughly on the counter. "What are you doing here?" An uncharacteristic coldness in his tone sent a shiver coursing down her spine. Patrick's voice had always held such emotion, the rich timbre broadcasting his feelings with the simplest words. In all the years she'd known him, Rhiann had never heard this distant tone.

Rhiann hugged the baby in her arms close to her chest, tears filling her eyes as she fought to keep her emotions from overwhelming her. She'd wished the time since they'd last seen each other might have given Patrick clarity and soothed the raw edges of his anger, but clearly not enough time had passed. Now she could only hope that he was professional enough to put their personal grievances aside and focus on her child's best interests, and she needed to keep a clear head today, so she stuffed her feelings away as best she could. She had known coming here was a risk, but there was no other way or she'd have explored it already.

"I need your help. Well, he needs your help. This is my son, Levi. He has a heart defect and the cardiologist at St. Thomas wants to do surgery to fix it. But if anyone is cutting my baby open, I want it to be the best surgeon I can find." She paused to swallow down an oversized lump, "And that's you."

"You expect me to save someone you love. How ironic." A single dark eyebrow raised as he stared down at her, his expression unreadable and as cold as marble. His eyes searched hers, for what she didn't know. Just as she was sure he was about to tell her to leave, to scream at her like he had the last time she saw him, his gaze flicked down to the baby in her arms, and the ice in his eyes melted the tiniest bit.

Continue reading
HEART SURGEON'S SECOND CHANCE
Allie Kincheloe

Available next month
www.millsandboon.co.uk

MILLS & BOON

True Love

Romance from the Heart

Celebrate true love with tender stories of heartfelt romance, from the rush of falling in love to the joy a new baby can bring, and a focus on the emotional heart of a relationship.

MILLS & BOON

THE HEART OF ROMANCE

A ROMANCE FOR EVERY KIND OF READER

MODERN

Prepare to be swept off your feet by sophisticated, sexy and seductive heroes, in some of the world's most glamourous and romantic locations, where power and passion collide.
8 stories per month.

HISTORICAL

Escape with historical heroes from time gone by. Whether your passion is for wicked Regency Rakes, muscled Vikings or rugged Highlanders, awaken the romance of the past.
6 stories per month.

MEDICAL

Set your pulse racing with dedicated, delectable doctors in the high-pressure world of medicine, where emotions run high and passion, comfort and love are the best medicine.
6 stories per month.

True Love

Celebrate true love with tender stories of heartfelt romance, from the rush of falling in love to the joy a new baby can bring, and a focus on the emotional heart of a relationship.
8 stories per month.

Desire

Indulge in secrets and scandal, intense drama and plenty of sizzling hot action with powerful and passionate heroes who have it all: wealth, status, good looks…everything but the right woman.
6 stories per month.

HEROES

Experience all the excitement of a gripping thriller, with an intense romance at its heart. Resourceful, true-to-life women and strong, fearless men face danger and desire - a killer combination!
8 stories per month.

DARE

Sensual love stories featuring smart, sassy heroines you'd want as a best friend, and compelling intense heroes who are worthy of them.
4 stories per month.

To see which titles are coming soon, please visit

millsandboon.co.uk/nextmonth